EARTHLY WORLDS

BILLY WRIGHT

William Wright/Earthly Worlds
Printed in the United States of America

This is a work of fiction. Names, characters, places, and incidents are a product of the author's imagination. Locales and public names are
sometimes used for atmospheric purposes. Any resemblance to actual people, living or dead, or to businesses, companies, events, institutions, or locales is completely coincidental.

Earthly Worlds/ William Wright. -- 1st ed.

LCCN: 2020906454

ISBN 978-1-7347770-0-0 Print Edition

ISBN 978-1-7347770-1-7 Ebook Edition

In loving memory of my youngest.

Tatum A. Wright 12/10/19 to 1/16/20

I love all my kids big and small.

ACKNOWLEDGMENTS

I would like to thank Mark, Travis and Colin for your hard work and for believing in my vision and bringing it to life with me.

PART I

ONE

A SHARP THUD KNOCKED Stewart out of his last shreds of sleep. Had something struck the side of the trailer? Something heavy like a stone or a board? He sat up in bed, rolling back the covers.

Beside him, Liz stirred with a few incoherent noises. As he stood, the floor creaked under his weight, his ears tuned for any sounds. The gray light of predawn filtered through yellow-flowered curtains, crept across brown wood-grain paneling.

Tendrils of mist swirled around his feet, obscuring the floor.

That was peculiar.

Red LEDs beside the bed glowed: 5:18.

No more sounds came. Or was that a strange kind of horn in the distance, tooting out a simple, staccato rhythm? Was he still dreaming?

The low-lying mist stretched through the bedroom door, past the kids' room and down the hallway toward the living room, clinging to the floor.

Liz's mumbling turned into words. "What is it?"

"I think I heard something," Stewart said.

"Again?" She rolled away from him with a sigh and curled deeper into the covers.

It would not be the first time that a strange sound had dragged him from sleep and sent him prowling outside, looking for he knew not what and finding nothing. Not even the first time this week. He suddenly felt like the boy who cried wolf. It had been a weird week. Maybe a family of raccoons had moved in or something. They could make a hellacious racket crawling around on top of the trailer.

Wearing boxer shorts and a Lord of the Rings T-shirt, he grabbed his old Louisville Slugger, which he kept beside his night-stand, and prowled down the hallway, his feet poofing cloudy craters in the mist. The chill of the desert night raised goosebumps on his arms and legs, even though he was inside. At midday, the Arizona sun would turn the trailer into a corrugated tin oven, but by this time of the night the cold had fully invaded.

He opened the door to the kids' bedroom. Two little lumps snuggled up in their bunk beds, breathing softly, watched over by a black Toothless the Dragon doll and the white, dog-like Falcor the Luck Dragon figure, one from the kids' favorite movie and one from his.

Stewart eased the door closed, gripped the bat, and walked into the living room. Halos of light seeped through the curtained windows. The rhythmic trill of a cactus wren sounded in the distance, answered by another from a different direction.

The low-lying mist had disappeared entirely, as if it had never been.

What could cause that thud he had heard? Someone throwing things at his house? Town ne'er-do-wells were not typically awake and functional at this time of day, nor did they venture much outside of city limits.

He pushed open the front door and stepped down the cinder-block steps—one of them wobbled under his tread—and stood at the verge of the awakening desert.

Nearby stood his battered old pickup truck—it was old enough to vote, Liz always said—its color washed out by a film of ubiquitous dust. Their trailer lay at the end of Cactus Wind Road, about half a mile from the outskirts of Mesa Roja. The thud had come from the rear of the house, near the master bedroom, so he circled the house toward the back side, able to ignore the gravelly, stony earth under his bare feet by thirty years of living in the desert. It was still too chilly for rattlers or scorpions to be active.

He looked past the wire-mesh fence he'd erected to keep the cottontails and javelinas out of Liz's garden, over the scattered, sun-faded toys his son and daughter had left outside, into the scrub and cactus of the Arizona desert.

A strange noise came to him, like harsh music or angry conversation heard through a wall. He peered around, looking for the source, but the only thing he could see was desert.

Something flashed in the shadows, maybe fifty yards away, like the glint of polished steel. He knew this area like the back of his hand, as he had been looking at it every day for almost a decade. Any polished metal was definitely out of place. He gripped the baseball bat a little tighter and walked toward the glint.

The sounds got louder, like grunts of exertion, metal clashing against metal. A fight. But not a street brawl, more like a medieval battle.

A shrill, brittle scream. A taunting laugh. A strange smell, like animal dung, rotten meat... and blood.

The sounds were not just ahead of him now, they were all around him.

The mist had reappeared, curling around his feet in wispy tendrils.

"Who's out there?" he called.

Then something struck the ground near his feet. A black arrow with half its length buried in the earth.

"What the hell...?"

A gigantic shadow loomed over him, a huge man—no, *not* a man at all. Eight feet tall, broad as the back end of his pickup, swinging a huge club, a face that was all gaping maw, jagged teeth, bulbous nose, and glowing green eyes.

He cried out and swung the baseball bat. It connected with something that felt like a boulder, and cracked in his grip.

Something sharp jabbed Stewart in the back of the calf.

The monstrous beast swung a spiked club that was half Stewart's size. Stewart hit the deck. The club whistled over him and crashed into metal and something softer underneath. A sharp cry of agony erupted from the blow and then receded, as if smacked into the distance like a line drive.

All around him, Stewart could hear the clomp of boots and feet. More cries of exertion and pain. He felt he could reach out and grab someone right beside him, but all he saw was shifting shadows, like car lights playing through a patch of mesquite.

Stewart looked past his upraised arm at the towering creature. It gazed down at him with those lantern-like green eyes. Then a look of surprise came over its face, followed by casting about as if for a place to hide.

The creature shouted to someone Stewart couldn't see, its voice like a mix of bear and gorilla in a string of hoarse, unintelligible syllables. Warm spittle showered Stewart's arm and hair. Then the creature stepped over him and leaped across a nearby boulder.

Stewart peeked over the boulder, but the creature had disappeared. All he could see were shadows dancing among the rocks. Was that the sound of footsteps receding?

As silence returned, the air was so still, all he could hear was his own breathing, the pounding of his heart.

He smelled bad breath, then realized it was coming from the spatter of fluid on his arm. He wiped it hurriedly on his T-shirt.

One look at his bat told him it was irreparably cracked, splintered, and slightly bent in the middle. He sighed. He'd had that bat since he was a kid. Most of his scant supply of happy childhood memories were associated with the Louisville Slugger. The only way he'd found other kids to play with was through his ability to hit a ball over the fence more often than not. As a boy, his lumbering size hampered his speed running bases, so his best option was to aim for the outfield bleachers every time. But then, there was that one game, the last game he'd ever played. His team had won the game, thanks to a ball he'd hit over the fence, but they'd somehow lost the whole thing.

Maybe the bat was salvageable. Maybe with some wood glue and a clamp he could repair it.

Then a cooling wetness on the back of his calf caught his attention. He was bleeding from a two-inch gash, as if he'd been cut by a small knife.

Weird. Had he caught himself on a sharp rock? The cut looked too clean for that. He'd better get inside and clean it up.

Before he stood, though, he grabbed the black arrow still sticking in the ground nearby and pulled it out. Black wooden shaft. Black fletching like raven feathers. An obsidian arrowhead, chipped to razor sharpness. As a bit of a rockhound, he knew his rocks.

You couldn't buy anything like this at a sporting goods store. This was handmade. And someone had shot it at him.

***

In the bathroom, he cleaned up the blood with a washcloth, foot propped up on the sink, then grabbed a handful of cotton balls and the bottle of hydrogen peroxide.

"What the heck happened?"

Stewart jumped at Liz's sudden appearance at his elbow.

Even bleary-eyed, she still took his breath away. "Jumpy much?" she said with a yawn. "What did you do?"

"Not sure," he said. "Something *really* weird just happened."

"Here, let me." She took the wad of wet cotton balls and dabbed at his cut. The peroxide fizzed white in the wound and stung like crazy. "You're going to need some stitches, babe."

"I don't have time for that. I gotta get to work."

"Work shmerk. If this gets infected, you're going to miss more than a couple of hours."

"Time for the Super Glue."

"Ugh! I hate it when you do that!"

Most people didn't know it, but Super Glue was used during the Vietnam War for battlefield triage, to seal soldiers' wounds on the way to a hospital. He had discovered this in an old novel.

Liz said, "At least let me finish cleaning it up." She dabbed fresh peroxide onto her cotton balls, then onto the cut.

Stewart gritted his teeth at the pain, and at the idea of having to call in to tell Mr. Richards about being late to work. Mr. Richards did not allow for time off. If you were on the job, you were *on the job*, and worse, he didn't like Stewart. It didn't matter that Stewart was the best locksmith in Mesa Roja, even better than Mr. Richards. Then again, maybe that was why Mr. Richards didn't like Stewart.

Liz squeezed the last dregs out of a tube of antiseptic ointment and rubbed it into the wound. "Okay, do your magic."

How had he gotten so lucky to have this angel give him the time of day, much less marry him? Not that her parents had approved. Mesa Roja was a small town, and if it was just a little too big to know everybody, you knew someone who did.

Stewart had always had a reputation as a "bad kid," at least that's what he'd been told pretty much every day of his childhood. Nowadays, his in-laws at least spoke to him, but the resentment over "ruining" their daughter's life emerged in every interaction.

Nevertheless, even after twelve years together, he still couldn't take his eyes off Liz's honey-gold hair, big brown eyes, and plump lips, always ready with a grin.

He took the little tube of Super Glue gel from the medicine cabinet and squeezed a tiny bead of it along one side of the cut. It burned like fire. Then he pinched the lips of the cut together, and they bonded instantly. Of course, as always, he glued his thumb and forefinger together, too.

She covered the wound with gauze and taped it up. "Don't forget Cassie's birthday present. She wants a doll."

"Got it." He would go shopping today after work. Since he drove the only vehicle and she carpooled to work, he was more mobile.

"So, what happened?" she asked. "Find some goblins lurking outside?"

"Well, funny you should say that..." He reached for the black arrow, where he'd laid it atop the toilet tank. But it was gone. "Where the hell did it go?"

"Where did what go?" Liz said.

He cast about the room, looked behind the toilet, in the corners. Had it fallen behind something? "I *know* I set it down right there!"

"What?"

"An arrow," he said.

"You were shot by an arrow?" Alarm rose in her voice.

"No, the arrow missed me, but—"

"Someone *shot* at you?" More alarm.

"I don't know. It was so strange." He couldn't muster the words to explain it. Liz often told people that Stewart was not a man of words. Words got in the way of the truth sometimes, and the truth was often too big to speak at once. He was usually happy to let her do all the talking. "I'll try to explain when I get home. It was so, so strange."

Of everyone in the world, she would be the one to believe him. Maybe by then, he could put words to it. She shrugged and stood up next to him. She was tall for a woman, over five feet eight, but still only came to his chin.

He pulled her close and kissed her, longer and deeper than the peck she was expecting. She molded to him and snaked an arm behind his neck.

When he released her, she said, "What was that for?"

He smiled and kissed her again. "Forever."

Two

AS STEWART PUT THE key in the pickup truck's ignition, he paused to look out over the scrubby, rock-strewn landscape that stretched away from this edge of Mesa Roja.

Had he really seen that...creature?

Had all of that been real?

The very real gash on the back of his leg suggested it was, but how could it possibly be?

Now, under the harsh morning sun, there was no place for uncertainty. Stark shadows still existed under the rocks and mesquite bushes, but there was no place for mystery.

He sighed and turned the key. "I am working too many hours."

The pickup roared to life. The muffler needed replacing but the engine still purred like a kitten—a very large kitten.

On the drive to work, he couldn't get the images of what had happened out of his head, the flashes of shadow, the smell of the monstrous creature looming over him, the slimy warmth of its drool on his skin, but most importantly, the sense he was surrounded somehow by *things he couldn't see.*

When Stewart arrived at work fifteen minutes later, walking into the weathered, main street storefront, Mr. Richards gave him a noncommittal grunt of greeting from behind the counter.

Stewart responded with his usual, "Good morning, sir."

The shop walls were covered with key blanks, a myriad of lock types, and other security-related gadgetry. The air smelled of metal, lubricants, and solvents.

Mr. Richards was dressed in his crisply pressed blue uniform with its embroidered patches emblazoned with his name, draped over a frame like dry, weathered branches. Stewart wondered how many hours a day the man spent in fastidious grooming. Such a meticulously kept appearance was much easier to maintain by someone who never actually did any work. And he made sure to remind Stewart multiple times a day that that was what Stewart and Eddie were for. He also made sure to remind Stewart almost as often about who had been the only business in Mesa Roja willing to give Stewart Riley a chance.

It didn't matter that Stewart's juvie record was sealed; the town was small enough that people still *knew*. Felonies had a way of clinging to a person, even if their exact circumstances were secret.

Mr. Richards handed him a sheet of handwritten scrawl incomprehensible to anyone but Richards himself and his carefully trained employees.

Stewart scanned it. Eight new locks on dwelling doors. Re-keying all the locks on a foreclosed business. Opening an abandoned safe. Inventory. "This is a lot for one day, sir. Can you send Eddie to do the new locks?" Those were the easiest of the jobs, but safe-cracking was not among Eddie's skills.

"Eddie's got his own sheet." Mr. Richards didn't look up from his computer screen.

Stewart glanced at the screen. On it was what looked like a job application. "Looking to hire someone new? We could sure use the help."

Mr. Richards closed the file quickly and looked annoyed. "That's none of your business. Just do your job."

Stewart drew back at the hard edge in Mr. Richards' voice. "Whatever you say, sir." Stewart *always* did his job.

Best to just get to work. So, he passed through the workshop and out the back door to the alley where his work van was parked. The sun was already hot. Arizona didn't have its reputation for nothing.

He spent the morning working his way through the job list, during which time he became thankful for a decade's worth of locksmith experience. Everything went smoothly, efficiently. There was no better locksmith in Mesa Roja. Stewart liked Eddie, a few bouts of negativity notwithstanding, but his coworker would take half again as long to do the same jobs.

About lunchtime, he decided to eat his lunch in the van on the way to the next job. Mr. Richards didn't like anyone eating in company vehicles, but Stewart was pretty sure he could eat a tuna sandwich without a major catastrophe. He took a side street that he rarely noticed through the decrepit part of town, where many of the buildings could have been straight out of the Old West. To some people they were "historic," to others, an eyesore. But Stewart liked them. They made him feel like a cowboy riding his horse through town. He could almost imagine hitching posts and gunslingers clapping their hats tight at a passing dust devil.

But then he spotted a store with The Cabinet of Curiosities painted in gold on the storefront window. He couldn't recall ever noticing it before.

And more importantly, sitting in the window were two dolls in beautiful dresses, just the kind of thing Cassie would love.

So arresting were the dolls that he couldn't take his eyes off them, until the blaring of an oncoming horn jerked him back into the moment; he had started to drift into the wrong side of the street.

He parked and walked back to the store. One adjacent storefront was an attorney's office, the other, a Western Art gallery. Through the window, beyond the dolls, he glimpsed shelves and shelves of untold curiosities, just like the name suggested. Toys, antiques, books, magazines, strange knickknacks, vintage clothes on mannequins that had worn them when they were new.

But it was the eyes of the dolls that drew his gaze. Like chips of backlit sapphire, droplets of evening sky, the blue of glacier ice, their eyes seemed to be looking at him. The dolls' faces were like twins whose features were subtly different.

He caught himself grinning. Cassie would *love* one of those. Given how beautiful they were, he probably couldn't afford them, but he had to find out.

He went inside, and a little brass bell above the door announced his entrance.

The air inside was cool, not the cool of air-conditioning, but the cool of an early spring morning. The place smelled of old hardwood, polishing oil, and gentle incense. Everything in here looked at least double his age, but there wasn't a speck of dust to be seen.

The man behind the counter peered over his glasses with a smile. "Good day, young man."

"Howdy," he said, scanning the shelves in wonder. He couldn't quite place the shopkeeper's accent. Eastern European perhaps.

The shopkeeper winked and returned to swabbing an old cowboy doll. A few wisps of white hair fringed his bald pate. His slumped shoulders and strange, rounded build, worn plaid trousers, button-down suspenders, and crisp white shirt gave him a peculiar, Humpty Dumpty-like appearance.

"Oh, wow," Stewart said, spotting a Boba Fett action figure that he wanted so badly as a kid, but he had never been with a foster family willing to buy one for him. His neck and shoulders tightened. An impulse shot through him to buy it for himself, right now, but he didn't have enough money to spare for that and a doll for his daughter.

"See something you like?" the shopkeeper said.

"You've got a lot of great stuff."

"But I suspect you came in for something in particular."

"How much is one of those dolls in the window?" Stewart said.

"I see you eyeing that Boba Fett." The shopkeeper smirked. "You don't look like a doll sort of fellow."

"It's my daughter's birthday in two days, so what I'm interested in is one of those dolls."

But the shopkeeper continued as if Stewart hadn't spoken at all. "You look more like a pugilistic sort. How about this pair of vintage boxing gloves used by Rocky Marciano when he defeated Joe Louis?" He pointed to a pair of weathered leather boxing gloves hanging in a glass case.

Stewart frowned and clenched his fists. "I don't fight for fun. Look, I just want to see one of the dolls. I've got to get back to work." Nevertheless, he wondered how such items as those particular boxing gloves ended up in a tiny shop in Mesa Roja.

The shopkeeper's gaze, suddenly sharp, narrow, and penetrating as an ice pick, turned Stewart's shoulders to knots. "Let me tell you a story that you will not believe."

"Is it a long story?" Stewart checked his watch.

"It is neither too long, nor too short, but eternal. It is the oldest story of all."

"Then I've probably heard it before. Can we move this along? If my boss thinks I'm taking an extra five minutes for lunch, I'll never hear the end of it."

"As I said, you will not believe it."

"Try me." After what he had seen this morning?

"Do you believe in magic, young man?"

The question put Stewart unexpectedly back on his heels. People didn't talk about magic, and they didn't ask if you believed in it, unless you were a child. "Let me put it this way. I wish I could."

"But you don't."

"I... I used to." But was that true? As a child, his belief in magic was the only thing that got him through. Had he abandoned that in the face of adulthood, the pressures of fatherhood, or was he just in a bad mood? "No, scratch that. I do believe in magic."

A tiny smile tugged at the corner of the shopkeeper's mouth. He came out from behind the counter, dragging one foot, and approached the window. "Then maybe all hope is not lost. What if I told you a great secret? It can only be understood by those who believe in magic."

Stewart sighed, wishing the old man would just get on with it. As the shopkeeper passed, Stewart smelled cotton candy, earthy spring flowers, and freshly scrubbed baby. What kind of old man smelled like that?

"There is a war going on," the shopkeeper said.

Stewart didn't think he was referring to America's endless wars of the last twenty years. "There's always one somewhere."

The shopkeeper clucked his tongue as if to silence Stewart. "The universe straddles three realms: the Light, the Dark, and the Penumbra, the place of shadow where Light and Dark meet."

Stewart held back the urge to scoff. *What is this, a New Age bookstore? Is he trying to sell me some sort of fantasy game?*

"But I'm just telling you a story, yes? Only a story," the shopkeeper said. "In the Light Realm reside beings of compassion, kindness, growth. *Love.* The Dark Realm is filled with creatures of hatred and cruelty, destructive forces, the utter absence of love."

"Sounds like you're talking about Heaven and Hell."

"That's...a somewhat narrow view, like understanding the truth of the universe through the prism of someone else's beliefs. Do you know the story of the three blind men and the elephant?"

"No."

The old man took another step toward the dolls, then paused to speak. This was excruciating. "Well, you see, the first blind man felt the elephant's trunk and declared, 'It's a serpent!' The second blind man grabbed the elephant's tail, and said, 'No! It's a rope!' The third blind man ran into the elephant's leg and said, 'No, 'tis a tree!' And then they all came to fisticuffs over the disagreement. Such is the nature of religion. But forgive me, I wax philosophical, and you just want to make your daughter happy." He took the two dolls from the window and carried them to the counter. "So the

Light Realm and the Dark Realm are not just places full of other-worldly magical beings. The inhabitants are part of that realm, *of* that realm, and vice versa. The realms are alive, constantly growing or contracting, depending upon which side has the upper hand. Sadly, the upper hand is almost always held by the Dark."

Stewart felt like he was in the middle of an enormous TMI session. Why was the shopkeeper telling him this stuff? "And why is that?"

"Because by its very nature, the Dark is ruthless, strictly self-serving, willing to go to any means, violate any boundaries, to achieve its aims. The Light side is often hampered by the desire to keep the innocent and vulnerable from harm. The Dark is happy to seize whatever upper hand it can."

"So, the Light side will take the gloves off when fighting the Dark, but they'll hold off if bystanders might get hurt."

"Precisely. The Dark holds no such compunctions. And it is the Penumbra always caught in the middle."

"What's that mean, 'Penumbra'?" Stewart asked, feeling the strange music of the word on his lips.

"That is our world, caught forever on the border between light and shadow, forever neither dark nor light, like the shifting edge of an eclipse."

Despite the abruptness and whimsy of it, something about the shopkeeper's tale thrummed a chord in Stewart's breast. He had often daydreamed about such things, about some eternal struggle between Good and Evil, and how he too often felt like a man caught in the middle. There was so much goodness in the world, but so much evil, too. Too often, it did feel like darkness predominated, with so much rampant cruelty, even among those whose job was to serve the public. Vile politicians, bad cops, abusive churches, greedy corporations, and that was before one even considered the overtly bad, like gangsters, tyrants, and criminals. His own life was marked with moments of regret, moments he had taken the path of violence or selfishness, but also moments of unexpected joy and wonder. He often felt like a pawn on a chessboard, or the rope in a tug-of-war. Everything the old man was saying would sound outlandish to almost anyone else, but not to Stewart. But how did this guy know how Stewart thought?

"Look, sir," Stewart said, "that's a great story, but I really gotta get back to work. How much for one of the dolls?"

"These dolls are a matched set. One cannot bear to be parted from the other."

Stewart doubted he could afford both, and girded himself to leave empty-handed. "How much?"

"You are fortunate in that we are having a buy-one-get-one sale, today only." That little smile tugged again.

Stewart pulled out his wallet and checked his watch again. "Please, I really have to go."

The shopkeeper gave Stewart a number that made him swallow hard. That was more than twice what he had planned to spend. If he paid that much, his truck would be running on fumes until his next paycheck.

But seeing Cassie's face would make it all worth it. He sighed and counted out the money.

The shopkeeper's eyebrows rose like white caterpillars arching their backs, but he spirited the money away behind the counter.

"I'm sure your daughter will be delighted with them. They are looking forward to meeting her."

What a strange thing to say.

The shopkeeper produced a beautiful bag of golden foil and put the dolls inside it.

"Thank you," Stewart said, taking the bag and turning toward the door.

"There's just one more thing," the shopkeeper said.

Stewart sighed again and turned. "What?"

"You have questions, do you not? You want answers to them, yes?"

"Questions about what?" Stewart's impatience was mounting.

"Why, about *life*, about the *universe*, about *everything*."

"Doesn't everybody?"

"Sadly, no. Many people find such questions bothersome." The shopkeeper placed a folded parcel of what looked like parchment on the counter. "This will answer your questions."

"Look, I don't have any more money—"

"This I offer you as a gift."

"Sorry, I don't think I need—"

"Oh, but you *do!*" The sudden hardness of the shopkeeper's voice, an insistence that wouldn't be denied, brought Stewart up short and stoked an ember of anger.

"Who are you to say what I need?" Stewart said, his own voice turning hard.

"What rightly constructed boy doesn't dream of digging for buried treasure? Just a look. I offer this to you free of charge."

"Twain," Stewart said.

The shopkeeper raised an eyebrow quizzically.

"That's a line from *Tom Sawyer*. 'There comes a time in every rightly constructed boy's life when he has a raging desire to go somewhere and dig for hidden treasure.'" Stewart had read that book many times as a boy.

"Why, indeed it is," the shopkeeper said with an enigmatic smile.

Stewart reluctantly came back to the counter as the shopkeeper unfolded a battered piece of parchment that looked for all the world like an old, pirate treasure map. But he recognized the outlines of familiar rivers, mountains, and canyons north and northeast of Mesa Roja. A dotted line meandered into the wilderness toward what looked like a lake with which he was unfamiliar. In the wilderness lay warnings: *Here there be monsters.* "You're kidding, right?"

"Take this map. Take the dolls. And take your family *here*." The shopkeeper stuck his finger on the *X* near the lake on the map. "Do that, and something extraordinary will happen. I promise you."

"Uh, okay." Stewart grabbed the map. He didn't have any more time to trade words with this guy.

The shopkeeper grinned widely, showing an expanse of white, sparkling teeth.

Stewart tucked the map into his shirt pocket and hurried back to the truck.

As he started the truck and checked his list for the next job, he said, "What a bunch of bunk."

And yet, there lay within him a boy who used to believe in such things. He *had* yearned to dig for buried treasure, dreamed of finding an ancient chest of Spanish doubloons, or an ancient cliff dwelling like Mesa Verde, which lay only a few hours' drive away.

Then his company phone rang with a phone call from Mr. Richards.

***

Mr. Richards' voice was like a brick lobbed at Stewart's head. "What are you doing parked on the street in *that* part of town?"

"Taking my lunch break," Stewart said calmly, but inside alarm bells were ringing that this might be one of his boss's occasional tirades. Mr. Richards was always wired pretty tight, but some days he was simply insufferable, unreasonable, irrational. Time for some new meds, perhaps.

"Are you *trying* to get my truck vandalized?" The tone in Mr. Richards' voice, suggesting that Stewart might be the stupidest lout ever born, set Stewart's teeth on edge.

"No, sir." The steering wheel cover creaked with the force of his wringing grip. There certainly didn't look to be any vandals around, especially in broad daylight. The only thing moving around him was the hot breeze and the waves of heat that went with it. It was simply a street that had seen better times, like so much of Mesa Roja. "I've been with it the whole time."

"Never mind. Lunch break is over. I just got a call from the customer telling me you haven't been there yet."

"I'm working the sheet in the order you gave me."

"Don't give me any of your smart lip, you dumb lummox. Get your butt over to the old taco shop on Alameda. The bank wants those locks changed pronto."

"Yes, sir," Stewart said, but he was already fuming at being called names. Was any job worth working for such an abrasive ass? It was like wearing sandpaper underwear.

Maybe it was time to start looking into his own business. He'd only been thinking about it for years. He had been watching Mr. Richards for so long, he had a solid grasp on how to run a locksmith operation—as well as how not to. Not being a dick was high on that list. He didn't bother trying to offer suggestions anymore.

The line clicked dead, and Stewart threw the phone onto the dashboard with a snort of disgust. Nevertheless, he started the engine and headed to the next job.

For the rest of the afternoon, Stewart resisted the urge to drive back to the shop and punch Mr. Richards in the head. He fantasized about walking in and laying his boss out with one shot. But then Stewart would go to jail. And he couldn't have that, not with two of the world's most beautiful kids at home. Time to swallow his pride. At least for a little while longer.

The rest of the day's jobs all went smoothly. The customers thanked him profusely at saving their bacon. When he finished the taco stand job, the man from the bank tipped him twenty dollars with a kind smile and firm handshake.

With his job list complete, he returned to the shop to work on the inventory and found Eddie alone minding the store.

Behind the counter, Eddie put his feet on the floor and his phone on the desk, then tossed back a long, blond lock of hair that habitually hung over one eye and gave Stewart a little nod. "'Sup, bro."

"Where is he?" Stewart asked.

Eddie shrugged. "I ain't his secretary."

Stewart had a moment wondering why Eddie felt safe doing nothing when the boss might walk in at any moment. He didn't resent it—to each his own—but something felt off. "Want to help me with inventory?"

Eddie shrugged again, perhaps his most habitual mannerism. "Sure."

"Thanks. How's your mom?"

"Mean as ever. Still smoking, even on chemo."

"She's a tough old gal." Eddie's mother was a woman made of weathered boot leather, with eyes like polished turquoise. Even fighting off Stage 3 non-Hodgkin's lymphoma, she would probably outlive all seven of her kids, of whom Eddie lay somewhere in the middle.

Eddie gave a wry smile. "Don't I know it. Where'd we leave off yesterday?"

"Deadbolts, I think."

Inventory was a hugely tedious job in which every key blank, every lock, every screw, every washer, had to be meticulously counted. Nevertheless, it required the kind of concentration that made time pass quickly.

It was nearing time to clock out when the back door chimed, announcing Mr. Richards' return.

At the sight of him, Stewart had a flash that the man was a walking scarecrow with button eyes, a frame of sticks inside a shirt stuffed with tattered rags and moldy straw, some strange rodent peeking out from between the buttons of his shirt. But it was not just a metaphor; it was as real, for half an instant, as the monstrous creature he had seen this morning. Then he was just Mr. Richards again.

"Stewart," Mr. Richards said, "in my office." He went straight into his cramped little office, more of a closet, really.

Stewart jerked stiff and his stomach flipped over. He put down his clipboard and followed Mr. Richards. Had he done something wrong? All the jobs had gone smoothly, as far as he knew. He still chafed at being called a "dumb lummox." His fists clenched.

As soon as Stewart stepped into the office, he caught a strange, earthen scent.

Mr. Richards said, "Shut the door."

Stewart shut the door behind him. He hid his clenched fists in his armpits.

"I'm sorry to have to do it," Mr. Richards said, "but I have to let you go."

An invisible truck tire slammed into Stewart's belly. That was absolutely the last thing in the world he had expected to hear. A thousand protests and questions sprang to the edge of his tongue, but the fact that Mr. Richards didn't sound the slightest bit sorry brought them all up short. So he just stood there, frozen, rooted, his insides starting to boil.

"Aren't you going to say anything?" Mr. Richards said.

What was he going to tell Liz? He had just spent half a week's pay on Cassie's birthday present. And now he was unemployed. A sick mix of guilt and worry churned into the anger building inside him.

"Well? Speak up!"

He chewed on several words, but only one emerged: "Why?"

"Because there have been complaints."

"From who? When? What job?" He didn't believe it, and his tone conveyed that.

"That's none of your business."

More protests joined those already threatening to spill out, but the futility of it stopped him again. This was so unfair, so unreasonable—like getting kicked out of school for a fight that never actually happened—there was no defense against it.

"There aren't any complaints," Stewart said. "You're a liar."

Mr. Richards' face flushed all the way to his collar. "Now see here—"

"I do my job and I do it well. You're a liar and an idiot."

"*Get out!*" Mr. Richards' voice went so shrill it hardly sounded human.

"I want my last check. Right now."

"The hell with your last check! I'll mail it to you."

"You just took food out of my kids' mouths. I'm walking out of here with my pay." He kept his voice as even as he could. He was easily double Mr. Richards' size. All he had to do to look scary was cross his arms tighter and loom.

Mr. Richards' voice was as brittle as glass. "Fine." His hands trembled, fumbled with a check register and a pen. He scribbled an unreadable scrawl, tore it off. Stewart snapped it out of his hand before he could hand it over. Then he spun and yanked the door open. Back straight. Eyes forward. Shoulders back. Like an innocent man headed toward the gallows.

"Dude." Eddie stared, wide-eyed, mouth agape. "I heard the whole thing."

Stewart stalked past him to the back where his truck was parked, the old wooden floor creaking under his tread.

Eddie followed him outside. "That sucks, man. A really crappy thing to do."

Stewart fixed him with a look. "Good luck, Eddie." Then he climbed into his truck and started the engine.

THREE

IN HIS TRUCK, with the beautiful golden gift bag next to him, paused at a stoplight, he considered going back to the Cabinet of Curiosities and returning the dolls. He could go buy a cheap plastic doll at the dollar store and that would have to be good enough. But it was already too late in the day. The shop would be closed, and the first thing he had to do was cash this check. The final check. The end of his income. It was too late in the day for Mr. Richards to call the bank and void it, so Stewart headed for the nearest supermarket to cash it.

Afterward, the modest wad of cash in his pocket pressed against his thigh as he drove home. It was all the money he had left in the world, and it didn't amount to much.

Neither did all the years he had worked for Mr. Richards.

All those years of *yes, sir* and *no, sir* and now, nothing. There was no rhyme or reason for it. If Stewart had botched a job or been a bad employee, that would be understandable, but not this. How could he have worked for someone all these years and have it suddenly vanish, *poof!* Like smoke. Had he missed the warning signs? Mr. Richards had never been a nice man, or a good boss for that matter, but the work was steady and his paychecks never bounced. Richards had shown glimpses of internal instability and insecurity, but he had never been so capricious. Stewart felt like he had stepped into the Twilight Zone just in time to get sucker-punched.

Tomorrow he had to return the dolls and try to get his money back. Cassie would never know. But the thought of giving back that beautiful pair of dolls made his heart ache. He kept imagining the adorable, gap-toothed grin spreading on her face like the sunrise when she saw them.

But in the meantime, he had to tell Liz. He had to figure out what to do. There was no time to grieve for the loss. His family didn't have time for that. They had no savings. Liz's part-time job at the day care would keep them in groceries for the short term, but he didn't dare miss payments on the trailer and lot.

When he arrived home, he sat in the truck for a few minutes outside the trailer house that was older than he was, tamping down his anger. He didn't want Liz to see how angry he was, how stricken. He wouldn't miss the job—in fact part of him was breathing a sigh of relief at never having to go back there—but that didn't stop him from feeling like a failure. He wasn't even good enough for an idiot like Richards.

Eventually, Liz's face appeared behind the screen door, looking for him.

She came outside with a concerned expression on her face, prompting him to get out of the truck. The sight of her buoyed his spirits. That look of concern confirmed that he would never be able to hide anything from her. "Everything okay?" she said. "You look like someone dropped a bomb on you."

"I lost my job."

Every implication of that simple statement flashed across her face in a handful of stunned seconds. She just stared at him. "Oh, baby."

She threw her arms around him and pulled him close. "It'll be okay. We'll get through. We always do. I can go full time at the day care for a while. Someone will hire you..."

He stopped listening and just held her. The warmth of her embrace suffused him, strengthened him, made him feel like a mountain that could weather anything. But words wouldn't fix this.

Inside the house, Hunter and Cassie were arguing about whether all unicorns had horns or just males, like deer. Their argument came through the screen of their bedroom window.

When she finally stepped away, she said, "So what happened?"

"I don't know. Mr. Richards lost his mind. Completely blindsided me. I made it to work on time. Every job went fine. I came back to the office, and he gave me the boot. He wouldn't give me a reason."

She scratched her chin thoughtfully. "Mrs. Rodriguez—god, her grandkids are so cute, but anyway—she told me that her nephew was applying for a job there."

"Why would he get rid of his best guy to hire someone new?"

"Someone cheaper maybe. Mrs. Rodriguez's sister and her family just came up from Mexico on the hush-hush. They're probably undocumented. I'll bet that old skinflint thinks he can train a new guy and pay him half what he pays you. Or less. Since the kid is undocumented, Richards can pay whatever he wants, and this kid with nowhere else to go won't be able to complain or push back. Richards could never push you around."

Stewart's memory flashed back to the job application he had seen on Mr. Richards' computer screen.

A few chunks of puzzle fell into place.

Liz burst into a tirade, "Rack-a-frackin'-angel-farts!"

Stewart couldn't help but chuckle. Liz's unique brand of profanity never failed to amuse him. When she was angry, she sounded like Yosemite Sam.

She sighed. "Well, let's go and let the kids cheer you up. I'll make a salad. You can grill some caveman burgers. After dinner, we'll burn Richards in effigy."

Just then, Stewart's phone chimed. "Eddie" appeared on the cracked screen.

When Stewart answered, Eddie gave a long slow, "Duuuude."

"No kidding," Stewart said.

"That was a really raw deal, bro. Want to go out for a beer or something to soothe the wound?" Eddie said. When Stewart hesitated, he added, "My treat."

"I don't drink," Stewart said.

"Well, you can drink club soda or something."

Stewart didn't feel like going out tonight, but maybe he could get a little more information out of Eddie. "How about you come over here and we'll chill in the back yard?"

"Done."

After he disconnected, Stewart told Liz, "Eddie is coming over."

"So, have you decided what to tell the kids?" she said.

He shrugged. "The truth."

"Is that gold gift bag in there what I think it is?"

He nodded and sighed. "I got a matched pair of dolls. Kind of expensive, but they're gorgeous. After what happened, I should take them back and get something cheaper."

"Let me see!" Liz clapped her hands before her.

Stewart pulled the bag closer, checking the trailer windows for spying eyes.

Liz pulled one of the dolls out and gasped. "Oh, dear Lord, honey, they're gorgeous!" Her eyes glowed in the evening light. She pulled out the second one and gasped again.

"Yeah, the shopkeeper told me they were a matched pair. He wouldn't sell me just one."

"Don't you dare take these back!"

"Really?" he said, then he told her how much he'd paid for them.

She deflated a little at that. "You're right. That's a lot. But they're so gorgeous. Oh, look at those sparkly dresses! And those eyes!" A sigh escaped her. "Cassie would so love these. But I see your point. It's going to be mighty tough around here until you get a job. Maybe the shopkeeper would let you put them on layaway for Christmas or something, make a couple of payments after you find another job. I'll leave that up to you."

"Okay." He stuffed the dolls back in the bag. "I'll leave them in the truck until tomorrow."

"Yeah, sleep on it," she said with another sigh. "So, are you ready to tell the kids? Plus, I made enchiladas."

His mouth watered at the mere mention of Liz's enchiladas. "Let's get this over with."

FOUR

THE MOMENT STEWART WALKED into the house, the mouth-watering aroma of Liz's enchiladas set his stomach roaring.

Cassie threw herself away from the kitchen table where she was coloring and flung herself against his leg. "Daddy!" She barely came to his waist, so he hoisted her up as lightly as if she were a doll and kissed her. She had her mother's honey-gold hair, brown eyes, and button nose. She flashed him a gap-toothed grin. "Want to see my unicorn? It's made of rainbows!"

He chuckled and said, "Sure."

She slithered out of his arms and snatched the coloring book from the table, holding it up. On the page was indeed a unicorn made of rainbows, colored occasionally outside the lines, but with great flair and airy beauty. What struck him about it was that she got the order of the rainbow colors correct. The sight of it buoyed the heaviness of his heart.

She was turning eight in two days. Where had all that time gone? How had she gotten so big?

"Hey, Dad," Hunter said, only barely looking up from his *Ninja Turtles* comic book. At ten years old, he was a skinny kid, genes he must also have gotten from his mother, because Stewart had always been the biggest kid of his age. His face, however, favored his father, with curly brown hair and an earnest brow.

How could he tell these kids their dad was a loser who just lost his job?

Might as well get it over with.

"Kids, I—"

"Daddy, Hunter says unicorns only have horns if they're boys. But I think girl-icorns have horns, too." Cassie looked up at him hopefully.

He rubbed his chin. This was an easier realm of thought than the mess built up inside him. "Well, sweetie, maybe you're both right. Maybe there are different kinds of unicorns. With some kinds of deer, only the boys have horns. But with reindeer, like Santa's, the girls have horns, too."

Cassie spun on her brother. "See!"

Hunter rolled his eyes. "Deer have antlers, Dad." His withering tone was so over the top that it was clear he was teasing. But he was apparently willing to concede the argument to his sister so he could peacefully go back to his comic book.

Liz said, "It's time for dinner, kids. Cassie, time to clean up your crayons. Hunter, set the table, please."

Hunter sighed, mightily put-upon, but he put the comic book on the coffee table in the living room—because the trailer was small, it was a short trip from the living room to the kitchen—and opened up the kitchen cupboard for dishes.

The boy was so tall, he could reach the cupboards now. Maybe he would grow into his father's height.

Stewart sighed. Why was he so afraid to broach the bad news? He didn't want to spoil dinner.

As they all sat around the small kitchen table, the sounds of cutlery and chewing settled over them all. Everybody loved Liz's enchiladas, even Hunter, who was a notoriously finicky eater. Liz kept glancing at Stewart, obviously wondering when he was going to drop the bomb.

It was an unusually quiet meal, as if the kids could sense something in the air. He waited until everyone was finished eating before he cleared his throat. He had never been one for preamble. "I lost my job today, kids."

Both children stopped in mid-chew and stared at him.

Mouth still half-full, Cassie said, "You look sad, Daddy."

"I am pretty sad, sweetie."

Her face crumbled into sadness for him. "Don't be sad!" she squeaked.

Hunter said, "So where are you going to work next?"

"I... I don't know. I need to start looking for a job tomorrow."

"What happened? Did your jerk boss have a tantrum?" Hunter asked.

"Hunter," Liz said, "that's no way to talk about people."

Hunter shrugged. "You and Dad call him that all the time."

Stewart said to Liz, "He's got you there." Then he sighed again. "I don't know what happened, Hunter. He didn't really give me a reason." Mr. Richards had been Stewart's boss for the entirety of the kids' lives. He had always been some nebulous figure, something "known to exist," like the bogeyman. Mr. Richards had never been one to socialize with his employees, so the kids had never met him.

"Maybe you can be a blacksmith now," Cassie said hopefully, still on the verge of tears. "And you can make swords and armor and horseshoes and..."

Liz laid a hand on Cassie's. "That's a great idea, honey, but it's not quite that simple."

"Why not?"

Stewart said, "Because we need money *now*."

Hunter sat up straighter. "But all the stuff you make is so cool!"

Stewart said, "No one around here to sell it to. Not too many sword collectors or knights in the middle of the desert."

"What about the internet?" Hunter said. "People sell all kinds of stuff on the internet."

They didn't have internet access at home. Without a computer, there was little point. The kids knew all about the internet from school, but it was all way beyond Stewart. He would have been more comfortable living in an earlier century.

Stewart had certainly had the same ideas himself—getting a computer, setting up a website or selling page—but all that stuff cost money, and he couldn't find the space in their finances to take such a risk. "It would take too long to set it up as a business before we started making any money."

Liz said, "Maybe someday. Right, hon?" Her hopeful gaze and warm hand on his arm chipped a crack in his gloom.

"Maybe someday," Stewart said. "But for now, I need to find a new job. I'll start looking tomorrow."

"It all depends on how things go, but there might be some changes around here for a while," Liz said.

Cassie looked alarmed. "Like what?"

Stewart said, "Like Mom might have to work full time for a while. Which means I'll have to take over the cooking."

Hunter's eyes bulged. "I hope you find a job fast!"

Cassie said, "You can wait to get me a birthday present until after you get another job."

Stewart's throat closed and his eyes misted. He opened his mouth to speak but nothing came out.

Liz came to his rescue and hugged Cassie. "That's very sweet, honey, but nothing for you to worry about. Your birthday is going to be epic."

Cassie pumped a fist. "Epic!" But she still looked a little worried.

***

Stewart had his modest forge good and hot by the time Eddie showed up. In the descending chill of the desert night, the warmth radiating from the enclosure of firebricks comforted him. The hissing roar of the propane furnace stoked the forge and the block of metal inside to yellow-orange heat. If his propane tank ran empty, when would he have the money to buy more?

Eddie sat in an old lawn chair with a bottle of beer cradled in his lap. He had brought Stewart a six-pack of his favorite root beer. Stewart was not a drinker, didn't like the taste of beer, so he appreciated the gesture. He didn't know Eddie that well, but sadly Eddie was the closest thing Stewart had to a male friend.

Gauging the heat of the billet from its color, he pulled the long block of layered metal out of the forge, put it on the anvil and started beating on it with a hammer, drawing it out, each blow smashing it flatter and lengthening it at the same time. If all went well, in a few days the block of metal would be in the shape of a hunting knife.

Out here in the back yard lay a small pile of scrap metal and failed efforts. He always tried to reuse the metal from blades or objects that didn't work out, reconfiguring them into something smaller, for instance, but that was not always possible. Out here in the back yard, under the tin-roofed shelter he'd erected to keep off the sun, surrounded by the tools of his hobby—the anvil, the grinding wheel, the workbench—he could let the worries of life wait until later. They would always be there. But here, shaping metal with his own hands, he could live in the moment.

Next door, perhaps a hundred yards down the road, the Collins's orange grove was in full bloom, its fragrant blossoms filling their back yard with beautiful scent.

Stewart and Eddie had already spent several minutes complaining about Mr. Richards, fruitlessly speculating about what had happened and why, and had settled into simple companionship. The bottom line of the conversation was that Richards was simply a bad person, with only neuroses and greed contributing to the whys and wherefores of his actions.

Eddie had been quiescent for a few minutes, watching Stewart work. Finally, he said, "So what's this 'Damascus' stuff you say you're working on?"

"Damascus steel," Stewart said between hammer blows. He would pull the billet from the forge, beat on it until it grew too cold to shape, then return it to the heat. He had drawn it out sufficiently now it was almost time to fold it again. "It's layered, like a sandwich. Every time you fold it, it doubles the number of layers."

"Like a samurai sword?" Eddie said.

"Sort of, except that I'm using nickel foil for the in-between layers." When it was finished and polished—again, if all went well—the layers would give the steel an almost wood-grain appearance. "Back in medieval times, it was the best steel in the Western world. The layers made it flexible and sharp. It holds an edge better, too. How it compares to the Japanese swords is up for debate."

"Sounds really cool. Someday I'll have to have you make one for me."

Stewart shrugged. "I sure could do it. This one is for Hunter. I hope I have enough gas left to finish it."

"So why do you do it?"

"Do what?"

"This. Nobody needs this anymore. Factories make perfectly good knives. Swords, too."

"None of those factory swords are made to be used. They're just decoration. The steel is all wrong and they're not sharpened."

"But we're not running around out in muddy fields trying to stab each other with swords anymore. What's the point?"

Stewart closed the door on the forge again and wiped his brow. "Don't you feel like there's stuff we're losing? There's no soul in a factory, where CNC machines just stamp out thousands of blades at a time. Not much point in a sword as decoration. Like making a gun that doesn't shoot."

"Never bring a knife to a gunfight."

Stewart rummaged around among the half-finished projects and experiments atop his workbench. He found a mostly finished blade, a little longer than his hand, a blade lacking only a final grind and a handle. He flipped his grip between blade and tang several times, enjoying the balance of it.

Then he threw it.

It stuck point first in the ground between Eddie's feet.

Eddie yelped and jumped out of his chair, sloshing beer everywhere.

Stewart chuckled.

"Not funny!"

"A little funny," Stewart said. "I didn't hear a gunshot, did you?"

Eddie pulled the knife out of the ground. "Point taken. Where did you learn to do that?"

"My childhood in the circus."

"What? I didn't know you were in the circus!"

Stewart chuckled. "Sorry, just pulling your leg."

"You don't talk about your past. Every time I ask, you deflect."

Stewart nodded. It was so hard to answer questions about his past. "Let's just say when I was a kid, I went through a really bad patch." His whole childhood was a bad patch. Then there was the worse patch, where he had to think about killing one of his foster fathers to defend himself, to survive. He still had scars on his legs and back from the wire coat hanger.

"Whereas *I* am an open book," Eddie said. "You hear enough dirt and drama on my family to fill the *National Enquirer* for a month."

That was also true. "I don't like to think about my past. I'm happy it's over. It needs to stay that way."

"I've heard some stuff, but I have a hard time believing it."

"I was an angry kid." With good reason. Shooting out streetlights with a slingshot was a favorite pastime.

"I get that. Bouncing around foster homes will do that to a person."

"I never knew my dad. When I was three, my mom and the baby died in childbirth." The truth was, Stewart only barely remembered her, just fleeting flashes of love and comfort, usually lost in a sea of fear and sadness. What would it have been like, to have a real sibling? "After she died, I bounced from foster home to foster home, some of them worse than hell."

"Harsh."

"Like I said, I don't like to think about it."

"So, you want to go egg Richards' car?"

Stewart laughed. "As satisfying as that would be, I think he would suspect."

"But he wouldn't suspect *me*," Eddie said with a dark grin.

"Nah, I think I'm content to let him wallow in his bad-person-ness. I've never met such a negative person before. Why do *you* keep working there?"

Eddie shrugged. "Not many jobs in Mesa Roja for someone with my incredible educational background." He shrugged again. "It's something to do."

"What do you dream of doing?" It seemed like such a personal question, too intimate.

Eddie laughed, a sharp bark. "Dude, I am *not* one of those people."

"One of what people? Dreamers?"

"I honestly haven't had a dream in years."

"You mean at night, or greater aspirations?"

"Both. I go to bed, I'm out, like I'm dead. As for aspirations..." He shrugged again.

Stewart frowned. "Don't you ever dream of things outside Mesa

Roja? Doing something with your life bigger than counting key blanks for Richards?"

"Sure, but I'm smart enough to know they'll never happen, so why beat myself up about it?"

Stewart stood and stared at him for a long moment. "Do you believe in magic, Eddie?"

"You mean like rabbits in hats?"

"No, I mean real magic, that there's more to the world than this place, paycheck to paycheck. Things we can't see."

"Not much point, is there?" He shrugged yet again. "I'm stuck here. My mom is here. My family's here. They're not going anywhere." Eddie was frowning now, too, as if Stewart's questions had cracked something loose. "Life is life. Keep your expectations low, and you'll never be disappointed."

***

Snuggled in their blankets, Hunter and Cassie lay in their bunk beds with the windows open to admit the cool night air, listening to the sounds of night.

Hunter could tell that Dad's bad news had really shaken his sister, as she was innately incapable of hiding anything she was thinking. Neither of them had ever seen their father looking so worried.

In the quiet, they could hear him hammering hot metal, talking to Eddie. Late at night, after Hunter and Cassie went to bed, was when Dad did most of his work. To Hunter, the sound of *tink-tonk-tink-tonk* was like a lullaby. It let him know that his dad was near, watching over them all, protecting them from the things that made little noises outside when they thought no one could hear, all the little scrapings and whisperings.

He tried to go to sleep, but Cassie's tossing and turning made the bed squeak. He would get close to nodding off and then she would rumple around and wake him up, and he would sigh.

"Go to sleep!" he said.

But she would only toss and turn some more.

At some point, his awareness rose from the quiet grayness between sleep and waking, the land of shadows, and he realized the hammering had gone silent and the voices disappeared.

Cassie had gone still and silent above him.

At least he thought so, until he heard her voice outside.

He climbed out of the bed and peeked over the mattress above. Only her plush unicorn occupied her bed. She *was* talking to someone outside. But who?

He went to the window and listened through the screen.

"...knew you were here somewhere!" came Cassie's voice.

And then another voice *answered her.* A voice small and high-pitched, as if a rabbit could talk, but it was too faint to make out the reply.

He took a deep breath and became a ninja, a shadow that moved, warrior of silent deadliness. Well, except for the deadliness. And probably the silence, too, because the floor creaked as he crept toward the door. He would have to practice his stealth skills more. Taekwondo was fun, but the ability to break boards was not exactly a deadly skill.

The back door was only a few feet across the hallway from their bedroom door. It hung open half an inch, unlatched. He pushed it open and stole outside barefoot. At least at this time of night, there were no scorpions around, and Dad kept the yard clear of cactus.

Cassie's voice came from around the corner of the house. "... know what I can offer you..."

More tiny whispers.

His feet were as silent as a native tracker's on the earth of the back yard. He reached the corner of the house and peered around.

There was Cassie, hunched near a pile of mesquite wood Dad used to grill steaks. Dad wasn't much of a cook for most things, but he knew how to grill meat fit for a king. But it had been a long time since they'd had steaks. Cassie squatted beside the woodpile in her Harry Potter nightshirt. Beyond her, Hunter caught sight of a little glow.

"My daddy really needs help," Cassie said. "Can you help him find a job?"

Whisperwhisperwhisper.

"Gee, thanks!" Cassie said.

Whisperwhisper.

Hunter edged farther out, trying to see who or what she was talking to.

"Do you want to be friends?" Cassie said.

Hunter would have sworn he heard a tiny *yes*, like the tinkling of a bell.

Cassie clapped her hands in delight. "Sweet!"

Hunter edged out farther, and that's when he saw the tiny woman sitting cross-legged on a small log. She was about the size of one of his Star Wars figures and... He rubbed his eyes, once. Nope, still glowing. He rubbed them again. Her skin glowed with an inner light like a firefly's, slowly pulsing with brightness.

"No way!" he said.

In an instant, Cassie turned and gasped.

The tiny woman disappeared like a firefly going out.

"Hunter!" Cassie whispered. "You scared her away!"

"Uh, sorry!" Hunter said. "What was I supposed to do when I saw you talking to a faerie?"

Cassie sniffed. "She's not a faerie."

"She looked like one."

"She doesn't have wings. And faeries aren't real." Then she whispered out over the woodpile. "Hey, come back!"

They waited several moments for a response.

Finally, she sighed and gave him an expression of profound annoyance. "You scared her away."

"Uh, sorry."

Cassie whispered out over the woodpile again. "If you're still out there, you can come back anytime!"

"Let's go inside before Mom and Dad hear us. We'll get in trouble."

"No, we won't. They would think it was cool."

"Not being awake this time of night, they wouldn't."

"Okay fine, but it's your fault."

"Okay, it's my fault. Can we go back in now?" Was that tiny woman one of the things he had heard moving outside the house? So many questions, a flash flood of them wanting to bubble out, but he had to get his sister back to bed.

Tomorrow on the school bus there would be time for questions.

FIVE

STEWART WAS UP BRIGHT and early, groggy from having slept little. What sleep had come was filled with dreams of uncertainty and endless trouble, an unceasing cavalcade of misfortunes that prevented him from accomplishing the most basic tasks. The arrival of dawn was an exhausted relief.

A tingle of foreboding drew him outside into the grayness to the area where he had imagined the huge, ugly creature the previous morning. He stood out there, hands on his hips, looking around, silently daring whatever was out there to show itself again.

Nothing happened. He went back inside, a bit saddened by the lack of activity.

He made breakfast for Liz and the kids before they went off to school and work, and only burned the eggs a little.

At the breakfast table, Hunter and Cassie kept exchanging meaningful looks.

"What, you don't like eggs?" Stewart said to them.

Hunter replied, "Oh, the eggs are fine, Dad."

Stewart gave both of them long looks, but they both innocently—too innocently—went back to eating their breakfast. Cassie surreptitiously gave her brother a *Shut UP!* glare.

After the kids had hurried off to meet the school bus, Liz gave him a long kiss before she departed for work herself. "Everything is going to be okay, baby," she said. "Go get 'em!" Her beaming smile warmed him in spite of himself.

He hugged her again, grateful that she had chosen to be in his life. His stomach twisted half a turn at her departure, but he certainly loved to watch her walk away.

The first order of business was dragging the old phone book out of a kitchen drawer, a holdover from when people still used landline phones. Then he went through the Yellow Pages and made phone calls to the handful of other locksmith operations in town. All of them already knew him, at least by reputation. None of them were hiring. He tried nearby towns as well, even as far away as Page. No luck.

The second order of business was to call all the hardware stores, which often employed locksmiths for their key-making counters. None of them were hiring. Then the department stores. Same story.

And so it went. By noon, the discouragement left him staring at the surface of the kitchen table.

With a heavy sigh, he went out to the truck. It was time to return his little girl's birthday present. As he twisted the key in the ignition, his stomach twisted with it. He drove away thoughts of what her face would look like when she saw the dolls. Meals on the table and gas in the truck were more important.

Or were they?

Was a life devoid of joy, a life bereft of magic, worth living at all?

It was so easy to forget what life was worth living *for* in the face of its daily onslaught of immediate needs.

No, he couldn't think about that now. Cassie would never know what she had almost gotten. Food and shelter came first.

One of the dolls looked up at him from inside the golden bag, its eyes—*her* eyes—a perfect cerulean blue. He could almost hear her whisper *Loser...*

He sighed again, but got the truck moving. On the way to the Cabinet of Curiosities, he turned up the radio loud to try to drown out his thoughts, but the songs grated across his nerves.

It was a day like any other in Mesa Roja. Hot, sunny, and quiet. The world had neither idea nor care that his life was in ruins. It churned along, oblivious to his plight.

He found himself at a stop sign at the end of the street where the shop lay, then chided himself for being so deep in his head that he missed the place. He made a U-turn and headed back toward the shop, this time keeping a sharp eye out for it. But then he started seeing buildings that he *knew* were on the other side of the Cabinet of Curiosities, buildings that he remembered clearly from the day before. How could he have missed it again? He drove another couple of blocks to be sure, but then snorted with frustration and made another U-turn.

Where *was* it?

He paused to consider clearly, to rack his brain and recall which buildings and businesses had been on either side of the shop. An art gallery with a lot of Southwest and cowboy paintings and sculpture. And a lawyer's office.

It took him less than two minutes to find the lawyer's office and the art gallery.

They were side by side. No Cabinet of Curiosities between them.

And the storefront wasn't just empty. *It wasn't there at all.* The lawyer's office and the art gallery abutted each other as if there hadn't been another whole building between them the day before.

Stewart's head spun.

He got out of the truck and walked up and down the street, looking for the shop, grasping the back of his head with one hand.

Was he going crazy?

Or.

Was it magic?

The thought slammed into him.

Like a balloon swelling inside him, the sensation that he had just ventured into the uncanny for the second time in two days filled his stomach, pressing on his heart and lungs.

Was this real?

Could it be real?

He leaned against the hot grill of his truck, the scalding heat instantly seeping through his clothes, as if to remind himself of what *was real.*

Magic was real. He believed in it. So why couldn't it happen to him? Why was he unworthy of experiencing it? His childhood memories were full of moments of miracle and mystery. But it was not a religious belief, like one of his foster families had tried to drill into him. This was not "faith," it was *knowledge.* It was a certainty that went all the way to his bones.

The question was: What was he supposed to do with this knowledge?

This new mystery did clear up one thing: he couldn't take the dolls back, and he found himself happy about that.

When he was Cassie's age—eight years old tomorrow—his foster father had locked him in a closet for twenty-four hours because he had stolen a donut from a box on the counter. It was chocolate glazed, the most heavenly thing he had ever eaten. The taste of it was still in his mouth as the man screamed at him, "Thou shalt not steal!" In that twenty-four hours of confinement, Stewart had both wet and soiled himself, and when they let him out, they beat him for it and made him scrub the closet with a toothbrush, and then use the toothbrush.

But in that dark closet, in the dead of night, listening to his foster parents snore, lying on the hard floor, Stewart saw something.

A tiny beetle, slightly larger than a ladybug. He would never have seen it in the dark, except that it glowed like a firefly. But he had seen fireflies before. Only their butts lit up. This bug's entire body glowed, and it trundled along like a dung beetle. Where it had come from, he didn't know, because there were no holes in the walls. An empty closet didn't seem like the place for a dung beetle, especially one that glowed like a lightbulb.

At one point in its path, it stopped, as if looking at him, waving its feathery antennae.

"Hang in there, Stewie," the beetle said in a voice so small he couldn't be sure he heard it. Its tiny shell coruscated with brilliant colors.

He sat bolt upright on the floor. "What?"

But it didn't speak again. It disappeared under the door.

He put his ear to the floor, trying to peer under the door, but he lost sight of the beetle quickly, and its glow faded.

Had it been a dream? He couldn't be sure. But today felt like that moment somehow, like a familiar scent you couldn't identify.

With a sigh, he uncrossed his arms and got in the truck. It was time to keep job hunting. He would stop at the lumber yard and few other places to see if they had any job openings. But it was a fruitless search; all he came home with was a handful of job application forms that they would "keep on file." On his circuit around town, his stomach rumbled, but he might as well start cutting back on meals right away. He could wait until dinner with Liz and the kids.

When he pulled up in front of the trailer, he saw the absolute last thing he was expecting.

Wearing Liz's wide straw hat to shade her from the blazing sun, Cassie sat on a folding chair at a folding table at the edge of the road. Taped to the table, written in a rainbow of crayons, was a sign that read GEROJ SALE. On the table lay an assortment of small items, mostly Cassie's toys that she had grown out of, but also some of her favorite storybooks.

She waved brightly at him, making him want to laugh and cry at the same moment.

"What are you doing, sweetie," he said as he climbed out of the truck.

"What does it look like, silly?"

He knelt beside her and touched her shoulder. "This is some of your favorite stuff."

"I want to help." Her eyes glistened.

He rubbed her small back. "That is so great for you to offer. I can't even tell you. But it's not your job. It's my job."

"I don't need this stuff anymore. I'm growing up."

"Yes, you sure are," he said. "Have you had any customers?"

She nodded vigorously. "Oh, yes! Mrs. Rodriguez bought two of my books for her grandson."

"How much money did you make?"

"Fifty cents! You want it?" She held out two quarters that had clearly been in her palm ever since.

"You just save all that up." He swept off her hat, kissed her sweaty little head, put the hat back on, and went inside.

Hunter was in the house, reading a Harry Potter book from the school library, lying on his back on the living room floor under the ceiling fan, his calves on the sofa. "Hey, Dad."

"Hey, Son. How was school today?"

"Am I going to be able to keep going to taekwondo class?"

"I hope so, but I'll be honest, it depends on how long it takes for me to get a job. If I'm still unemployed in two weeks, we might have to put martial arts on pause for a while."

"Oh." He sounded disappointed in a way that carried more of a story behind it than he was letting on.

"Is everything okay at school?"

"Sure."

But Stewart could tell from the boy's tone that something was afoot. "Are you sure?"

"Yep," Hunter said, extending the 'Y'.

Stewart let it go, for now, and set about combing the kitchen for something to make for dinner.

***

After a meal of impeccably grilled hamburgers with a side of burnt mac-and-cheese, Stewart and Liz sent the kids off to their rooms and retired to the back yard, with the cooling of evening coming on, for some grown-up-style conversation.

Sitting side by side in a couple of old lawn chairs, they looked out over the rocks and scrub.

"Thanks for cooking," she said, squeezing his hand. "Any luck today?"

He shook his head.

"So what is it?" Liz asked. "Spill it."

Her tone was kind, but Stewart knew he couldn't hide from her that something really weird had happened today. It was more a matter of how to tell her.

She waited patiently while he worked up the verbal steam. "So, I tried to take the...things back today." He looked over both shoulders for any small eavesdroppers.

"And...?"

"The shop wasn't there."

"You mean closed up?"

"I mean, not there. As if it never existed."

"An empty storefront?"

"No. I mean, the whole building."

"Torn down overnight?"

"*No.* I mean, the building I remember going into doesn't exist. I remember what was on either side. I remember the shop in the middle. Today, no shop in the middle. The businesses on the sides, it's like they... It's like they squashed it out of existence."

She looked at him for several seconds, searching his face. "Weird." After a few more seconds, she said, "Oh, you're serious."

He nodded. "And then, I never told you what happened yesterday morning. I went outside, right over there, because I heard something. Maybe it started like I was in a dream, but I was out there, near that boulder. And it was like I was in the middle of a battle. There was noise, and yelling, but I couldn't *see* anything. And then there was this...monster, half again my size, he just appeared out of nowhere, ugly as a Gila monster's hind end. He took one look at me. That's when my leg got cut, I'm not sure how. I looked away for a second, and then the thing was gone. The sounds started to fade. And then it was like...it never happened."

She listened intently.

"What?" he said.

"I think that's the most words I've heard you speak at once since our wedding."

He couldn't help but grin at the memory of the speech he'd written for her—one paragraph long—at the tiny reception they threw in the Community Hall after their elopement. Her parents wouldn't consent to a wedding.

"And you know what else?" she said.

"What?"

Her eyes flashed with wonder and fascination. "It sounds absolutely *magical.*"

"Really? I'm not sure I—"

"Oh, come on, Stewart! You used to talk about magic all the time when we first started dating. That's how I knew you were different from other people. How I knew you weren't what everybody said you were. Magic, my loving husband, makes the world go around. Most people just don't see it. But *you* did. You used to talk about all the crazy things that happened to you. I still remember the story about the glowing beetle."

"You remember that?"

She turned toward him, her voice earnest. "I remember *all* that, baby. Please don't tell me you've stopped."

"Stopped what?"

"Believing in magic."

He sighed and looked out into the desert. "I just don't know. We could sure use a little right now."

"Maybe we just have to settle down and look." She took his hand again and leaned back in her chair, glancing toward the house. "So where is the big present now?"

"Still in my truck. Hiding."

"Bring 'em in after we put the kids to bed."

They sat outside and watched dusk sweep across the landscape. Later they went through the nightly routine of trying to shoehorn their children into bed. Cassie always wanted a drink of water, or another story. Because of the situation, Liz indulged her with a few more pages of *The Hobbit*. And then Cassie wanted a third installment, but Liz finally declined, kissed the little girl on the head, and extricated herself.

"Time for sleeping, sweetie," Liz said. "You have a big day tomorrow."

Cassie's eyes glowed. "Epic!"

Stewart watched from the doorway as Liz kissed her, then came in to do the same. Hunter turned off his reading lamp and held out his fist for a knuckle bump. Stewart obliged him, and then blew it up.

The adults waited half an hour before bringing in the golden bag. Liz sighed again at the sight of the two beautiful dolls. Then she happened to spot something else in the bottom of the bag.

She drew out the map. "What's this?"

Six

"**SOMETHING THE WEIRD OLD** shopkeeper gave me," Stewart said. "He almost wouldn't let me leave without it."

As Liz unfolded the map, her eyes sparkled. "If nothing else, it's nice work. It looks handmade."

He nodded.

"Why did he want you to have it so badly?"

"He said I should take my family here." He poked the *X* near the lake on the map, the lake that didn't exist. "If I did that, 'many questions would be answered.'"

"What's convincing about it is that *some* parts of the map are real. Here's Mesa Roja. Here's the Colorado River. 'Here there be monsters.' That's funny." She pored over it, her face painted by a faint smile. "Here's the highway. Here's some sort of side road leading off into what looks like a forest. But this isn't Lake Powell, and this town surely can't be Page, unless the scale is completely wrong... What kind of questions did he tell you would be answered?"

"'Life, the universe, and everything,'" he quoted.

"Good grief, that's a line from *Hitchhiker's Guide to the Galaxy*. Couldn't he be more original? But those do seem to be the kind of questions most on your mind, my dear husband. So, what are you going to do?"

"Keep looking for a job—"

"No, silly. I mean, about the map."

"Honestly, it hadn't even occurred to me to follow it. Too much else on my mind."

"He gave it to you for a reason."

"Yeah, well, I don't believe in fate."

She grinned at him and snaked her arms around his neck, batting her eyelashes. "Oh, come *on*. Don't you believe in magic anymore *at all?*"

He chuckled. "Oh, I believe in *that* kind." She was all the evidence he needed.

"Wouldn't it be fun to take the kids on a little road trip? We could go camping, exploring, have an *adventure!* Doesn't that sound like fun?"

"Sure, but we can't exactly afford the gas. If we follow the map as far as we can, that's probably at least a hundred miles there and back. Besides, you have to work and—"

"I have a couple of days off saved up. Just think! We haven't been camping since Cassie was three!"

Stewart grimaced at the memory.

She slugged him playfully. "Oh, come on, she can't possibly get that sick again."

All Stewart remembered of that trip was fountains of vomit and diarrhea. The poor kid had been so sick, they almost took her to urgent care. Without health insurance—neither of their jobs offered it—they couldn't afford a hospital visit. It had been enough to drive all desire for another camping trip far, far from his mind.

"Hunter would *love* it!" Liz said.

Maybe he could get the hunting knife he'd been working on for Hunter finished in the next few days. The boy didn't know that Stewart was working on a twin to his own hunting knife. He got the idea from the way Hunter's eyes lit up with avarice and admiration every time he saw the Damascus-steel hunting knife Stewart had made. "I'll think about it. Let's see how things go."

"Meanwhile, Cassie's going to be over the moon about these dolls. I'm glad we still have them." Liz took them from the bag and laid them on the kitchen table.

They were so beautiful, with their lifelike skin and eyes, their beautiful, lacy dresses, soft, flaxen hair, the innocent expressions on their faces, one with a little smile, the other a little sad. They didn't look mass-produced, because their faces were similar but not identical, as if they were sisters.

Liz said, "I think I'll just add a little pretty tissue paper to this nice bag they came in..."

As she worked to prepare Cassie's birthday present, however, Stewart's attention wandered back to the map. One of the mountains beyond the lake looked like it had the face of a snapping turtle.

***

The waters of Smithfield Quarry were ice cold, somehow, even in the Arizona heat, which is why it was so popular among the local kids. The twenty-foot cliffs, crystal-clear water, and terraced road down into the pit made for nice scenery and plenty of places to roll out a picnic blanket. Too small to be a real tourist draw, it was like Mesa Roja's best kept secret.

Stewart was ten. He was with his fourth foster family. These adults hadn't beaten him yet. The scars were healing.

His birthday fell within a few days of another of the foster kids' birthdays, a cross-eyed boy named Jeff, who was a year older, wore thick glasses, lacked a chin, and had teeth that jagged toward each other like rodent's teeth. To celebrate both birthdays, the foster parents magnanimously took their foster brood—maybe six kids in all ranging from four to eleven, Jeff being the oldest—out to the quarry for a picnic and some swimming. Stewart couldn't remember any of their names—he had only been with this family for a couple of months—but he remembered Jeff. The two of them shared a love of comic books. Most of the comics in the house were lame ones like *Richie Rich* and *Archie*, but they were better than nothing at all. The two boys read the covers off the Spider-Man, Superman, and Avengers comics, but Stewart was creeped out by the comments Jeff made about some of the female superheroes. It would be a couple of years before he even understood what Jeff was talking about.

They all laid out some blankets on the side of the road circling the water in one of the shady areas. The high cliffs nicely shadowed one crescent of water along the shore of the lake. The roadside was gravel and powdered rock, and the air smelled of moistness. A few yards away, the edge of the road dropped straight down into the crystal-clear water about twenty feet below.

The four-year-old foster kid always made a fuss, and today was no exception. She cried a lot, even at night when they were supposed to be sleeping. Stewart didn't remember her name, but he remembered the haunted despair in her eyes. He didn't know how to help her, so he went and sat at the edge with his feet dangling over the water.

"Stewart! Come away from there! You'll fall in!" his foster mother called, but she was too busy with the little girl to pay attention to whether he obeyed.

He just sat there enjoying the waves of air changing temperature across his body, looking down into the dark depths of the water, wondering if there might be sea monsters from the earth's core down there, or mermaids.

He could smell the cold hot dogs and potato salad from the Tupperware containers, the pickle relish, the brownies. This foster mother was a pretty good baker.

And then two hands on his shoulder blades, a big shove, and then he was spread-eagled in midair over the water. Tumbling.

He hit with a resounding slap, and the water exploded up his nose, into his mouth. He was choking. He didn't know which way was up. The icy cold lake numbed his flesh. He flailed and kicked, but there was nowhere to stand or grab. Everything was a dim blur.

The sensation of hands or something like them brushed the flesh all over his body. Were they lifting him or trying to drown him?

He remembered a little fish so green it might have been made of chips of emerald, glinting with sunlight. It swam into his face, poking his cheek. The sight of it told him which direction lay the sky.

He flailed some more, but he was going down, down...

His lungs screamed for air. If he opened his mouth, the water would rush in and that would be the end.

The belly of a whale drifted above him.

No, not a whale. Its flippers were oars.

The sensation of something touching him all over—and it was *not* water—intensified, squeezing or embracing him, as if he were inside the ring of an inner tube that was being inflated, and it made him feel buoyant. Tiny bubbles like in a soda fizzed in the water around him, caressing his skin, lifting him.

But it was too late. He had to breathe. The water grew dark.

A rough hand seized him by the collar of his shirt, lifting him. The bubbles danced and cavorted. He felt lighter than air.

Then he lay in the bottom of a rowboat.

The side of his head throbbed with pain.

A distant voice: "Is he okay?"

A nearby voice answering, "I think so. His eyes are open. He's trying to breathe."

Warm water vomited out of Stewart's mouth and nose, and then he could breathe again, and he lay there sobbing and gasping at the sky, across the hard ribs of the rowboat as they dug into his back, and he saw the back of a man in a plaid shirt as he worked the oars. He smelled of old sweat.

Gravel grated against the keel of the rowboat.

Arms hooked under his and lifted him. The sun was so bright. Heads encircled him, leaned over him.

"Stew, are you all right?"

"Say something!"

"Why'd you jump in the water?"

"What happened?"

"He's bleeding."

Stewart raised a hand to the throbbing lump above his ear.

"Must have bumped his head."

"How did you swim back up with a lump on your head like that?"

That question he knew the answer to. "Magic," he said.

A few of the onlookers laughed.

"He must be feeling all right now, making jokes."

Onlookers wandered back to their lives, excitement dissipating.

His foster father helped him sit up. The gravel of the lake shore hurt his legs. His head swam with the movement.

"That was a silly thing to do, Stew," his foster father said. "You gave us all a terrible fright."

Behind them all, looking sheepish, Jeff hung back.

Stewart looked back toward the water. A palm-sized fish gleamed emerald a few yards from shore, swimming back and forth.

***

When he awoke in the dead of night, covered in enough sweat to make him believe for a moment that someone had just dragged him out of Smithfield Quarry, the fish was the last thing to fade from his memory.

It was a familiar dream, but his heart was still pounding. He sighed and slung himself out of bed, evoking a murmuring sigh from Liz. His tossing and turning would keep her awake. Better to do something with himself. The dream was still too close for him to try going back to sleep. He had had this dream before, but this had been the most intense in years.

He went outside, still rubbing his eyes and flexing his muscles to wake up, fired up the forge, and set himself to working on Hunter's Damascus hunting knife. After last night with Eddie, the folding, welding, and drawing out were finished. It was all down to the grinding, then tempering, then etching, then polishing. As he ground the roughly blade-shaped chunk of steel into its more final shape, he could already see the "wood grain" of nickel and steel emerging. It was indeed a beautiful sight.

So absorbed was he that he didn't notice Liz until she was standing before him with an expression of mixed amusement and worry. She was fully dressed for work.

He switched off the grinding wheel and grinned at her sheepishly. "Huh. It's daylight."

"Yeah, no kidding, Profoundly Observant One."

"Couldn't sleep."

"And Captain Obvious as well!" Her tone was good-natured, but there was worry behind it.

"I'm all right," he said. "Just had a bad dream."

She came close and kissed him. "I'm off to work. Kids are already off to school."

"Wow, I *have* been a little absorbed."

"Yeah, we could hear you tinkering back here. How's it going?"

He held up the thing that now looked very much like a hunting knife, but without a grip. "Almost ready for tempering."

"Well, don't let it give you any attitude." She paused with a smirk. "Get it?"

He blinked.

"Temper?"

He chuckled. "Oh, geez."

She guffawed and slapped her knee. "Hah! I kill me. With that, I bid you adieu." She curtsied and turned away. "Tip your servers. I'll be here all week."

He grinned at her and turned the grinder back on. "Beat it."

She departed to meet her ride at the entrance to the main road.

The sun gave him another hour before the heat reached the quitting point, and then it was time to get back on the job hunt. Before he did that, however, he drank half a pot of coffee and ate two peanut butter sandwiches.

And then the phone rang.

He answered it, thinking it might be one of the many businesses at which he'd applied to work.

A nasal voice came over the line, "Is this Mr. Riley?"

"It is."

"This is Principal Snyder from Barnett Elementary. I'm sorry to inform you that your son Hunter just got in a fight at school. We need you to come and pick him up."

Seven

AS SOON AS STEWART got off the phone with the principal, he called the day care where Liz worked.

"What's up, hon?" she asked.

"Hunter got in a fight at school. The principal just called."

"What?"

"He might get suspended or expelled over this."

"*What!*"

"I'm coming to get you."

"Right. Did they say what it was about?"

"No."

"Then I'll be waiting out front," she said. "And don't spare the horses."

They hung up and Stewart jumped in the truck, low-level alarm dinging in his chest. The seat and steering wheel were already fry-an-egg hot from sitting in the sun. Hunter had never been in a fight before. At worst, he could be willful with his teachers or classmates when he thought they were wrong or being unfair. In contrast, by the time Stewart was Hunter's age, he had been in a few fights, mostly with kids who started them to try to prove themselves against the biggest kid in school. Hunter was truly a good-hearted kid, so Stewart was mystified at what could have happened. It had to be some sort of bullying.

Could it have something to do with the weird looks Hunter and Cassie had been trading lately, when they thought no one was looking? The boy had also seemed worried about not getting to go to taekwondo class anymore.

He pulled up in front of Sunshine Kidz eight minutes later, where Liz stood arms crossed against the split-rail fence surrounding the modest playground.

As she climbed in, they gave each other worried looks. When they arrived at the school, they went straight to the principal's office, where they found Hunter slumped in a chair near the secretary's desk. His lip was swollen and pink. At the sight of his parents, he sank deeper into his chair and looked as if he was about to cry.

Liz knelt before him and took his hands in hers. "Are you all right, kiddo?"

Hunter's posture straightened, and he nodded.

She hugged him and then examined his swollen lip.

The boy couldn't look at his father, trying to hold it all inside, but anger and shame leaked from his eyes.

The secretary, a plump lady with too much makeup, a bouffant hairdo, and a dress that made her look like a rounded clump of flowering prickly pear, gave them a wan smile. "I'll tell him you're here." She picked up her telephone receiver, but the door to the principal's office opened with slow gravitas.

Principal Snyder somehow made five feet six look even smaller, as if he were denser, more compact than a normal person. Salt-and-pepper hair fringed a shiny pate, making his protuberant ears look even bigger, almost like clamshells, and beady eyes flicked back and forth between them from behind thick-rimmed, squarish glasses that made his facial structure appear even more marmot-like. He was new at school this year, hired from Tucson or Phoenix and moved all the way to Mesa Roja. He was unmarried and drove a Ford Pinto so sun-bleached and dust-scoured it was difficult to tell what the original color had been. Mesa Roja was not a big town; Stewart had seen him around.

Today, Principal Snyder's solemn expression suggested Hunter was about to be sentenced to the gallows. It felt so overblown to Stewart he found his muscles tightening, his teeth clenching. Surely someone should have been hospitalized to warrant this kind of severity in the air.

Hunter slid out of his chair, appearing almost boneless. Liz put her arm around him, and the three of them entered Snyder's office. The air smelled a little sour, like old sweat, or an onion going bad.

Principal Snyder offered his hand to Stewart. "Dr. Ellis Snyder."

Stewart shook it. It felt like a damp sock. "Stewart Riley. This is Liz."

"How do you do?" Liz said, shaking the principal's hand.

"I wish this could have been under more pleasant circumstances," Snyder said, gesturing them all to sit.

They sat before Snyder's desk with Hunter in the middle. He still would not meet his father's eye.

"So what is this about?" Stewart said.

Snyder began, "As I told you, Hunter and two other boys—"

"Two!" Liz said.

"They jumped me," Hunter said sullenly.

"What was it about?" Stewart said. "They started it?"

"That's not the story they tell," Snyder said. "They said Hunter came at them in some sort of karate posture and—"

"It's *taekwondo*," Hunter said. "And they started it."

Liz said, "Where are the other boys?"

Snyder said, "They have been sent back to their room."

Liz said, "So Hunter is the only one in trouble?"

Snyder's gaze flicked to Stewart. "Under the circumstances—"

"Why are we still waiting for the whole story?" Liz said. She was about to get fiery. Stewart liked to watch her get all fiery on other people. It wasn't much fun when it was directed at him. "Maybe we should start at the beginning."

Snyder's face tightened. "Fine. Hunter, please proceed." He sat down behind his desk and straightened his suit jacket.

Hunter opened his mouth. "Well—"

"It seems your son suffers from an excess of imagination," Snyder said.

Both Stewart and Liz stiffened at the interruption.

Stewart leaned forward and put his elbow on Snyder's desk. "I'd like to hear it from him."

Snyder edged back, presenting his palms.

Hunter glared at him. "See, there were these two fifth-graders from Mrs. Donnelly's class, real idiots—"

"Now, Hunter," Liz said.

"They *are*, Mom! They were teasing Cassie on the playground at recess. They made her cry. I...got mad." Hunter wrung his hands tight.

"What were they teasing her about?" Liz said.

"She was over by the fence by herself, in the shade by the piñon trees. She was singing, just minding her own business, and these two idiots went over and started razzing her—"

"Hunter," Liz said.

Hunter sighed. "Fine. These two mentally challenged gentlemen. They made her cry. So I went over and told them to stop. Charlie White says, 'Your sister sounds like somebody dragging a cat through a keyhole.' Joey Alton says, 'Yeah, it hurts my ears.' I said to leave her alone. They said, 'Make us.' So I got into my stance and I *kihap*ed and—"

"Your son is clearly the aggressor in this incident," Snyder said.

"What about the two boys harassing my daughter?" Liz said. "Look, Mr. Snyder—"

"*Doctor* Snyder."

That was the point Stewart started fantasizing about popping the little man's head like a balloon.

"Look, *Doctor* Snyder, we raised our kids to protect each other," Liz said. "If you've got a couple of hooligans terrorizing an eight-year-old girl, and you're blaming *her brother* for protecting her, we have a serious problem."

"Unfortunately, the school district has a zero-tolerance policy against violence of any kind—"

"Then why does *my son* have a fat lip?"

Snyder peered through his glasses at Hunter as if noticing it for the first time. "Oh, well. I'll have to have another talk with those boys. They assured me they had not touched him."

Liz's eye-roll was practically audible. "Have you talked to Cassie? What does she say happened?"

"Your little girl is even more fanciful than your son, I'm afraid.

She says they were arguing about 'magic.'" The man's air quotes dripped with disdain. "What she claims happened can no more be trusted than stories of imaginary friends."

"Tell us what she said," Liz said.

"She says she saw some 'little people' near some kind of burrow at the edge of the schoolyard. We encourage imagination, but we all know there are limits, don't we? Such fantasies can be tolerated in one Cassie's age, but Hunter should have grown out of them by now and be looking toward his future as a productive adult."

Stewart didn't have to open his mouth. With one glance, Liz knew his mind. Her voice became hard and sharp as flint. "Well, we disagree, *Doctor* Snyder. Let kids be kids. Later in life, there are plenty of people like you who will kick them around plenty and cripple their imaginations."

It was time for Stewart to play Good Cop. He could almost see the smoke boiling from her ears as he laid his hand on her arm. "What she means is, what's going to happen to Hunter?"

Snyder's eyes narrowed. "He is suspended from school pending a full report to the school board."

Hunter's face went milk-white, fists clenched in his lap.

"And then what? Who makes the decision?" Liz asked.

"I will make a recommendation to the board, and they will decide his final disposition." The principal picked at one of his cuticles. "Hunter, would you mind waiting out by the secretary's desk? I need to speak to your parents."

Liz squeezed Hunter's hand. Stewart patted his back. His posture looked like that of a puppy that been kicked. Hunter shuffled out of the office and shut the door.

Snyder cleared his throat. "May I suggest...some counseling for your son? These kinds of ideas are not healthy in a well-balanced, productive youth."

"You're suggesting *my son* needs therapy because *your school* tolerates bullies?" Liz snorted. "May I suggest you come back with a reasonable decision," Liz said, every word meticulously enunciated. "Do you really want to see your name in the *Mesa Roja Messenger*? It'll feature prominently in a story about a boy kicked out of school for standing up to bullies, and the bullies get to stay in school. Better still, how would you personally like to be internet famous?"

Snyder jumped to his feet. "Are you threatening to slander me or this school?"

"It's not slander if it's true," Liz said. "Today's Friday, so I guess you have the weekend to think about it, *Doctor* Snyder. I'm taking my kids home. They'll be back on Monday."

Stewart stood up and gave Snyder a long, quiet look, a gaze the principal could not meet. He let himself loom there for a long moment.

Snyder said, "The apple doesn't fall far from the tree, I see. Good day to you both."

"What the hell does that mean?" Stewart said.

"You have a...history, don't you, sir?" Snyder brushed his hand toward the door. "Good day."

***

"I'm sure glad you did all the talking, babe," Stewart said as they walked up to the truck, Cassie holding his hand and Hunter holding

Liz's. "If it were up to me, I'd have thrown him through the window," Stewart said.

"*I* wanted to throw that smug, self-righteous, pompous, pus-faced, shark-a-lop-tipus through the window, too."

Cassie giggled into her hand. "Mommy, you talk so funny sometimes."

They all four piled into the truck, with the kids sharing the middle seat belt. As Stewart fired up the engine and backed out of their parking space, Liz said, "Okay, kids, it's time to spill it. After that meeting with the principal, we still don't know what really happened."

Stewart cranked the truck's decrepit air conditioner, which would blast air as hot as a hair dryer until they were almost home.

Hunter and Cassie glanced at each other. She elbowed her brother, prompting him to begin. He said, "Those two have been picking on Cassie since school started this year. They go out of their way to be jerks."

Cassie nodded vigorously at this. "They're mean. Cobweb always tells me to ignore them but—hey!" She elbowed Hunter back.

"You two!" Liz snapped. "I've had about enough beating around the bush today. What is all this about?"

Cassie glanced at her brother. "Hunter doesn't want me to tell you."

"Tell us what?" Liz said.

"About the little people," Cassie said.

Liz glanced at Stewart, who remained silent and pretended to focus on driving. "Is Cobweb one of these little people? You mean, like faeries?"

"No, not faeries. Faeries are just from stories, like Tinker Bell. Cobweb is real."

"They won't believe you, Cassie," Hunter said with a sigh.

"Yes-huh! They will, too!" Cassie said. "Won't you, Mommy?"

Liz nodded. "Just tell me all about it."

Cassie settled into her tale. "I was over by the fence because there was a little hole in the ground and Cobweb told me that her people lived in holes in the ground in Arizona because they don't like hot, and they love it when I sing to them and I was a little lonely today so I started singing by the hole, thinking they might come out and say hi, and that's when Charlie and Joey showed up and started calling me names. They said I was a terrible singer, and that really hurt my feelings." Tears welled in her eyes, but she sniffed once and wiped them away. "That's when Hunter came and told them to shut up. What happens if Hunter gets kicked out of school? Will I get kicked out of school, too?" Her voice cracked and her face crumbled toward a wail.

"No, honey," Liz said quickly. "Hunter is not going to get kicked out of school. Hunter? What happened next?"

"Well, like I said," Hunter said, "I told them to shut up and leave her alone. They laughed. I got in my stance and *kihap*ed."

"He yelled to scare them," Cassie said, "but it didn't."

"They both grabbed me and tackled me. They punched me in the lip. We haven't done what to do about tackles in class. I see the adults working on that kind of stuff sometimes, but..." His voice also cracked, and his face crumpled. "I didn't know what to do, so I just tried to fight back, but they just held me down and..."

He wiped his eyes and crossed his arms tightly.

"What happened, baby?" Liz said kindly, cupping his cheek. But he just sighed.

Cassie said matter-of-factly, "That's when Joey held him down and Charlie farted on his head."

Hunter wiped his eyes again and squeezed his arms tighter.

Stewart hoped Hunter didn't notice his mom's barely restrained burst of surprised laughter. The humiliation was already almost more than the boy could withstand.

"It was so stinky!" Cassie said. "But Hunter got a couple good kicks. It was enough to make them stop. Then they just laughed and went away. But then the playground teacher was coming."

A few blocks went by in strained silence. Finally, Stewart said, "Hunter, I'm proud of you. You did the right thing, protecting your sister. If it happens again, you have my permission to go full black belt on them."

Liz nodded. "Well, maybe not full black belt. But yes, what Dad said. You did the right thing. We're proud of you both."

Cassie piped up, "So you believe me about the little people?"

"Absolutely!" Liz said. "I'd love to see them, too."

Cassie elbowed Hunter again. "See! I told you they'd believe me! Peaseblossom says only kids can see them. Grown-ups can't."

"Why is that?" Stewart said.

Cassie shrugged. "I dunno. Maybe they'll let you see them if I ask them nice on account of it's my birthday." Then her eyes gleamed. "Hey! Can I invite them to the party?"

"Of course you can, honey," Liz said. "How big are they? How many pieces of cake do you think they'll need?"

"We're gonna have *cake?*" Cassie crowed, eyes wide.

"Why wouldn't we have cake, honey? It's your birthday," Liz said.

"I figured because we were broke and stuff," Cassie said.

Stewart's eyes misted. He laid his hand on his daughter's knee. "Cassie honey, we will *always* have cake. No matter what."

EIGHT

CASSIE INSISTED ON HELPING Liz make the birthday cake, a confetti angel food cake with strawberry frosting. Before it went into the oven, Cassie had as much of the batter on her face as went into the cake pan. As she bounced off to invite the little people to her party, Liz couldn't help but laugh. Stewart had told her about Cassie's "Geroj Sale." It was just so adorable.

But then an idea came to her.

Stewart was in the back yard now, working on a knife. He must be in a bit of emotional turmoil to be working out there in the heat of the day. It was so difficult to tell sometimes with him. He kept his emotions so close to the vest he'd be a great poker player if he believed in gambling.

Liz went outside to him, shielding her eyes against the afternoon glare. "Hey, babe! Just had a little eureka moment. Tell me what you think of this idea."

He paused his efforts polishing the blade of a new hunting knife. It looked like wood grain made of mirror.

"Wow," she said, "that looks fabulous."

"Thanks," he said. "What's up?"

"You know that storage unit full of Gramm's stuff?" Liz said. Her dear grandmother had passed away almost two years ago, bequeathing all of her stuff to Liz. Across town, there was a small storage unit full of furniture. She had never mustered the heart to go through and dispose of it, it seemed so morbid. Liz had been the favorite grandchild, the most trusted. Gramm and Liz's mother had never seen eye to eye on anything. Liz put her hands on her hips. "Maybe Cassie had the right idea. Maybe it's time for me to do something about that stuff. We could have a yard sale next weekend."

Stewart scratched his chin. "Not a bad idea. Are you sure, though? I mean, she was a sweet ol' gal and she really loved you."

"I know." Liz choked up a little just thinking about it, eyes misting at the thought of her grandma. "But if we can empty that unit, that's one less monthly bill, plus we need the cash. She left me that stuff for a reason." She had held on to it long enough.

"Your mom will be..."

"Furious, I know. But it's not her call."

Stewart smiled a little at that. Her mother had been vociferous, outspoken, and shrill in her disapproval of Stewart. Nowadays, they had reached a sort of detente, but he still nursed a bit of a grudge. It had been Gramm who gave Liz a little elbow and a wink on Stewart's behalf.

Liz went on, "How about we go tackle the storage unit first thing tomorrow? I'll put the yard sale in the paper next week and advertise on the internet. I'll call the radio station community calendar, too."

He nodded. "Sounds like a plan."

***

After dinner, the four of them sat around the kitchen table. Stewart dimmed the lights, and Liz lit the candles on the beautiful pink birthday cake, complete with rainbow sprinkles and HAPPY 8TH BIRTHDAY CASSANDRA spelled out in red piping on the top. Cassie bounced in her chair, eyes glowing at the sight of it.

Stewart wondered if he was feeling as much anticipation as Cassie. He could hardly wait to see her face when he gave her the dolls.

Liz set the cake on the table before her.

Cassie couldn't peel her eyes off it.

Stewart looked around the room, checking corners, nooks, and crannies for a sight of anything unusual. "Are your friends here, Cass?"

Cassie looked around. "I went out to their hole and invited them, but they weren't home."

"Ah, that's too bad," Liz said.

"I'll take them a piece of cake later," Cassie said.

"That sounds like a wonderful plan," Liz said.

"Let's do this!" Hunter said. "That cake looks so good. Do you have strawberries and whipped cream, too?"

"As a matter of fact..." Liz made a *voilà* gesture at the bowl of strawberries and can of whipped cream on the countertop.

Both kids looked ready to die of anticipation.

"All right, let's sing," Stewart said.

"Sing! Sing!" Cassie said, bouncing.

So the three of them sang *Happy Birthday* to her, and when it was over, she blew out her candles in one breath, giving a fist pump at her success.

Liz set about slicing the cake while Stewart produced the sparkling golden bag.

Cassie's eyes almost bugged out at the sight of it, little jewels in the dim lights. "What is it?" she breathed.

Stewart handed her the bag, his heart pounding in his chest. He couldn't keep from grinning.

Cassie took the bag and opened it. With a gasp, she looked at him and said, "*Two* dolls?"

"Take them out of the bag," Stewart said.

Cassie yanked one and then the other out of the bag and sat them against each other on the table, staring at them, unblinking.

Stewart was struck again by the perfection of their faces, the meticulous beauty of their dresses, the startling depth of the eyes. The old shopkeeper had an eye for wares, that was for certain. Even Hunter's jaw hung open.

Cassie stared at the dolls. But she didn't smile.

Stewart's heart skipped a beat.

Her lips parted and turned downward, lower lip quivering, eyes glistening.

"What's wrong, sweetie?" Stewart said in growing alarm, a sick pang in his gut over whether all his worry and angst over the dolls had been for nothing. "Don't you like them?"

"They're..." Cassie began.

"What, sweetie?" Liz said, glancing at Stewart.

"They're just so *beautiful!*" she said. Then she started to cry.

"Oh, sweetie..." Liz said, tears and laughter bursting out of her, too, as she hugged the child to her chest, giving Stewart a grin and eye-roll of incredible relief.

Amid tears and sniffling, Cassie reached out and hugged both dolls to her chest and squeezed them tight.

"This is my best birthday *ever!*" Cassie unleashed another gust of crying and sniffling.

Stewart wiped a tear and swallowed a lump in his throat. He met Liz's gaze, and she gave him a grin and a heartfelt thumbs-up.

***

The next day, they went to the storage facility, all four of them.

Stewart rolled up the steel door, revealing the collection of old furniture, boxes, and untold bits of stuff. The size of the task immediately slumped his shoulders. It was going to be a long week.

Hunter said, "Man, this stuff even smells old."

The scent of old furniture, paper, and who knew what else had come wafting out as the door opened.

Cassie had a doll tucked under each arm. "Mommy, can I play with my dolls?"

Liz nodded. "Stay where we can see you, okay?"

"Ugh! This place is *boring*," Cassie said, casting her gaze to the ceiling.

It was just a long row of red-painted doors, concrete floor, and high industrial ceiling. It *was* boring, but at least it was air-conditioned. Cassie went off a little way and sat on the floor with the dolls.

Stewart surveyed the contents of the storage unit. It was a 10-by-10-foot unit, stacked halfway to the ceiling. The furniture was too new to be truly antique but too old to be in fashion, with the exception of an old dresser and vanity mirror that Gramm had had from her mother.

With a sigh, Liz said, "Let's dig in, shall we?"

"We can start hauling this stuff home in the truck," Stewart said. "I can do it during the week, too."

Liz let out a deep breath and nodded.

An hour later, Hunter looked bored out of his mind, sitting next to Cassie, chin in hand, no doubt wishing he had thought to bring some comics to read. The hallway around the storage unit was filled with a scattering of furniture and stacks of boxes. Liz was taking it all pretty well, it seemed. Sometimes she teared up and sniffled, other times she held up something of Gramm's and said, "Oh, Stewart, look at this."

Gramm had been an interesting woman, the daughter of Slavic immigrants. When her husband died, she had traveled extensively on the life insurance money, and brought back boxes of relics from all over the world. Balinese wood carvings, Japanese dolls, a beautiful Chinese embroidered silk dress, an Argentine gaucho's *bola*, a Mexican sombrero, kitschy replicas of the Eiffel Tower and the Tower of London.

Some of it might have a little value if they could find buyers for it.

But then Liz found what looked like a Japanese jewelry box of black lacquer, inlaid extensively with intricate, mother-of-pearl designs.

"Wow, that's pretty," he said.

But what was inside made Liz gasp. "Oh, my gosh. Stewart, I think this is gold."

His ears pricked up immediately at the sound of that. He'd been hoping all morning they might uncover something of real value to stead them until he could find a real job.

She lifted what looked like a pendant out of the box. Hanging from a gold chain was a two-inch gold oval, inlaid with silver in a vaguely organic pattern; in the center of the pattern lay a richly colored blue stone. He was no art or jewelry expert, so its origin was beyond him, but it certainly looked like real gold. And he was enough of a rockhound to recognize a sapphire when he saw one. The stone looked like two or three carats. This was exactly the kind of thing he'd been hoping to find, but now that they found it, the thought of parting with it didn't sit well with him.

"We need to get this thing appraised," Liz said.

"Are you sure you don't want to keep it?" Stewart said. "It's probably the only thing in here worth real money."

"You're right... Oh, I don't know!" The indecision twisted her face and she bit her lip. He liked kissing those.

"I think your mom would kill you if you sold that," he said.

"I'm not sure Mom even knows about this, or else she'd have asked me about it. I've never seen this before. And I didn't think Gramm was the sort to collect this kind of thing. Where do you think it came from?"

Stewart shrugged. "I'm pretty sure that's a real sapphire. No clue what it might be worth. Depends on the quality of the stone, but maybe a couple thousand dollars?"

She whistled. "We are *definitely* getting it appraised." Then her eyes almost glowed and a grin spread across her face as she looked at him.

"What?" he said.

"We're going to be okay!" she said.

"Well, yeah, but—"

"No, no, ya big goon. The map!"

"What about the map?" It was sitting atop his dresser at home beside some pocket change and a bottle of cologne.

"We're going to have a little money for gas after this. We have a tiny, little cushion. We can follow the map!"

"Oh, you're serious."

"Of course, I'm serious. You've been in a funk for days. There's the whole school thing hanging over us." She lowered her voice and glanced to make sure the kids weren't listening. "I'm a little worried about Cassie and her little people, to be honest. We need a little road trip, a little fun. It'll be like hunting for pirate treasure!"

Her enthusiasm tugged loose a grin on his face. "It *does* sound like fun..."

She looked at the pendant again, stroked it with her thumb. "Thank you, Gramm." Then she put it back in the box.

That's when Stewart saw the little man peeking from behind the old, floral-print sofa.

Stewart blinked and focused.

The little man was about a foot high, with a little round face, little mutton-chop whiskers, a little black top hat, his expression changing from curiosity to shock and dismay as he realized Stewart could see him.

Stewart must have made a noise of surprise, because Liz said, "What is it?" She turned to look where Stewart was staring.

He had looked away for only a split second, but when he looked back, the little man was gone. Stewart jumped around boxes and a stack of chairs to get farther into the space for a better look at where the little man had been standing.

But there was nothing there. Stewart cast about, looking behind the sofa, behind everything still in the storage unit, but there was no sign of the little man.

"Stewart!" Liz said. "What on earth?"

"Thought I saw something."

She drew back. "It wasn't a rat, was it? Or a mouse? I don't smell any mouse poop..."

He sighed and rubbed his eyes. "I'm not sure."

She put her hands on her hips. "Yes, you are. You just don't want to tell me."

There was no fooling her. "I thought I saw a little guy about this high." He held his palms about a foot apart. "With a top hat. And whiskers."

She snickered. "You sure it wasn't a leprechaun?"

"You're right. It sounds stupid."

"I was thinking more along the lines of 'curiouser and curiouser.'"

"No, it sounds stupid," he said, but even as he spoke the words, they sounded hollow. He remembered that face as clearly as he could see the hideous sofa in front of him. Another thing he was certain of, it was gone now. Somehow, he knew that for certain.

NINE

WHEN MONDAY CAME, Stewart loaded both children into the truck for school. They had received no formal notification of whether Hunter had indeed been suspended, so Stewart was going to behave as if everything was fine. Maybe it would all just quietly disappear.

"Is Hunter still in trouble?" Cassie asked.

Hunter sank deeper into his seat.

"I don't know, sweetie," Stewart said. "But he's not in trouble with me."

"Thanks, Dad," Hunter said, still sullen and worried, but appreciative. "What do I do if those idiots come after me?"

"Fart on their head!" Cassie said.

Stewart looked his son in the eye. "You do what you got to do, Son. But here's what I want you to remember forever, from now until you're an old man. Are you listening?"

Hunter looked him square in the eye. "Yeah, Dad."

"Never throw the first punch. You throw the *last* punch, and only the last punch. No more than that. Do you understand?"

Hunter considered this for a moment. "You mean never go farther than I need to. If they stop, if they quit, if they give up, it's over."

"Right."

"Are kicks okay?" Hunter said.

Stewart chuckled. "Use the right weapon for the right situation."

Stewart walked each of them to their classrooms, Cassie first. Hunter's teacher, Ms. Mecklenberg, greeted him with a smile and a wave as if nothing had happened. Hunter looked back once at his father, and Stewart could see the lift in his shoulders. With a sigh of relief, he left the boy there and went to the storage unit to begin hauling Gramm's stuff back home. He would store everything in the house and carport until the weekend. It would take him several trips to haul it all, but he had the time. He also took the sapphire-and-gold pendant to a jeweler to have it appraised. On the drive, he took a moment to really study it. It was indeed a beautiful thing. It looked like there was engraving on the back, some sort of writing, but he couldn't read it, didn't recognize any language. It might be just scrollwork.

When the jeweler gave him the appraisal, he kept his jaw from dropping open.

That night, when he told Liz the appraisal figure, her jaw dropped open.

She sat on the couch, clutching her hands. "Wow. I really don't know what to do now. We need the money, but..."

He had had all day to think about it. "How about this? Tomorrow I go put it in a safety deposit box. Let's see how the yard sale turns out, and if we really need the cash, we can talk about it again then."

Liz nodded. "The weird thing is that knowing how much it's worth makes me want to keep it. Is that weird? Gramm left that to *me*, and I never even knew about it..."

"Maybe I'll even have a job by the end of the week," he said. "Then it won't matter."

***

But he didn't. Between stops in his job search around Mesa Roja, he hauled more of Gramm's things home. By Wednesday, however, he had exhausted all the employment possibilities he could think of, with nothing on the horizon beyond a few vague niceties like "we'll call you soon." Warehouse jobs, construction, all kinds of manual labor, no one was hiring. Truckers were in demand, but he didn't have a commercial driver's license. It would take time and money he didn't have to get one.

On Thursday, he started looking more concertedly for work in neighboring towns, a process made more difficult by all the employers who wanted him to fill out his application in person. His truck slobbered up gas like a Saint Bernard at its water dish. Paying for all that gas would guzzle what little money they had left. He was already using more fuel than normal by hauling all of Gramm's things, never mind that their living room was already stacked halfway to the ceiling with musty boxes and furniture.

By Friday, he was once again thoroughly disheartened. Worry settled over him like a lead blanket. He told himself that his loss of appetite would help make the food last a little longer, for the sake of the kids. Should he have done something different that day with Mr. Richards? Could he have kept his job? When everyone was home, he spent more and more time outside, feeling the pressure of his inadequacy, his unworthiness, every time he looked in their faces.

Liz, however, was getting more and more excited. She and the kids were having fun putting price tags on everything. She told everybody at the day-care center about it, even the parents. "Everybody loves a good yard sale!"

Aside from jeering at a distance, Hunter and Cassie had gotten no more trouble from the bullies at school. Apparently the two boys had gotten the memo about laying off.

The day of the yard sale came quicker than expected. On Friday night, he brought the last bit of junk home from the storage unit and closed it up. Gramm had been a bit of a pack rat, it turned out, particularly when it came to old magazines. Stewart sifted through boxes of magazines that were older than he was. No silverfish, mold, or mouse nests, luckily.

Hunter was excited to see the magazines, though. He hefted a full box of old *Popular Science* and *National Geographic* back to his room and started reading. Soon he poked his head out. "Hey, Mom, can we keep these? It's like sticking my face in a time machine."

Liz laughed. "Sure."

On the morning of the yard sale, Liz and Cassie were outside on their lawn chairs in the shade of the carport. Cassie made a cooler full of lemonade, sweetened with prickly pear syrup, and sold it to an appreciative clientele for fifty cents a cup. Stewart couldn't help but smile at her entrepreneurial spirit, a trait she certainly hadn't inherited from him. He hated getting in front of people and trying to sell anything. Give him a job to do and he would happily go do it, as long as it didn't involve persuasion, selling, anything like that. He liked metal, he liked earth, he liked concrete things he could make with his hands. Such things were all he was good for.

He wasn't ready to give it to Hunter yet, but he put the finishing touches on the hunting knife. About eight inches long, the Damascus blade turned out beautifully. It was razor-sharp, flexible, and the microscopic layers meant that it both took and held an edge, the kind you could shave with, which was why Damascus steel had been in such high demand in medieval times. He fashioned the handle from desert ironwood, which also had a pronounced, gnarled grain, but was very dense and hard to cut and shape, harder even than maple and walnut. That was also precisely why it made such a great knife grip.

The sheath he made from a few scraps of leather left over from other projects. He was not a skilled leatherworker, so it was very Plain-Jane, but he sewed it with real sinew, which gave it an archaic, Native American look.

Cassie's dolls had been such a tremendous hit that he wondered if he could get two home runs in a row. It wouldn't be Hunter's birthday for a while, but he planned to give the knife to his son when they went on their camping trip.

The camping trip. He still couldn't convince himself that it was a great idea. It just felt wrong to go on any sort of vacation when he didn't have a job. It made him feel like a deadbeat, a failure, somebody who ran from his problems.

But then he thought about the map. He had no silly illusions that it was authentic. It was just a toy, a fabrication... But toys were toys because they unlocked adventure and imagination.

When had he stopped playing with toys? When had he put away childish things? Had he ever, completely? He still dreamed grand stories of taking his children on trips and showing them things like the terracotta warriors of China, Machu Picchu in Peru, the lost city of Angkor in Cambodia, the Great Pyramids, all the wonders the world had to offer, and he could imagine himself in a leather jacket and fedora like Indiana Jones, or maybe he could be an explorer and save tribes of gorillas in Africa from poachers. When he got really fanciful, he could imagine himself in a suit of armor battling ogres and dark elves on some strange battlefield. All these things he could imagine. He could show Hunter and Cassie these amazing things, because he was their dad, and they made him feel like he could do anything. He was not just a "bad kid" from a skid-mark town in the middle of nowhere. To them, he was no such thing.

All this rumination kept him in the back yard, staring out into the desert, long after he had finished the knife.

For some reason, the customers and neighbors wandering through their yard sale annoyed him. It was like they were vultures picking through a carcass. Gramm wasn't even his grandmother, but he'd loved the old bird.

At dusk, Cassie came and took him by the hand. "Daddy, come and look at everything that's gone!"

He smiled and let her lead him out front, where he found her to be correct. Much of Gramm's furniture was gone now, except for that awful, floral-print sofa. In the daylight, it gave his eyes a cramp. He couldn't remember everything that was missing, only that there was much less stuff there now than there had been this morning.

"Guess how much money we got!" Cassie said.

"How much, sweetie?"

"Two thousand dollars!"

His eyes must have bulged.

Liz chuckled and said, "Kiddo is a little overzealous and added a zero."

He laughed. "So, two hundred then?"

"A little over, but yeah. I can't complain."

He found himself growing tense, teeth clenching. "It's not enough." All that *work!* All that *gas!* He spun and walked back to the house. His hands were shaking.

Liz called after him. "Stewart?"

He didn't answer, just kept walking. He wanted to walk out into the desert and never come back.

Liz was following him now. "Stewart! Where are you going?"

He didn't know.

"What's gotten into you?"

He didn't know that either. It was as if a ton of bricks had just fallen on his head, each of them carved with things like:

You're a loser.

You're no adventurer.

You can't go on some silly camping trip.

You can't afford it.

You don't have the money.

You have to find a job.

Everything is a waste of time.

You don't deserve a woman like her.

You don't deserve such great kids.

You'll never amount to anything.

You'll never take them on any adventures.

They will grow up hating you.

An endless litany, raining upon him.

"Stewart!" Liz seized his arm and tried to stop him, but his strength was easily twice hers. He pulled his arm away. Her gasp of fear began its shift to anger.

Let her anger come. He deserved it.

"What the burp is going on?" she said.

He stopped a few paces away from her, near the rocks where he'd seen the huge ogre or whatever his diseased mind had confabulated for him. "I don't know."

"Why are you so angry? After all your hard work this week, I thought you'd be happy we got rid of most of it."

He didn't know why he was angry. It was as if every negative thought he'd ever had had been loaded into a machine gun and fired at him in an unending barrage.

"I know it's not your thing, but I need you talk to me," she said.

He pulled the map out of his back pocket. He didn't remember putting it there. Unfolding it, he stared at the lines traced into geographical shapes both familiar and unfamiliar. *Here there be monsters.*

"This is why I'm angry," he said.

He tried to tear it in half, but it was somehow tougher than boot leather.

"Stewart!"

"Sometimes I just want it to die!"

"Want what to die?"

"The magic."

She sat on a boulder beside him and took his hand. "Why?"

"Because life would be easier. Clinging to hope is too damn hard."

"Oh, baby," she whispered.

"Here I am, still without a job. How long before the kids are ashamed of me? How long before they start thinking I'm a good-for-nothing dad? I never had a dad. I never had any kind of male role model, so how am I supposed to know how to do it?"

She stood and tried to look up into his eyes, but he couldn't meet her gaze. "Stewart, you are a way better dad than mine ever was. And I *love* my dad. But a strong man he was not. He still lets Mom and everybody else walk all over him. He's a good, sweet soul, but do you think he's happy? I remember one time, Mom humiliated me in a department store, I don't even remember what it was about, except that she made me feel about two inches tall, and he just smiled and said, 'Yes, dear.' He didn't stand up for me. I was too shocked to be furious with him. Then Mom sneered at him and humiliated him, too, right in front of several people. But he just wandered off and we lost track of him. I looked for him for an hour, found him sitting alone in a changing room. He'd been crying. He always knew what was right, but what he didn't have was the strength to stand up for it. When I was a kid, there was still some life in him. But somewhere along the line, it's like he gave up, and part of him just withered and died."

Giving up was easy. It was what Stewart wanted to do. He wanted to give up and let that hopeful, magical piece of him wither and die, starved on the vine. His eyes misted over at that. "Do you ever think..." He couldn't bring himself to finish it.

After a long moment, she said, "Spit it out."

"Do you ever think you made the wrong choice?" He met her gaze then. "You could've had anybody you wanted."

She held his gaze. "But I picked you."

And here she was, this beautiful woman, who strangely liked hanging out with him. The question was, why?

"Let me explain it to you this way," she said. "Baby, you are a *mountain*. I had the quarterback, power forward, and half the marching band mooning over me. I was a vain little princess back then, so the attention was fun sometimes, I'm not gonna lie. The quarterback, Bill Myers—"

"Runs the car dealership. And the all-state power forward—"

"Has five kids by four different women and doesn't pay child support on any of them."

"I didn't know that."

"I work in a day care. I'm losing my point..." Her eyes cast about, pointed internally, until they found it again. "Right. You're a mountain, Stewart. All those other guys, the best of them are little hills, and most of them are speed bumps. I'm not sure my metaphor is working here. It takes a lot of time and effort to climb a mountain, but it's worth it. I climbed a couple of fourteeners in Colorado on summer vacations. It's tremendous work, kinda dangerous if you're not careful. You got sheer cliff faces, hard-scrabble trenches, boulder fields, thousand-foot drop-offs, but boy, when you hit the summit," she stroked his cheek, "the view is *amazing*. Absolutely nothing like it on this planet."

"So that's a really long way of saying you like a challenge."

She laughed, the full, heartfelt laugh that helped him overcome his uncertainties every single time.

He said, "You're the only one ever wanted to climb this particular mountain."

She shrugged. "And it's not just that climbing you is a pain in the baby donkey—"

"Baby donkey?"

"What's another word for donkey?"

"Oh."

"Let me finish my train of thought."

"The tracks are still under construction." He snickered.

She punched him. "Here I was being all sentimental and earnest and you're cracking jokes."

"I like your sentimentality and earnestness." He hugged her close.

When they released each other, she sighed. "What I was *going* to say was that watching you deal with people like my mother, like your boss, is that you are like a mountain, able to withstand whatever storm came your direction, like the weather patterns for half of North America would just break and go around. Nothing seemed to be able to alter your course. Nothing fazes you. Except yourself. Maybe I should have said you're like rocks on a beach, standing up to the waves and everything. My metaphor keeps breaking down."

"I like the mountain one better." He took a deep breath and looked around, surveying the desert colors of falling night. "I'm sorry. I don't know where all that anger came from. It's almost like it didn't come from me, like someone was whispering in my ear."

"The devil on your shoulder."

"Something like that."

"Maybe there are angels, too."

"If there are, their voices aren't as loud. Besides, there's only one angel I need." He looked into her eyes again.

A goofy grin spread across her face. "See? Just when I think I need to give you a good whacking, you say something like that and make me all gooey."

"You are my warm, caramel angel."

She rolled her eyes, but her cheeks flushed red. He hugged her close and kissed her.

He said, "We should go back and head for bed."

"The kids are still awake."

He laughed. "That's not what I meant."

She waggled her eyebrows at him. "You sure you don't want to hang out, out here in the dark a little while, and make out?"

"What I was going to say was we need our rest, because tomorrow we're getting up early to pack for an adventure." He took the map out and looked at it again.

"Really?" Her eyes sparkled.

He put the map away. "Then again, I like the way you think."

PART II

Ten

THE JUBILATION WHEN STEWART and Liz told the kids the plan erased any remaining misgivings.

Hooting, jumping, cabbage-patching and floss-dancing, all made the adults laugh until their faces reddened.

Liz sent them back to their room to pack for a couple of nights' worth of camping.

"I'm taking my dolls!"

"I'm taking my comics!"

"You can't take your comics! They'll get ruined."

"Then you can't take your dolls, doofus!"

"Enough!" Liz called. "Dolls and comics are okay. Dinosaurs, mastodons, and hippopotamuses are not."

"*Whaaat?*" came the chorus from the back room.

Liz winked at Stewart and he chuckled.

Cassie came out into the living room, looking at her mother with one eye narrowed. "Mom. What are you talking about?"

"Dinosaurs, mastodons, and hippopotamuses will not fit in the truck. Therefore, they are not allowed."

Cassie rolled her eyes and marched back to the bedroom. "I don't have any of those things!"

Inside the house, what followed was a frenzy of "Can I take this?" and "Stop touching my stuff!"

From the back-yard shed, Stewart started dragging out the dusty accoutrements of their last camping trip. Tent, backpacks, water bottles, sleeping bags, all the little tools like flashlight, batteries, hatchet, matches, and mess kits, but also things like toilet paper, sunscreen, and mosquito repellent. He spread everything out on the ground to make sure no tarantulas or other creepy-crawlies had taken up residence in the family's camping gear. It would not go well to discover any intruders when it was time to bed down at a campsite.

Even as he did all this, his heart felt buoyed, as if the dark, angry thoughts that had consumed him earlier in the evening were but a distant memory. Before bedtime, he had everything packed back up and loaded in the truck so they could leave bright and early in the morning.

He and Liz sat at the kitchen table, drinking some chamomile tea, looking at the map, comparing it to a state road map, plotting out their route and the possible campsites along the way. Meanwhile, they could hear the kids tossing, turning, and whispering back in the bedroom.

"You think they're excited?" Liz said.

Stewart chuckled and pointed at a spot on the shopkeeper's map. "Check out the Colorado River. It looks like, as it gets close to the Utah border, the river has a different course. Up until this point, the shopkeeper's map looks fairly accurate—"

"Did you hear that?" Liz cocked her head toward the open kitchen window.

Stewart listened, too. After all the strange stuff he'd seen lately, the hairs on the nape of his neck rose instantly.

Liz said, "It sounded like whispering, but outside."

Then outside, a tremendous metallic crash raised a yelp from Liz as she leaped to her feet.

"Something is in the garbage." Stewart jumped up and ran outside into the dark.

After dinner tonight, he had placed the metal garbage can at the end of the driveway for tomorrow's garbage pickup. They sometimes had the occasional raccoon or javelina try to get in the garbage, so he always made sure the lid was on tight.

What he found, however, was not the efforts of an enterprising raccoon or javelina. The garbage can looked like someone had fired a bowling ball into it at fifty miles per hour. It was completely smashed, lying on its side, the garbage bag burst open, scattering garbage in a twenty-foot fan.

"What the hell?" he said.

Had someone hit it with a car? He hadn't heard any engine.

He cocked his ears into the silence of the night.

Was that whispering he heard in the bushes?

"Hey!" he called. "Come out of there where I can see you!"

The whispering stopped. It hadn't sounded like adults or teenagers, too high-pitched.

He approached the noise, wishing he'd grabbed a flashlight on the way out of the house.

It sounded crazy, but Cassie's stories of little people rose to mind—and the memory of the weird little man with a top hat he thought he'd seen in Gramm's storage unit. Was he hallucinating? A hallucination couldn't do that to a garbage can.

"I said come out of there!" he said.

Something burst out of the bushes like a roadrunner, not a real one but more like the cartoon. A burst of leaves, a dust cloud streaking away from him, and gone into the night.

He blinked and stared, a chill trickling down his spine. No animal could move that fast.

Then he jumped as something else burst from the bushes, streaking in a different direction to disappear just as quickly in the dark.

When he could get his feet to move again, he hurried toward the bushes to see if whatever they had been had left any evidence behind. The air near the bushes smelled of cinnamon and cloves, and the ground was newly scuffed by the passage of feet.

He turned back toward the house to retrieve a flashlight, when he spotted movement under his truck. Kneeling for a better look, he thought at first it was a porcupine because of the spines, but then he realized they were not quills or spines, but darts. It was...

His mind struggled to wrap itself around what he saw.

It looked like a naked mole-rat, but the size of a dachshund, and pin-cushioned by at least a dozen shiny, black darts about three inches long. Its wrinkled skin was the color of sour milk, and it lay on its back, four limbs in the air, staring at the undercarriage of his pickup, gasping, writhing like a creature in its death throes. The white whiskers of its face gave it the look of a kung-fu master from some old martial arts movie. It was maybe the most hideous thing he had ever seen. Its forelimbs ended in what looked like little hands, tipped with nasty-looking claws. No, not claws—blades of dark, lustrous metal fixed to its hands by little gloves.

From the screen door, Liz called, "What is it, Stewart?"

"Uh, I *really* don't know."

"Mommy!" Cassie shrilled in growing alarm.

Liz spun and disappeared inside the house. "What is it, sweetie?"

Cassie's voice carried real fear, but the bizarre creature before him held him in place. He wanted to drag it out so he could examine it, but he was afraid to touch its pale, wrinkly hide.

But then the sound of crying through the bedroom window, a howl of alarm and heartbreak, drew him away to see what was the matter. He went back into the house.

Cassie's voice echoed. "They were *right there!*" she wailed.

When Stewart entered the bedroom, Liz was hugging Cassie close, and the girl's eyes were wide. "What's going on?"

"My dolls!" Cassie cried. "They're gone! Hunter took them!"

"No, I didn't!" In the top bunk, Hunter's eyes were wide and confused. "I swear!"

Stewart frowned at him.

"Dad, I swear!"

Breathlessly, Cassie said, "I put them on top of my dresser so I don't get their clothes all rumply at night." She pointed a little finger at the empty space atop her dresser. "They're gone!"

Liz stroked her hair and spoke with a soothing voice. "I'm sure they'll turn up. I mean, it's not like they walked off."

"Hunter did it!"

"No, I didn't!"

Stewart studied his son, and if the boy was lying, he'd been taking acting classes. Flipping on the light, Stewart checked all the corners, under the bed, in the closet, and then expanded his search to the rest of house.

He spotted them immediately upon entering the living room. Both dolls were sitting on the couch, as if carefully arranged. With a sigh of relief, he picked them up and carried them into the bedroom. "Found 'em!"

Cassie, on the verge of the kind of hysteria that would not be easily soothed, melted into a pile of relief, holding out her arms to receive them. He handed them over and she hugged them fiercely.

At least now they would all get to sleep tonight.

"They were on the couch," he said.

She hugged them tight with a sigh.

"See?" Hunter said. "I told you it wasn't me!"

"I don't remember putting them there," Cassie said.

Liz said, "The important thing is that they're not lost. Go back to sleep now. And if you want to keep them in your bed, that's okay. I'm sure they wouldn't mind if their dresses get a little wrinkly. Will you?" She stroked one of the dolls' hair. "We can always iron them."

Cassie scooted back into bed, still clutching both dolls, and Liz tucked her in.

As Liz stood, Hunter said plaintively, "It wasn't me, Mom."

Liz stroked his cheek with motherly warmth. "Good night, you two. Now get your rest. We're hitting the road bright and early."

Stewart shut the bedroom door and said to Liz, "Come on, you *got* to see this."

Strangely, the living room smelled of cinnamon and cloves, but what he wanted was to show Liz the bizarre creature under the pickup. First he grabbed a flashlight from the kitchen junk drawer.

Following him outside, Liz said, "Is it what got into the garbage can?"

"You won't believe this." He knelt beside the pickup and shined the flashlight underneath.

But there was nothing under there but rocks and dust.

He said a few angry words as he jumped up and circled the truck, shining the flashlight about for any sign of the dying creature he'd seen just minutes ago. Had it dragged itself off?

Too many weird things had happened for him to write this off. He'd gotten a good look at the thing. It was so ugly, as if made of spite, that he would never forget it. It looked like a creature whose entire purpose was to do harm. And something had killed it.

"Let me guess," Liz said. "Whatever it was, it's gone now."

He gave her a plaintive look.

"I'm starting to get the feeling that there's stuff going on all around us that we can't see," she said, looking out into the desert darkness.

"Now who's Captain Obvious?" he said.

"*Touché.* It's like there's something out there watching us."

He nodded. "It can't all be in my head. A streak of crazy can't do that to a garbage can."

"Unless you have telekinetic mind powers."

"I don't have a lot of time to practice those."

"It's a shame. You'd make a great Jedi."

He chuckled, then sighed at the sight of scattered garbage. "Let's get that cleaned up and then go to bed. I'll go get a rake for the garbage and a hammer to straighten out the garbage can."

ELEVEN

JORATH EL-THRIM STOOD before the Master, trembling, on the mirrored expanse of chromium floor. He could not peel his gaze from the Master's Machine as it worked. Its sole purpose was the systematic destruction of a living being, its power drawn from the life of those placed in its clutches.

The Master's audience hall stood so swathed in shadows that its boundaries would not be visible to anyone without a dark elf's eyes, but Jorath could see the rib-like pillars along the metal walls, reaching up into the cavernous arches above. Globules of light floated in the air, spreading pools of illumination, produced and marshaled by the will of the creature upon the throne.

On a high dais of polished bronze and steel stood the Blood Throne of Baron Tyrus. The monolithic throne of blood-red copper, with its slowly waving halo of thorny metal vines, animated whenever its master occupied the throne, rose twice the height of even a creature as tall as Baron Tyrus.

Baron Tyrus watched the Machine work, anticipation gleaming in his featureless crimson eyes like polished rubies catching the red glow of the Machine's inner workings. His chalk-pale face and bald head looked like sculpted marble, as if he were one of the Medusids' victims. He would have been strikingly handsome if he still resembled flesh. Stringy black wisps of mustache, meticulously trimmed and waxed, flowed into a spiked beard that looked like sharpened obsidian. His robes glittered with shards of diamond woven into the fabric, glittering with the light of the globes and the inner glow of the Machine. His long-fingered hands, encrusted with jeweled rings, were steepled before his sharp chin, his thin lips pressed together in anticipation.

The screams of Jorath's superior, Dorash, were beginning to subside as the Machine did its inexorable work. It truly was a demented wonder, the Machine. Designed and perfected over a thousand years by Baron Tyrus, its sole purpose was to drain every drop of blood, every trickle of life force, from those placed in its clutches, but keep them alive and awake for days, weeks, even months, never spilling a dram. It was a thing of meshing gears, blades, drains, pinions, restraints, and needles, everything twisting, squeezing, slashing, stabbing at whatever speed most amused Baron Tyrus in a given moment.

Jorath had been watching the Machine work for over an hour. At first, Dorash had begged for mercy, an act that highlighted his immense foolishness. The tiniest scrap of mercy did not exist within the creature known as Baron Tyrus. It was foolishness that brought Dorash to this terrible end and brought dishonor to the House of Thrim.

A row of dark elf guards, Jorath's underlings, held fast the other two prisoners. The spindly, cadaverous creature clad in burlap with a face of charcoal scrawled upon its sackcloth skin, trembled in its bonds. Did such a dry, desiccated creature contain any lifeblood to drain? The Machine could reduce it to scraps of burlap and straw in moments.

The other prisoner was a goblin, short and squat, hunched and rounded. Its bald head accentuated its protuberant ears, like broken clamshells they were. Its bulbous nose and snaggleteeth made it a deliciously hideous creature. But goblins were not to be discounted for their ugliness, for like most of its race, its black eyes harbored a devious cunning. Even now, it was doubtless scheming a way out of its imminent, agonized demise.

The Machine eased to a halt, its glow diminishing to a slow, rhythmic pulse, and what was left of Dorash hung in its clutches, gasping his last.

Baron Tyrus's voice was a distant thunderstorm, an earthquake. "Captain Dorash El-Thrim."

Seeing Tyrus's face move—one did not expect the face of an alabaster statue to show animation—sent a fresh chill over Jorath's flesh.

But the sound of it awakened Dorash from his near-death stupor. "Yes, Master!" he yelped. "I serve only you, Master!" There was so little strength left in him, it was as if he marshaled all of this strength simply to speak.

"And that, poorly," Baron Tyrus rumbled. "You are a cretin, Dorash. I gave you a single purpose: prevent the human from going on his journey. You enlisted the aid of more incompetents." His ruby gaze swept toward the scarecrow and the goblin, who quailed at its bottomless fury. "And together, you failed."

"But, Master!" the goblin mewled. "The human could *see* things."

"That is why I sent you!" Tyrus snarled, his razor teeth glinting in the light of a globule hovering near the throne. "That is precisely why he is so dangerous to my plans."

"He...had...protectors!" Dorash gasped.

The Dark Lord snarled, baring his awful teeth. "And with all the power and weapons I gave you at your disposal, you still failed. Look!"

A chromium globe descended from the shadows above, hovering in the air before the throne. In it, Jorath could see the images reflected of onlookers' faces, weapons, the glow of the Machine.

The globe's surface rippled like quicksilver until it formed the image from the Penumbra. Four humans, the man, his wife, and their two children, climbing into a mechanical conveyance in the light of the rising sun. They were all smiles and excitement, at the beginning of what they anticipated would be a grand adventure, free of danger, clueless to the forces that were gathering against them.

The view in the globe came from a vantage point atop the family's tin house, where an Eye had been placed. Rooted as it was in the magic of the Dark Realm, the Eye would be invisible to those born of the Penumbra. Baron Tyrus had been watching this human family for some time. Why, Jorath did not know, except that the man, Stewart Riley, was considered a threat to be eliminated. It would have been easy just to kill him, but for the Dark Realm to act so directly against a Penumbral human would jeopardize the Veil between worlds and alert their enemies that schemes were afoot. There were always schemes afoot between Light and Dark, but a direct action in the Penumbra would attract attention.

"As you can see," Baron Tyrus said, "they have departed. They will be more difficult to track now that they are on the move."

Jorath summoned every ounce of his courage and ambition,

used them to beat down his fear, and raised his voice. "I can do it, Master."

Baron Tyrus's terrible gaze fixed upon him.

Jorath swallowed the dry lump in his throat. "I have tracked others in the Penumbra, and in the Borderlands as well. I know their creatures. I am familiar with the humans' mechanical contrivances." Dorash's demise would be Jorath's opportunity. He had been waiting almost two hundred years for that fawning fool to displease Baron Tyrus. Promotions were rare among beings as long-lived and resistant to disease and injury as dark elves.

In the Machine, Dorash wept.

Baron Tyrus's voice rumbled over Jorath. "So, you seek to reclaim the honor of the House of Thrim."

"I do, Master," Jorath said. "My cousin has proven himself weak, stupid, and ineffectual. I am none of those things."

"We shall see, *Captain* Jorath El-Thrim."

Jorath genuflected. "Thank you, Master."

"You may assemble your minions. Your cousin chose poorly." Baron Tyrus indicated the scarecrow and the goblin.

"Thank you, Master," Jorath said, still kneeling.

The scarecrow and the goblin began to tremble and blubber once again.

Baron Tyrus turned back to the Machine. "Before you depart, however, I have one more task for you, Captain."

"Of course, Master," Jorath said.

The Machine began to move again, the light within to pulse brighter. Dorash had apparently rested enough to muster a shriek that echoed into the hall's high reaches. The Machine's arms, blades, and needles picked up speed. It operated in unnerving silence, every moving part lubricated. The hall's only sounds were Dorash's dying wails and gasps, and when they faded could be heard the sound of flowing liquid, slowing to a trickle.

Dorash hung slack.

The Machine eased to a halt.

The Master said, "Jorath El-Thrim, serve me."

Jorath approached the Machine. Inside a niche on the side of the Machine rested a golden goblet, encrusted with multicolored gems which glowed with stolen life force. The well of the goblet was twice the size of Jorath's head, and it brimmed with dark elf blood, Dorash's blood.

Jorath cupped the goblet in both hands and lifted it carefully, reverently, painstakingly, from its cradle. The power trapped within the goblet's gems tingled in his palms. He dared not spill a drop as he took it and approached the throne.

Always moving, always alert, the nimbus of thorny metal vines around the throne extended toward Jorath, shivering with threat.

Jorath swallowed his fear and tried not to think about what those vines could do to him. He bowed and presented the goblet to Baron Tyrus.

Baron Tyrus received the goblet in both hands. Strangely, Jorath had never noticed before that the Master's fingers each possessed an extra knuckle. The Master raised the goblet to his polished-marble lips and drank. But while he did so, his gaze drilled squarely, piercingly, into Jorath.

If Jorath failed, he knew what his fate would be.

Twelve

THE MORNING WIND WAS already hot, so both pickup windows were rolled down.

Stewart's mood was light-hearted, despite the weird occurrences of the night before. Bleary-eyed and barely awake, they had left their house this morning just as dawn was breaking over Mesa Roja.

"Where does the map lead, Mommy?" Cassie said. "Where's our house?"

As usual, the kids sat between him and Liz, sharing the middle seat belt. In another year or so, that arrangement would be uncomfortably snug for both of them. When that time came, he might have to trade off his old truck for something his whole family could comfortably sit in. He always wanted to save money for a used SUV or a minivan, but there were always bills, always unexpected expenses. When this old truck finally gave up, he didn't know what they would do.

Liz laid the map over her lap and traced a line with her finger. "This is the road we're on. This is Mesa Roja, so our house is about right here."

"But where does it *go*?" Cassie asked.

"That's what we're going to find out!" Liz said with a grin. "Isn't it exciting?"

Cassie nodded vigorously. Then her eyes widened as if just re-alizing something. She leaned over and whispered something in Liz's ear.

Liz said to Stewart, "Oh, charioteer, it is time for a pit stop."

Stewart nodded in acknowledgment. It would be good to get out and stretch his legs. "I'll pull over at the next place we see."

This stretch of highway leading generally north toward Utah was sparse in the way of human habitation, the kind of area you could find yourself afoot if you didn't pay attention to the gas gauge.

Hunter had been quiet, slumped down, straddling the stick shift, face in a paperback book among Gramm's things, something called *The Illustrated Man*. Stewart had asked him near the start of the trip if the book was any good, and the boy tore his attention away from it long enough to grunt his assent.

About half an hour ago, Liz had poked the boy in the ribs. "Hey, you should be paying attention outside. The scenery!"

Hunter gave her a withering look. "Mom. I've seen the desert."

Stewart and Liz traded *can't-argue-with-that* looks.

A dusty, wind-swept gas station appeared as the highway curved around the skirt of a mesa. "There's our pit stop," Stewart said. He slowed the truck and eased up to one of the pumps, older than he was.

Cassie said, "I don't want to go potty here."

Stewart smiled at her. "It's this or behind the next bush we see. Sorry, kiddo."

"It'll be okay, honey," Liz said. "I'll go with you."

Cassie gave each of them an *are-you-crazy?* expression, then sighed in acquiescence.

Stewart shut off the engine and got out, stretching his legs, appreciating the cooling wind on his sweat-moistened back. Liz and Cassie hopped out the other side and hurried for the main building, which looked about ten years overdue for a coat of paint.

"Hey, Hunter," Stewart said. "Raise your periscope. I got something to show you."

The boy blinked and looked at Stewart, rubbing his eyes. "Yeah?"

Stewart reached under the tarp covering the pickup bed and pulled out the hunting knife.

Hunter scooted out of the truck and jumped to the ground.

Stewart handed him the knife.

The boy drew the blade from its sheath, and his eyes widened at the polished Damascus steel, about eight inches long and two fingerbreadths wide, the gorgeous ironwood handle with its prominent wood grain. "Wow, Dad! That's beautiful! Is this what you've been working on?"

Stewart nodded. "What do you think, Son? You think you're old enough to handle a knife like that?"

Hunter's eyes blinked a couple of times, then bulged with burgeoning hope. "Dad!"

"Without cutting your finger off or stabbing yourself in the leg?"

Hunter's head bobbed up and down.

"Or hurting your sister?"

More vigorous nodding.

"Let me show you how sharp it is." Stewart took the knife, laid the edge at an angle to his forearm, and promptly shaved a patch of hair clean away.

"Wow!" Hunter breathed. "Can I try it?"

"Sure, but be *really* careful."

Hunter took the knife and applied it to his forearm as he'd seen Stewart do. The edge was indeed sharp enough to shave the downy peach-fuzz that covered Hunter's forearm. He rubbed the bare patch with his thumb, and then reverently slid the blade back into its sheath.

Then he threw his arms around Stewart's waist. "Thanks, Dad!"

Stewart chuckled and hugged him.

Then the boy unbuckled his belt and slid it through the sheath's belt loop.

Stewart pointed to a little loop over the knife grip. "Keep that loop over the handle so it won't slip out by accident."

The boy did so, and as he finished buckling his belt again, he seemed to grow two inches before Stewart's eyes. "Thanks, Dad." Then he pelted away to show the rest of the family.

Meanwhile, Stewart filled the gas tank. He put in a few gallons more than he was expecting for the distance they had traveled. The decreased mileage must be because of the truck being loaded with people and camping equipment.

As he was headed inside to pay for the gas, he saw Hunter run into Liz and Cassie coming out of the toilet, which lay outside around the side of the building.

Hunter cocked his hip prominently to display his new prize, while trying to look nonchalant.

"Hunter!" Liz said. "What is *that*?" Her tone made it clear she was exaggerating her shock and dismay.

"Dad gave it to me."

Cassie crossed her arms and pooched out her lower lip. "You're not old enough for that."

"I am so!" Hunter said.

Liz winked at Stewart. "Are you sure about this, honey? I mean that thing's so sharp he'll probably cut his finger off."

"Mom!" Hunter rolled his eyes in protest.

Liz raised a finger and spoke with over-exaggerated archness. "Hush! Zip it! *Silencio!* It's my job as the mother to say such things. If you cut yourself, your sister, your parents, or anything that ought not be cut with that little sword, you will not see it ever again. Do you understand?"

Hunter nodded vigorously, suppressing a grin of excitement.

Cassie eyed the knife and her parents with narrowed eyes. Then she sniffed and walked back toward the truck.

Liz gave Hunter one last meaningful look and followed the girl.

Stewart had his hand on the gas station door latch when he heard Cassie say, "Hey, Mommy, the pickup has a runny nose."

He turned at the strange comment to see Cassie squatting and pointing under the pickup. Liz knelt as well and followed Cassie's gaze. She was pointing at a small puddle of liquid forming under the engine.

He sighed and walked back to the truck. "Ugh, what now?"

Liz looked over her shoulder at him. "She's right."

He knelt and ran a fingertip through the small puddle. One sniff told him what it was. "It's gas."

"Something is leaking?" Liz said.

"Looks like it." He slid on his back under the vehicle, across the gritty slab of sunbaked concrete, feeling a whisper of threat. A fuel leak on a hot engine was dangerous. How long had it been leaking? Was that why the truck's mileage had decreased?

"I'll go in and pay for the gas," Liz said.

"Thanks," he said, sliding deeper under the truck. He maneuvered himself as close to the puddle as possible without touching it. Another drip of gasoline helped lead his gaze to the source of the leak.

A hole in the fuel line.

"Hunter, hand me a tissue or something like that," he said, wiping the fuel line clean with his thumb, only to have it wetted again by the slow but constant drippage.

Hunter crawled into the pickup, opened the glove compartment, and grabbed a tissue from the Mom Kit, as Liz called it, and handed it under the pickup. "Can I see?"

"Crawl under here, Son, and I'll show you what we're looking at."

The boy eagerly soiled his clothes by scooting under the pickup beside his father.

Stewart pointed to the hole in the rusted, metal fuel line, which ran from the fuel tank, along the inside of the chassis, then up along the engine to the top, where the thirsty carburetor waited. "See the hole?"

Hunter said, "Yeah, but why does it look like the metal was snipped or something?"

Stewart looked closer. The boy was right. The hole was not a rust-through or a break. The edges of the hole were clean, straight, as if someone had taken a tiny clipper to it.

Perhaps a small wrinkled creature with razors of dark metal attached to its fingers?

"That's weird, right?" Hunter said.

"Yeah."

"Can we fix it?"

"It's that or be stranded somewhere."

"We're not going home, are we?" Hunter said hopefully.

"That depends." The weight of possibly having to call off the whole trip settled onto Stewart's chest.

He slid out and went into the gas station. A jack-a-lope that looked older than Stewart stood sentinel near the entrance. The place's wares were a wild assortment of this and that, not unlike the shop where he'd bought the two dolls. He found Liz paying for the fuel. The owner was a rosy-cheeked old man in a dusty baseball cap with more smile than he had teeth to fill it. A toothpick rested in the corner of his mouth, for what purpose Stewart couldn't fathom. His pale eyes twinkled with welcome from deep, crinkled sockets. He wore faded, frayed overalls and a Led Zeppelin T-shirt.

The old man said, "Everything all right, young man?"

"Looks like we have a leaking fuel line."

The old man's eyebrow arched like a fuzzy gray caterpillar. "How bad?"

"Bad enough to take seriously." Stewart looked at Liz. "It's either fix it or limp back home." The more he thought about it, the more it felt like sabotage, adding up with all the strange events of the last couple of weeks. Something or someone was trying to stop them from going on this journey.

"Mind if I have a look?" the old man said.

"Any help would be appreciated," Liz said.

The old man grinned at her and slid out from behind the counter.

Outside, he crawled under the truck with a few grunts of effort. He only looked for a few seconds before he slid back out again and extended a hand for someone to pull him to his feet. Stewart took it and pulled. The old man's hand was dry, callused, strong, the hand of a man who still worked.

Brushing off his overalls, the old man said, "I might have just the thing. Hang on to your britches." Then he went back inside and returned shortly with a small plastic tube. "This here's epoxy putty. It hardens in about ten minutes and isn't affected by gas or water. It should plug the hole until you can fix it proper."

Stewart felt a gush of hope. Liz gave him a buoyant grin.

The old man squeezed out two dollops of stuff, one black, one silvery gray, from separate containers inside the tube and kneaded them together into a ball the size of a large grape. Then he crawled back under the truck. Stewart knelt and watched him squeeze the putty around the fuel line over the leak, continuing to knead it with his fingers, smoothing the edges. It looked like dark-gray chewing gum.

Then he took the toothpick from his mouth and used it to score a shape onto the putty. It looked vaguely familiar, like a capital Y with an extra upright line, like an upside-down peace sign. Then he licked his dirty thumb, touched the character—the *rune*—and whispered something Stewart couldn't hear.

A tingle raised the hair on Stewart's arms.

With a groan of effort, the old man slid back out into the scorching sun. "I think that'll do it. Should hold for a good long while."

"What did you just do?" Stewart said.

"Why, I fixed your leak," the old man said with a wink. He met

Stewart's gaze for a moment, as if acknowledging that Stewart had recognized what he had done.

Liz gave Stewart a look. "Thank you, Mister..."

"Call me Benny," the old man said.

"Thanks, Benny," Liz said. "We're on a little family excursion, and I'm so happy we didn't have to cut it short."

Benny said, "C'mon back inside out of the sun for a few minutes while the putty gets hard. Don't want you running off if it ain't gonna work. We'll come back out and check it in about ten minutes, see if it's still leaking. We can send you down the road then."

Cassie had been sitting in the driver's seat with her legs dangling out the open door.

Benny winked at her. "You like lemonade?"

Cassie nodded. "*Everybody* likes lemonade, you know."

"Ain't that the truth," Benny said. "I keep some in the fridge, just for days like this."

"Days like what?" Hunter said.

"When it's hot," Benny said.

"This is Arizona," Hunter said.

"Exactly!" Benny laughed and beckoned them to follow him inside.

Stewart said, "You all go have some lemonade. I'm going to look the pickup over."

Liz gave him a long look, but followed Benny inside.

Stewart couldn't forget the sight of the strange little creature lying dead under the vehicle the night before. What other damage might it have done? Brake lines? Tires? If it had cut the brake lines, too, he would have known it long ago. Same with tires. Rough Arizona highways were murder on tires.

And what about the tiny rune inscribed in the putty? He didn't dare disturb it for fear of ruining Benny's repair job. What was its purpose? And who was this Benny character, really?

Thirteen

THE SUN WAS NEARING the horizon as Stewart drove his family across the empty landscape, swimming in thoughts of runes and strange, nasty-looking critters. Nevertheless, it felt good to be back on a road trip with people he loved. Crisis averted, for the time being. The only radio they could get was an AM broadcast from some oldies station. With so little traffic on the road, he let his gaze drift out over the sea of sagebrush, saguaro, and scorpions, boulders churning from the earth like the backs of great whales.

Cassie was asleep against her mother, and Hunter was admiring his new treasure for the tenth time.

Liz said, "According to the map, there should be a turnoff soon. There's this drawing of a campfire right here. Might be a campsite." She had been studying the map off and on since they left the gas station. She rubbed her eyes, probably weary from so long in a hot vehicle.

Stewart took a drink from the water bottle—it was never a good idea to go far without one—keeping his eyes peeled for a turnoff. Then he spotted a rusted, sun-faded sign that read: BENT KNIFE CAMPGROUND 6 MI. An arrow pointed toward a narrow dirt road that led perpendicularly away from the highway. The sign was so badly weathered and sun-faded it was barely legible.

He hit the brakes to make the turn onto the dirt road. "It's a good thing you're following the map so close," he said. "I probably wouldn't have noticed the sign."

"Navigation is my job," she said, reaching over the children to stroke his shoulder and neck. "And massages."

Her touch sent warmth and relaxation through tensed muscles.

"We've got to be getting close to Utah," he said.

"Yeah, but I haven't seen any signs. And cell service is gone, so no GPS."

The lurch of dropping onto an unpaved surface jolted Cassie awake, and she rubbed her eyes. "Are we there yet?"

"We're almost to a campground, honey," Liz said.

"Do we have marshmallows?" Cassie said, still groggy.

"Yes, I packed us marshmallows," Liz said.

"Oh, okay," she said, then snuggled back up against her mother's side.

The dirt road led off into a maze of boulders and scrub, but the road was so rough he had to slow to little more than jogging speed. Six miles of this kind of road would take at least half an hour. It would be getting dark before they reached the campground.

About a mile down this path, Cassie said, "It's going to shake my tummy out."

"Do you feel sick, honey?" Liz said.

"No, but..." Her voice trailed off.

Stewart slowed down even more, negotiating curves and undulations, dodging holes and boulders. "Hang in there, everyone."

The sun touched the horizon, and shadows spread across the land.

"I was hoping we'd be there in the daylight," Liz said. "It sucks setting up a tent in the dark."

Stewart nodded. "Me too."

The road dipped into an arroyo, the sides of which were covered in thickets of sage and juniper. Towering cacti rose like fingers into the darkening sky. Shadows spread across the sandy floor of the arroyo as it deepened.

"Are you sure we're still on the road, babe?" Liz said.

"These look like tire tracks to me."

"You realize if there's a flash flood we might be trapped wherever we're going..."

He couldn't dispute that, although this was not the season for monsoon rains.

The arroyo's sandy bottom made the driving easier, so he was able to pick up a little more speed until the path traced back up onto the land above. The path led into a valley between rocky hills that looked purple in the dusk, the shadows of sunset spreading up their sides.

For another twenty minutes or so, Stewart kept the pickup trundling forward as the trail switch-backed up the side of a hill. As the road crested a ridge, however, the hill became a mountain, sweeping upward at least two thousand feet, the slopes blanketed by pine trees.

The air cooled with the coming of night.

Flowering bushes draped the roadsides, reaching high above as the mountainside sloped up and away.

Cassie sighed. "Daddy, how far is it? I'm tired."

"Maybe two more miles, sweetie," Stewart said. "We'll be there soon."

As the truck rounded a switchback turn, he spotted a profusion of scarlet flowers blooming from a thicket along the roadside just ahead. The bright, brilliant red caught his eye and held it.

Liz saw them, too. "Look at the pretty flowers, kids!" The truck drew nearer, and Liz said. "They look like roses."

"That is one huge rosebush," Stewart said. The entire growth was easily the size of their house.

As they passed it, two deafening pops made him jump. A moment later, two more. The truck lurched and skidded, and the steering went sloppy. Fortunately, their slow speed let him maintain control and pull over to the side of the road after about thirty yards.

A sinking dread formed in the pit of his stomach as he realized they had just lost all four tires.

Liz's eyes were wide, her mouth open. "Is that what I think it was?"

Stewart jumped out and saw two flat tires on the driver's side. A quick check of the passenger side revealed the same.

He stood there scratching his head. "Four flat tires."

Liz's voice rose with incredulity. "Did someone put something in the road?"

Alarm was growing on the kids' faces, Liz's, too. He needed to head that off, keep everybody calm. "It's all right, everybody. I'll just call for a tow truck."

"Aw, Dad! We have to go home?" Hunter said.

Liz said, "That's a great idea, Stewart, but it's kind of late in the day and we're way out in the middle of nowhere. You might have better luck with that tomorrow."

He grabbed his cell phone from where it lay atop the dash and checked the signal.

No service. Zip. Zilch.

He said, "No reception anyway." He gazed up the mountainside, into the thickening blanket of pine trees. "We might be able to get some reception if we go higher up."

"So what do we do?" Liz said.

Stewart took two deep breaths, let them out, scratching his head. Then he said, "Everybody up for a hike?"

"In the dark?" Cassie said, eyes wide.

Stewart said, "It's that or we all get to sleep in the pickup."

"Don't worry, sweetie, we have flashlights for everybody," Liz said.

"All right, everybody out," Stewart said. "Everybody is going to have to carry what they can."

"Good thing it's mostly backpacks," Liz said. "I don't think we'll have to leave anything behind."

"Essentials only," Stewart said, untying the tarp, folding it aside, and opening the tailgate.

Hunter bailed out, the gleam of adventure in his eye. "This is gonna be fun!"

"Are there bears?" Cassie said.

"No, there are no bears, sweetie," Liz said, but she gave Stewart an uncertain look.

"Nope," Stewart said, "no bears this far south."

"But there are coyotes!" Hunter said.

"Mommy!" Cassie said.

Liz sighed at Hunter and gave him a stern look. "Coyotes never bother people, sweetie. We hear them at our house all the time, right?"

"Okay," Cassie said uncertainly.

Liz got out and circled the pickup. "What did we run over, anyway?"

Stewart grabbed a flashlight out of his backpack and shined it down the road the way they had come. The light of dusk still lingered, but had turned the landscape into a palette of shadows. He walked down the road with the flashlight.

The hazy circle of light passed over something dark and twisted crossing the road. It lay partially obscured by shadows, dust, and potholes, but it was clear. He knelt beside it. A thick bundle of what looked like cables, all in all about the thickness of his wrist, snaked across the road, in and out of the dust.

But they weren't cables.

They were thorny vines. And the thorns varied from an inch to two inches long. The thorns looked absolutely nasty, so black and barbed he dared not touch them. He traced the vines back to the rosebushes on the roadside. They were indeed outgrowths of the rosebushes. His tire tracks went straight across them.

But how had they gotten twisted and intertwined like that? And why would they have grown straight across the road?

The more he looked at them, the more it seemed they were... moving.

He stood back with a gasp of revulsion. As soon as he tried to focus on the movement, however, it seemed to stop. Almost like catching the movement of a clock's hands from the corner of his vision.

It was a trap.

Someone had placed those vines deliberately.

But who?

The same people who'd snipped his gas line?

The same people—no, creatures—that had attacked him outside his house?

The little top-hatted figure in Gramm's storage unit?

The weirdness was too much.

Then he felt eyes on him somewhere in the darkness. Watching.

He shined the flashlight into the bushes, peering as deep and far as his sight could reach.

"What is it, Stewart?" Liz called.

"Nothing." He turned and walked back to the pickup.

Liz zipped up her backpack and lugged it around her shoulders. "Did you see what blew the tires?"

He shook his head and wouldn't meet her gaze. From his backpack, he retrieved his hatchet. She would see the lie instantly, but for the sake of the kids, maybe she would let it go. For now.

If he left those vines there, there would be a tow truck tomorrow with shredded tires, and anybody else who came along this road. Not that he expected anyone tonight. This area felt more desolate than he was expecting. The vines were tough, but they yielded to the hatchet's bite. When they were severed, he hooked the length of the twisted mass with the hatchet blade and dragged it off the road, still loath to touch those barbs without thick leather gloves. They looked venomous, like scorpion stingers.

Back at the pickup, he found everyone nearly ready to start hiking. Each of them had a backpack filled with their clothes, water, mess kit, and sleeping bag.

Two little doll heads poked out of the top of Cassie's backpack as she slung it around her shoulders.

Hunter said, "You can't take the dolls. Dad said essentials only."

"They *are* essential!" Cassie retorted. She turned to Liz. "Mommy!"

"Sweetie," Liz said, "when you're on a hike, everything you carry gets heavier and heavier the longer you walk."

"But they're really light! I can carry them!" Cassie said.

"That's just my point," Liz said. "They won't feel so light on a long hike."

"I'll carry them and I won't complain, I promise!" Cassie's eyes glistened with entreaty.

Liz sighed. "All right then. No complaining."

All that remained to be carried was their plastic cooler full of food and water.

Stewart hefted the cooler onto the ground. "We're all going to take turns carrying the food. You kids can share the load when me and Mommy get tired. All right?"

Cassie said, "Are the marshmallows in there?"

Stewart nodded.

"All right, then," she said.

Stewart slung his own backpack over his shoulders and buckled the straps across his chest and waist.

Liz said, "Intrepid explorers! Let us sally forth!"

"Who's Sally, Mommy?" Cassie said.

"Not a 'who,'" Hunter said. "'Sally' is a verb."

"What's a verb and why is it named after Sally?"

Hunter rolled his eyes. "Oh, my God!"

Liz laughed and tousled the little girl's hair.

Stewart picked up the cooler and led the way up the road, toward the campground that he hoped lay about two miles ahead.

Fourteen

OVERLOOKING THE ROAD, Jorath El-Thrim knelt on the bough of a pine tree, peering between veils of needles, as the four humans hiked off into the night. His dark elf vision saw his prey and their surrounding landscape as clearly as a raptor's in daylight. For this reason, dark elves preferred the night. Their large, dark eyes were well suited to see in the dark, and they could shift the color of their skin to make it easy to hide. Goggles worn in daylight protected their eyes from the sun but obscured the sharpness of their vision.

The dark, supple leather of his jerkin and boots, mottled to camouflage him in the foliage, was as silent as his tread as he slid along the bough to maintain his view of the human family. Beside him on the branch lay the copper dish wherein he had burnt the knotted rope and rosebuds that had been the material components of his spell.

The rosebush had done its work. The trap had been sprung. Now, without their mechanical conveyance, the humans were vulnerable. The young ones would be weak and easily dispatched, once Jorath's forces arrived. A being with his powers could slip back and forth between realms easier than most, but less powerful beings required passage through where the Veil was thinner. The tingling weakness still in his limbs from the shift persisted, however. The fuzziness of his thoughts, ever present when he visited the Penumbra, made him feel as if he'd just chewed an entire bale of nightwort leaves. It was a result of his separation from the magical essence of the Dark Realm, which made missions to the Penumbra so distasteful. He could hardly wait to go home.

Of the humans, the father was nervous, wary, with an aura more powerful than any Penumbral human Jorath had ever seen. All of these humans were exceptional, but the large male would be a force to be reckoned with, if he somehow managed to cross into either the Light or the Dark Realm.

It was apparent now why Baron Tyrus was so steadfast in his desire to keep this Stewart Riley trapped in the Penumbra. He would be a powerful ally to whoever found a way to help him unlock his power. No doubt, this was why the enemy had cast its net of defenses around him and his family. Little things, subtle things, things that would be imperceptible to average Penumbral humans.

Jorath had many questions, such as who or what had slain Dorash's knibling saboteur last night? Kniblings were cautious, wily creatures, but also vicious, which was why they made such effective servants for certain kinds of tasks, such as sabotage. Dorash had been a fool, but he had not shirked his duty. Those who directly served the Master knew the stakes of every decision they made. Jorath did not intend to be a fool like Dorash, or to die like him. The dishonor on their House brought down by his demise would resonate for centuries—unless Jorath could destroy this human and his family.

In the distance, night dogs yipped and sang—here in the Penumbra, they were called coyotes. He raised his voice to the sky and responded to their inane chatter with his magic-laced commands, sounding like one of them to any non-coyote ear.

Once the night's work was done, the thread of magical command lurking under Jorath's howls would dissipate and the coyotes themselves would not remember what they had done here tonight. The magical imprint left on the Penumbra would be minimal, untraceable.

But he must beware. These humans might have as many hidden protectors as they had predators.

***

As they hiked up the road, pine trees closed against the sides. Their roots must reach deep to grow so tall in such a dry area, Stewart thought. The road climbed steadily. It was a perfect night for a hike, with a full moon hanging above them like a lantern amid a tapestry of stars, turning the road into a shadowed silver ribbon. The stars were so bright they seemed to shimmer with iridescence. With their path so clearly lit, they didn't have to worry about wandering off the road, even with their flashlights turned off. The cooling air would make their future campfire a welcome thing. The air smelled of pine needles and resin and the wildflowers growing alongside the road. He kept his eyes peeled for signs of any more of those rosebushes, however. If those thorns could puncture tires, they could pierce the sole of a shoe. How mobile were those vines?

The yip of a coyote sounded high up on the mountainside, among the pines, soon answered by a chorus of coyote voices in the distance. It was almost as if coyotes had the ability to throw their voices. One animal could sound like several. The yips and howls sounded very close, within a couple of hundred yards, so close it made everyone stop and listen.

Cassie stayed close to her mother, while Hunter ranged a few dozen yards ahead.

"You hear that?" Stewart said.

"Are those coyotes?" Cassie asked, eyes wide.

Liz said, "Yeah, and one of them sounds like it's just up the slope."

"But they don't hurt people, right?" Cassie said.

"Right."

They walked on, while the coyote conversation continued all around them. Stewart had the strong sense that they were speaking a language just as full of information as English, and he wondered what they were saying.

When his hands and arms felt like noodles from carrying the cooler, he called a rest and Liz took over.

"Mommy, I'm *tired*," Cassie said. "Are we about there?"

"It won't be long, sweetie," Liz said. "You're an intrepid explorer, right? Like Dora?"

"Dora is for babies, Mommy," Cassie said.

"You used to love Dora," Liz said.

"But then I grew up," Cassie said. She sniffed and marched ahead to catch up with Hunter, who was serving as the party's scout about thirty yards ahead, while the adults were the pack mules.

As Cassie left earshot, Liz said to Stewart, "So are you going to tell me what happened to the tires?"

"Something weird," he said, flexing his hands to restore blood flow from gripping the cooler handles. "Are you sure you want to know? We crossed into the Twilight Zone before we even left the house."

"Lay it on me, buster."

"It was that rosebush. A really thorny vine stretched across the road. And it wasn't there by accident."

Liz stopped and stared at him. "The phrase that comes to mind is, 'spit just got real.'"

He couldn't help chuckling even though he couldn't disagree.

"So, who do you think it is?" she said. "Somebody messing with us? A prank?"

"Pranks don't ruin a whole set of tires. I think it's something we can't see. All the little weird things. Something is going on. Even that old guy at the gas station. He carved a little rune on the putty he used to fix the fuel line."

"You didn't tell me that."

"I don't want to scare the kids. That's why I didn't tell you about the vine in front of them."

"If the kids are in danger—"

"I'll protect them. I'll protect *you*. No matter what."

"You *are* kind of like having my own personal Viking."

He thumbed toward the hatchet hanging from a carabiner on his backpack. "Brought my axe."

"Let's go then, Bjorn the Beefy. The kids are getting a little far ahead."

They continued on after the children. After about fifty yards, Liz said, "Hey, how about grabbing a handle? This thing is heavier than it looks."

He took one of the cooler handles, and they carried it in tandem, switching grips when one hand grew tired.

As they walked, however, he couldn't shake the sense that someone or something was watching them. All he told Liz was, "Keep your eyes open, okay?"

"Right. Someone sabotaged the road. Check," she said. "Tell me again why we're not hiking back to the nearest town?"

"Because the nearest town is what, thirty miles? Across the desert? We can't take the kids across the desert that far." At least, it wasn't in the top five options. He checked his phone again. "And still no reception."

"But we're walking *farther* from that town, even the gas station."

"We need to get a camp set up so the kids can get some rest. If I still can't get any phone reception, tomorrow morning I'll hike back to the highway and flag somebody down." It would be safer for the kids to stay in the shady coolness of a forested mountainside than to march across the scorching desert. He could bring help back for them.

Liz nodded. "Meanwhile, we're still just having a little family adventure, right?"

"Right."

About fifteen minutes later, a whoop of exultation echoed from ahead. Hunter called, "We found it!"

"Woohoo!" Liz called.

Liz and Stewart soon caught up with the kids. The Bent Knife

Campground consisted of a flattened clearing bordered by weathered logs, large enough for three or four cars to park. There was one cinder-block outhouse, which was characteristically aromatic, and three fire pits. None of the fire pits looked as if they had been used in a while, although one of them had a scattering of dusty charcoal.

Stewart picked a flat spot farthest from the outhouse for their tent.

An owl hooted in the dark, drawing a gasp from Cassie. She stood frozen like a mouse caught in the open.

Hunter hooted back, but the owl did not respond, so he industriously turned his attention to helping with the unpacking. "Dad, can I help put up the tent?"

"Sure," Stewart said.

When that was half-finished, he said, "Dad, can I light the fire?"

The boy's earnestness to help didn't necessarily equate with being helpful, so Stewart said, "First, go gather up some wood." One look around the campsite showed there were plenty of fallen branches. "Grab as much as you can."

"Can I chop it?" Hunter said.

"Sure, I've got a hatchet right here. But first, go get some."

Hunter took his flashlight and scampered off into the shadows under the trees. A pang of nervousness washed through Stewart. Was it a good idea for him to take his eyes off any of them? But there was enough old wood lying around to get a good fire started. The boy wouldn't have to go more than twenty yards in any direction.

Liz called after the boy, "You stay right here where I can see you!"

Big sigh. "Okay, Mom."

Stewart made sure to keep an eye on the boy's flashlight as he meandered among the tree trunks, filling his arms with branches.

***

An hour later, the tent was erected, the fire was crackling merrily, and the four of them sat around the fire pit, roasting hot dogs on sticks. Narrow strips of starlight filtered down through the canopy of pine branches, but under the forest canopy it was almost pitch black.

"I'm so hungry I could eat three of them cold," Hunter said.

"Hold your horses, kiddo," Liz said. "They're way better roasted over a fire."

Hunter sighed. "You hear that growling? That's my belly."

"No, it's mine!" Cassie said, grinning with anticipation.

"Hey, Dad!" Hunter said. "Yours is turning black!"

Stewart blinked and looked at his hot dog, pulling it out of the flames. Even the stick had blackened to the verge of catching fire. His attention had been on scanning the darkness of the surrounding forest. Something in the air, an unnamable tension, had straightened the hairs on his arms and neck. He had quietly laid his hatchet next to him on the ground.

Despite the blackened exterior, he grabbed the hot dog with a bun, pulled it off the stick, and bit off half of it.

"No ketchup?" Hunter said, as if unable to imagine anyone eating just a hot dog in a dry bun.

But Stewart's taste buds caught fire. The blackened skin of the frank was all the flavor he needed. The bun was simply the delivery truck.

He couldn't shake Liz's scrutiny, however. No doubt she hadn't forgotten the vine, and maybe she even sensed the threat in the air.

The kids munched their hot dogs, fanning their mouths at the heat.

"We should do this at home every night," Cassie said.

"Yeah," Hunter said with his mouth full.

"You wouldn't get tired of hot dogs?" Stewart said.

"Nope!" Cassie said.

Then Hunter pointed into the darkness. "Hey, look. What's that?"

Beyond the edge of the firelight, under the deep shadows of the pine trees, a pair of eyes reflected the firelight, yellow-orange orbs floating in the black.

"Probably a raccoon," Stewart said. "Maybe he smells our hot dogs."

But unlike any raccoon he'd ever seen, these eyes did not fade away again into the night when they were noticed. They remained fixed on the campsite with a steady intensity.

And then another pair of eyes appeared directly above the first pair, these closer together with a crimson tint, fading in and out of existence like faulty lightbulbs. Hovering there perhaps three feet above the ground, simmering with intelligence, those eyes made Stewart snatch up his hatchet.

"Mommy, Daddy! Look! Over there!" Cassie shrilled.

Stewart looked to where she pointed just in time to see more eyes skulk close enough to catch the firelight. Three more sets of four, each with two above, two below. As if the upper pair belonged to something riding the lower.

Cassie screamed and clutched her mother.

They were surrounded by eyes, and the eyes were coming closer.

FIFTEEN

CASSIE SCRAMBLED UP LIZ like a cat climbing a tree.

Stewart snatched up his hatchet and stood, tensed and ready, moving to interpose himself between his family and the coyotes. Except that the half-circle was collapsing into a ring.

Liz tried to whisper soothingly to Cassie, but the girl was in a frenzy. Liz jumped up and hoisted Cassie onto her hip. The girl clung to her like a monkey as Liz snatched up a firebrand and held it like a flaming truncheon.

Hunter grabbed a flashlight and shined it toward the encroaching circle of eyes. The circle of light played briefly over sharp coyote faces, but there were gnarled shapes clinging to the backs of the coyotes. Yips rippled around the circle like the spread of laughter, and the coyotes edged back from the light. Stewart couldn't get his eyes to focus on the things riding the coyotes. They seemed to be made of smoke, or somehow unseeable, or maybe it was like the childhood dreams where he really needed to see whatever dream monster was coming for him but his eyes wouldn't work, wouldn't open, wouldn't focus and the only way to escape was to wake up into the cold blackness of a bedroom shared with other foster kids, and on some of those nights he'd gone to bed hungry rather than submit to whatever degradation the Abusive Foster Parent of the Month had in store for him.

Stewart rubbed his eyes and peered harder into the night.

"Oh, Mommy, they're so ugly!" Cassie shrilled.

"What, honey, they're just coyotes!" Liz said, still trying to soothe her.

"No! The things! On their backs!" Cassie said.

"Yeah!" Hunter called. "Little monsters on their backs!"

This sudden revelation sent a bolt of lightning through Stewart. *The kids could see them,* whatever they were.

"What do you see?" Stewart said.

"They're ugly!" Hunter said. "Like warty gnomes, but with huge, nasty teeth and ears like bats!"

Chittering, whispering gibberish passed around the circle of creatures. There was no mistaking the consternation in the creatures' tone, as if they were saying, *They can see us!*

The coyotes hesitated at the edge of the firelight, as if awaiting a command to charge.

But then an agonized yip erupted from a coyote somewhere in the darkness. There came a scrambling, scratching noise, as if its claws were tearing up the forest floor. It loosed another yip, and then a decidedly non-coyote squeal erupted, like a javelina caught in a bear trap.

The glowing eyes disappeared as they turned toward the noise. Snarls of warning and anger filled the blackness. Sounds of scrambling, movement, paws tearing up the needle-carpeted earth.

Another yip, this time crunched into silence.

A chorus of high-pitched gibbering filled the air, a commotion coming so hard and fast and from all directions that he couldn't follow it.

There was nowhere for Stewart and his family to run. They were miles from anywhere—

"Liz!" he shouted. "Get the kids in the outhouse!"

It was the only shelter within miles, and its walls were cinder block.

"Follow me! Run!" he said.

She did not question, seizing Hunter by the arm. Stewart clutched the hatchet and ran toward the building, Liz close behind him, even with Cassie bouncing on her hip, clinging with incredible tenacity. "Hunter! You're on flashlight!" Stewart said.

Hunter managed to stay on his feet despite his mother yanking on his arm, but with the other hand, he shone the flashlight toward and around the outhouse.

Several coyotes crossed into the firelight in pursuit. And they had strange, gnarled riders on their backs, gripping little pistol-shaped crossbows. Whatever kind of bolt those things fired would not be larger than a pencil, but even a sharpened pencil could go deep into flesh.

Moments later, Liz reached the outhouse door. It was metal with a real latch and a deadbolt on the inside.

"Lock this door!" Stewart said as he spun to face any oncoming threats. This far from the fire, night closed around him as glowing eyes came and went among the tree trunks.

"Dad!" A flashlight appeared at his side on the end of Hunter's outthrust arm.

Stewart took the flashlight in his left hand. The outhouse door slammed shut behind him, and the deadbolt clicked into place. The door was sheltered by the sloped eave of the roof, which was supported by a four-by-four-inch wooden pillar on each corner.

A pair of low-slung canine shapes stalked toward him, dark riders silhouetted by the campfire on the coyote's backs.

Something clunked into one of the pillars and stuck there, a shiny black spine slightly thicker than a pencil, with little black feathers as fletching on the tail end.

He shone the flashlight at the oncoming creatures. Small, three-fingered hands flew up and shielded great luminous eyes, as big and round as a bush baby's, but obsidian black. Hunter's description had been spot-on.

The coyote steeds paused, blinking against the light.

But then their riders loosed shrill battle-cries, and the coyotes leaped forward. Incoming, they dodged the swing of his hatchet, lunged at the backs of his legs, trying to hamstring him. He swung the hatchet wildly but couldn't connect. The gnarled little creatures were shockingly quick.

Something sharp jabbed his thigh. He seized the end of a tiny lance and used it to yank the hideous rider off its mount. The creature loosed a plaintive bleat as it arced through the air and slammed against the side of the outhouse. The riderless coyote lunged and retreated, snapping and snarling.

In the forest around them emerged a commotion like Stewart had never heard before, a cacophony of coyote voices mixed with their strange riders'—but also something else. He caught a noise almost like a spinning buzz saw, but it moved among the trees as quick as a flitting bird.

Stewart swung the hatchet but missed his target, embedding the blade in one of the pillars with a hard thunk.

In the moment his weapon was immobilized, the other coyote

dashed in and seized Stewart's pants leg in its teeth, dragged his leg out from under him until he flopped onto his back. He went down hard against the earth, gravel jamming against him. The coyote kept pulling and dragging, stretching him out.

The creature on its back leveled the small crossbow at his face.

The hatchet tugged free.

He kicked at the coyote's face with his free leg. The crossbow twanged. The coyote tried to dodge Stewart's kick, but didn't relinquish its grip on his leg, throwing the creature's crossbow bolt off-target. The bolt thunked into the earth about a foot from Stewart's head.

Stewart doubled his body like a folding knife, bringing the coyote's head into range of his hatchet. It released him and jumped back, snarling and wary, yellow eyes gleaming like sparks.

More yelps of pain and squeals of frustration rang out in the surrounding forest.

The creature he had thrown against the wall was gone, as was its mount.

A howl rang through the night, as if summoning.

The coyote before him edged back, teeth bared. The rider holstered its crossbow and leveled a lance about as long as Stewart's leg, as if preparing to charge.

Then the coyote spun and ran off into the night.

The sounds of paws thudding over the earth receded. Silence descended.

Stewart stood, trying to catch his breath, slow his thundering heartbeat. He hadn't been in a fight since high school, and it was easy to forget how quickly less than a minute of frenzied struggle sapped your energy.

He said, "You guys stay in the outhouse for another minute or two. I think it's over, but I'm going to have a look around."

"Okay," Liz said. "Are you all right?"

"I'm all right," he said.

"Hurry, Daddy," Cassie said. "It stinks in here."

"It's safe in there," he said. "Just hang on a minute."

He walked into the forest, shining his flashlight in all directions. The needle-carpeted forest floor was torn up. Some of the tree trunks sported fresh gouges in the bark. Difficult to guess what had made them, but they didn't resemble claw marks. He found several black crossbow bolts embedded in the trees and the ground.

Then the shiny crimson of blood spread over a patch of fallen pine needles. The farther out he ranged, the more bloodstains he found.

But no bodies. No dead or wounded coyotes, nor any evidence of their riders.

He made a broad circle around the campground, but found no further sign of the coyotes, their riders, or whatever had driven them off. All that lay in the shadows of the towering pines was silence.

Knocking on the outhouse door, he said, "All clear."

Liz flung open the door and threw her arms around him, tears of relief on her cheeks. Two small bodies jumped around his waist.

"Something drove them off," he said. "I don't know what. I couldn't see whatever it was."

"You're bleeding, Daddy!" Cassie said, drawing back in disgust.

The front of his thigh was soaked with blood. "Yeah, one of the little devils got too close."

"Let's find the first-aid kit," Liz said.

They all returned to the campfire, but their eyes were still peering into the darkness. Liz entered the tent and promptly returned with the little nylon package that read *FIRST-AID KIT*.

Hunter shined the flashlight on the wound as Liz knelt before him. "Here we are with yet another strange leg wound," she said. "Looks like a puncture."

Stewart nodded.

Cassie's eyes were wide with fascination. "Does it hurt, Daddy? Did they stab you?"

"It looks worse than it is," he said. "I'm fine."

She eyed him skeptically but watched as Liz went to work. "You should probably take your pants off."

After a couple of minutes to swap into a pair of gym shorts, he sat back down and let Liz begin the cleaning and bandaging process.

Both kids watched with fascination as Liz smeared on antiseptic ointment and taped a patch of gauze over the puncture.

"What was it, Dad?" Hunter asked.

"They had little spears. Like I said, one got too close."

"Did you...you know, kill it?" Hunter said.

"No, I grabbed the spear and yanked him off his, well, off his coyote. He got away."

"You said coyotes wouldn't bother us!" Cassie said, crossing her arms, lower lip sticking out.

"Normal coyotes don't have monsters riding them," Liz said.

"To those little guys, it would be like fighting a giant," Hunter said.

Stewart nodded. "I hadn't thought of that, but I suppose so."

"Daddy, you're really brave," Cassie said.

He hugged her close and kissed her forehead.

When Liz was finished, he stood and said, "Now, Hunter, you and me are gonna find enough wood to make that fire ten feet high. All night long."

Hunter stared at him. "We're *staying* here?"

Cassie crossed her arms again and squared herself toward him. "Daddy. What if they come back?"

Liz fixed him with a look. "They have a point, babe. You expect us all to stay here and just go to bed after that?"

"The other option is to pack up and hike down the mountain in the dark. We're all exhausted. I don't think those things are coming back." The thought of stepping on venomous, prehensile, thorny vines while blundering around in the dark gave him pause.

Clouds drifted across the sky now, shrouding some of the light they had enjoyed on their hike up the mountain. A six-mile hike in the dark sounded even less appealing than an hour ago, what with potential enemies in every direction. At least here, they could take shelter in the outhouse.

A few minutes later, he and Hunter were scouring the area far and wide for firewood. He didn't let the boy more than ten feet out of reach. The sheer strength of the coyote that had grabbed his leg was still fresh in his mind. It was the kind of strength that could easily drag a child away.

Then Cassie's distant voice came out to them. "Hey, my backpack! Where are my dolls?" Alarm grew in her voice.

He heard Liz say, "Maybe the coyotes tried to drag it away. Did you have any food in it?"

"Mommy, my *dolls* are gone, not the food!"

"You sure have a hard time keeping track of those things," Liz said.

"But they're *gone!*"

"Then grab a flashlight and let's look around. It's not like they could have run off, right?" Liz said.

Two flashlights started bobbing and swinging around the campground.

Meanwhile, Hunter and Stewart made several trips back and forth to the fire pit, where they stacked up the pile of firewood until it was almost waist-high. Stewart broke and chopped the branches into suitable lengths, threw a bunch on the fire, and watched with satisfaction as the flames grew.

He gave Hunter a high-five. "Great work, Son. Now it's time for pajamas."

"But, Dad, I'm not tired," Hunter said. "Like, at all."

"You will be," Liz said. "Once we get settled down. It's been an exciting night."

How she managed to stay in Mom Mode in the face of everything that had happened today amazed Stewart. That woman had fortitude.

Cassie was already wearing her pajamas, sitting on a stump, clutching her knees and looking sullen.

Hunter said, "How are we supposed to 'get settled down' with a bunch of little monsters out in the woods?"

"I'm going to guard you all night long," Stewart said. "I'll be sitting right out front, keeping the fire up and my eyes open."

"All night?" Cassie said.

"Yes, all night," Stewart said, rubbing her soft hair.

"All right." She knuckled her eyes, and they hugged and kissed goodnight. "And we'll look for my dolls tomorrow?"

"Absolutely. We'll look everywhere. It'll be easy in the daytime." He picked her up and hugged her again.

A flashlight clicked on inside the tent. "Okay, kiddos," Liz said. "Come inside and grab your toothbrush."

While Liz and the kids went through the nightly bedtime routine, albeit in a strange, dark place, Stewart rolled a fat, stumpy log near the tent entrance to sit on, threw more wood onto the fire, took a deep breath, and watched.

Sixteen

STEWART COULDN'T BE SURE that he hadn't nodded off a couple of times, but he always caught himself. Whenever that happened, he would rebuild the fire to a blaze as tall as him, and then walk a perimeter with the flashlight, swinging his arms to get the blood pumping.

It was after 4:00 in the morning that a distant noise echoed up the mountainside, difficult to tell the distance. He knew only that it sounded almost like a car accident, like the crash of metal against metal. The noise must have come all the way from the highway, because he'd seen no evidence of any vehicles since they turned onto this road.

The chill air seeped into his bones until he returned to the circle of the fire. As grayness slowly, imperceptibly replaced the darkness between the trees, Stewart walked one last patrol. Today he would look for high ground to find some cellular reception, call for a tow, and get the pickup back to town. He was saddened their adventure would be cut short, but he didn't want to put his family into any further danger. Best just to go home and keep looking for a job.

After about half an hour, as the grayness brightened, Liz emerged from the tent, rubbing her eyes and stretching. She looked so beautiful with her hair disheveled, so vibrant even half-bleary from sleep. She came over, sat in his lap, and snuggled up to him. Her warmth was so welcome after a night spent chilled on one side and roasted on the other.

"Everything quiet?" she said.

He nodded and hugged her close. "I still can't get any reception, so I'm going to look for some high ground and try to find some. We must be in some sort of bowl."

"We'll sit tight here until you get back," she said. "It'll be just like a day at the park or something."

"I don't think whatever those things were will bother you in the daylight," he said. "All of the weird stuff has been at night, or dawn."

"When are you leaving?"

"Soon. If I go too soon, the tow services might not be open for the day."

"Have I told you how brave you were last night?" She looked up into his eyes.

He shrugged.

"You could have been in the toilet with us, hiding until they went away," she said.

"I'm not sure that would have helped."

"Maybe not, but it never once crossed your mind to do anything but defend us with your life." She stroked his stubbled cheek.

It was true.

She kissed him on the mouth, warm and soft. His heartbeat surged, and blood pounded in his ears as he squeezed her close. The urge to wake the kids up, kick them out of the tent, and send them on a little hike for about half an hour rose up within him, but he controlled that, and just held her, and let her hold him.

***

Hunter rolled out of his sleeping bag to the sounds of activity outside, and the smell of bacon and eggs frying.

Mouth watering and stomach roaring at the smell of breakfast, he crawled over Cassie's sprawled form. Cassie moaned and dragged the back of her hand across her face before she subsided again into motionlessness.

Outside, he found his mom squatting beside the rack she had arranged over the fire, stirring a big skillet full of bacon and scrambled eggs.

"Good morning!" she said with a smile. She stretched out an arm and beckoned him into it. He sidled up and accepted the warm hug.

"Where's Dad?"

"He already took off to call a tow truck."

"Oh." He tried not to sound disappointed. He'd been hoping his dad would invite him along.

"Your dad told me to tell you before he left. It's your job to protect me and Cassie if the coyotes and goblins come back."

His voice brightened. "Really?"

"Yes, really. He left you the hatchet and you still have that snazzy hunting knife he made you, right?"

He nodded vigorously. "And they showed us some cool weapon moves in taekwondo!"

She rubbed his back. Then he bounced off toward the toilet.

As he approached it, he spotted something lying on the ground a few paces away, a splash of light-colored cloth leaning against the base of a tree. He walked closer. Cassie's dolls sat propped against the tree as if they had been placed there. On closer inspection, he saw their dresses were torn and stained with dirt and a few spots of rusty brown. The ruined dresses would make Cassie very unhappy, but she'd be glad to get them back.

He picked them up, caught for a moment in their sky-blue eyes and flawless cheeks, then he carried them back to the campsite.

"Hey, Cassie!" he called. "Look what I found!"

As he approached the fire, Mom's eyes widened and she gasped. "Where did you find them?"

He pointed. "Over by the outhouse, by a tree."

Cassie crawled out of the tent, rubbing her eyes. She spotted the dolls in Hunter's hands instantly, gasped, and came running, eyes glimmering with relief.

"Oh! My! Gosh!" She seized them and hugged them to her chest.

"Found them over by the outhouse," Hunter said.

"But we looked over there!" she said.

Hunter shrugged. He thought she might be right, but he had not covered that area himself.

She gave him a hooded look. "Thanks."

He said, "At least we found them." For a long time last night, after they had gone to bed, she had lain in her sleeping bag quietly sniffling. He had felt sad for her.

"It looks like the coyotes were chewing on them or something," Cassie said, examining the tears in one of the dresses, the fabric stiffened as if from dried drool.

"We'll fix up their little dresses as soon as we get home," Mom said.

"Okay," Cassie breathed, hugging them again.

"Now," Mom said, "you guys go get dressed. Breakfast is almost ready."

As Cassie walked back toward the tent, a chill went up Hunter's spine. He couldn't help but think that the eyes of one of the dolls moved to look at him.

***

Stewart couldn't believe what his eyes were telling him.

He stood motionless on the road, his legs ready to crumple.

A boulder the size of a Volkswagen Beetle had rolled down the mountainside, plowed into the pickup, and came to rest atop it.

The cab was flattened, the frame bent, the rear axle snapped, all the glass shattered, the engine crushed.

The path the boulder had taken down the mountainside was clear, a bouncing trench that led up through twisted masses of pine trees into heights he couldn't see.

What was he going to tell his family? *A boulder fell on our pickup.* How could he tell them the truth? On the other hand, how could he lie to them?

After what they had all experienced, no one would believe this was just bad luck. They had all seen most of the crazy things he had seen. The kids were seeing "little people." He was pretty sure he had also seen one in Gramm's storage unit. The bizarre little saboteur under the pickup the night before. The grotesque creatures *riding coyotes*. If he tried to tell a single soul, they would have him locked up as a crazy person.

Should he take his family back down to the highway and try to flag down a ride? Some would call that the sensible move.

But his intuition was buzzing with something he couldn't put his finger on.

Ever since he bought the dolls, met the shopkeeper, opened the map, and embarked on this trip, he felt as if one set of invisible forces was herding him toward something, and others were blocking his progress at every turn.

Was one side preferable? The old shopkeeper had talked about Light and Dark, but what if he was telling a series of carefully constructed lies? What if it was all just nonsense? Should Stewart allow himself to be herded at all? Should he take his family and set off on a different course?

Threats surrounded them on all sides. None of these attacks or incidents were random. For all he knew, the same forces were squelching his cell phone reception. All these incidents and attacks felt carefully orchestrated. But last night, something in the dark had intervened, or else the coyote cavalry might have killed him and his whole family, dragging them off to vanish without a trace. It was a chilling thought, the idea of being eaten alive by a pack of coyotes, which were normally cowardly, reclusive, and solitary. The idea of something, anything, coming after his kids set his teeth on edge and turned his fists into hammers.

Sometimes, the best way out of a situation was not to retreat, but to go through it. *When you're going through hell, keep going,* as the saying went. He'd spent his whole life going through hell, wondering if there was an end to it.

It seemed a quiet voice in one ear was telling him to take his family, follow the map to its destination, and trust that everything would work out okay. He couldn't exactly see how, given that their only vehicle had been destroyed, and he had only liability insurance on it. Even if they made it back home, their family was now without transportation. It also seemed that a much louder voice was in his other ear, telling him to go back, go home, get back to doing sensible things like looking for a job and being a productive worker, a good consumer.

He snorted at that last, because he resented being forced, thrust, shoehorned, into a box someone else made for him.

Deep breaths flowed in and out of him, calming, centering, without him having to think about taking them. He had so often found that the quiet voice was more often the right one, because it was his truth emerging from a boiling morass of everyday worries and crises. If only he thought to listen to it more often.

He closed his eyes and listened to the forest, the whisper of pine needles in the breeze, the chatter of distant birds, the pulse of his blood in his ears, felt the breeze rustling the hairs on his arms and head, smelling the pine needles both in the trees and carpeting the forest floor in layers of decomposition, embracing the way they were being reclaimed by the earth. He ignored the stench of spilled oil and gasoline from the ravaged pickup, moving away from its intrusive tang.

Continuing his deep breathing, he hiked the two miles back up the switchback road to his campsite. Liz immediately saw in his face that something terrible had happened.

Cassie was playing with her dolls and Hunter was practicing his taekwondo forms, so they only waved at his return and went about their activities.

Stewart took Liz out of easy earshot and told her what happened. Her hand cupped her mouth, and her eyes went wide.

"Is it really that bad?" she asked.

"Junkyard-bound."

"What do we do?"

"You still have the map?"

She nodded. "You want to keep going."

"Yeah."

"You want to take our kids into the wilderness." She said it slowly, digesting each word.

"That's what my intuition is telling me."

She took a deep, thoughtful breath, crossing her arms, riding the same quiet train of thought that he had. "If the coyote monster attack was trying to keep us from going forward, there might be more of the same coming."

He nodded. "But there's something on our side, too. I didn't fight them off last night. Something else did. We're in the middle of something."

"And if we keep going, we'll find out what it is." She chewed her knuckle.

"Through it is the only way. This feels...important."

"Do you have any idea how many parents would be screaming at us and calling Child Services for even considering this?"

"Those parents would be wrong."

She chuckled at that, then sighed as if she couldn't believe what she was about to say. "So, what do we tell the kids?"

He pointed into the forest. "Adventure is thataway."

SEVENTEEN

THE KIDS TOOK THE news in stride. Stewart simply told them, "We're going to keep going and see where the map leads."

And they went, "Okay!"

And that was that.

He didn't tell them about the pickup, but neither had they forgotten the attack. That much was plain as they packed up the camp, casting wary eyes into the forest at every opportunity.

The dolls' reappearance sent a little tingle up his arms. Twice now the dolls had disappeared inexplicably and then reappeared. That he had gotten them from the strange shopkeeper, the same one who'd given him the map, could not be a coincidence. They had to be part of the unseen orchestrations going on around his family, but the question was, whose side were they on?

Stewart strapped the cooler to his backpack with a length of rope. It was a little unwieldy and unbalanced, but he could adjust, and it was easier than carrying it by hand.

"Hey, kids!" Liz quipped at the sight of him. "Check it out! Dad's a pack mule."

Stewart brayed accordingly, making the children giggle.

They had enough food and water for a couple more days, thanks to Liz's tendency to over-pack and over-prepare. At this higher elevation where the air was cooler, under the shade of the trees, they would need less water than if they were trudging across the desert, but he would have to keep a close eye on their water supply. Fortunately, the nearby stream looked crystal clear, so they filled their bottles before setting out. He also had a small fishing kit in his backpack. There might well be trout in some of the larger streams.

It was midmorning by the time they broke camp and set out. With every step away from the campsite, Stewart felt them leaving civilization—everything that was known—behind. They weren't just going into the wilderness, but into the unknown.

The air was crisp and alive, redolent with scents of pine and earth. The sun-dappled forest floor was open and easy to traverse.

On the map, the nearby stream was clearly marked, and it seemed all they had to do was follow it. Setting off across the wilderness without a clearly marked trail made him nervous, but his intuition kept telling him it was the right thing to do. Common sense told him it was very much the *wrong* thing to do. They could run out of food or water. Someone could fall and injure themselves. The goblins and coyotes could come back, and this time there would be no outhouse for protection.

The shopkeeper had said that when they reached the lake near the X on the map, Stewart's questions would be answered. He was full of questions, driven by the niggling sense that he was surrounded by things he couldn't see, and that the best word to describe them was "magic," even though it felt woefully inadequate. The scale of the map was unclear, so he couldn't be sure how far away the lake was.

The land steadily climbed as they followed the stream, which was as clear and cold as snow melt. Cassie skipped along next to Liz. Stewart let Hunter range out a little ahead, as the boy seemed to revel in his role as the party's "scout," but never too far ahead, always remaining within sight. Given everything that had happened, the boy was smart enough to take his parents' admonishment seriously. They stopped for a few minutes every hour or so to rest. Cassie whined about being tired, but Stewart could hardly fault her, as she was the smallest of them, requiring more and faster strides for the same distance.

At about noon, the world turned upside down.

Up ahead, Hunter froze, cocking his ear. He put one hand on his hunting knife. He looked back toward the family, waving his hand for them to stop and be quiet. Stewart motioned to Liz and Cassie to remain still, then he crept forward to join Hunter, the carpet of pine needles muffling his tread.

Crouching against the trunk of a pine fat enough to be a redwood tree, Hunter strained to listen, peering off into the gloom under the canopy. Their trek had been relatively free of undergrowth so far, but ahead lay a mass of thickets and deadfall. The stream burbled out from under a thick mass of thorny bramble. The air before it smelled sweetly of flowers. Roses? Stewart knelt beside the boy. Hunter pointed toward the bramble, and it was in the fresh silence that Stewart was able to catch the sound of something moving in there.

Something big.

Something moving closer, but slowly, taking its time about it. Leaves rustled and branches snapped. Stewart glanced over his shoulder to make sure Liz and Cassie remained where they were, about thirty yards back. Whatever it was sounded big as a bull-dozer, because he could see the branches shoved aside, the thicket swaying.

"Is it a bear?" Hunter whispered, voice quavering.

"Bigger than a bear," Stewart whispered, his voice as soft as he could make it. He squeezed the boy's shoulder and tugged him back toward where Liz and Cassie crouched behind a tree.

Together they crept backward, never taking their eyes off the thrashing foliage.

Then Stewart caught sight of something moving amid the thicket, sweeping back and forth across the top, something brown and pronged. It moved with ponderous slowness but unstoppable strength as it tore through vines and thorny brush.

Antlers.

But not just antlers.

Great, scooped antlers so broad they stretched farther across than the length of a car. Antlers dripping with soft, green moss. But they were not deer or elk antlers. They belonged to a bull moose.

A bull moose that stood at least twenty feet high.

Hunter began to emit a breezy squeak. Stewart clapped a hand over the boy's mouth. Both Cassie's and Liz's eyes were as wide as he'd ever seen them. Liz hugged Cassie to her.

The beast stood breast deep in thorny brambles, but unfazed by them, protected by a thick, earthy-brown coat so deep and dense it might have had small creatures living in it. Its long beard and wise gaze made it look almost like an old man. It chewed placidly on what looked like thick ropes of vegetation. But then Stewart saw the blood-red rose blooms on the vines. The same color as the rosebushes that had shredded the pickup tires.

Had another trap been laid for them in the depths of that thicket?

Their path would have led them into the thicket if they wished to stay close to the stream, as the map suggested they should. Would they have stepped on the poisonous thorns, which would cut through the soles of any shoe? Would the vines have come alive somehow and attacked?

The majesty of the creature brought a lump into his throat as if he were looking at something primeval, as if he had just crested a hill and seen a valley full of dinosaurs below him. The massive creature's deep brown eyes were the size of volleyballs, and harbored immense wisdom.

The moose ripped great mouthfuls of leaves from the thicket and brambles, its great square teeth tearing through branches as if they were soft green grass. Stewart had thought that moose spent a lot of time in marshes eating aquatic plants, but this one seemed to be tearing through the tough, woody thicket as if it were the tenderest of shoots.

They could only watch, mouth agape, hearts pounding at the wonder of it.

Moose were by no means docile creatures. A moose could be aggressive when threatened, cornered, or when its calf was nearby. Even a normal-sized one could easily kill a human. One this size could send an elephant trumpeting for the nearest horizon. Stewart kept his family behind the trunk of a pine tree, hoping the creature wouldn't notice them, fixated as it was on its meal. It may have simply viewed the human spectators as beneath its notice, like crickets or mice.

But how could such a creature exist in modern-day America? Had moose ever grown so large, even in prehistoric times? Could it be some sort of mutation? Stewart didn't know. And what was a moose doing this far south? Arizona was not their habitat. His mind buzzed with such questions.

For maybe ten minutes they sat breathless and watched the enormous moose tear through the thicket with the sound of snapping branches and stripping leaves, its legs like furry tree trunks.

Little by little, it finally moved away through the thicket until they lost sight of it among the trees. It took a long time for the sounds of its passage to disappear, however, and none of the family moved until it had gone.

Hunter was the first to rouse from his stupor. "That! Was! So! *Cool!*" He jumped up with both fists outthrust.

Liz breathed, "That was the most incredible thing I've ever seen."

"Mommy, was that a dino-moose?" Cassie said.

Liz and Stewart both laughed. Liz said, "That's what we'll call it."

Stewart shrugged off his pack in case he had to move quickly. "You all stay right here. I'm going to go check out the path ahead. We need to keep moving."

"But, Dad," Hunter said, "I'm the scout."

"You stay here and guard Mom and Cassie," Stewart said.

"Hey, that's sexist," Liz said with one raised eyebrow.

"Yeah, Daddy!" Cassie said. "We're not princesses. Mommy is like Wonder Woman."

Stewart chuckled. "Okay, fine. You got me, Amazon warrior women. Anyhow, I'm going to make sure the dino-moose is gone." He raised a finger to his lips for silence while he did.

Unclipping the hatchet from its carabiner, he crept toward the swath of destruction the dino-moose had left behind. Reaching the edge of the thicket, he saw the moose had torn through the underbrush like a bulldozer. He also got a closer look at the rose-bushes that had been hiding just inside the edge of the thicket. Never had a plant looked so malevolent to him, even as it lay in splintered ruin. Its tendrils, very much like the ones that shredded his tires, fanned out from a thorny hub that had been packed with blooms the color of congealed blood. Now, however, that plant had been half-uprooted and soundly stomped into the ground by cloven hooves the size of truck tires. Rose petals covered the forest floor like blood droplets.

The moose's passage crossed the stream in the direction they needed to go and then led away into the forest, with no further sign of the creature or any other threats.

Before long, they were on their way again, but more cautiously this time, taking their time to walk quietly. The encounter with the dino-moose had squelched Cassie's chatterbox tendencies.

As they trekked, a sense of warmth suffused Stewart's limbs, as if with satisfaction or excitement. The air smelled fresher, sharper, and the greens of the pine needles seemed to gleam like emeralds.

They checked the map often, and both adults felt confident they were following the correct path.

Stewart noticed that Liz stopped several times, turned to look at something, then shook her head with consternation. "You see something?" he asked her.

Her smooth brow furrowed. "I keep thinking I see things out there behind the trees, running from cover to cover, like animals or something. But every time I look, try to focus on it..."

"Every time you try to focus on it, it's gone," Stewart said.

"Right."

"I've been getting that since the dino-moose," he said. And he had. Sort of. Maybe he was getting used to it. The truth was, that had been happening to him for a while, ever since he'd been stabbed in the calf by some unseen creature that early morning.

Cassie gave both of them a knowing look, then giggled and rambled onward.

The gobbets of sky peeking through the coniferous canopy took on a brilliant blue like Stewart had never seen before, as if it were free of dust and pollution. It was the kind of blue he'd only ever seen in pictures of sapphires and turquoise.

The pine trees began to give way to redwoods, and the air grew cooler, moistening with the scent of dew.

"Look, Daddy!" Cassie said, pointing at some bushes that sported profusions of pinkish-red berries catching a shaft of sunlight. "What are those?"

As they approached, he said, "They look like raspberries."

"Really? I never seen raspberry plants before!"

"Can we eat some?" Hunter said. "I'm getting hungry."

Liz and Stewart checked them out.

"They look ripe to me," Liz said. "And there are so many!"

Cassie reached for a handful, eyes gleaming with hunger. "Hey! They got stickers!" She yanked her hand back, stung.

"Yes, so be careful," Stewart said.

Cassie's face twisted. "The green ones are *yucky!*"

"Well, don't eat those," Liz said.

"This is great," Hunter said. "I was getting hungry."

"Scouting is hard work," Stewart said, shrugging off the unwieldy weight of the backpack, stretching out the kinks in his back and shoulders. This unexpected find pleased him. It would take a little pressure off their food supplies. He ate several mouthfuls himself. The way the raspberries burst with sour, gritty sweetness in his mouth, so plump and juicy, made him crave the next handful. He had been getting hungry himself.

In their respite, he surveyed the area and it came to him that these trees were like nothing he'd ever seen. Many of their trunks were ten feet in diameter, and they stretched so high into the sky he could not easily gauge the distance.

"What's wrong, babe?" Liz said, studying him.

"These kinds of trees don't grow in Arizona."

"Well, maybe we're in Utah now. We've hiked a few miles."

"They don't grow in Utah either." He looked high, trying to determine how tall this tree was.

Birds flitted among the branches, singing, chirping, whirring, squawking, little bursts of movement and color. At least, he thought they were birds. But some of them didn't move like birds. They were too quick and distant for him to distinguish details, but some of them moved more like dragonflies, some of them more like bats. But they were too big to be dragonflies, and bats were not usually active during the day.

"Hey, Dad," Hunter said, "check out the side of this tree." He was looking at the opposite side of the redwood tree.

Stewart circled the raspberry bushes to see what the boy was looking at.

A patch of bark on that side, reaching about ten feet up and six feet wide, had been worn almost smooth as if by incessant rubbing, except for a series of gashes scratched deep into the bark, parallel gashes in groups of four.

Hunter saw them, too. "What are those?"

"This tree belongs to someone," Stewart said, a tingle of wariness raising the hairs all over his body. "Probably the raspberry bushes, too."

"Who?" Liz said.

Something about the gashes troubled him even more than what had certainly left them. Stewart took a few steps back to get a fuller look. The scratch marks reached almost ten feet from the ground. And there seemed to be a pattern to them, almost in the shape of a rune. But that couldn't be.

"Who?" Liz repeated.

"A bear," he said. A big one.

EIGHTEEN

"A BEAR!" CASSIE SQUEAKED. "You said there wouldn't be bears!"

"Don't worry, honey," Stewart said. "It's probably not close since the dino-moose was just around these parts." He had no idea if that was true, but he couldn't have Cassie losing her marbles two days' walk from anywhere. If everybody kept calm, he had one less thing to worry about.

Liz gave him a pointed look, however, as if to say she didn't quite believe him. "It's best to keep moving, though, in case he comes back," she said.

His lips pink with raspberry juice, Hunter wiped his mouth with the back of his hand, gave a little burp, and said, "What do we do if it shows up?"

"Don't turn your back and run," Stewart said. "Speak softly and back away the direction you came. Keep your eye on it so you can watch what it's doing. And most of all, *stay together*. Big groups are scarier to bears."

"How do you know this, anyway?" Liz said.

"My junior year of high school," Stewart said, "the science teacher was—"

"Kind of a barf-head," Liz said. "I remember."

"What Mom said. I ever tell you about the bet we made?"

"Oh! About getting an A?"

He nodded. "Not just an A, but *all* A's."

Hunter said, "What was the bet?"

"See, the science teacher hated me. He thought I was stupid because I loved to play football and I didn't try that hard in school. Too many teachers like Principal Snyder. I had too much else to worry about."

"Like what?" Hunter said.

"Like whether I was going to get anything to eat that day. By this time, I had run out on my last pair of foster parents."

"Why, Daddy?" Cassie said.

Because it was either leave or set his foster father on fire while he slept. The man had taken to beating him with a wire coat hanger to "whip that sass outta that boy," threatened him with telling the police he was a thief and sending him to juvie. All Stewart had done was to demand to be fed on a regular basis, and when meals were withheld for no reason, he sneaked into the kitchen late at night. And Stewart could be mighty scary, even at 16, all two hundred fifty pounds of him. And he knew it. But he couldn't tell his children that part of the story. So, he said, "They were really mean to me. Terrible people. Anyway, one day, the science teacher called me 'stupid' in front of the entire class. I was tired of his crap, and I made him a bet in front of everybody. If I ended junior year with all A's, he would buy me tacos every day for the entire summer. If I didn't, I'd drop out of the football team senior year. We were studying biology. I wrote a paper on the behavior of bears. It was the best paper I ever wrote. I got an A on it. And

I got an A in Mr. Barf-head's class. And all my other classes that year."

Liz chimed in, "Your dad made the school paper for that."

"So did Mr. Barf-head pay up?" Hunter asked.

"I made sure he did. I went by his house every day. I think by that time, maybe he'd changed his mind about me. And it's a good thing, too. Those tacos were pretty much the only thing I had to eat that summer. He had me do a few odd jobs around his house a few times, paid me a little for it."

What he had never told his kids was that he'd lived on the street for a while, sleeping in parks, until he finally found a part-time job and eventually made enough money to afford a room in an honest-to-goodness boarding house. He'd had no idea such things still existed, but he'd found one, befriended the lady who ran it with a few odd jobs, and lived there during his senior year of high school.

"So, I know a lot about bears," Stewart said. "But let's keep moving, huh?"

***

They kept onward, following the path of the stream, which grew narrower the higher they climbed. The water was so clean and clear, they didn't hesitate to drink it.

On breaks, Stewart and Liz pored over the map. While its dark lines seemed to clearly mark their path up to now, it could not assuage their worry over whether they were doing the right thing by following it at all. Now that they were firmly in the wilderness, with at least a two-day hike back to civilization, the pressure Stewart felt continued to increase. At some point, this could easily go from a family bonding experience to something much, much worse. The children's spirits were still high, though. The sense of adventure dampened the complaining about the endless walking and climbing. He had to give the kids credit; they bore their loads without a single whine.

The "something worse" came sooner than he expected, at about midafternoon when the stream disappeared, despite the map showing it should still be there.

The four of them just stood and stared at the cleft between two massive boulders, from which the stream sprang, bursting from the mountainside itself.

Stewart stepped right down into the cleft, which stood perhaps ten feet high, five feet wide, watching his footing on the slick, wet rocks. The stream was narrow enough here that he could leap across it, but he couldn't follow it into the mountain.

He sighed and scratched his head.

They let the kids munch on a bit of lunch while he and Liz conferred out of earshot.

"Did we take the wrong stream? Have we missed a fork?" Stewart asked.

"There haven't been any real forks. A few tiny ones that Cassie could step over." Liz scratched her head and sighed. "I just feel like things have gotten very weird. I mean, those aren't even birds up there." She pointed into the canopy high above where the bat-winged things and dragonfly wings flitted and buzzed loud enough to echo all the way down. She gave him a hard look. "I feel like we've wandered into Neverland or something."

He nodded, took a deep breath, let it out. "Yeah."

"Which may explain the lack of cell phone reception," she said.

He nodded. "Can you feel something in the air? Like static electricity?" The sensation of all his little hairs standing on end had been with him for a while, as if the air itself was poised for something. "Magic maybe."

"You think that's magic?" she asked.

"I don't know what else to call it. Power. Potential. Energy. But it's not like electricity either."

Just then, a sound sent claws of ice skittering up his spine.

A deep, rumbling chuff. Like an old man rolling over in bed, but an old man that stood nine feet tall and weighed over half a ton.

There was no mistake. It had been the sound of a bear. And it was close, within a hundred yards. Since a bear could outrun a thoroughbred, it could cover that distance in a handful of seconds.

Liz had heard it, too, and she clamped a hand over her mouth, eyes springing to the size of hubcaps.

Squeezing her arm, he dragged her back toward the kids.

"What do we do?" she whispered.

"We run," he whispered back.

"What? You told us not to!"

"Maybe it hasn't seen us yet. Maybe we can get out of its path, let it go its merry way."

Hunter and Cassie watched their parents approach, eyes widening with alarm, sensing that something *bad* was coming. They had heard it, too.

"Dad, what—" Hunter managed to say before Stewart clamped a hand over his mouth.

Liz scooped up Cassie and both their packs and began to run away from the sound.

"Go!" Stewart hissed to Hunter.

"Where?"

Stewart pointed after Liz, then grabbed the cooler containing most of their food.

The chuffing growl sounded again, closer this time.

Hunter bounced a couple of times as if gathering his momentum, staring at his Dad, staring into the forest, then he spun and ran after Liz.

A thought crossed Stewart's mind like a shooting star, bright and brief. Maybe he could distract the bear, which was certainly already coming this way, with a package of hot dogs.

That's when he heard the thump of its movement on the forest floor, great clawed feet tearing up the carpet of pine needles. It felt so close he could hear its breathing, or maybe he was imagining that.

He flipped open the cooler, snatched a package of hot dogs, ripped it open, and flung them away from him in a twenty-foot arc. Having to search out each individual frank by smell might give the bear enough pause for Stewart and his family to get away.

For good measure, he threw out several hot dog buns as well.

Then he slammed the cooler shut, snatched a handle, and took off running. Liz and the kids were almost a hundred yards ahead of him now, dodging among the pine trunks. Liz had put Cassie down but gripped her arm, half-dragging the girl along. He could hear Cassie sobbing with fear.

They angled downslope, which lent further speed to their feet. But he had no illusions about being able to outrun a bear.

The slope steepened, forcing him to slow down and watch his step or else lose it.

Then he looked up, and his heart skipped a beat. Liz and the kids were gone.

And he didn't dare yell out to look for them.

He increased his pace again, struggling to catch up, slipping and sliding on pine needles as he went.

But then he rounded a wrinkle in the slope and found them, kneeling next to a group of boulders leaning together at odd angles.

At the sight of him, Liz's eyes brightened, and she gesticulated for him to hurry. When he reached them, she said in a hushed voice, "Hey, look! We found a cave!" She was still panting from the run.

"We could hide in here," Hunter said, down on all fours as he peered through the small entrance.

"Yeah, or we could be trapped in there," Stewart said as he came to halt.

Liz said, "A bear couldn't fit through that opening."

Hunter's voice echoed as he crept inside. "And there's a rock right here we could move over the opening like a door. And it's really big in here, plenty of room."

"Are you sure it's not a den for something else?" Stewart said.

"Doesn't look like it," Hunter said. "I don't see a nest or anything."

A rumbling chuff echoed down the mountainside, and that made the decision for Stewart.

"Let me check it out," he said. He dropped the cooler, shrugged off the pack, and wormed his way inside.

Hunter was right. The opening was barely big enough for him to fit through. A bear couldn't without considerable digging, if at all. The chamber amid the boulders was about the size of the interior of their tent, the floor covered in a couple of inches of old pine needles. Ribbons of sunlight peeked between the boulders, so if it rained, they would get wet, but the opening was the only way in, and there was indeed a stone about the size of a car tire he could shift to block the opening.

Wriggling back outside, he said, "All right, everybody inside." He found them all looking up the slope toward another chuffing growl. "Now!"

That spur was all they needed. Seconds later, the kids were inside, dragging their packs in behind them. Liz went next, tugging her pack through the tight opening.

Stewart tried to shove the cooler through the hole, but it would not fit. He had to leave it outside. And he could hear the bear's footfalls now. But he wasn't about to leave the bear any more of their food, so he opened the cooler, chucked its contents into the cave, then shoved his pack in ahead of him.

His scrabbling feet felt dangerously exposed as he crawled inside, hearing the bear's trundling, thumping gait pounding down the slope. His heart jumped into his throat, choking off his breath. He could almost feel the heat of its breath on his calves and ankles as he thrust himself into the space, surprisingly cramped now that it was full of them and all their gear.

Even as he spun to look back, a huge shadow fell upon the opening, and a *whuff* of hot breath blew a puff of dirt and leaves into the space after him.

Nineteen

A SNOUT AS THICK as Stewart's leg poked into the opening, a sensitive black nose twitching, snuffling. The nose was easily the size of a dinner plate.

Cassie started to cry. Liz clamped a hand over the girl's mouth. Hunter had his hunting knife in hand. Stewart was lying on a packet of luncheon meat. A package of bread lay pancaked under him.

The bear poked its nose far enough into the opening that it could lay one eye on them. The glimpse of enormous teeth between the dark lips drove Stewart back against the rear boundary of the space. There was something about the fur on its nose that seemed off, but Stewart was too frantic to grasp it. The big brown eye blinked, regarded them.

"I don't think our group is going to scare *that* thing, Dad," Hunter whispered, eyes like golf balls.

Then as if ascertaining something only the bear understood, the huge snout withdrew and began to snuffle around the area outside the opening.

Stewart's galloping heart began to slow. Cassie's crying quieted to a whimper. Liz clutched her and stroked her hair.

Liz whispered, "What's it doing?"

Hunter moved toward one of the gaps between the boulders, just wide enough to peer between.

"Hunter!" Liz whispered. "Get away from there!"

The boy peeked outside, then gasped at what he saw. "Dad! Look!" he whispered.

Stewart crawled up behind him—the ceiling was too low to stand—and peered out.

The first thing he saw made no sense to him, so he blinked and rubbed his eyes.

He looked again.

It certainly looked like a bear in form, but it was huge, bigger than the biggest Kodiak grizzly ever recorded, the size of a minivan. Grizzly bears did not roam this far south. But it sounded like a bear. Even the smell of it, earthy, musky, resembled a bear.

But bear fur did not change color, did not coruscate with patterns and movement like a cuttlefish or an octopus. The beast's coat was a constantly shifting mosaic of brilliant hues, shifting through palettes of earth-tone browns and greens and then bursting with Day-Glo splashes as it sniffed around the cooler.

The cooler thumped and clattered as the bear opened it and stuck its nose inside. Plastic crunched and shattered. It made a disappointed grunt, and the colors shifted back to a rippling forest camouflage.

"Liz!" Stewart whispered, "You gotta see this!"

"I wanna see!" Cassie gulped, wiping her cheeks with her palms.

The two of them scooted forward to find an aperture. At the sight of the bear, they fell silent and gaping.

"Do you think it's friends with the dino-moose?" Cassie asked.

Stewart couldn't answer, because all logic and reason had fled over the nearest mountain.

With a quick wrench of its claws, the bear turned the cooler into wreckage, and then sniffed through the pieces.

Stewart reached back for the flattened package of bread, tore it open, then ripped off a chunk comprising several slices mashed together, which he chucked outside.

The bear came closer, sniffed it once, and devoured it. Its coat flashed with bright colors again, hypnotic and pulsating. Then it caught Stewart's eye. Stewart blinked and rubbed his eyes, because what just happened…

The bear had winked at him.

Then it turned and ambled away, the exploding colors of its coat once again subsiding into browns and greens.

It was a couple of minutes before anyone could speak again.

"Did you all just see that?" Stewart asked.

Liz whispered, "I don't think we're in Kansas anymore."

"Mommy, we live in Arizona," Cassie reminded her in a hushed voice.

Stewart could breathe again, and his heart stopped trying to leap out of his chest.

"What do we do now?" Liz said. Both adults knew they were lost at this point. Off the map. In a wilderness that he was pretty sure wasn't the real world. Populated by gargantuan creatures.

He eased back to lean against the rocks and squeezed the bridge of his nose. The real question was: Should they try to retrace their steps back to the campsite, and then down the road and back to the highway?

But could they? After that frenzied flight, could they even find the stream again? If they decided to push ahead, where would they be pushing ahead toward?

They had certainly found adventure. They had found magic. They had seen a dino-moose and a rainbow grizzly.

While he was lost in thought, Liz prized apart the cracker-thin slices of bread, slapped some luncheon meat in between them, and gave them to the kids to eat, and they all munched in silence. Liz kept glancing at him. She knew he sometimes had to quiet himself, sweep away mental debris, and wait for the truth to coalesce.

He closed his eyes and listened to the quiet voices within himself.

The bear could still be out there. He was sure of many things now, but he could not be sure the bear had winked at him.

But even if it hadn't, it had lost interest in them quickly. It hadn't tried to get at them. Its attitude was more curiosity than hunger or aggression.

Finally, he said, "You all stay here. I'm going to venture out, scout around a little. Maybe I can find our stream again."

Liz's eyes widened. "You want to *split up*?"

"I won't go far. I just want to have a look around."

"But, Dad, I'm the scout," Hunter said.

"Not this time, Son. Sorry."

With one last peek for threats, he grabbed his hatchet and crawled outside. He took careful note of his surroundings, the lay of the land, the position of the nearby boulders. It would be easy to get lost again if he ventured too far.

He headed around the skirt of the mountain slope, thinking he would make a wider arc downward, just to see what was around before returning to the enclosure.

The forest was silent, except for the buzzing and flitting and chirping of the creatures above and the breath of the wind in the redwoods. These trees possessed a size and majesty he had never seen before, stretching high, high, at least a hundred feet. The lowest branches were at least thirty feet up. He would need a jet pack or wings to get up there.

As he passed around a low, rocky ridge, he lost sight of the cluster of boulders where his family hid. He walked another hundred yards or so, careful to keep himself orientated.

What he discovered on the other side, however, seized his attention.

A trail.

What he couldn't immediately discern was whether it was game trail or a manmade trail. It was about as wide as a cattle path, just enough to walk single file, but was clean and clear of rocks, easy to follow. In one direction, it snaked upward and switched back out of sight, and in the other it meandered down the slope and disappeared among the trees.

He knelt and studied the trail. There had been a recent rain shower that cleared the dust of the trail, like shaking an Etch-A-Sketch, but there were cloven hoof prints, probably from deer.

For about a hundred more yards, he followed the trail downhill. And that was where his heart bounced with hope. At a spot where the trail snaked around a cluster of boulders lay a small cairn of carefully arranged stones standing maybe a foot high. The stones were stacked meticulously, carefully balanced in a single column, rising to smaller and smaller until the apex was a pebble the size of his thumbnail.

This was a trail that people used, unless the coyote-riding goblins had some sort of artistic bent. Someone had paused here long enough to fashion this little marker. For what purpose, he couldn't know, but it gave him hope.

He hurried back to the boulders where his family hid, retracing his steps. As the sanctuary came in sight, Hunter's voice yelled, "It's Dad!" As he tramped closer, they all crawled outside to meet him.

"I found a trail," he said, and then told them where. "I think we should follow it."

"What about the bear, Daddy?" Cassie asked.

"Honey, the bear went thataway." He pointed with each hand in different directions. "The trail is thisaway. I hope we won't see him again. But we'll keep our eyes and ears open, okay? No talking. We can hear better that way. Can you do that?"

She nodded, face worried.

It would also be better if they didn't give away their presence to who and whatever might be around, but he didn't say that. The glint in Hunter's eye, however, told Stewart the boy understood that very well.

"Let's pack up and get moving," Stewart said, looking for the position of the sun. Gauging from its location in the sky, the time was 2:00 or 3:00 p.m.

While the kids shrugged on their backpacks, Liz pulled out the map and examined it again.

"Oh, no way," she said. She looked at Stewart, eyes wide. "The map *changed!*"

"I can't say I'm surprised at this point." He leaned over her shoulder and looked. Their path had moved away from the stream and now meandered over the side of the mountain.

Some distance away down the mountainside, the map showed the outline of a bear. Some distance behind them now lay the outline of a moose.

"'Here there be monsters,'" Stewart said.

"Mommy, is the map magic?" Cassie stood on tiptoes to peek over Liz's hand.

"It sure is, honey," Liz said.

"Wow!" Hunter breathed. "A real, live magical map!"

"And maybe even a giant-rainbow-bear detector," Stewart said. He couldn't be sure, but the bear's silhouette might have moved away by a few hairsbreadths. "Okay, let's go. Mom is bear detector and navigator. Hunter and I will be the scouts."

"What about me, Daddy?"

"You are the rear guard, Cassie. Your job is to watch and listen behind us. Can you do that?"

Cassie nodded vigorously.

"All right then. Remember, lips shut and ears open."

It was only a few minutes' walk to the trail, and their spirits picked up as soon as they found it, as if it were a touch of intelligent presence, the fingerprint of civilization in the wilderness.

For a couple more hours they followed the trail, which led generally downslope with a few areas of rocky undulation. But they found more cairns spaced along the trail, some of them taller with more stones, others shorter.

The trail led them into a deep, wide mountain valley, and the going was so much easier than threading their way through the maze of massive tree trunks. The opposite side of the valley was an emerald tapestry of mountains and forest, toward which the sun descended. This meant they were traveling roughly north or northeast. As the sun dipped toward the saw-toothed horizon, it painted orange ribbons across the carpet of needles at the feet of the redwoods, and the sounds of the forest changed. The chitter and chirp of the canopy above hushed to an occasional call and response. The air grew cooler, moist, and smelled of rich fertile earth, flowers, and even honey.

Liz kept checking the map, reporting periodically that the bear and the moose outlines did not appear to be getting any closer. About half an hour of light remained when the trail led them to the bank of another stream, prompting her to wonder aloud, "Do you suppose this might be the stream that leads us to the lake? We're supposed to go to the lake, right?"

"That's what the shopkeeper told me," Stewart said.

"What are we going to do when it gets dark?" Liz said, growing nervous. "Those coyotes could come back."

He'd been thinking about the same thing himself, looking for suitable campsites as they went or another shelter like the one that had protected them from the bear, but had seen nothing suitable. The ground was too steep, too rocky, and at the same time, too wide open to serve as both a campsite and a defensible position. If those coyote-riding goblins caught them in the open, without the defense of a cinder-block toilet, the outcome would be much worse than the night before. Stewart's wounds ached, but they were nothing he couldn't endure.

They continued down the trail, paralleling the stream's flow for maybe another quarter of a mile, when they came to a fork in the trail. At the juncture stood another stone cairn, but unlike any they had seen thus far, these stones were engraved with more runes resembling those the old gas station attendant had embedded in the putty to fix the fuel line.

"Hey, Dad?" Hunter said, interrupting Stewart's reverie. "Did you notice the river is flowing the wrong direction?"

"What do you mean, 'wrong direction'?" Stewart said.

Hunter shrugged and pointed.

Liz exclaimed, "Are you telling me the water is flowing *uphill*?"

He was right.

"Then which way is the lake?" Liz grabbed a handful of her hair and squeezed it. "Is this stream flowing *from* the lake, or *to* the lake? Oh, doodles, my head is spinning." She sat on her haunches and stared at the gurgling stream, throwing the map over her shoulder.

The stream was maybe twenty to thirty feet across, about knee deep, and so crystal clear he could see the dark, streamlined shapes of fish maneuvering in the current, ranging in size from minnow to trout, some of them as long as his forearm. It might be time to go fishing. After all of today's trek, hunger was chewing on him.

But the water flowing uphill, defying gravity, disoriented him, made him a little dizzy. Could it be an optical illusion? No, the uphill slope was too steep for it to be an illusion.

A fish flipped out of the water and disappeared again with a splash of silver and emerald.

Cassie pointed. "Is that a fish? It was really pretty."

"Like the bear?" Stewart said.

"No, more like the greenest green I ever seen. Hah, I made a poem!"

He knelt at the river bank, peering into the water.

A brilliant, emerald-green fish leaped into the air and splashed, its scales glimmering like chips of gemstone. It was big, about the length of his forearm, thick as his wrist, but sleek, strongly resembling a koi in shape.

It leaped again, and after the events of today, it became easier to believe its bulbous quarter-sized eyes were looking at him.

"If I didn't know better," Liz said, "I'd say it's trying to get our attention."

Twenty

"**WHAT MAKES YOU THINK** it's not?" Stewart said. He had never seen such a gymnastic fish in his life.

Then the fish whipped upstream about thirty yards—downhill—and launched into another flurry of arching leaps, twists, and flops.

"It *does* want us to follow it!" Cassie said with a giggle.

"What if it's a trick?" Liz said.

Stewart nodded. "I had the same thought." It was so hard to know what to believe, especially in a state of increasing fatigue. As dusk drew on, the weight of the day's events and the lack of sleep the night before hung on his limbs and eyelids. Weariness weighed him down.

Liz must have seen it on him. "We need to set up a camp somewhere so you can rest. Maybe if we follow that fish, we'll come to a place that's flat enough to at least sit down."

"Yay!" Cassie jumped up and sprang after the fish.

"Stay close, baby girl!" Liz called.

The closer they got to the fish, the more it moved away. The path grew wider as they went, as if more traveled.

Stewart's shoes seemed to turn to lead, slowing his tread, even going downhill. All his reserves of energy had abruptly run dry.

Liz and the kids gradually outpaced him. He found himself day-dreaming, just a little, of a nice flat patch of cool, green grass, the kind that felt like a cushy mattress, but protected by a circle of boulders, a space just big enough for the family, with a nice little fire pit in the center.

Then a white light burst in his vision, and a spike of dizziness brought him to his knees.

"Stewart!" Liz cried, turning at the sound of his collapse and grunt of distress. "Are you all right?" She ran back to his side.

He jammed his fingers into his eyes against the pain and blinding flashes bursting behind his eyelids. Dizziness washed over him. The ground beneath him felt like a rowboat in heavy swells, swells crashing over the landscape, over him, through him, making his skin tingle, his hairs stand on end.

Her warm hand on his shoulder quelled the tossing enough that he could open his eyes without throwing up. He blinked through tears and squeezed her hand to steady himself.

"What is it?" Her voice sounded almost frantic.

"I don't know...just got...really dizzy."

"You look like you're about to pass out!"

"Uh, yeah... But I think it's over now." The white spots in his vision faded into rainbow particles, then disappeared.

"You want me to help you up?" Liz asked. The kids stood on either side of her, worried.

He shook his head. "Need to try it myself." Gathering his strength, he stood, concentrating on steadying himself. He took a couple of deep, slow breaths. "That was—"

"Terrifying!" Liz threw her arms around him, her face alight with fear. Then she whispered for only him to hear, "I don't know what I'd do if I lost you."

Meanwhile, the sliver of emerald green leaped out of the water again. "Let's keep going," he said, "before it gets too dark to see anything."

They moved on down the path again, sticking close to Stewart this time.

Ahead, the fish seemed careful to keep them in sight.

After another fifteen minutes of walking, they rounded a sharp bend in the trail, below which the river narrowed and sped up, tossing whitewater over jagged boulders. Thirty yards ahead, to the side of the trail, stood a cluster of more boulders, each at least fifteen feet tall.

Stewart's dizziness returned for a moment, and his mouth fell open. He grabbed Liz's arm as he approached the circle of stones. Between two boulders stood a gap just wide enough for him to slip through sideways, an entrance that faced the trail and the river. Within the circle of boulders, open to the sky, lay a lush swath of bright green grass, and in the center, an old fire pit ringed by stones. The space looked to be about fifteen feet across, plenty of room for them to sleep, but close enough to be sheltered from a horde of goblins on coyote-back.

"Stewart, what is it?"

He touched one of the boulders at the entrance, as if he could feel its antiquity rising out of the earth. He rubbed his face, his eyes.

Hunter darted past him into the space. "It's like Stonehenge, but small! I read about Stonehenge in one of Gramm's magazines."

Of roughly uniform size and shape, the boulders did make a circle, but except for the entrance, they were spaced closely enough they formed a wall.

The setting sun shone through the trees and splashed orange through the opening onto the floor of the space.

"Let's camp here," he said, glancing at Liz.

"Are you sure?" Liz said, rubbing the back of her neck, her voice nervous. "It feels almost too convenient."

"I'm sure," was all Stewart said, because what he wanted to tell her felt too weird, even after everything that had happened today. He wanted to bounce it off her, in case it was too absurd, before he said anything in front of the kids. He didn't want them thinking their father was a nut case.

"First priority," he said, "Hunter and I will gather some firewood before it gets too dark."

"Aye aye, sir!" Hunter said with a salute.

Half an hour later, the sun was gone, but their circle of stones was lit by a crackling fire that cast an orange glow up the sides. The air cooled and made their fire a comfort that went all the way down into their caveman instincts. Shelter. Warmth. Food. Tribe. It was good in ways that few things in the modern world could match.

The bear's visit had taken a chunk out of their food supplies. All they had left was a few granola bars and dried apple slices. Liz made the kids brush their teeth and settle down for bed, but keep their clothes on. No pajamas. They unrolled their sleeping bags on the soft grass, which acted like a springy, fresh-smelling cushion. He could see from the looks on their faces they were worried, but weariness would soon overcome that.

He took Liz down to the water, where he removed his hiking boots and socks and put his feet into the stream. The dash of chill cooled and soothed his blistered feet, and staved off the exhaustion that threatened to make him pass out on his feet.

She sat beside him and did the same. "Okay, spill it."

He squeezed her hand. "Remember that dizzy spell I had?"

"Yup."

"Right before that, I was daydreaming about finding the perfect campsite. A protective circle of boulders, soft grass, a fire pit." He gestured toward it. "And here we are."

She considered this for a moment, sucking on her teeth, scratching her head. "So, are you saying you dreamed this up, or was it some kind of premonition?"

"Those seem to be the possibilities, yes."

"So, which is it?"

"I think maybe it was like fulfilling my own wish, creating it." He didn't have the words to express that sense of immense *shifting* that blasted up through his feet when it happened, rocked his sense of the world under him, like standing in a crashing ocean wave but the wave was invisible and made of earth.

She looked out into the night, listening to the music of the night creatures, frogs and crickets and gods knew what else. "Could be it's this *place*. I keep wondering when the Tin Man is going to jump out."

"Which means we should be on the lookout for a wicked witch, right?"

"At least we haven't dropped a house on anybody yet," she said, "so we've got that going for us."

"But those creatures might come back tonight. Maybe they'll be riding flying monkeys this time."

They chuckled at that. He rubbed his eyes again.

Seeing this, Liz said, "It's my turn to keep watch tonight. You need some rest, or else you won't be any good if those critters do come back."

He couldn't argue with her. "You know you're amazing, don't you?"

"Of course." Her grin lit up the night. "But wherefore comes this burst of husbandly appreciation?"

"I just said to you one of the strangest sentences ever spoken out loud, and you took it in stride, like I said I was going to the grocery store."

"It would be weirder for you to actually go to the grocery store."

He chuckled at that. He hated grocery stores, maybe because he'd three times been accused of shoplifting in Mesa Roja's biggest supermarket. Twice they had been wrong.

She said, "You're right, though. That was a strange sentence." Pulling her feet out of the water, she hugged her knees and sighed, looking back at their children falling asleep in the firelight. "Now, you go get some sleep before you pass out and fall in the water. I don't think I could drag you out. I'll wake you if there's trouble."

***

Following the human family into the Borderlands between the Penumbra and the Light Realm made Jorath profoundly ill, like feeling poison coursing through his blood, infusing his bones, coating his tongue, making him dizzy, sapping his strength.

Fresh wariness gave him pause after last night's disastrous attack. Jorath had not yet pinpointed their nature, but the humans had protectors. Those protectors had destroyed enough of his goblin lackeys that the rest had been routed, and refused to venture from their burrows again even under threat of death.

And now the man had somehow found a way to channel the Source tides and alter the landscape itself. The ripples and undercurrents had felt like Jorath was losing his footing in a sudden riptide. It could not have been a purposeful event, but he saw now why the Master was so interested in this human. Stewart Riley had power. If he ever came into that power, he would make a formidable enemy.

It was time to tamp that power back down where the man could not reach it, to bury it again under everything that prevented him throughout his life. Anger, desperation, worry, tedium.

Jorath meditated on this, sitting cross-legged in a tree across the stream from the glow of the campfire crackling among the stones. The woman sat in the entrance facing out into the night, vigilant.

Jorath sent probing tendrils from his mind, visible only to someone with a similar ability, across the distance, reaching for the man's mind. Even in sleep, Stewart's mind was disquieted, and this disquiet created the chinks that allowed Jorath's tendrils to slip within. The tendrils wormed inside and drank deep of thought and memory and conveyed the essence of them back to Jorath.

Oh, but there was delicious Darkness in this man, almost in equal share with the Light. The balance might still tip to either side. With enough Darkness, the man would open himself to the influence of the Master. But the man knew of the Darkness and kept it shackled with a will of steel, so much so that his family might not even know of it. But shackles could be weakened, even broken. And if released, that Darkness would breathe freedom. There was no Darkness in the other three humans. Stewart often depended on their Light to keep his Darkness in check. Setting it loose in him might drive a wedge between them, help tip the balance. Then he would belong to the Master.

Jorath took this knowledge flowing into him, reshaped it with his own will, and reversed the flow.

***

Stewart was eight years old, and his life was pain and fear.

Older boys chased him across the schoolyard where other kids were playing soccer, and no one cared. He fled off the school grounds, but still they chased him. And when they caught him, they pushed him down, kicked him, stole the pack of watermelon-flavored Bubblicious he had skimmed from his lunch money to buy. The leader's name was Jed, and he tore the package of gum open and shared the pieces with his buddies while Stewart lay on the ground feeling tiny and helpless.

Fury sparked within him.

He jumped back to his feet, and the fury built him a bigger body until he stood twice the height of his tormentors, with muscles like a professional wrestler. He seized Jed and another boy by their skulls and slammed them together. The boy who had kicked him in the belly, he kicked onto the roof of a nearby house. The fourth boy broke and ran, but Stewart brought him down by flinging Jed at him.

He smiled in satisfaction.

In this larger size, he fit in perfectly with the high school football team, and he wanted the quarterback's beautiful girlfriend, but he could not remember her name because her curves and smile and breathtaking eyes fogged his brain. His arms lengthened and he bent down to chase her on all fours like a gorilla. She ran, but he caught her, reached for her tentatively, longingly, but she screamed and slapped him, and this angered him again, but the blow so surprised him all he could do was watch her run away in her cheerleader skirt, a vision of petal-soft legs and flying hair. But when she looked over her shoulder to see if he was pursuing, there was only terror in her eyes.

So he trudged through the back alleys of town so no one would see him this way.

The moment he walked through the front door of his foster home, his foster mother started screaming at him how stupid and ugly he was, so he roared at her in fury. She shrank in size by a third, her face and hair turning ghost white. She fled out the back door. Then his foster father charged at him, calling him a monster, flailing at him with a wire coat hanger bent long and thin. The wire lashed across his face, his arms, leaving bright red welts. It hurt a lot. He grabbed it in mid-swing, ripped it out of the man's hand, and grabbed the man by the throat. The man's legs flailed and his hands clutched Stewart's thick wrist. Stewart carried him outside and threw him into a pile of burning leaves. Then he went back inside, took the pan of lasagna out of the oven and ate most of it. He shared a little with three foster siblings, who were all very grateful.

Then he went to work cleaning out piles of cattle manure from the barns at the feedlot, but he stepped into a watery, waist-deep hole, and the noxious slurry filled his rubber boots, soaked through his jeans, and mired his feet in place. He was stuck. In a small motorboat, Mr. Richards rode out to him, screaming at him the whole way, the propeller splattering manure in all directions behind him. But it wasn't really Mr. Richards; it was a scarecrow made of moldy straw and sun-bleached tatters, with a face as blank and empty as a burlap bag, but shrieking vitriol nevertheless. Stewart tried to reach him, but couldn't. The manure held him fast, and worse, he was sinking. He tore his feet out of the boots and slogged through the manure swamp. The manure was too thick for Mr. Richards to maneuver his boat. Stewart seized the boat and flipped it upside down. Then he stomped the scarecrow down into the bottom of the waist-deep manure and held the creature there until it stopped squirming.

Covered head to toe in oozing stench, he shambled onto dry land like some swamp monster made of mud and cow dung. The cheerleader was there with her quarterback boyfriend, and they both laughed at him.

"You don't know me!" he yelled at her.

Then he wiped the poop from his face, and ran on all fours for the rock quarry that was right over there, where the crystal-clear water could wash this manure and stench off him. He jumped into the water, but the swimmers screamed in fear and chased him with kayaks and beat him with paddles. So he climbed out, scrambling up the sheer, stony cliff face to gesticulate at them with a long, misshapen arm, roaring like King Kong.

When he reached the cliff top, two little monkeys were up there crying, "Daddy! Daddy!" They were so cute, so precious, so he scooped them into his arms, but they shrieked in terror, biting and clawing as they wriggled free and fled. They flung rocks at him as he cried with rage and hurt.

His flesh burst into flames, but not flames that burned him. They were flames that burned everything and everyone around him. The little monkeys squealed and fled from the blaze of heat that set the nearby grass alight.

He found the cheerleader and her quarterback boyfriend kissing on the hood of his Camaro.

The cheerleader looked surprised. "Stewart!"

The quarterback boyfriend sneered at him. "This isn't Halloween, loser."

But then the gorilla torch-beast grabbed him, listened to him scream as his flesh burst into flame, crisping and sizzling and—

"Stewart!"

Something grabbed his arm and he flung it off as if it were a doll.

Except that it *was* a doll.

"Dad!"

"Daddy!"

"Stewart!"

A chorus of terrified voices.

A beautiful little doll in a delicate dress of lace and silk.

But as she struck the stone wall of their campsite, she bounced off it like an acrobat and sprang upon him, wrapping her cold, hard legs around his neck, seizing his ear with one hand like a tiny monkey's claw, squeezing, pinching, twisting. In her other hand was an obsidian needle poised to plunge into his right eye. The doll's cold, cobalt gaze drilled into his left eye, a finger's breadth away, her cherubic face chilling in its blankness. But in those eyes, those quite living eyes, he read a single intention.

If he made another move, the doll would blind him.

Twenty-One

STEWART FROZE, blinking in confusion.

The orange glow of the fire's coals glimmered in the doll's polished eyes, eyes that were at once cold blue glass but somehow full of intelligence.

"Stewart, what's happening?" Liz's voice, close to panic, was nearby but the doll's blank face filled his vision.

The point of the needle hovered, just out of focus, an inch from his eye.

The hot, pulsating rage of his dream began to fade, but slowly. He wanted to seize the doll and smash it against a boulder, but he didn't dare. The thing was too fast.

"What do you want?" he said, holding stock still.

But the doll didn't speak, its face a porcelain mask.

"Daddy, you were scaring us," Cassie said.

"Yeah, you sounded like a monster," Hunter said.

"Stewart, I think the doll is protecting us. From you."

He gasped as his stomach filled with lead, steel cables cinching around his chest, cutting off his breath. "Oh, no." It came out as whispering wheeze. "What did I do?"

Liz's voice quavered. "Uh, you were yelling, and grabbing handfuls of grass like you were tearing something to shreds, waving your arms and..."

"Daddy, you almost knocked me into the fire," Cassie peeped, on the verge of crying.

His mouth fell open as the nausea of self-loathing washed over him. The fury of the dream, the vividness of it, the *fun* of it, slashed an open wound in his psyche. He had *enjoyed* destroying his tormentors. He had reveled in the freedom of letting the shackles of propriety and civilization fall away to release the ferocity of righteous retribution for all the wrongs he had suffered. In his childhood, there had been so many. Liz and the kids had soothed those, let him bury those old hurts, but it was as if something had shaken up a soda bottle, disturbing all the sediment of long-buried wrongs, and uncorked it. But it released acid and fire.

The uncertainty in Liz's voiced cinched his chest tighter. If she ever for a second thought he would hurt the children, it would kill him.

His voice cracked, "I'm so sorry, Cassie baby, I was having a terrible dream. I didn't mean to hurt you." Even as he said the words, he clenched his teeth at the tears of guilt. He hated violence against women or children, hated anyone who committed such acts, so the mere thought of hurting her, even accidentally, filled him with such shame and guilt he wanted to die. "I would never hurt you! Any of you!"

"Please don't hurt my daddy!" Cassie said. "He didn't mean it!"

But the doll did not move. The needle's point did not waver.

Then an unfamiliar voice spoke, a small voice. "That'll be quite enough now, lassies."

The doll on Stewart's face eased back. Its expression had not changed, could not change, but it released him and did a back flip onto the ground between his knees. Quick as a blink, the needle disappeared somewhere within its dress.

But then he saw the second doll, poised behind his back to thrust a needle into his kidney. His mouth went dry. If he had threatened the children even the slightest bit more, those dolls would have taken him out.

With preternatural speed, the dolls scuttled away to stand between him and Cassie, quiescent, but wary.

The new voice came from a small figure standing in the entrance of the circle, a little man in a scaly, emerald-green waistcoat, fists on his hips, one eye narrowed as he surveyed the scene. His waistcoat glimmered in the light of the coals, the same color as the fish's scales. He stood about knee high and wore a top hat set at a jaunty angle. Mutton-chop sideburns adorned his bulbous, rosy cheeks.

With a blink of surprise, Stewart realized he'd seen the little man before. In Gramm's storage unit.

The four of them stared.

The little man sighed and rolled his eyes. "Aye, aye, get yer ganders and then get over it." He waved his hand.

The rapid succession of strangeness hit Stewart like hammer blows, but he could focus on only one thing. He wiped his eyes. "Cassie, I'm so sorry." He held out his arms.

She didn't hesitate to run into them and hug him. Hunter still eyed him warily, however, his eyes still full of fear that was not from killer ninja dolls or the little man Stewart would swear was a leprechaun. Something in Stewart had terrified his son, and the shame steamrolled him again.

As he got to his feet, lifting Cassie with him, still hugging her tight, kissing her soft cheeks, he felt the attention of the dolls freshly focused on his every move, ready to strike in an instant. Cassie clung to him, assuaging some of the awfulness swirling in his belly, but not all of it.

"Who are you?" Stewart said to the little man.

"Should I have ye call me Seamus or Paddy or Darby or something other kind of cliché?" the little man said with a smirk.

"Is one of those your name?" Hunter asked.

"No, laddie. My name is not for you. But how about ye call me..." He rubbed his chin thoughtfully. "How about 'Bob'?"

Cassie asked, "Are you a leprechaun?"

"My people are called that in various parts, aye."

"You sure do look Irish," Liz said.

"Now let's not be hasty," Bob said with a wink. "Call it an affectation, a style choice, like changing your underclothes." A snap of his fingers caused a quick swirl of mist around him. When the mist dissipated, he stood before them wearing a sparkling robe of green silk brocade with a circlet of silver stars around his neck. His skin had gone from rosy-cheeked paleness to the color of coffee. With another snap, he wore the buckskins and beads—also emerald green—of a Native American, with long black hair and weathered red-brown features. With another, an emerald-green kimono embroidered with golden thread to look like fish scales, with two tiny swords thrust through his sash. With a final snap, he returned to his original appearance. "Depends on me mood, it does, and the spirit of the moment. My people do get around."

Cassie asked, "Do you know Peaseblossom and Cobweb?"

"My kinfolk they are," Bob said with a smile. "They told me all about *you*, my dear."

Cassie blushed and nuzzled Stewart's neck.

Stewart said, "So, uh, Bob. What are you doing here? We have a lot of questions."

"So I'd reckon. Apparently, I'm here to be referee." Bob gave the two dolls an arched eyebrow. The dolls lowered their heads in unison. "Fairer to say, perhaps, I'm here to help ye with all the things ye don't know. Which amounts to mostly everything. And just in the nick of time, it seems. Ye got yerselves a dark elf on your trail."

"Aren't elves the good guys, like in *Lord of the Rings*?" Hunter asked.

"Not these fellows, boyo. Chief henchmen for the Dark Lord, they are. Nasty as they come and twice as cunning."

"So, you're here to protect us," Liz said.

"'Protect' might be too strong a word. 'Tis not within me power. But steering you away from him, that I can do."

"Is he the one who wrecked my truck, laid the traps?" Stewart said. "Brought the coyote-riding creatures down on us?"

"What kind of creatures?" Bob asked.

Hunter said, "Ugly little guys, about this big, with spears and crossbows. A whole pile of them."

"Oh, dear me." Bob frowned and looked worried.

"What is it?" Stewart asked.

Bob's voice grew ominous. "This dark elf, he brought power with him, if he can summon Dark creatures into the Penumbra. Baron Tyrus must want you all in the worst way. And he sent him a dark elf to do his dirty work. He's out there right now, probably watching us, perhaps listening. I cannot cipher what he's up to but I can feel his presence. Like a vulture breaking wind."

"So what do we do?" Stewart said, holding Cassie close.

"The sooner we get ye out of the Borderlands, the better," he said.

"And go where?" Stewart asked.

"To the Source."

"And where's that?" Stewart pressed.

Bob sighed with impatience. "English is such an inadequate language sometimes. 'Where' is just not quite the right word. But nor is 'when,' nor 'what,' nor 'why.' Think of it like your sun, that big glass marble that gives light to everything in these parts. The Source is the place where Light comes from, and shines over all the worlds, yers, mine, the Penumbra and the Borderlands."

"Is it on the map?" Liz asked, unfolding it.

"You'll see it as a lake, but that's only part of how it really looks. Calling it simply a lake, 'tis like looking at a picture of a lake versus seeing the lake in all that it is, surface to bottom, shore to shore, encompassing everything living in it. Because ye're human, ye'll only see the picture version, but they won't hold that against ye."

"'They'?" Liz said.

Bob doffed his top hat to scratch his black-fringed bald pate. "Well, *everybody*." Then he shrugged. "Don't ye worry, lassie, ye'll see. Shall we be off then?"

***

They hurried down the riverside trail by the light of the moon, feeling more nervous and vulnerable after having left their stone fort behind. Silvery light shone down through the gap in the canopy, bright enough to cast shadows and make the going easy. Even high above, the moon looked larger than normal, and the face of the Man in the Moon looked strangely more defined.

They kept close together, and Liz still looked at Stewart with no small amount of fear. He needed to talk to her about what had happened, but it was more important for them to be moving.

Bob said, "That dark elf might still be on our heels, but 'tis better to present a moving target, is it not? When we get close enough to the Source, he'll have to turn back."

"Why?" Hunter asked.

"Because creatures of the Dark Realm cannot abide the Light, any more than vice versa. Even now, he no doubt feels like he's got himself a belly full of angry eels."

"How do you know it's a he?" Cassie asked, holding Liz's hand as they walked. The dolls walked now on either side of her like fierce little bodyguards, their short legs somehow keeping up with miraculous ease. Stewart could hardly peel his gaze from the way they moved, so unnatural and natural at the same time. Never mind the fact that until a couple of hours ago, he thought they were actually *dolls*. What they were, he didn't know, but they certainly weren't dolls.

"Because dark elves," Bob said with a shudder, "they're all boys."

"That's strange," Liz said. "Why are they all boys?"

A horrified look bloomed on Bob's face. "Ye don't *really* want to know, do ye? In front of the wee ones?"

Liz cleared her throat. "I suppose not."

The relief on Bob's face was plain, as if he hated even thinking about it.

"Can you change your shape to whatever you want?" Hunter asked.

"For the better part, aye, as long as 'tis something me own size. 'Tis like dressing up for All Hallows Eve every day. Do ye like All Hallows Eve, me boy?"

Hunter nodded. "You mean Halloween? I love dressing up and trick-or-treating."

Bob winked again. "Ye might call me the 'trick' in that arrangement."

As they walked, Stewart's mind wandered the crystal-clear shards of his savage dream that had somehow crossed over into his waking world, and the wreckage he might have made of his life and his family if they had not awakened him. He felt incredibly lucky that he had not hurt Cassie, only scared her. If that kind of trust was ever destroyed, it was nearly impossible to rebuild it. He had just missed falling into an abyss he hadn't known was there.

After an hour's walking, though, Cassie started to complain. "Mommy, I'm so tired." So Liz picked her up and carried her, backpack and all.

The same fatigue was plain on Hunter's face, so Stewart offered to carry him, too.

"No, Dad, I can do it," the boy said, his face full of determination.

Within minutes Cassie had fallen asleep in Liz's arms. Hunter trudged onward doggedly. They traveled in silence, keeping their eyes open and ears sharp for trouble. With short rests every hour or so, they kept going through the night, thankful for the mostly downhill path.

On one of these rests, Liz left Cassie propped against Hunter, the two dolls standing sentinel at their feet, then she took Stewart by the arm and led him a short distance away. "We need to talk," she said, her face determined and worried in equal measure.

They sat on a boulder at the river's edge.

He took a deep breath, feeling like his body weighed a thousand pounds. "I'm so sorry. I don't even know what I did, but the thought of hurting you or the kids makes me want to throw up."

"You don't remember anything?"

"I remember awful, awful dreams, fighting, rage, and then waking up in a choke hold by a doll."

"It started out you were tossing and turning, moaning in your sleep. You were all over the place. But then the moaning turned into something else, almost an animal growl, and then this evil laugh, and then you were tearing up the grass. You woke up the kids. They tried to wake you up, but you grabbed Cassie by the shirt."

"It was an accident!" he said in a cracked hush.

"Yeah, you were just grasping for whatever was there, but she got too close, and you were swinging your arms around and you're so strong that she almost stumbled into the fire pit. All of us were terrified. It still scares me to think about it."

He rubbed his face, his eyes, wishing the images from the dream were not still lurking behind his eyelids. "I'm so sorry." He wanted to say *It wasn't me!* But that would have been a lie.

She looked at him for a long moment, searching, frowning. "The thing is, it was so...so mean, so brutal, like a rabid animal ready to kill anything that got close, no matter who or what."

"That's how the dream was." He couldn't hold his voice steady. "I wish I could change it."

"I've never seen any of that from you before. When we started dating, I heard stories about your past, but I didn't know what to believe. I just thought you were a cute, kind, misunderstood guy who was getting a bad rap. But over the years, I've come to know you well enough to know something is lurking in there, something you control with an iron leash."

"I don't want to talk about that stuff. I had to leave it behind. I was happy to. I needed to."

"But maybe you haven't dealt with it. Maybe you just stuffed it all, and it's been deep down inside festering this whole time."

He couldn't look at her, this goddess who inexplicably loved him. The urge plowed into him to run into the forest and disappear so he could never hurt or frighten them again.

She put a warm hand on his, and that touch broke the dam of emotion. Tears filled his eyes, and his breath caught, because he didn't deserve the kindness. He deserved to be locked up, put in a straight-jacket in a deep hole, and forgotten. How could he have been so stupid as to think he deserved someone like her? Like the kids?

For a while, she just held his hand while the waves of despair and guilt washed through him.

"Did you...?" He faltered, unable to bring himself to ask the question.

She squeezed his hand gently and waited for him to gather the strength to say the words.

"Did you ever think...even for a second...that I could do that on purpose?"

Tears glistened as she leaned in and kissed his forehead. "Not for a second."

He pulled her close, buried his face in her hair, and let the tears come.

PART III

Twenty-Two

THE LONG WALK INTO dawn was not the most arduous travel of Stewart's life, but the difficulty grew with every step he took, almost as if he was fighting against himself. His stomach clenched, but it wasn't fear or hunger, more a vague unease.

The rising sun warmed his face, a wonderful sensation after a night of chill and fear.

As the sun prepared to crest the distant mountain peaks, its rays painted the sky the most brilliant colors he had ever seen, so many that he couldn't name them, couldn't recognize them. The colors painted streamers of cloud into scraps of rainbow.

It brought them all to a halt.

"We're leaving the Borderlands," Bob said, releasing a deep breath and smiling. "'Tis good to be home."

In the burgeoning light, Stewart noticed the trail had changed texture. It was no longer simple, hard-packed earth and pebbles. A more regular texture emerged from the earth, too small for cobblestones, with a feel that it was...organic. The closest thing he could liken it to was ray skin, the pale, scaly leather he had sometimes used to cover knife handles, but here at a larger scale. The scales were maybe the size of silver dollars. Before he could stop to consider whether this trail was fashioned of the skin of some gigantic creature, the sun broke the horizon, spilling brilliance over everything.

"Oh, wow," Liz breathed.

The kids froze in slack-jawed amazement.

The landscape exploded with colors so vibrant, so intense, they hurt Stewart's eyes. In this fresh sunrise, the feet of the redwoods were swathed in wildflowers. The river turned a cerulean blue he'd never seen before. The thick bark of the massive redwoods flourished in lush reds and browns and ochers, the canopy above sparkling with emerald. The sunlight brought life to all those creatures living up there, and a profusion of them sprang into the air, a kaleidoscope of wings.

The landscape revealed a splendor of misty waterfalls and lush grottoes.

And it all jammed an ache into his heart.

It was too much.

He didn't deserve to be here. Not after what he'd almost done to his daughter just a few hours before, after what he'd wanted to do to all the people who'd ever tormented him. His belly squirmed.

He had sunk to one knee, he realized, when Liz came up to him. "Are you okay?"

When he looked up at her, he gasped in wonder. She drew back at his surprise. "What? What is it?"

In that moment, she was the most beautiful he'd ever seen her. Not even their wedding day could compare to the vision who stood before him. Her brown eyes dark and soft as a doe's. Her tousled hair like spun gold dipped in honey. Her cheeks as soft as the petals of a rose. It was as if she glowed from within, as if the sunlight had awakened something that was already there, and now it was spilling out of her and taking his breath away.

She blushed and glanced away. "What?"

His mouth wouldn't work well enough to answer.

"What's the matter, Daddy?" Cassie said, rubbing her eyes with tiredness.

Stewart could only stare. The same was true of his baby girl. The same magic that imbued Liz turned Cassie into the sweetest cherub, so beautiful and wise she belonged in a Renaissance painting. He half-expected to see her produce a lyre and wings to sprout out of her back.

Hunter looked like a little Peter Pan, at once fierce and kind and alert, a young man who mixed compassion with courage, who would grow up to be someone like Robin Hood, a protector of the weak and a scourge of the corrupt. Stewart felt such pride in him in that moment that he wanted to shout to the universe *This is my family!*

He struggled to wet his mouth enough to speak. Finally, he managed, "You all look...amazing!"

The three of them looked confused, until they looked at each other.

"Mommy, you're so *pretty!*" Cassie said.

Liz blushed deeper. "Thank you, baby, but I feel just the same... Well, maybe not..." She looked at her hands and arms. She turned to Bob. "Something's happening. I feel...really *good*."

Bob gave her a wise look. "That's the Source. We're crossing over, and its power is flowing through you at full strength now."

"But what about Dad?" Hunter said. "Dad doesn't look so good."

Stewart might have been offended if his son wasn't correct. All around him, he felt the invisible flow of something—he had to call it magic—an intensely creative force. But it wasn't flowing through him. He felt like a river boulder, getting wet but only parting the flow as it swirled around him.

Bob stared deep into him. "The fingers of the dark elf linger in yer mind, laddie. Look at yer hands."

Stewart gasped to discover they looked ill defined, as if he could see through his fingers, his skin translucent at the edges. "What's happening?"

"The dark elf's touch awakened something in you," Bob said. "The Dark side is all about destruction, disruption, corruption. The Light side creates, the Dark side destroys and corrupts. I daresay you're feeling a fresh penchant for mayhem?"

Stewart didn't want to, but he nodded.

"Them that walk the Dark path can't come to the Source, and vice versa," Bob said. "A bright enough light banishes all shadows. A dark enough shadow can douse a light."

Liz's voice rose. "So, you're saying he can't even be here?" She grabbed Stewart's hand protectively. Where she touched him, corporeality spread through his flesh.

"Not exactly," Bob said. He gestured at Stewart's hand, which looked more solid now. "As ye can see, yer presence helps keep his internal Darkness at bay."

The kids crowded around him, laid their hands on him. Almost instantly, Stewart felt better, as if the ground under him had solidified, as if his flesh had solidified. The snakes in his belly stopped writhing.

He hugged all three of them to him, more grateful than he had ever been.

When he let them go, he said to Bob, "So am I in danger of falling back into the real world?"

"If ye mean yer world, the Penumbra, then aye, it is possible. But I think the Dark Lord's power can't reach ye here. Ye've only the darkness ye toted along."

"Could I come back?"

"Clear the Darkness out of yer soul and aye, ye could return. But that's not an easy thing. Been there a long time, it has."

"Don't let that happen, Daddy!" Cassie said tearfully.

"I won't, baby," he said, stroking her hair. "I feel better now. I have you." He hugged Hunter again, too. "All of you."

"Let's shake an expeditious leg, shall we?" Bob said. "There's folks waiting on us."

As they all started down the path again, Stewart asked, "Who's waiting for us?"

"I'll be letting them introduce their own selves," Bob said.

"So your side, the Light side, brought me here for a reason," Stewart said. "If I'm so Dark on the inside I can barely stay here, why bring me at all?" He couldn't bring himself to ask, *Am I dangerous?* He already knew the answer to that question.

Bob paused before replying. "Them that knows, it's for them to say."

"I thought you were supposed to answer questions," Stewart said.

Bob just sniffed and kept walking—or jogging, rather. His short legs had to move at triple speed to keep up with Stewart's long stride.

The two dolls skipped along like tiny schoolchildren on either side of Cassie. Stewart shook his head at the weirdness of it.

"Oh, no! Dad, look out!" Hunter stopped and pointed. "It followed us!" An enormous hulking shape emerged from the dense flowering shrubs across the river. It could leap over the water and be upon them in an instant.

The giant grizzly bear's coat of many colors let it blend in with its surroundings almost perfectly, but a creature half the size of the family's trailer house was not particularly stealthy.

Bob waved genially at the bear.

The bear paused and waved back with a paw the size of a truck tire.

"Oh, you're kidding," Stewart said. "That thing is on our side?"

"Mighty fine goblin repellent, ain't he?" Bob said.

The bear made a scoffing noise, as if offended at having his role thus belittled.

"Come now," Bob said, "we mustn't dawdle."

Stewart stared, mesmerized at how the bear's camouflage shifted so quickly, so precisely. At times, he almost lost sight of it, even though it walked in full view. "How much farther is it to where we're going?"

"That depends," Bob said. "One thing ye must know about this land is that 'tis not really land. The journey is as much an internal one created by all of us, by all of our intentions and beliefs..." He gave Stewart a pointed look. "By our baggage."

"That's really confusing," Hunter said.

"Stay here long enough, it'll come to ye, me boy. Think of it as a journey inward as much as a long walk. In some ways, it only *looks* like we're on a ramble."

"Not helping," Hunter grumbled.

***

Stewart didn't know how long they walked because his sense of time diminished.

What he knew was that there were unicorns.

But not horse-sized unicorns. The size of them fell between the size of goats and horses, like a small, spindly pony, but no less beautiful for their unexpected size. They grazed in verdant glades among bursts of wildflowers, like alabaster statues imbued with movement. Their horns caught the sunlight like diamonds. Winged creatures flitted among them, which Stewart thought to be insects at first, with wings like dragonflies.

But then a unicorn meandered close enough for him to see one of the winged creatures land on the unicorn's back. It was, in fact, a tiny, human-like shape with wings like a dragonfly's, sage-green skin, and hair in rainbow hues. The creature grabbed onto the unicorn's hair and stretched out to sun itself.

"Look, Mommy! Little people!" Cassie pointed at them.

"I beg your pardon!" Bob said with great indignation. "Those are *pixies!* Quite wonderful they are, in their own way, but they are, shall we say, like comparing monkeys to humans."

"But they're so cute!" Cassie said with a giggle.

On down the uphill-flowing river, into a valley so broad the far side was only barely visible through the mists of distance, they continued on their way.

Hunter said, "It's weird, Dad. I'm not tired anymore. It's like energy is just flowing through me all the time."

"Me, too!" Cassie said, bursting into a skip.

Stewart felt no such relief, however. If anything, his weariness was only increasing. His eyes were full of sand and his limbs were made of stone. He imagined the cause to be the fact that there was too much Darkness in him to flow through and replenish his strength. But Liz and the kids seemed to be perfect conduits for it. Seeing this tangible evidence of their purity of heart made him love them more, while making him feel less and less worthy.

As they went, Stewart's worries and fears diminished, however. It was like everything they saw was designed to coax his inner ten-year-old into the open.

Everywhere he looked was something wondrous to the eyes. Awe-inspiring vistas of mountains and forest. Industrious denizens in villages of the strangest appearance. The denizens looked human—until one looked closely, when all the tiny differences became apparent. Eyes sparkling with colors no human eye ever had. Skin and hair colors as varied as a box of crayons. He had difficulty identifying what their dwellings were made of. They appeared to be stone at first, but this stone, like the path underfoot, looked somehow alive, organic, as if they extruded it from the earth.

In one village, the dwellings were minuscule, suitable for people of Bob's stature. In another, where the people were very tall, perhaps eight feet, their dwellings matched their tallness. In another village, everyone seemed to live in a couple of large buildings like beehives. Everywhere was a flurry of activity: gardening vegetables, tending fields of grain, mending this and that. Here and there were people painting, sculpting, stoking kilns full of the finest porcelain. From every village they passed came the sound of music.

They sang in the fields, and in villages and glades; they strummed strange, stringed instruments and piped on flutes and horns.

It was all so beautiful, so idyllic, so exciting and yet peaceful, he found himself not believing it.

How could such a place exist? Where were the hard-pressed workers, the peasants? Where were the places of punishment? Where were the poor? Where were the diseased and downtrodden? Where were the outcasts?

Stewart saw no livestock anywhere. Did these people not eat meat? He saw nothing resembling even a chicken. What he saw were lush vegetable gardens and orchards full of blossoms and trees heavy laden with fruit.

The luscious-looking apples made his twisted stomach stir.

The endless wonders filled him with hope and awe, but there was a niggling corner of his mind, like a worm in an apple, that made him fear this was all some elaborate illusion, and the truth was coming like an avalanche to bury him.

He didn't dare hope too much that there would be a place where dreams came true, where evil couldn't reach, where everyone was content and fulfilled.

But even as these thoughts plagued his steps, the sight of what came into view as they topped a final ridge drove all such thoughts away.

Twenty-Three

JORATH'S SUDDEN RECALL TO the Master's presence was like a thousand fishhooks in his flesh and soul, dragging him through a keyhole in space and dimension.

One moment, despite how his increasing nearness to the Light sickened him and made his limbs feel made of stone, he'd been leaping from tree to tree in the Borderlands, following high above his quarry. The next moment, incredible agony slashed through him, and he was pulled into blackness.

He awoke already strapped into the Machine, held immobile, surrounded by a thicket of needles and blades. The Machine hummed against his flesh, quiescent for now, but ready to begin his long, agonizing demise at the Master's slightest thought. The darkness around him smelled of hot metal and blood.

"The human and his family have crossed the Veil, out of the Borderlands." The Master's voice was a red-hot boulder, its passage echoing in the metal vaults of the cavernous chamber.

Jorath's voice was a dry croak. "Forgive me, Master! They had much aid! And I was too far from your presence to overcome their defenses. It is my most fervent wish to serve you!"

"What shall your punishment be, Jorath El-Thrim? How long should I let my Machine work its magic upon you? How small should your pieces become before I allow you to expire?"

Jorath could see nothing except the dim outlines of onlookers standing in the hall, swathed in shadow at the foot of dais, many of them doubtless trembling with anticipation at the imminent spectacle of his agony, others plotting their own short-lived ascension just as he had. The Master's throne stood out of sight. Jorath could sense the power and intention flowing back and forth between the Machine and its Master, as if the Machine were a gauntlet upon the Master's hand.

Was Jorath afraid? No. He had known this end was possible. It had always been so. His people accepted it as a condition of their exalted status among the Creatures of the Dark. But he had acquitted himself well against forces that even the Master had not anticipated.

"Master," he said, "may I speak?"

"Do indeed. Regale us with your pleas."

Jorath took a deep breath and steadied his voice. Even in the face of his own death, he would not further dishonor the House of Thrim. "For a thousand years, Master, our enemies have not been so active in their designs as now. They have been content simply to react and defend, and only then to the minimum, giving us the advantage in every confrontation. We have grown accustomed to their reluctance to engage us openly. I believe their tactics are changing because they know *we* have the advantage. Your brilliant designs have borne fruit. They are desperate. They know their power wanes. Now we have the perfect agent in their midst, and neither he nor they know it."

"What agent is this?" The tiniest shred of interest emerged in the Master's voice.

An arm covered in blades and pincers paused before Jorath's face like a serpent, as if sniffing him.

"Stewart Riley, Master. Before he left the Borderlands, I flayed his mind and found exactly what I needed to darken his path. He nearly became ours at that moment."

"What prevented this?" Baron Tyrus said.

"His family. Their ties are strong. But not unbreakable. He controls his darker nature for their sakes."

"Not unexpected, but intriguing nonetheless."

Jorath's bonds released him, and the Machine dumped him face-first onto the metal dais. He struggled to control his shock. The Master could be as capricious as the wind. Was this a reprieve, or was the Master toying with him? He got to his feet, turned to the throne, and knelt. "I remain always at your service, Master."

Baron Tyrus rose from the throne, silent as a shadow, and loomed over Jorath like a tower of bleached bones stacked on end. "Come, Jorath El-Thrim." Sounds of disappointment whispered through the hall from the onlookers deprived of their spectacle. The Master walked away toward the rear of the hall.

Jorath scrambled to his feet and stumbled after, his hands and feet still numb from the tightness of the Machine's bonds.

The Dark Lord disappeared into an alcove, Jorath scrambling behind. In the alcove was a hidden, thick steel door. The metallic clunk of many bolts, sliding open one by one, sounded muffled through the barrier, then it swung silently inward to blackness.

Beyond the portal lay blackness only an elf's eyes could penetrate, the blackness of caves and warrens, pits and labyrinths. The

Master's smooth, silent stride carried him so quickly Jorath had to run to keep up.

The tunnel shot straight as a blade through the subterranean blackness. Other vaulted halls branched away into realms Jorath barely knew. He had only heard whispers of this part of Baron Tyrus's fortress, the place where the deepest secrets of all the universes lay hidden, cataloged, concealed, for eternities of time and dimension. Sounds echoed strangely to Jorath's ears, as if echoing through something that was not air, or bouncing from and among things that were not metal or stone.

For a long time, Jorath followed the Master, until they emerged into a cavern where a river of lava provided the only light. The dull orange glow reached a vaulted ceiling far, far above his head. The intense heat would have roasted the flesh from his bones had he not cast a protective spell that sent the heat flowing past him, as if it were river water and he, a stone.

In the center of this huge cavern stood... Well, Jorath did not know what it was, but it was roughly half-spherical, perhaps thrice as tall as the Master. He studied it with his magical sight. It was faceted, black as obsidian, but it didn't look like stone or crystal, because... He rubbed his eyes. Because the facets were moving, vibrating, shifting size and orientation. Focusing on the facets was difficult because they seemed to devour vision itself, as if color and substance had no meaning for what they were.

This was a barrier of some sort. A shell of pure Darkness. The Dark between stars. The Dark between universes. The Dark between thoughts.

The Master crossed a narrow stone bridge arching over a torpid, orange river toward the barrier. The air rippled with heat. The heat itself seemed to part for the Master's passage. Jorath hurried to catch up again.

The cavern was unspeakably ancient. Its walls and ceiling showed the smoothness and regularity of the hammer and chisel's touch, or perhaps the sculpting hand of magic, but in places, stalactites had grown over the construction, perhaps by the movement of water, or perhaps by the drip of molten stone.

A strange sensation gripped Jorath as he approached the barrier, as if he were walking steeply downhill, even though visually it was clear he was not.

The Master paused at the barrier, closed his eyes, laid his hand upon it. The nearest facets crumbled like black smoke, opening a space for them to pass through.

Inside, orange lava-light filtered up through cracks in the floor to reveal a cage resting on spidery legs of black iron. Within the cage, a small figure knelt motionless.

Through the grid of iron bars, Jorath caught a better glimpse of the occupant.

Her face was small and pale, her flesh smooth and covered in a strange, magical sheen, like the surface of a soap bubble. The sheen was a protective spell, not unlike the one protecting Jorath from the heat. In this enclosure, fueled by the heat of the lava, the air might be hot enough to melt lead.

A child.

Of what race, he could not be certain, but she was of the Light side, perhaps halfway to adulthood. She wore a simple white shift soaked with sweat. Her hair was plastered to her head and face, perhaps by sweat, perhaps by the protective bubble. Her eyes held closed and still. Was she even aware of their presence? Her cheeks were drawn, gaunt, like a shriveled fruit. She knelt on the bars of the cage floor, emaciated hands and forearms resting on her thighs, fingers entwined into a pattern of deep meditation.

Questions swarmed through Jorath's mind, but he waited for the Master to speak.

The Master produced a flask of clear crystal. "Drink, child. You must be thirsty." He offered it between the bars.

The child remained still, eyes closed.

Jorath moved closer for a better look.

The beauty of her face, even in its desperate state, seized his attention. She was the most beautiful child he had ever seen. Hatred roared forth so intense Jorath grabbed the hilt of his sword and half drew it, intending to impale her through the bars. The sight of this ancient enemy threw his deepest instincts into a froth of killing rage.

But the Master said, "You sense who she is."

"Yes, Master!" Jorath was almost breathless. "Titania's spawn! But, Master! How did the child of the Queen of Light come to be here?"

The ramifications beggared Jorath's imagination. What machinations, what schemes, what profundity of raw power could have brought this child into the Master's power? In a few eons, she would inherit her mother's place as the Queen of Light.

The Master's waxy lips twitched a hairsbreadth toward a smile.

"And she's still *alive*!" Jorath breathed. Had he been in a similar position, taken deep into the Light Realm with only his own power to protect him, he would have long since fallen back into the Dark. "How long have you had her, Master?"

"Too many questions, underling."

The child remained still, did not reach for the flask of water.

Jorath could see the crimson tinge in the water. Had the Master infused it with a couple of drops of his blood? A smile of appreciation found its way to Jorath's lips. The Master was trying to corrupt her, to bring her to the Dark, thus not only depriving the Light of one of their greatest sources of power but also bringing that power to the Dark *and* striking a profound blow to the Light's weak, tremulous heart.

"Oh, Master!" he breathed in worship.

But the child did not take the flask. Perhaps she was too clever and saw through the Master's ruse. Perhaps she was so deep within her trance that she was unaware of their presence. Perhaps her power was such that she could indefinitely protect herself from the chamber's scorching heat.

Could the Master compel her bodily to drink his blood?

Perhaps, but that was not his way. Baron Tyrus much more enjoyed seduction and trickery than brute force and savagery. He was averse to none of those, but he played games that were millennia in scope. He reveled in defeating his enemies at their own games. The Master wanted to make her *want* to drink his blood, because the moment she did so, she was his.

"Take it, my dear," Baron Tyrus. "You must be so thirsty, and this is the coolest water you have ever encountered. Only a single sip would bring you the sweetest relief."

The child did not stir. Her entwined fingers did not twitch.

"Perhaps, then," the Dark Lord said to the child, "you would like me to release you?" From within his robes, he withdrew a key. It looked to be fashioned of the same kind of black emptiness as the barrier, so slippery his gaze could not hold it, except to grasp the impression of spines and barbs. This, the girl opened her eyes for.

The intensity of her gaze, even in her weakened state, made Jorath queasy. The yearning in her gaze was like the force of gravity, but she was examining the key as well, and with similar intensity.

The Master gave a taunting laugh and put the key away.

The child closed her eyes and returned to her meditative posture.

The Master said, "This child is why the Enemy has entreated the aid of the human man. So I believe."

"To what end, Master?"

"To save her, you fool. Although what they think a mortal human can achieve, I cannot fathom."

"It would be a fool's errand, Master."

"He does not know that. It is his nature that made them choose him. His spirit is home to enough Darkness that he would be equally at home here."

"So, you still wish to turn him."

Tyrus nodded. "Of course, that would be my preferred outcome. But destroying him and his family also serves my purposes. They will send him. You must attempt to stop him."

"But how, Master? They are all in the Light Realm now."

Baron Tyrus focused his attention on the bars of the child's iron cage.

Quick as a blink, mechanical arms sprang from the substance of the cage, much like those of the Machine, seized her wrists, jerked her hands out of their meditative pattern, and hung her spread-eagled from the cage ceiling. She gasped in pain, eyelids snapping open to reveal eyes like jewels. They caught the light like diamonds and mixed it with the pain of the air. Her skin reddened, her hair steamed, and her pale shift darkened at the edges. Her gasp became a cry of pain.

The bars parted so that Baron Tyrus could reach through them with the gleam of a talon-like blade. A quick snick of the blade across the child's arm opened a wound that...

It *was* blood, to be sure, but not entirely in the sense that mortal, corporeal beings imagined blood.

It flowed, liquid-like, into a silver chalice the Master held under the wound, but it also bubbled and sparkled with colors that intensified Jorath's nausea.

At the moment of the cut, the child's cries silenced, and she looked Baron Tyrus straight in the eye. Her expression became one of disappointment and stoic reproach. If she were still in pain, it made no mark on her.

Her blood dripped and shimmered into the chalice.

"Have you enough?" she said, in a voice so light and deep that it made Jorath's bones ache.

The Master took the mostly full chalice, and her wound closed as if she had willed it.

Heat blisters appeared on her legs and arms, her beautiful face.

The iron arms released her, snapping like springs out of sight.

She resumed her posture of meditation, entwined her fingers once again, and closed her eyes.

The Master held out the chalice. "This, Jorath El-Thrim, is how you will stop the humans. Stewart Riley will join us—or die."

Twenty-Four

LIZ FELL TO HER knees, tears trickling down her cheeks. "It's so... It's like every fantasy dream I ever had as a little girl!" The yearning in her voice sounded of doll houses, dragons, and childhood adventures.

Stewart stood beside her and stroked her hair.

A glimmering, mist-kissed lake caught the sunlight, stretching into the vast distance where untold mysteries remained to be uncovered. Emerald forests hugged the sides of the valley. Distant waterfalls flowed upward into the lush reaches of the surrounding mountains.

The sun looked larger in the sky, and its brilliance seemed to press down on his flesh, like the quality of the sun in the high mountains, more intense, like tiny fingers pressing on him. Even though the sun filled the sky with light, the stars were so bright they shone through the cerulean blue.

He had thought the redwood trees of the Borderlands to be huge, but those across the lake made them look like saplings. A half-mile high, trunks fifty yards thick, branches and boles shaped and interwoven into homes and thoroughfares, bridges and balustrades. Jewels gleamed in great mosaics embedded in their trunks. Gazebos of pristine white wood entwined with vines and leaves.

It was a city, but like no city on Earth.

It was alive.

Not just with inhabitants, and not just because it stood housed within living trees, but because it was constantly growing and changing, yet somehow never tearing apart the bridges and causeways that connected the gigantic trees. An immense, gushing flow of creative energy flowed around and through it.

"Don't trip over your jawbones," Bob said with an impish grin. "'Tis quite a sight, says I. Come now." He coaxed them along the path toward the city.

"Does it have a name?" Liz said.

Bob paused, took a deep breath, and gathered himself. What came out of his mouth was not a single language, but a dozen, a hundred, a thousand, all at once, layered over each other in impossible ways.

It was as if Stewart were hearing its name in many, many dimensions, all of them scattering through time and space in ways he could not perceive with human ears. Nevertheless, something within sensed its passing. Out of the harmonious cacophony, Stewart picked out a phrase he understood. "The City."

Cassie held her ears. "That made me woozy."

"Hearing True Names can do that to humans," Bob said. "Especially when the Name is as old as the universe itself. Ye'll get used to it, lassie. Stay here long enough, ye'll be able to speak it yerself."

Meanwhile, Stewart stood stock still. What had passed over him—he had to call it sound for lack of a better word—had rung him like a gong, and not in a pleasant way. It was as if all the sharp, broken, jagged bits of his inner self had resonated all at once, tearing into the soft, smooth parts deep inside him, bursting to painful life like a kennel full of ill-tempered dogs startled into barking. Every part of him ached now—joints, muscles, organs, even his eyes and ears.

It was the first but not the last time he felt such raw power. And it was only the *name* of the place.

He wasn't supposed to be here. After what he had experienced, the evil dreams, the awful experiences, the wrongs he had committed, he didn't belong here.

And the City *knew it.* The scope of the City's consciousness went beyond even the word *consciousness,* like the difference between a lake and an ocean.

The vastness of what lay before him—the trees, the lake, the habitations, the architecture—went beyond human senses. What he saw were projections of their Truth into the three dimensions that humans could perceive and comprehend, like drawing a sphere on a two-dimensional piece of paper.

"Come along now," Bob said. "We're almost there."

Stewart helped Liz to her feet, and she wiped her eyes. Was she seeing the same City that he saw? Or was her version different from his? As she faced him, the sight of her caught his breath, and he could only stare in unbridled wonder. She was the most beautiful woman he had ever seen, who had ever existed, and love for her swelled his chest and turned his pulse into a stampede.

She caught his stare. "What?"

He kissed her. It was all he could think of to do.

When Liz pulled away, she blushed a little and smiled. "Watch yourself, mister."

Hunter mimed a gagging face. Cassie giggled.

As they walked, Stewart tried to control his discomfort with deep breaths, clutching Liz's hand as if it were the only life pre-server in a storm-tossed tumult.

Thoughts plagued him. Was this real? Was he dreaming? Was he trapped in a nightmare so insidiously deceptive it was going to crush his soul when he awoke? Just like his life had done.

Hunter and Cassie were skipping ahead up the path, their eyes wide with wonder, and all Stewart could think about was whether it was all an elaborate ruse to lure them to their destruction. Was some hideous monster going to leap out of the idyllic landscape and kill them? Or worse, was he on the verge of some psychotic break? Was the monster he had become in that evil dream about to burst to life and wreak havoc on everything around him?

These questions clotted in his belly and lay there squirming in a cold ball like a nest of rattlesnakes. The air itself seemed to exert greater pressure on him, muffling sounds and squeezing his flesh.

"Don't get too far ahead, kids!" Liz called after the children. At times, they seemed so far ahead they might disappear into the landscape. An instant later, they were only a step or two away. The sudden shifts in perspective made his head swim.

"There's nothing here to hurt them, me dear," Bob said, ambling along as if this were but a leisurely ramble. "The Dark cannot reach us here."

Liz kept glancing at Stewart with concern. "Are you all right, babe?"

"Hanging in there."

She squeezed his hand tighter, holding on to him.

Profusions of flowers and ferns lined the path, alive with tiny critters that flitted and jumped and crawled.

Behind them, the kaleidoscope Kodiak bear strolled, the size of a bus, sniffing the air with a look of contentment. Its coat coruscated with DayGlo colors, an ever-shifting canvas, apparently feeling no need now for camouflage. Skin crawling with worry, Stewart kept glancing back to see if the bear was preparing to attack them.

The nearer they drew to the City, the more the kids checked on him. "Dad, are you okay?" Was his discomfiture so glaring? "Daddy, what's wrong? Come *on*, this is so great!"

"I'm fine, kids." He gave them the best smile he could. "It is *really* wonderful."

Bob's scrutiny was Stewart's constant companion. The little man seemed poised at any moment to spring into action, as if Stewart was a threat. Could Bob sense the currents of doubt and violence coursing through Stewart's mind?

Distance was difficult to judge as they approached the City, but at one moment, Bob rounded on Stewart. "Ye've got yerself some willpower, me boy."

Relief gushed through Stewart, hoping that Bob's confrontation might assuage the illness and unease he felt.

"Willpower might be enough, but it might not," Bob said. "Know this." He tapped his head with his cane. "That dark elf's fingers are still digging around in yer mind. Much of that yer feelin' ain't comin' from you. That Darkness in you, 'tis there, but right now 'tis lookin' bigger than it truly is. His spell is still in there, stirring up sludge that's settled to the bottom. I can sense the good in you, Stewart. Don't let that blackguard get the better o' ye."

"Can you help me?"

"'Tis beyond me ken, but where we're going, there's them that might lend their aid."

Liz hugged him. "Hang in there, baby."

His mouth was dry as the Arizona desert. "I'll try."

***

The immensity of the City threatened to swallow them as they approached its outskirts. The great trees stretched impossibly high. The lush, living smell of the foliage and lake filled Stewart's heart with hope. Everything here was connected through the invisible flow of magic, every being, every creature, every tree, flower, and blade of grass. The sublime harmony of it all moistened his eyes.

On the outskirts, clusters of homes rested alongside the lake's outbound tributaries. Everywhere was the sound of music and activity, laughing children, boisterous conversation without rancor. Could people truly exist this way? Without greed and selfishness? Without deception and treachery? The passing of Stewart and his family prompted many an amiable greeting. Many of them even greeted the bear as if he were an old acquaintance. The two deadly dolls marching on either side of Cassie waved to onlookers as well, their faces blank as ever, but their eyes alight with joy and anticipation.

Stewart tamped down into a hole in his mind the writhing black serpent that refused to believe any of it.

They rounded the corner onto a broad thoroughfare when Stewart held in a deep-throated expostulation of surprise.

In a pleasant plaza, a group of—well, he could only describe them as ogres, as they were eight feet tall, with a warty hide, barrel chests and gnarled limbs—a group of four ogres were sitting around playing a game that might have been something like four-player chess. They were clad in brightly colored trousers and waistcoats, their huge feet bare. One of them wore a broad-brimmed hat with a long white plume. But one of them stared at Stewart in recognition, its smile a mess of slobber and crooked teeth.

Then the creature's face snapped into recognition for Stewart, too.

It was the face of the creature who had stood over him that morning in the desert.

It jumped up from its tree-stump stool and bounded toward them, arms outstretched.

Stewart tensed to flee, but the look of joy on the ogre's face could not be denied. It was speaking in a bass, guttural tongue, incomprehensible, but the hug it threw around Stewart could not be misunderstood. Its size dwarfed him, and it could have crushed him like a bug, but it hugged him with the relief and joy of encountering a long-lost friend.

Stewart patted its rough hide awkwardly. "Uh, how you doing, buddy?"

Then it held him at arm's length, a little tear in its eye, then it spun just as quickly and ran back to its companions, telling them the story of meeting Stewart in its own language.

Liz and the kids stared, mouths agape.

Hunter said, "You know that guy?"

"Uh, sort of?" Stewart said.

Then he told them the story. When he finished the kids stared at him in similar wonder. He felt abashed at not telling them sooner. "Sorry, I thought you wouldn't believe me."

Cassie hugged his waist and grinned. "I got to meet the Little People. You got to meet the Big People."

***

The broad thoroughfare brought them deeper among the great trees, until the road rose into a winding series of bridges and walkways stretching between the trees. The bridges and walkways appeared to be fashioned of a wood as pale as ivory, beautifully wrought and polished in motifs of interwoven vines. Up into the canopy these bridges took them, stretching and spiraling.

The air was redolent with the smell of flowers, fresh-baked bread and pastries, spices, and greenery. A moist breeze blew off the lake, the perfect temperature to cool them from the warmth of the sun.

The tree trunks bulged with habitations, nodules shaped from the living wood, great towering mansions like Versailles or Buckingham Palace that rose rather than sprawled.

Toward the largest of these tree mansions Bob led them.

The bridge underfoot stretched across an emptiness hundreds of feet from the ground.

Cassie and Hunter ran to the balustrade and peered over.

"Be careful!" Liz called.

Both kids chorused, "Mom!" in that annoyed voice children use on overprotective mothers.

Stewart joined them and looked down from the dizzying height. Winged creatures flitted past below, some of them too quick to discern their nature, but there were birds from the size and shape of hummingbirds to condors passing below.

Ahead of them at the end of the bridge rose a mansion perhaps twenty stories tall. The nature of the City made judging scale difficult. The walls of the mansion resembled the ivory wood of the bridge, but they were shaped into a stunning array of bas-reliefs. Those bas-reliefs filled the face of the mansion with stories of heroes and heroines, quests and trials, homecomings and reconciliations. Trying to examine them all even cursorily would have taken months—even if they weren't moving.

The closer their party drew to the gate, the more Stewart could see the bas-reliefs shifting, as if the stories being told were still in progress.

Liz and the kids were just agog, heads on swivels. There was too much to see for their human minds to take in.

"Come now, let us move a mite more expeditiously," Bob said, gesturing to them with his cane. "Time is malleable here, but 'tis not on our side."

As they approached the gates, the sheer grandeur of this living mansion made Stewart feel dwarf-like, stunted. Thick wooden double-doors swung inward to greet them.

Beyond the gates stretched a vaulted hall filled with lights and stairways, the walls decorated with paintings and sculptures. The floor was an elaborate parquet of a thousand colors, depicting what, Stewart could not yet see.

Stepping into view, a rotund figure said, "So, here you are."

Stewart shouldn't have been so surprised, but the wonders had been coming too hard and fast. "What are *you* doing here?"

The shopkeeper waggled his caterpillar eyebrows.

Stewart answered Liz's inquisitive stare. "He's the one who sold me the dolls and the map."

From just behind him emerged a doll that resembled the two next to Cassie, but standing about twice as high, wearing a gown of the finest silk and lace that sparkled with greens and blues.

Cassie's dolls leaped with joy and sprang forward, throwing their arms around...their mother? Their porcelain faces and limbs clicked and clinked and clacked as they all hugged.

"Aww," Cassie said, wiping a tear.

The shopkeeper said, "Lady Jocinda is delighted you have brought her children home."

The three dolls paused their joyful reunion, turned to the human family, and curtsied.

Stewart said to them, "Thank you for protecting Cassie, protecting all of us."

The two dolls curtsied again.

"Indeed," Bob said, "they did a right fine job of it. Lady Jocinda, ye should be proud."

Lady Jocinda clutched her porcelain hands over where a human heart might be and bowed her head.

Cassie said to the dolls, "It's weird that we've been together all this time and I don't even know your names."

Bob pointed at one. "That one is Jaclyn." Then the other. "That one is Jazlyn."

Stewart wasn't sure how to tell them apart. Maybe Jazlyn had slightly longer hair and bigger eyes, but he couldn't be sure—and after the way they'd handled him, he didn't want to get close enough for a good look.

Then Cassie's voice grew sad. "Does this mean you're not my dolls anymore?"

Jaclyn and Jazlyn shook their heads emphatically and rushed forward to throw their arms around Cassie's legs.

"But I don't want to take you away from your mommy again," Cassie said.

Bob said, "The lassies took this job willingly, my dear. They're your guardians until you decide you no longer need their service."

"Oh," Cassie said, a sense of responsibility creeping into her voice. "I'll make sure to take good care of them, Lady Jocinda."

Lady Jocinda bowed her head in acknowledgment.

"You must be starving," the shopkeeper said. "You've crossed three whole worlds on foot, after all."

Liz swallowed hard and collected her voice. "I have so many questions."

"Isn't a companionable meal the perfect place to answer them?" the shopkeeper said. Then he gave Stewart a weighty look. "And now that you're here, you and I have much to discuss."

"We do?" Stewart said, feeling stupid at his slack-jawed response.

"You don't think you were brought here for no reason, do you?" the shopkeeper said.

Twenty-Five

INSIDE THE TREE MANSION was more artisan-made beauty than he imagined could have existed. The floors and grand staircases of polished wood were somehow still alive, their wood grain shifting and changing like the city outside. Paintings, murals, sculptures in wood and stone, mosaics, bas-reliefs, tapestries. Some covered in stories, others simply abstracts that seized Stewart's subconscious attention and struck him deep, lodging half-guessed impressions in his psyche.

The immensity of the mansion, with its many floors above and below, countless rooms filled with art and activity, made him feel insignificant, almost naked. What the activity was, he could not guess. The bureaucracy that oversaw the universe? Were there other humans like him who had the eye of the Queen and her court?

On the breeze came the scents of flowers, pine resin...and food.

The shopkeeper led them into a grand dining hall with a ceiling three stories high, where a dining table of modest size was set for six, dwarfed by the cavernous space. The silvery white tablecloth gleamed. All the dinnerware was of painted porcelain. Cutlery was fashioned of wood so dark it might have been ebony. Awaiting them were platters full of bread, bowls of fresh fruit, some types of which he didn't recognize, and steaming tureens of savory soup.

Sunlight poured through skylights, painting shifting patterns on the floor. Paintings covered the walls. The dining table itself had legs that looked as if it might trot away at any moment.

Stewart remembered something he had read as a child. "So, if we eat any of this, do we still get to go home?"

"Stewart!" Liz hissed. "That's rude!"

But the shopkeeper smiled. "You're referring to the faerie tales that say if a mortal finds himself in the Faerie Realm, he should not eat anything he finds, or else be trapped there and unable to return home forever."

Stewart nodded, glancing at Bob, who was growing in size sufficient to sit properly on one of the human-size chairs. "And Little People were usually the culprits."

Bob said, "That's a tactic oft employed by them that hold to the Dark path. Taint yerself with enough of the Dark, and it becomes mighty difficult to leave."

"The same isn't true here?" Stewart asked suspiciously.

"Stewart!" Liz said. "These are our hosts!"

But he ignored her. The sense that this was all too good to be true nagged at him.

The shopkeeper said, "We aren't interested in forcing anyone to do anything. Eating our food, for instance, might make it easier for someone to return, but it won't trap them here. In your case, it might make staying here easier."

Stewart still looked insubstantial, fuzzy around the edges, as if the subject of a soft-focus lens, and he felt much that way, plagued by a buzzing tingle that wouldn't relent. He hoped the food would help quell the tendrils of distrust and wariness.

Bob and the shopkeeper took seats at the ends of the table, Stewart and Liz on one side, the kids on the other. As Cassie slid up onto a chair, Jaclyn and Jazlyn took their places on either side of her. When they weren't moving, they appeared inanimate, like real dolls. The uncanniness of it gave Stewart a chill.

The shopkeeper gestured toward the food. "You must be famished. Please."

The family wasted no more time tucking in.

The soup smelled of onions and lentils, rich with herbs. A portly, rosy-cheeked chef dressed all in white with a towering cap wheeled out a cart laden with a covered porcelain tray. Lifting the lid, he revealed what looked like stuffed bell peppers, except they were the size of footballs. The kids' eyes bulged. The stuffing proved to be a collection of different grains, rice, barley, quinoa, all generously seasoned with savory herbs and spices. Crystal carafes were filled with cool water. The bread was still warm from the oven, at once crusty and soft, the fruit fresh, sweet, and juicy.

The Riley family's gustatory bliss was sufficient for the chef to trundle off with an expression of self-satisfaction.

For a while there were only the sounds of a breeze whispering through the skylights, and of chewing.

"Hunter, chew with your mouth closed, please," Liz said.

"Yeah, use your manners!" Cassie said, chomping on a gleaming, red-and-green-striped apple the size of her head.

Hunter glowered at his sister, but obeyed his mom's admonition.

Bob said, "A long walk like that does stoke the appetite."

After the razor edge of their hunger had been dulled, Stewart said to the shopkeeper, "So what should we call you?"

The shopkeeper dabbed at the corner of his mouth with a napkin. "My human name is Claude."

"Clod?" Cassie said, eyes wide.

"No, my dear," the shopkeeper said with an indulgent smile. He repeated his name, emphasizing the difference in the sound of the vowels.

"So, Claude," Stewart said. "How did someone from…this place wind up working in an antique shop on a back street in Mesa Roja?"

"Just lucky, I suppose," Claude said, a smile tugging at the corner of his mouth.

Stewart frowned, his patience for equivocation long since gone. "Oh, come on."

"I jest."

Stewart sighed. "Sorry, I'm just a little keyed up. It's been pure weirdness for two weeks."

"For a lot longer than that, don't you think? Your entire life, I'll wager," Claude said. Stewart squirmed under the old man's intense gaze. "Seeing strange things you couldn't be sure were real. Feeling the flow of magic coursing around you, but being unable to touch it. Sensing the vastness of how much your human picture of the universe was lacking. Am I anywhere in the ballpark?"

"Smack on the pitcher's mound. But you haven't answered my question."

"Very perceptive. The short answer is that I was sent to Mesa Roja to find you, and when I did, to watch you."

"Me? Why? I'm nobody."

"That is your choice, up to this point. Anyone is capable of great deeds. Human history is full of unexpected heroes who rose to the demands of the time. Individuals can change the course of history, and in fact I would wager that all history's turning points did so on the choices of motivated individuals. You can choose to be nobody. Many people do. Or you can choose to act when an important choice is presented to you."

"I get the feeling you're about to throw me one of those."

"In a moment. But first I must explain some things. I trust by now your mind is sufficiently opened?" Claude gave another little smile.

"Just don't let your brain fall out!" Cassie said.

"You are a very wise little girl," Claude said to her.

"Why did you come to find *me*?" Stewart said.

"Because of your imagination. All those intense daydreams when you were a boy, they had power. You didn't know it, but they helped shape the world around you in ways that most humans can't manage. That kind of power draws attention, and not just from us. Just as I was sent to watch you, Baron Tyrus sent his minions not only to watch you, but to steer you away from realizing your power. You had a difficult childhood, I know. Many of those tragedies and traumas were inflicted purposefully upon you."

The words settled upon Stewart's shoulders and chest like bags of cement. How often had he thought that someone really was out to get him? "Why?"

"To fill your mind with doubt, pain, and distraction. To destroy your imagination, your creativity. Without imagination, you cannot hope to touch the Source. The Dark Lord placed his minions close to you, in unexpected places. Perhaps you can think of a few potential candidates?"

Stewart met Liz's gaze, and they nodded. "No doubt."

Liz asked, "Who is this Baron Tyrus? He's the Dark Lord you just mentioned?"

"Baron Tyrus, ah yes. If ever there was an embodiment of malice and greed, it is that creature. Queen Titania no doubt knows more of his history than I, as they are of an age, but I can tell you he is an ancient vampire, older than human civilization in the Penumbra, although direct temporal connections are difficult due to the malleability of time."

"Malleability?" Liz said. "I thought time moves forward at the same speed for everything and everyone."

"No, no, dear lady," Claude said. "Haven't you had days that fly by and others that advance at a slug's pace?"

"Well, yes, but—"

"That is the power of the mind at work upon the locality of your universe, affecting the flow of time in your immediate vicinity. It could have been you. It could have been someone else having that effect. Allow me to say, time, space, matter, the building blocks of your reality, are not nearly so concrete and imperturbable as humans believe."

"You're talking about quantum theory," Liz said.

"In a manner of speaking, but quantum theory is only a facet, a projection—"

Bob jumped in, "Like the True Name of the City."

Claude nodded. "Bob is correct. Quantum theory is one way of looking at the universe, but it cannot encompass everything, because its forces act only at the smallest of scales. I've read much on the subject. Modern Penumbral physicists are seeking a Universal

Equation to explain all the forces of the universe. They'll be at it a while longer, I'll wager. What they do not yet know is that even if they find their Universal Equation, it will only apply to the Penumbra, so it will not be 'universal' at all."

Silence fell as they ruminated on this. The kids chewed their food, looking expectantly back and forth at all the adults.

Stewart finally asked, "So this Baron Tyrus. He's been trying to hurt us, stop us, stop *me*. Why?"

"He wishes to hurt all of us, destroy us, for the sheer joy of it," Claude said. "Never underestimate the allure of cruelty. He is like a vicious child who loves torturing animals, but with infinitely more power. On a grander scale, he wishes to destroy the Light so that the Dark will reign supreme. But his Darkness cannot harm us here, for the same reason that we cannot harm him."

Bob said, "He can, however, warp minds to his will, much like that dark elf did. He is a corrupter, a malign influence, a purveyor of destruction for its own sake."

"And worse, he has a plan to destroy us," Claude said, "to destroy the City, to claim the Source for himself. With that power at his disposal, he could reshape the nature of the universe to his whim."

"So what's his plan?" Stewart asked.

A female voice boomed through the hall. "That we do not know, but it begins with my daughter."

It was as if a sun had emerged inside the dining hall.

A female flowed like liquid sunbeams down one of the grand staircases, but she could never be mistaken as human. She was nine feet of all the feminine beauty in the universe, wrapped into one form. A thick cascade of hair hung to her waist, the color of which varied with the angle of light.

Stewart couldn't tell if she brought the light with her or emitted it herself, but her gown sparkled and rippled like liquid diamonds, so bright she was difficult to look upon. Motes of light circled her head like tiny moons. Her skin seemed to change color like her hair, but it was only the colors he could perceive at any given moment, that much he knew. Her eyes gleamed with yellow-white light in a face that seemed to glimmer. Her beauty made his heart ache, his knees go weak. Her existence went as far beyond the concept of *woman* as sunlight was to a flashlight. Her shape was beyond mere form, her grace difficult to encompass, like the sway of a willow tree in a gentle wind made flesh. She was all the mysteries of the cosmos on two long legs.

Claude and Bob stood and bowed to her.

"My esteemed Queen," Claude said.

Stewart and his family all jumped to their feet, chair legs skidding, and they bowed as well.

The Queen's voice boomed with the music of stars and moons, oceans and waterfalls, birdsong and the laughter of children. "You are all welcome here, humans. We are delighted to see Claude and Bob have successfully shepherded you to the Light Realm."

Bathed in the light of her beauty and the bottomless power of her gaze, Stewart couldn't help but remember how he had almost fallen out of the Light Realm entirely. In her presence, he felt like a jumbled wad of dust bunnies, old wasps' nests, javelina droppings, and cobwebs piled six inches high, useless and unwholesome.

Claude cleared his throat. "It was not a foregone conclusion that we would be successful, Your Universality."

"Indeed, my Queen," Bob said. "A mighty powerful dark elf dogged our track through the Borderlands."

"And there were goblins on coyotes!" Cassie said. "With spears and crossbows and—"

Hunter shushed her.

"You shush!" Cassie said with one narrowed eye and a determined lower lip. She looked back at the Queen. "It was all terribly scary, but my daddy saved us."

"I have no doubt he is a very brave man, my child," the Queen said, amused, her voice like the ebb and swell of tides, of wind and soft rains. "For years we have watched him grow, laying the path for him someday to come to us."

Frustration rose up in Stewart. No one had yet answered his most fundamental question. He kept his voice as even as he could. "Uh, may I ask why, Your Universality?"

"The Dark Lord has stolen my daughter," she said, the sound of rain turning to thunderstorm. "For fifty of your years, he has held her, keeping her close to his bosom where nothing of the Light can touch her. He is hatching a scheme to destroy the Light. He steals her power and gives it to his minions. All the time, their probes come closer and closer to the Source. Our realm shrinks and the Dark Lord's expands. Soon, he may have a way of sending a minion directly into the realm of Light. If he somehow absorbs all of her power, he may have the strength he needs to destroy us and bring all the universes to Darkness."

"Are you certain she's still alive? Wouldn't she be grown up by now?" Stewart said.

The quirk of her lips revealed her patience with his ignorance.

"If she were dead, I would know. We are bound, even though I cannot touch her or speak with her, a connection can be made."

"If Dark beings can't come here, how did they take her?" Stewart asked.

"That remains a mystery," she said, her gleaming eyes flashing brighter. "All I know of her is that she is still a child, and that he keeps her in a cage, surrounded by molten rock, forced to protect herself from scorching heat every moment. The effort saps her power. And always he comes to corrupt her. Your question about eating the food of the Dark side was an apt one, Stewart, because the Dark Lord tries to feed her his blood."

"Ew! Yucky!" Cassie said, her eyes full of horror at the picture the Queen had just painted.

The Queen's magnificent eyes transfixed Stewart again, so that he looked away. "You are our best chance for saving her."

"I'm just a guy from Small Town, Arizona."

"Even so, Claude has told you of the power you possess. That alone is not enough, however. What you also possess are the skills needed and...the touch of Darkness. You can enter the Dark Realm and move about just as freely as you do here."

"If there's that much Darkness in me, how can you trust me?"

She gave him a long look as cold as the light of distant galaxies, as penetrating as cosmic rays, with a voice to match. "I have seen many futures. I have seen enough to know I have no choice but to trust you."

The sound of it gave him fresh chills.

Claude spoke up. "You are also a locksmith, a blade smith, a metallurgist. The Queen's daughter is in a cage with only one key in existence, and it is carried on the person of the Dark Lord himself. Stealing it from him would be impossible. But a *new* key might be made."

"So, we're going to make a key here and someone is going to take it into the Dark Realm and open your daughter's cage?" Stewart said.

"No," the Queen said. "The key can only be made in the Dark Realm, and it must be made by you."

His mind reeled with the implications of everything she had just said. He was supposed to go into the Dark Realm, make a key to fit a lock he'd never seen before, on a cage surrounded by lava. It sounded like a suicide mission.

Cassie started to cry. "They're going to hurt my daddy!"

Stewart circled the table, picked her up, and hugged her. "Nobody is going to hurt me, sweetheart."

She sniffled against his neck. "They already did."

"Shh, I'm fine, I'm fine."

Her little arms encircled his neck and squeezed. Tears filled his eyes.

But at the same time, the thought of a little girl much like this one trapped in such a cage for fifty years, half-broiled by the heat of lava, filled him with the kind of anger that wouldn't go away, the kind that built and built and built until he set it loose. People who abused kids deserved nothing but destruction.

Maybe the Queen had chosen the right guy for this job after all.

He put Cassie down and faced the Queen. "I have a great big pile of questions I need answered first. But I'll do it."

"Stewart!" Liz said. "Shouldn't we talk about this?"

He nodded. "Yes, we should, but it won't affect the decision."

Moments passed as their eyes met. Then resolve settled behind hers. She nodded with understanding, recognition, knowing him better than anyone, but there was no acquiescence in it. "You're right. And we have to come with you."

Twenty-Six

"**YOU'RE KIDDING, RIGHT?**" Stewart said.

Liz shook her head gravely.

"I can't take you and the kids!" he exclaimed. "Didn't you hear anything they said?"

"I heard *everything* they said." Liz kept her voice incredibly even. He knew that tone, used when she was exerting incredible self-control to remain steady while he was flying off the handle. "My love, my sweet Viking, you wouldn't even be sitting here right now if it weren't for me and the kids."

"But—!" Then it hit him. He leaned against the table to support himself. Without her centering, calming, uplifting presence, he would have fallen out of the Light Realm, to be stuck in the mortal world—the Penumbra—without them.

The moment stretched and stretched, trapping him. He couldn't take her and the kids into that kind of danger.

He straightened and looked up at the Queen—doing so directly took an effort of powerful will. "I am sorry, uh, Your Universality, but the deal's off. I can't do it."

"Stewart—!" Liz said.

But he kept talking. "Liz is right. Without them, I couldn't have gotten to the City at all. And I'm not going to walk up to Baron Tyrus's doorstep *with* them. No way."

The Queen's voice rumbled like distant surf. "I see."

"We'll to have find another way," Stewart said into an utter, interminable silence.

After a long, tense pause, Claude cleared his throat. "For fifty of your years, there has been Darkness growing in your world. The forces of greed and ambition turn the Earth into a wasteland, acre by acre. Goodness feels as if it is passing away into nostalgic memory. Kindness and compassion disappear under waves of hate, bigotry, and greed. A handful of people hoard wealth for themselves while the planet burns and millions starve. Mankind's worst impulses are fueled and stoked and given rein by people positioned to profit from the rage."

"So, you're saying that this downhill slide began when the Princess was kidnapped," Stewart said.

"Her very existence brings Light to all the Universes," Bob said with a rhapsodic lilt to his voice. "Now, she is like a candle under a jar, slowly dimming, starving, until her light goes out forever. That will be soon."

Claude went on, "If the Dark Lord is successful in siphoning all the power away from the Princess until she ceases to exist, your world will fall into an abyss of war and blood and degradation the likes of which has never been seen. Desperate men do desperate things, and enough nuclear weapons exist now to render the surface of the planet uninhabitable to life of any kind. Someone *will* use them first, sparking the final conflagration."

The Queen's voice rolled over them. "I have seen many futures where the Penumbral Earth is reduced to a poisonous cinder. Most of them, in fact, end this way. *All* of those possible futures are the result of my daughter's cessation. The only way to prevent it is to save her. I have searched many, many timelines for others who might accomplish this. Only *you* have a chance. Others lack the skills, or the affinity for magic, or the force of will."

"You think I have an affinity for magic?" Stewart asked.

"It is foolish of you to ask the question," the Queen said. "Have you learned nothing?"

Stewart looked at his children, both staring at him with their innocent eyes and hopeful angelic faces. A bit of adventure in the mountains was one thing. But how could he knowingly take them into deadly peril?

Claude said, "We will protect you all for as long as we can."

"Aye," Bob said, "ye won't be alone. Pooh has already agreed to—"

"Who's Pooh?" Stewart said.

"The bear."

A manic laugh burst out of Stewart. "That bear's name is *Pooh*?"

"Best not to joke about that," Bob said. "Gets testy, he does. He loves those books."

The Queen spoke: "His True Name is…" What came after was a sensory avalanche of power, loyalty, cunning, and tenacity that quelled any further laughter. Amid the humans' stunned silence, she went on, "We will send our army with you to the very border of the Dark Realm."

"So how do we get there?" Liz said. "Walk all the way back to Earth, and then through the Borderlands to the Dark side?"

"There is one direct path between the Dark and Light Realms," the Queen said. "Through the mouth of Chukwa, the Cosmic Tortoise."

Cassie clapped her hand over her mouth. "You mean we have to go into its mouth? It'll *swallow* us?"

Hunter paled. "And then come out the other end?"

Bob stepped up onto his chair and waved his cane. "Getting a bit ahead of ourselves, we are." He pointed at Cassie and Hunter. "You, dearies, are far too pure of heart to enter the Dark Realm by any means. Ye'll fall out of that realm just as surely as a dark elf would fall out of this one. We need your father because he's the only one of us who can exist there."

Claude said, "What we will do is take you to the Tortoise with a force of our best troops to protect you."

"You have an army? I thought you were like pacifists or something," Stewart said. "All about the nonviolence?"

Claude said, "Hardly. Have you not seen what Jaclyn and Jazlyn can do? Unlike the forces of the Dark Lord, we fight only to protect those who cannot protect themselves. That is the noblest purpose of the warrior, is it not? To safeguard the weak?"

"But if we're in the Light Realm, why do we need protection?" Stewart said.

"We still do not know how they got away with the Princess," Claude said, sounding uncomfortable. "They may have ways that we do not know, especially now that they have her. They might be able to slip something in for a short time using her essence as a kind of Trojan horse."

"That's a little scary," Liz said matter-of-factly.

Bob and Claude nodded vigorously.

She fixed her gaze on Stewart. He already knew what she was going to say. "Baby, we have to do this," she said. "We'll be with you every step of the way. Up until we get to the turtle."

Hunter said, "A *tortoise*, Mom."

Liz rolled her eyes. "Fine. Tortoise. Why?"

"Because tortoises live on land," Hunter said, with a grin. "*National Geographic.*"

Stewart took a deep breath and let it out slowly. All eyes were upon him. He rubbed his face, his eyes. "So where is the Princess being held? How do I find her?"

Claude's shoulders deflated as if in relief. He withdrew what looked like a gold pocket watch on a gleaming silver chain from his waistcoat pocket. He offered it to Stewart. As Stewart touched the chain, a tingle passed up his fingers. He opened it to see a dial like no clock he'd ever seen, showing the Sun and Moon, rather than hours. It currently appeared to read noon, its dial pointing straight up, with midnight at the bottom of the dial. In the center lay what looked like a compass needle that spun lazily.

"The compass in the center," Claude said, "will lead you to the Princess." Then he fixed his gaze on Stewart. "The rest of the dial tells you how much time remains for you."

"Before I die?" Stewart said.

"Before the last of your Light is leached away, and you become a creature of the Dark Lord, never to return."

"I won't be able to come back?"

"You won't want to. Nor would your family recognize you if you tried."

Stewart chewed on that for a moment. "How much time will I have? Hours, days?"

"That depends on you," the Queen said. "How much Darkness will you allow into yourself? How much Dark magic will you use?"

"How do I control that?"

"With your actions, and to a lesser extent, your thoughts. Any acts of cruelty you commit or dark thoughts harbored for too long will shorten the time you have."

"I can hold those off."

"Perhaps," the Queen said, "but you must be on your guard. The forces of Darkness are corrosive, and the human mind prone to clinging to dark thoughts and adverse events, rather than seeing wonders and beauty around them."

"So, assuming I somehow find the Princess's prison, how do I make the key to open her cage?" Stewart asked.

An image exploded in his mind like a concert loudspeaker bursting to life at full volume. He flinched and staggered, then an image coalesced about the mental noise. A jagged construct of wrought iron, a thing of spines, angles, and blackness, but unmistakably a key. This merest flick of the Queen's mental power had almost brought him to his knees.

Her voice followed the image. "My daughter has seen the Dark Lord's key and sent me the image in a dream."

The image had burned into Stewart's memory so deeply he would never forget it. His mind started churning on how to construct it.

But the Queen said, "There is one complication. The Dark Lord's prison is powerful in ways the human eye cannot see. Her cage not only imprisons her, it is bound to her. Your key must not only open her cage, but destroy it, or else she will remain bound to it."

"How do you expect me to do that? Make a key out of TNT?"

"You must forge a key infused with love."

Stewart frowned, voice rising in frustration. "How do I do that?"

"Love can shatter any bonds. You are the magic smith, Stewart. We have faith in you," the Queen said. "It is settled. For tonight, take your rest, gather your strength. The Royal Guard will be prepared to depart with you tomorrow."

***

That night was the finest night of Stewart's life, with the exception of his wedding night. The breeze through their chamber window was cool and fresh, the kind that encouraged snuggling deeply into downy bedclothes. The view from their room took their breath away. The sparkling expanse of the City and the Lake lay beneath them under the starry tapestry of night, with a magnificent, glorious moon so clear and big he felt he could reach up and touch its textures.

The kids were asleep in their bunk beds, which seemed to have been extruded from the walls and floor just for them, and a luxurious four-poster awaited Stewart and Liz. But they stood outside leaning against the balcony, breathing in the sights. They didn't need to say anything, content to enjoy each other's warmth and company. Both were committed to their course. She never once stopped touching him, a hand on his arm, her head on his shoulder, as if conscious of the fact she was literally his anchor in this world, and that he could disappear at any moment.

Strains of intricate music filtered up from somewhere below, a lullaby soothing as a mother's kiss.

Finally they went to bed, her leg draped over his, and Stewart dreamed.

He was twelve years old in Lyndon B. Johnson Middle School.

In a school year marked by rare, relative stability in his life, he'd joined the baseball team. They seldom won a game, but he loved it. Putting on the uniform made him feel like a major leaguer, one of the heroes of old, like Babe Ruth. On the team, he was somebody, he was valued, and his teammates didn't care that he was a foster kid, because he could throw *really* hard, and with pinpoint accuracy. He could make a throw from center field all the way to home plate, and on two occasions threw a third-base runner out at the plate. He was also the team's star batter. He had such a good eye that he could follow a pitch, see its rotation, gauge his swing, and gather his strength, as if time itself stopped, as if the ball were hanging in midair waiting for him to crush it over the center-field fence.

It was the biggest game of his middle school career, the LBJ Middle School Jaguars in the conference playoffs versus the St. Mary's Knights, their arch-rivals. The Jaguars were down 5-3 in the bottom of the last inning, the sixth. Their star pitcher had taken a line drive to the bread basket and staggered off to the bench in tears, which had swung the momentum to let the Knights take the lead in the top of the inning.

In the bottom of the sixth, runners poised on second and third, two outs, Stewart would be the winning run or they would go home in defeat. He stepped out of the on-deck circle, swinging his favorite bat, trembling with the pressure, supercharged by it. It was all up to him.

The first two pitches were so far off the plate, he almost laughed. With as much pressure on him as on Stewart, already tired after pitching three innings, the pitcher was sweating bullets. The third pitch was intended to be a ball, but it just hung there like a sweet, juicy tomato. Stewart gathered every bit of his strength, wound up, and let swing.

The bat kissed the ball with the sweet spot, so perfect and effortless that he knew instantly it was going over the fence. The bat snapped in two a few inches above the handle.

He watched the ball go with a sense of wonder as a sharp tingle shot through his limbs. He almost imagined that it left a trail of sparks behind it.

His teammates were screaming at him to *Run! Run!*

So he did, but leisurely. He kept his gaze on the ball. It was still on its upward arc when it crossed the left-field fence.

Cheers roared.

Two runners came home.

He rounded third, but something was wrong. The opposing coach was screaming at the umpire about cheating. Stewart crossed home into a cheering pack of teammates, a forest of high-fives. But the opposing coach's screaming churned up a sick feeling in his gut.

The opposing coach came running out to the plate and snatched up the two pieces of the aluminum bat Stewart had used. "This is an illegal bat! No one hits a ball that hard! No way!"

Stewart's coach ran out of the dugout. "What are you talking about?"

"I demand this bat be checked!" He slid his fingers up and down its length.

Stewart stood agape as the opposing coach dumped a cylinder of cork out of the meat end of the broken bat.

A hush fell over the throng. A protest went up from the spectators.

All eyes fell upon him, the cheater. But he had no idea what corking a bat meant. All he knew was that it was his favorite bat.

The umpire called him out and voided the runs he'd batted in.

In the dream, the lights in the ball park went out, and he was standing alone at home plate. Everyone else went home, and he just stood in the blackness and shame until time itself stopped.

He awoke in the dark of night, feeling a baseball in his hand for a brief moment, but then it was gone.

In real life, the teacher who served as his baseball coach got fired, and probably no one blamed Stewart, but the shame of it clung to him like a stench he couldn't wash off. He'd cost LBJ Middle School the only shot at a playoff berth they'd ever had.

The ball he'd hit was never found.

He never played baseball again.

***

Unlike every morning that he could remember back home, Stewart awoke feeling completely refreshed, as if he'd had precisely the amount of sleep he needed, rather than constantly feeling at a deficit due to work schedule and family demands.

Just as he opened his eyes and swung his legs to the floor, Cassie jumped down from her bunk bed, ran over, and threw her arms around him.

He hugged her back. "What's this for, honey?"

"You're going to save the Princess," she said, cheek pressed against his T-shirt. "I know you will."

She hugged him for a long time. He shot a glance at the two dolls leaning against the bunk bed post, looking for all the world as if they were inanimate objects. He shuddered.

A knock at the thick wooden door of their chamber announced the arrival of a cart laden with breakfast. Steaming, aromatic herbal tea, sugared pastries, fruit, and Stewart's favorite, plain black coffee. Spirits were high, if a little nervous.

As they were finishing their breakfast, another knock came at the door. It was Bob this time. "I come bearing gifts!"

Behind him was another cart. He stepped inside, gestured to the cart, and it followed him inside of its own accord.

Upon the cart were packs for each of them to carry on their journey, complete with food, water, and bedding. But then Bob's expression turned grave. "Some protection ye all need, thought I. So, I petitioned Queen Titania and she fashioned ye a bit of armor. We hope ye won't run into any trouble on the way to ol' Chukwa's gob, but better safe than sorry, aye?"

Liz and Stewart nodded at each other.

"Real armor?" Hunter breathed. "Lay it on me!"

Stewart couldn't help but smile. To the boy, this was still a grand adventure, perhaps a game. Stewart had no such illusions, but he couldn't bear to destroy the children's.

Bob presented each of them with a shirt of the most brilliant mail Stewart had ever seen. The interlocking rings caught the light like...

"Diamonds," Bob said. "I'll wager each of these mail coats is worth a king's ransom back on Earth. Made this herself, she did. And I'll raise ye a bet that nothing can penetrate it. Won't save ye from crushing, but it'll turn aside any arrow or blade. Put it on under your clothes so you don't draw attention to yourself."

Inside the coat of interlocking rings was an undergarment of petal-soft silk that kept it from chafing. It fit like a T-shirt custom-made just for him, the sleeves reaching to just above his elbows.

"Have ye any weapons?" Bob asked.

"My children are *not* going to fight!" Liz said sternly.

"Ye might think different with another host of goblins in front of ye," Bob said.

"Don't worry," Hunter said. "I've got Dad's knife." He grinned at his mother, who gave him serious stink-eye.

"My lady," Bob said. "Something for ye." He pulled out a slender sword about the length of her arm, a rapier with a beautiful basket hilt to protect her hand. "Ye might wish to protect the little ones."

She took it dubiously.

"And you, good sir," Bob said to Stewart. "Ye've the look of this sort of fellow." He handed Stewart a battle-axe.

The haft was the length of Stewart's arm, the blade single-bitted with a curved spike opposite the blade. Carved runes covered the blade, catching the light in their crevices.

"This took a turn for the *Lord of the Rings*," Liz said.

"We hope it won't come to it, obviously," Bob said.

"We're not bringing swords to a gunfight, are we?" Stewart said. "The goblins we faced had some nasty little crossbows."

"The Royal Guard has ye covered there. But our guns operate on magic, not gunpowder. Ye don't have those skills yet."

Another figure appeared in the door, Claude with arms outstretched. He grinned, "Ah, good, you're still here. I was afraid I'd missed you." He approached Stewart. "I've two things for you, from the Queen." He handed Stewart a crystal vial full of amber liquid. "This you will need to purify the metal you use for the key. A special oil for you to use in the tempering process. The Dark Realm is a place of metal and corruption, corrosion. Anything you will find to forge your key will already be tainted by the Dark Lord's influence, so it will not suit your purpose. Purify the metal with this."

Stewart took it and stuffed it in his pocket. "Thank you."

"And one more thing. Took me some doing to find it." Claude tossed something to Stewart, who caught it reflexively.

"A baseball?" Stewart said.

"That is *the* baseball," Claude said earnestly.

"You mean the one I—"

"The one you hit over the fence."

Stewart flushed with anger, then stomped it back down. "But what good is that? It's just a stupid baseball."

"That was a day that time itself stopped for you. *You* did that, with magic you didn't even understand. But your victory was stolen from you, and you've been carrying that baseball around in your mind for almost twenty years. You've infused it with the power to give time a bit of a breather, you might say. But once only."

Stewart shrugged and tucked the baseball and vial of oil into a shoulder pouch he found among the packs.

The sound of a trumpet burst through the window from far below.

"Speaking of time," Bob said, "'Tis time to go."

Twenty-Seven

THEY SET OFF FROM the City without fanfare, but carrying a feeling of foreboding. They had only just arrived and had been sent away on a dangerous mission. Columns of bright elves, the Queen's Royal Guard, rode both before and behind, riding scarlet unicorns.

Stewart had never imagined unicorns as looking fearsome, but these did, with blood-red coats that shimmered into deep violet, gleaming black eyes, manes, and horns that looked like polished obsidian. Like the other unicorns Stewart had seen, these were considerably smaller than horses, somewhere between the size of a donkey and a Shetland pony.

As they were all mounting their steeds back in the City, Hunter asked, "Hey, Claude, how come the unicorns are red? I thought all unicorns were white."

"Most unicorns are white, my boy," Claude said, "but these are unicorns of war. White unicorns respond to the innocent and pure of heart. Red unicorns respond to the brave and the stout of heart."

Hunter said, "Can I ride one?"

Claude said, "If you are brave and stout of heart, one may well come to you. Otherwise, best to leave them alone."

The crimson unicorns were clad in light barding of lacquered metal scales laced into a felt undercoat. The unicorns were small, but they fit the size of their riders perfectly.

The bright elves stood to about the height of Stewart's stomach. Their features were sharp, their ears pointed, their eyes glittering with intelligence and solemn duty. Any one of them would lay down their immortal lives at their Queen's behest. Some of them wore coats of armor similar in construction to the unicorns'. The armor's design made them resemble miniature samurai, an effect heightened by their curved swords and skirted helmets.

A smaller contingent of Royal Guard—scouts, he supposed—wore no armor at all, but carried a weapon that resembled a rifle. Claude had said they used magic to fire the projectiles, contained in a magazine atop the stock.

Stewart rode a tall horse, Liz, a shorter one, and the kids, small ponies. Cassie carried Jaclyn and Jazlyn in saddlebags specially made for them.

A great road stretched before them through the mountains, leading toward a distant mountain range that looked impossibly high, its peaks swathed in snow. Their path looked as if it led them straight toward Shangri-La itself. Stewart wondered if that was what the Himalayas looked like from a distance.

The giant kaleidoscopic bear, Pooh, walked his own pace at the fringes of their party, sometimes ahead, sometimes behind, but always somber, always alert. His ever-shifting camouflage made it easy to forget he was there.

Under their clothes, Stewart and his family all wore the armor they'd been given. The extra weight chafed on his shoulders a little, despite the soft undershirt, but he was growing accustomed to it.

"It's not even scratchy!" Cassie said.

Stewart still cringed at the idea of his little girl having to wear armor, but if she was enjoying it, he wasn't about to discourage her. The sheer weight of the diamonds they were wearing meant that the armor would be worth millions of dollars on Earth. Could diamonds even be formed into rings? Not by any means he'd ever heard of.

Their spirits were high as they traveled. He'd always wanted to take the kids horseback riding, but could never afford it. He had to admit he was enjoying the sense of adventure coupled with a sense of purpose. Maybe, for once in his life, he could do something that mattered.

They traversed lush valleys swathed in old-growth forest and bamboo groves, cut by babbling brooks and frothing cataracts of whitewater flowing the wrong direction. Villages grew sparse the higher into the mountains they went. Unlike their walk to the City, he felt the land moving past him much more quickly, as if his mind were becoming attuned to the journey.

The food he'd eaten in the Queen's mansion and the food they'd brought with them made him feel more substantial, more acclimatized to the Light Realm. The bright elves had brought with them sacks of round, flat bread, about as thick as a finger. Even days old, it smelled and tasted fresh out of the oven. They loved to dip it in seasoned oil. It was so delicious, Stewart looked forward to meal stops. His edges had lost their fuzziness, but the sense of nagging unease wouldn't leave him alone, that he would be discovered as an impostor and cast out of the Light Realm forever. But he wanted to be here. He hoped that was enough.

Bob rode what looked like a long-haired greyhound, but this dog looked more primitive somehow, more wolf-like. Nevertheless, its demeanor was sprightly and friendly. Bob took to riding alongside Hunter and Cassie. They peppered him with questions, and he did his best to answer with patience and equanimity.

The Royal Guard rode in silent vigilance. Stewart had never been around trained warriors before, much less non-human ones. They moved with a strange deliberateness and inhuman fluidity. Even half his size, they could doubtless slice him to ribbons if given reason.

Stewart guided his mount to ride alongside their commander, marked by the scarlet horsehair crest on his helmet, and introduced himself.

"I am most pleased to make your acquaintance," the bright elf replied in a surprisingly smooth, sonorous voice. Stewart didn't know what he was expecting the bright elf's voice to sound like, but it was not that of a late-night radio DJ. "I am Wyn Ar-Chaheris. My family has always served the Queen, for as long as any of us can remember."

"And how long is that?" Stewart asked.

"Time is fluid. It is difficult to say in Penumbral years."

"Yeah, Claude tried to explain it, but I'm not quite getting it."

A tiny smile curled the corner of the commander's mouth. "Perhaps someday you will."

"How long have you been the commander of the Royal Guard?"

"That is easier to reckon. Perhaps a thousand of your years. Time becomes less malleable over smaller spans."

Stewart could not wrap his mind around a lifespan like that. "I can't imagine how living as long as you, changes your perspective on life, the universe, everything."

"We discuss such things often, given that the Penumbra is populated by comparatively short-lived humans. For us, it is easy to become bored, which leads to experimentation with greater and greater extremes of behavior simply to avoid the madness of monotony. Those who lack integrity or force of will sometimes fall to the Dark Realm. It is a tragic thing."

"So, you're saying that even your people can turn to the Dark side?"

"It happened to my cousin." The commander's voice hitched for a moment. "It was a terrible thing." His tone said that his tolerance for this line of conversation was at an end.

"So, can Dark side people come back to the Light?" Stewart was thinking of himself, and what he might have to do after crossing over into the Dark Realm.

"It has never happened, although I suppose it is possible. A Dark side creature who went against the wishes of the Dark Lord and tried to redeem itself would be hunted and destroyed immediately, long before it could reach us. Unlikely that it would even reach the Borderlands."

They rode on for a while, and Stewart listened to Claude entertaining the kids with stories. Some stories he recognized. Others were shades of stories he recognized. Heroes and heroines and myths and legends. Some sounded like Greek myths, others Native American, others from cultures he didn't know, but in them he recognized the core of the stories and the power those stories carried to shape human beliefs, to shape the world itself.

As they traveled, their road grew narrower, less well made, from well-fitted flagstones to loose cobblestones to a dirt track. The towns and villages shrank, the inhabitants few, the City and the Lake lost in the misty distance. It was difficult to believe they'd gone so far in only one day.

As dusk approached, Commander Ar-Chaheris called a halt to camp at a broad sward of lush grass surrounded by a mix of pine forest and bamboo groves. The Royal Guard scouts immediately dispersed into the forest, no doubt seeking evidence of threat.

The commander said, "Nothing will approach our camp in the night without them knowing and warning us. We'll be safe."

They all dismounted.

Cassie yawned and rubbed her eyes. "My butt hurts."

"Mine, too," Hunter said.

Stewart's backside and thighs felt tenderized as well. Casting an eye behind him, he saw no lights of the City, nor of any of the towns and villages they had passed along the way. They were alone in an alien land, an alien *dimension*. The mountains ahead looked jagged, forbidding, immense, and impossibly high on a scale his mind found difficult to encompass, as if they reached halfway to the moon.

As night fell, the Royal Guard set up a lively, comforting encampment, with bright watch fires and stone-baked bread in magic ovens molded from stones of the earth. There was nothing to fear here, so why not make a party of it?

Claude offered him a water pouch to drink from. "This will help whatever ails you." The rotund shopkeeper was moving slowly and stiffly from a long day in the saddle.

"What is it?" Stewart asked.

"Water. But it's from the Source."

As Stewart upended the pouch and took a mouthful, it filled him with an energy he couldn't describe, at once a burst of confidence, vitality, and strength, as if he could move boulders barehanded, accomplish anything he set his mind to.

Claude waggled his eyebrows.

Stewart said, "That's...like nothing I've ever tried before. Is it full of magic?"

"It's the Source itself. It *is* magic."

"What if I take some of this into the Dark with me?"

"It'll be just as powerful there as it is here. But it will eventually become corrupted and provide you only magic for dark purposes."

"How long before that happens?"

Claude shook his head. "I don't know."

"How long before we reach the Tortoise?"

"Again, I don't know. We traveled far today. It depends as much on our collective state of mind as anything. If we let our spirits flag, it will take longer. What I do know is that the road will disappear and we'll be in the wilderness. Unlike Earth, we've little to fear in the wilderness."

"That's where they'll strike," Stewart said tonelessly.

"What? What did you say?" Claude's gaze was suddenly sharp and penetrating.

Stewart shook himself and blinked. "Did I say something?"

"You said, 'That's where they'll strike.'"

"Uh, I..."

The shopkeeper's gaze was steady, pointed. "I do believe you've just scried the future, my boy. Do you not remember?"

"It was like I zoned out for a moment. When I came back, you were staring at me."

"Perhaps you've still a connection with that dark elf who fiddled with your dreams."

"Wouldn't that mean he still has a connection with me?"

Claude's expression turned grave. "It would."

Several of the bright elves produced flutes, lutes, fiddles, and drums, and struck up a series of jigs, reels, and the occasional ballad. Watching the elves dance gave Stewart a chill up his spine, because while they looked like miniature humans, they did not move like humans. All of them moved with an uncanny precision and a quickness that deceived the eye.

Stewart, Liz, and the kids settled down into bedrolls and blankets under the open sky. Contemplating the worrisome things he and Claude had discussed, he lay looking up at the sky, head couched on his hands, gazing at these constellations he did not know, at the moon that was too close. He savored the warmth of the nearby campfire, the softness of the grass under his bedroll.

The two kids lay between him and Liz. Hunter was already snoring softly when Stewart heard Cassie say, "Mommy, the sky is too big!"

Liz leaned over and kissed her, and Stewart smiled as he drifted off.

***

Liz couldn't remember when she'd felt more alive. Not when she was a kid, not when her kids were born. Her mother had always been ready and able to slap down any bursts of joy when Liz was growing up, and since she'd had kids, life had been an endless grind of daily obligation, such as feeding and clothing small people who couldn't do it for themselves. She had never once regretted having children, and there were moments of joy to be found even in the doldrums. But this was different, like life squared, every color, taste, scent, sensation heightened. It was like her entire body thrummed with potential and purpose.

She tried to fight against it, but the daily grind—getting the kids to and from school, working in the day care, the nagging worries of near-poverty—often reduced the passing days to a blur of drudgery and obligation. Even marriage maintenance was hard sometimes, pushed aside for the needs of the moment. She couldn't remember the last time she and Stewart had had a night out to themselves as grown-ups, like when they were dating. Nowadays, especially since Stewart had lost his job, they couldn't afford a babysitter. At times like this, she missed who she used to be, and who Stewart used to be as well. Daily life ground him down, too, but in different ways than her. It made him more cynical, less trusting, snuffed out the boyish hopefulness in his soulful eyes that had attracted her when they were teenagers.

But all this had *awakened* them. How could she feel good about going back to their old life? She was having *fun,* and so were the kids. Her mother would be appalled.

Watching Stewart shed bits of his negativity, smile by smile and hug by hug, assured her that they were, in fact, doing the right thing, in spite of the danger. It was as if the weight of crushed dreams and foul memories was falling away from him. Throughout their relationship, she'd caught glimpses of the man he could be, only to see them crushed. He was a sensitive soul, which was why cruelty struck him so deeply, caused him to shut down and withdraw into himself. But everything he'd experienced as a child had built a rage in him that he kept carefully in check.

Now, seeing his spirits buoyed did the same to hers, but what would happen when their journey was over? He would leave them to go to the Dark Realm, possibly never to return. She couldn't think about that, couldn't think about raising these two kids on her own. But there was no doubt in her. Everything hinged on her husband. He was an amazing man, but still only one man.

For several more days the ground rose beneath their feet. Unlike Earth, where high altitude caused headaches, nausea, breathlessness, and sleeplessness, here they had no signs of altitude sickness. The road dwindled to a footpath and then ultimately disappeared. The air chilled dramatically, however, especially at night, as they approached the snow line. As they neared the timberline, the trees grew shorter and gnarled, hardly as tall as a man, frozen into wind-swept shapes. The air bit through their clothes here. Liz pulled her hoodie tighter around her, anxious for the bright elves to fashion their shelter for the night. She had watched the way they coaxed the plants out of the ground, encouraged them to twine together into a tight-knit weave with a smoke hole in the ceiling and only a small hole for an entrance.

One dusky evening found them at the foot of a towering, snow-rimed peak that was flanked by two others of roughly equal height. Before them loomed a cliff that stretched at least half a mile high and a mile across its face. They would have to find their way around it tomorrow.

She heard Hunter asked Bob, "How far do we still have to go?"

"Depends," Bob said. "The Great Tortoise keeps his own counsel."

"What does *that* mean?" Hunter asked.

"It means we've been walking on him for days. He'll show his face when deems it fit."

Hunter's eyes bulged and he stared at the ground, as if looking for signs of Great Tortoise Shell underfoot.

They ate their bread and drank their Source water and bedded down for the night, just as they had done every night since leaving the City. How many was it now? Days and nights were difficult to follow here.

As they all settled into sleep, Liz couldn't ignore the dread crawling up the back of her neck. As they lay spooned together for warmth under their woolen blankets, she squeezed Stewart's hand, wondering if this would be the last time she ever would.

If she didn't know better, she might have said there was the breath of evil on the air.

***

High atop the cliff looking down on the encampment, Jorath El-Thrim sat at the precipice. The watch fires flickered below, a patch of light against the night's gathering dark. Alarm spells, undetectable to anything but a dark elf, circled the camp's perimeter.

His skin thrummed and burned with the power required to hold him here in the Light Realm. The spell covered every scrap of his skin, painted in the language of the celestial spheres with ink made from the blood of the Light's Princess.

Through his lingering connection to Stewart Riley's mind, Jorath had gleaned enough vague and splotchy detail to know what the enemy planned. He had emerged from the Great Tortoise two days in advance of the Light side's expedition. And he was not alone.

He settled himself, looking down from high above. His tendrils of mind and will remembered their anchors in the human's mind. Jorath had almost succeeded in unleashing the human's darker nature and completely preventing his entry into the Light Realm. This time, there would be no failure. If Jorath could set loose the human's inner demons, whip them into a frenzy, the man would disappear from the Light Realm as if he never existed, slipping back to the Penumbra. Or, if Jorath's efforts were particularly successful, he might slip into the Dark Realm to become a creature of the Master. In either case, the Light would lose their only hope.

The Master had been amused when Jorath told him of their intention to rescue the Princess.

Now, the human slid toward slumber in the arms of his wife. She would not be able to save him this time.

Jorath waited until the moon passed out of sight and the only light came from the distant, uncaring stars.

His minions awaited his command.

Jorath stood, stretched out his arms, and conjured an entity made of nightmare, a bat of smoke and shadow and webs that glided on the wind, circling down, down over the encampment, over the shelter of the human family. The Royal Guard would sense it, but they would not be able to stop it before it sank into Stewart's mind and dug in its talons.

Down, down, down the shadow bat spiraled. Jorath looked out through the creature's eyes at the upturned faces of the elves, whose expressions bore alarm and confusion.

It spiraled lower, lower, slipping through the walls of the shelter as easily as a breath of breeze, unseen by anyone, and settled onto the man's skull, where it sank in like water into a sponge.

High atop the cliff, Jorath settled onto all fours, and initiated his own transformation.

TWENTY-EIGHT

LIZ WAS HAVING TROUBLE sleeping, so she sat in the entrance to the hut of living foliage. Cassie had passed out, and Hunter lay snoring. Stewart appeared to be asleep, but the way he lay there twitching suggested he was in the midst of a dream. She hoped it was not one like the night he'd almost hurt Cassie.

The night was simply luminous, numinous. The beauty of the stars and moon gave her goosebumps with its simultaneous alienness and familiarity. The landscape was a dark, undulating carpet that swept away down the mountain slopes into the misty distance.

Silhouetted in the light of watch fires, some of the bright elves stood guard around the campsite here at the base of this huge cliff. The cliff made her feel like her back was to the wall. If something came at them, there was nowhere to run.

A horn sounded from somewhere in the surrounding forest, two quick blasts, an intruder signal from the bright elf scouts. It was the first such occurrence on this journey.

The camp sprang to life. The Royal Guard burst out of their small huts, weapons already in hand, helping each other into their armor. Floating globes of light appeared and illuminated the scene to near daylight. Several bright elves approached Liz and their hut, forming a circle of protection around it.

Liz shook Hunter's foot. "Wake up, guys. Something's happening."

Hunter sat up, rubbing his eyes.

"Wake up your sister," Liz said.

Hunter reached over and shook Cassie. She groaned and slapped his hand away. "Come on!" he said.

A noise in the woods drew Liz's attention. A chorus of hoarse, high-pitched cries. The enormous bear—Liz could not cope with the idea that his name was Pooh—roared in alarm from somewhere in the darkness. The waving of the treetops revealed his location, crashing through trees and undergrowth.

Across the camp, one of the scouts emerged into the clearing and ran up to Commander Ar-Chaheris, delivering a report that Liz couldn't hear. But she did hear a strange whine in the distance, like projectiles. More cries rose, shouts of anger, bleats of pain.

Commander Ar-Chaheris shouted commands. The bright elves were awake and alert, fully armored now and holding their guns.

Hunter's voice erupted behind her. "Dad! Dad! Dad, wake up!" Then his face turned to her, glowing with fear in the firelight. "Mom! Dad won't wake up!"

***

Jorath cocked a furry ear, listening to the sounds of battle among the trees, lifting his snout into the breeze.

His mounted goblins would lead the bright elf scouts on a merry chase. The goblins would not be able to remain in the Light Realm for long, but they would last long enough. Even Jorath felt the quiet sizzling and tingling of the magical war-paint on his face and paws, the same that had been smeared on the faces of the goblins and their coyote mounts. The war-paint had been made from the blood of the Princess of Light, and served to allow them to remain in the Light Realm, but only temporarily. When the war-paint's magic was exhausted, he would slip back into the Dark Realm.

The frustrated roars of the great bear echoed through the trees as its charges and attacks were thwarted by the goblins' superior quickness. High-pitched chortling echoed in the forest's dark recesses.

But that was all a distraction from the real attack.

He climbed down the cliff face silent as a cat. His iron claws dug into the rock face and into every available crevice, his low-slung body sliding over the rocks like liquid menace toward the little hut directly below him.

***

Liz crawled into the hut, knelt beside Stewart, and shook him. He emitted a fitful snore. "Stewart! Wake up!"

The clash of arms echoed across the mountainside. The firing of the bright elves' guns sounded like the snapping of steel cables. What were they shooting at?

"What do we do, Mommy?" Cassie asked. Jaclyn and Jazlyn moved to the doorway of the hut, their dark, glittering eyes soaking up the action outside. They had little obsidian knives in their hands.

Liz said, "You glue yourself to my leg."

"I don't have any glue," Cassie said with a snicker.

Now was not the time for jokes, but Liz couldn't blame her for trying to lighten the mood.

Hunter gripped his hunting knife, crouched just behind the dolls, scanning the night for threats.

Liz took her water pouch, uncorked it, and squirted some into Stewart's face. "Wake up!"

He coughed and sputtered, throwing an arm out and slamming her into the wall of the hut. Leaves fluttered down from the domed ceiling. Stewart's eyes remained closed. Sweat glistened on his brow, and his breathing came in short intakes and expulsions.

The roar of the great bear grew louder, as did a small chorus of squeals and shouts from the bright elves.

"What's happening, Hunter?" Liz asked.

The boy's eyes were wide. "Pooh just chased a bunch of little creatures—I think they're goblins—out of the woods, and they're fighting with the elves! Holy cannoli! He can turn his fur into armor!"

Cassie jumped up beside him, peering outside. "Wow, look at his fur! It looks like shiny, jagged rocks!"

"Yeah, like armor on a dinosaur!" Hunter said.

The bear's thunderous rumbles retreated into the distance again.

Meanwhile, Liz did everything she could to awaken Stewart, but in vain. This was no normal sleep. She even pinched his nose and mouth shut, but he unconsciously flung her aside again. Her husband's physical strength terrified her. If he ever chose to unleash it, she didn't want to be anywhere nearby.

Then suddenly a tremendous weight crashed onto the four bright elf guards outside, smashing them to the ground, not ten feet from where the children knelt.

Cassie and Hunter screamed and flung themselves backward.

Three of the guards struggled to right themselves, but the fourth lay motionless under the weight of a huge, hairy beast, perhaps half the size of Pooh. But this was not a bear. Its face was pure fury, a snout full of needle-like fangs twisted into a horror of dark, murderous purpose. Its fur was a mangy black coat, with a pale stripe down its face, almost like a badger. But it was a badger the size of a Volkswagen, with claws like steak knives. With one swipe of its claw, it knocked one of the guards aside, slamming him into the cliff wall with a terrific crunch.

The remaining two raised their guns and fired point-blank at the thing. Up close, the weapons made the strangest noise, but the beast howled in pain and rage as the elves' flechettes disappeared into its coat. The elves fired again and again, shouting the alarm as they did.

Liz snatched up her sword belt, whipped out the rapier Bob had given her, and jumped past the kids.

The blade gleamed, its razor edge catching the moonlight. It was pretty, but right now she wished for a ten-foot spear to keep this thing at bay. Or a machine gun.

The beast swatted again at the elves, but they were too quick, dodging and rolling out of the way. It snarled its frustration, then took a deep breath, and spat a line of scarlet fire across the two guards. One of them managed to roll away and came to his feet slapping at the flames licking at his breastplate. The other took the brunt of it, screaming as he was engulfed in crimson flame. Liz's gorge rose into a violent retch, but she choked it back, took her rapier hilt in both hands and leaped toward the beast, sword point foremost.

A foot of the blade disappeared into the creature's side. Its jerk of pain threw her off her feet and yanked the sword out of her hand. The rapier landed a couple of paces away, and she dove for it.

The remaining guard raised his gun and fired again, but this time he was too slow for the beast's backhand. Its massive paw swept him into the air. He sailed for ten paces and landed hard against the rocky ground, where he remained still.

Liz stumbled to her feet, her heart pounding so hard she could barely breathe, clutching her rapier with both hands inside the basket hilt. She stood between the beast and her family. "You have to go through me!"

The monster turned to face her and crouched, slinking forward with amusement in its eyes. Liz couldn't peel her eyes away from its claws, six inches long and gleaming like serrated steel.

In the distance, a cry of warning went up, but she didn't dare look away from the giant badger-wolverine monster. Spots of dark moistness glistened from its wounds, but didn't seem to slow it down.

Suddenly it lunged for her. She dodged aside, but its blow took out one entire side of the hut, splintering wood in all directions.

She interposed herself again between the monster and her children. "Run, kids!" she yelled.

Another animal bounded up beside her, growling and snarling. It resembled an Irish wolfhound except that it wore a vest of glittering emerald green. It snapped and barked, baring its teeth.

Hunter and Cassie scrambled to their feet and dashed out of the ruined wall of the hut toward the closest trees.

A tiny voice niggled at the hindquarters of Liz's mind—this thing had dropped from above, it could *climb*.

Quick as a cobra, the monster's claw slashed out and knocked her rapier out of her hands, numbing her arms to the elbow. It lunged forward with a roar and hit her again, this time catching her in the side below her ribs. It felt like a sledgehammer knocked her through the opposite wall of the hut. She came to a stop buried in the wreckage, unable to breathe for the agony.

A few feet away, Stewart still snored.

Thirty yards away, the kids were climbing a tree.

The wolfhound darted behind the monster and clamped its jaws into the monster's furry flank.

Pain blazed through her torso. Her jacket and shirt hung in tatters, revealing the coat of diamond armor underneath, still intact. But that didn't mean her ribs were intact, or her internal organs.

She levered herself onto her hands and knees, shedding wreckage.

The badger-monster was spinning in a circle, vainly trying to dislodge the wolfhound's fangs from its haunches.

Dark wetness soaked the front of her jeans.

She heaved herself upright, grabbed a broken stick and flung it at the monster. It slapped ineffectually against the monster's side, but she got its attention.

"You leave Bob alone. If you're after me, bring it on!" she cried.

Several bright elf warriors were charging up the slope toward them. Would they reach her in time?

She grabbed up another stick, this one with a splintered pointed end. Somehow it was heavier than it looked. "You might eat me, but I'm going to choke you on the way down!" Her legs were weakening. She didn't know how much longer she could stand.

The kids had reached the highest point of the tree, maybe twelve feet from the ground. The tree swayed dangerously under them. This monster would make short work of it, if it chose to go after them.

Then the closest of the bright elves paused to fire their weapons at the creature.

Their flechettes sliced into its body and pinged into the rocks around her. The beast howled in fresh pain and frustration.

Bob the wolfhound held on to the creature's haunch with all the ferocity he could muster, growling and tugging.

The remaining strength drained from her legs, and she sank to her knees.

The bottom of her diamond doublet was wet with crimson. "That can't be good," she said. Reaching under it, her fingers touched the lips of a terrible gash. One of the beast's claws must have slipped underneath the bottom edge of the mail. A strange thought rambled through the thickening fog of her mind. Now she'd have a scar that would look like she'd had a C-section. If she lived.

Bright elves fired their weapons into the creature's furry bulk. Liz saw the moment the monster's courage wavered and broke.

It launched itself at the cliff face, leaped upward, and clung to the rock like an enormous spider. It scuttled upward with a speed only a bird could match, leaving a dark, wet smear up the cliff face behind it. Bob crouched at the base of the cliff, barking up after its flight.

The blood looked shockingly red on her shockingly pale hands. She tried to stand but collapsed again.

Cassie came running up to her, sobbing, "Mommy!"

Hunter was close behind. "Are you okay?"

She couldn't let them see all the blood, so she collapsed onto her side and curled into a ball. "I'm fine. Just need to rest for a while."

But they weren't buying it.

Cassie saw the blood, and her sobs shrilled. "Mommy!"

Twenty-Nine

HUNTER COULD ONLY STAND there looking at his mother with his mouth agape.

The Royal Guard warriors surrounded them, firing their weapons up at the retreating wolverine-monster.

All Hunter could do was stare at all the blood soaking his mother's jeans and stop himself from crying. His hands were clenched into tight balls of dough.

Dad wasn't moving.

Sounds of battle still echoed from the surrounding forest, the cries of the goblins, shouts from the bright elves.

Come on, do something, he told himself, but his body seemed paralyzed.

Cassie was kneeling beside Mom, pleading, "Mommy, get up! Get up!"

"I don't think that's a good idea, baby," Mom said. "I'll be okay, just need somebody to patch me up."

The Royal Guards stopped firing. The monster had climbed out of range.

Claude came running, along with a bright elf named Telwyn. Hunter had met him a couple of days earlier and they talked at length about the bright elves' armor and weapons.

The two of them knelt beside Mom and eased her onto her back. She groaned.

Cassie cried louder.

Bob's voice appeared right next to Hunter, knocking him out of his stupor. "My boy, let's take your sister over here and let the healers work, shall we?"

Hunter nodded and went forward to take Cassie's hand. "Let's go over here and see if Dad's okay."

She sniffled and came along, tears and snot streaking her face, her breathing short and shuddering. Jaclyn and Jazlyn stuck to her as close as socks. He led her over toward Dad, but she hung back, clearly remembering what happened last time she tried to wake him up. Dad lay where he had fallen asleep, twitching and mumbling in the throes of a terrible dream. His face was wet.

From a safe distance, Bob poked Hunter's father with his cane. "'Tis the dark elf, I'm afraid. Got his fingers in yer papa's mind, he does."

A flash of blue-white light from behind brought a gasp from Mom.

"Eyes front, lad," Bob said gently.

Hunter wiped the wetness from his eyes and nodded.

Bob went on, "We might be able to give the dark elf the boot, but it will take some time. His clutches apparently run very deep, or else they would have been broken when ye entered the Light Realm. A crafty villain, this one."

In the distance, a bright elf horn sounded. Elven shapes emerged from the forest, mustering in the lights of the floating globes, some of them helping wounded brethren.

"I reckon I'll need yer help, me boy," Bob said, settling onto the ground near Dad's head, where it was harder for any flailing arms to reach him.

"How can I help?" Hunter said.

"I need yer magic, yer sister's, too."

Hunter and Cassie looked at each other uncertainly.

Hunter said, "I don't have magic."

"Nonsense. If ye didn't, ye wouldn't be here. Now, come and sit. Get comfortable."

Hunter and Cassie sat down on either side of Bob.

"Now, children," Bob said, "give me yer hands."

Hunter took Bob's tiny hand in his, so small it was like a doll's hand. Jaclyn and Jazlyn stood behind them, vigilant.

"Ye're in the Light now," Bob said, "close to the Source, so all you have to do is reach out and touch it. Magic is all imagination and will. That's step one. To do that, just close your eyes and take a few deep, slow breaths."

Hunter did that.

Bob's voice was soft and hypnotic. "Take another deep, slow breath, let it out... Empty yer mind of thoughts. Ye'll have some, but just wave at them and let them follow yer breath right on out..."

Hunter followed Bob's instructions.

"Ye're settling deeper and deeper, rooting into the earth. Can ye feel that?"

Hunter nodded.

"Let the sparks come in behind yer eyes. They're mighty pretty. So many colors. Can ye see 'em?"

Cassie giggled. "Uh-huh!"

Hunter couldn't. Too many other thoughts in the way.

As if sensing Hunter about to say no, Bob said, "If ye don't, that's all right. Might be ye got too many thoughts cluttering up the works."

Mom bleeding and badly hurt, Dad comatose, monsters everywhere. Yeah, Hunter had a few intruding thoughts.

"Just let 'em go, let 'em wander off like stray monkeys..."

In Hunter's mind, thoughts transformed into monkeys, chittering, scratching, then wandering off.

Then, behind his eyelids, he saw a spark arcing through the shifting colors like a shooting star.

Elation leaped up. More monkeys wandering in, wandering off. Another spark. Monkeys in, monkeys out. More sparks.

"I see them!" he whispered.

"Good, now see if ye can catch one. Imagine a baseball glove or a butterfly net or a fishing hook, whatever ye think might be best to catch them, gather them up into a ball."

Hunter reached out with long, stretchy arms like a rubber superhero and started grabbing them, gathering them to his chest, where they formed a warm, pulsating ball over his heart.

Cassie giggled again, breathless with wonder.

"Gather as many as ye can, make a ball as big as ye can," Bob whispered.

The sparks coalesced in Hunter's imagination to a beach ball, glowing and throbbing with warmth.

"Now, children, hug that ball tight."

Hunter squeezed the warm ball like it was his mother, and it sank into him. Toasty warmth burst through his body, up and down his limbs, flushing his face, tingling across his scalp. He breathed out in pleasure.

But then a cry from Mom yanked him out of that quiet, relaxed space, back onto a rocky mountainside surrounded by monsters.

Cassie jumped up and ran to her mother's side.

Telwyn's hands lay on Mom's stomach. Mom's face was a sweat-sheened grimace of pain.

Hunter trembled, his heart thudding. He suddenly realized the very real possibility that his mom could die. She might never see another sunrise, and his eyes teared up again.

Claude's voice was grim. "There's some kind of magical poison in the wound. We can't heal her."

Telwyn's smooth, angular face held a frown. "With enough time and enough magic, we might root out the poison, but our adversary has not departed."

"I'll help you," Cassie said.

"Sing to me, baby," Mom breathed. "I always love to hear you sing..."

Cassie asked Claude, "Will that help?"

"For some, singing is its own kind of magic," Claude said. "It might be that that is your talent."

"Okay," Cassie said. "It'll be the Cassie Jukebox."

Mom chuckled feebly, then winced. "Oh, don't make me laugh." A few quick breaths later, she said, "Sing your little heart out, baby."

Cassie took a deep breath, held Mom's hand, and launched into "Somewhere over the Rainbow." At first, her voice was soft and tentative, but by the second verse, it was full and confident and ringing through the night like bells. She knew a whole list of Disney songs from her favorite movies and heroines, "How Far I'll Go," "Let It Go," "Try Everything," and "Touch the Sky." The voices of Moana, Elsa, Officer Judy Hopps, and Merida would soon come bubbling out into the night.

And her singing drew sparks. Hunter could feel them coming. "Go, Cassie, go," he whispered.

Bob's voice turned him back toward Dad. "Let us get back to our task at hand, lad."

Hunter settled himself again, closed his eyes, and reached for the sparks. Surprisingly, rather than a distraction, Cassie's voice helped him focus, and the sparks behind his eyelids returned quickly. He gathered them to him again, hugging in more globes of warmth.

Bob said, "Excellent, lad! Magic works best when it comes from yer intuition, the quiet voices deep down. That's the well yer imagination is drawn from. So, when there's something ye want to do and ye want magic to do it, trust yer intuition. Now, find yer father's mind. It's right here in front of ye, and it's mighty turbulent. Just reach out with yer awareness. Feel how ye can sense things close around ye right now, like the air, the breeze, the grass, the rocks, both of us."

"Yes..." Hunter said, he could sense them. Bob's presence was like a sizzling coal right beside him.

"Now," Bob said, "reach out and extend that awareness to your father. Find his mind."

Hunter only barely reached out and found himself diving into a thunderstorm, a fury of wind and lightning.

Bob's glowing shape plunged into the storm with him, clasping his hand.

The power of the storm shocked him, frightened him. Was this what Dad was going through? Or was it like this all the time?

No, came Bob's thoughts, *he's trapped in this by the dark elf's spell. We must find him and set him free.*

They dove through the swirling blackness until a tiny, flickering light appeared, like a candle in the tumult. Together they angled toward it, buffeting the howling winds and dark intentions.

The candle swelled into a decrepit house, like a haunted mansion. Lanterns flickered in some of the windows, then faded out to emerge in others. The front of the house resembled Dad's face with eyes wide and front door open.

Hunter and Bob swooped through the entrance and lit upon the floor of the foyer, which rumbled and jumped underfoot.

Bob's thoughts came to him: *The dark elf's magic is in your father's mind, little pieces of it hiding in cracks and crannies, like roaches in an old house. Every single one of those roaches needs to be squished.*

Hunter spotted something scuttling across the floor and through a nearby door. He chased it around the corner and found a beetle the size of his shoe. He leaped into the air and stomped upon it with both feet. It collapsed under him with a crunchy squish, then disappeared in a puff of smoke. *I got one!* he crowed.

Excellent, lad. Now, let us get to work.

***

High atop the cliff, Jorath El-Thrim writhed in pain, his massive, furry body riddled with flechette wounds. It had taken every last iota of strength he possessed to escape to the summit of the cliff.

But he could not afford to fail.

This was his last chance.

His goblins had taken losses, but they had regrouped in the forest out of reach of the enemy scouts to await his command.

The rising sun of dawn would dissipate the magic that held them all in the Light Realm. Jorath would slip back into the Dark Realm, where the Master would devour him for his failure.

To conserve his power, he reverted to his normal shape. His bestial form shriveled away, leaving an array of flechettes scattered around him on the ground, but his wounds remained. He had enough power remaining to sustain his life, but not enough to launch another attack. He lay upon the rocky ground, gathered the dark motes of his magic, and willed his flesh to knit. It would be a slow process.

But then, a centipede the length of his arm scuttled over a boulder and chittered at him with sounds too high-pitched for any human to hear, announcing its presence. But it wasn't just a centipede. It was a linguapede bearing a message from Ackthor, war chieftain of the goblins. It spoke in perfect mimicry of the goblin's voice. "My lord, we have a wounded elf prisoner."

In that moment, hope bloomed anew.

Jorath seized the linguapede, its chitinous length squirming in his grip. He focused his will upon imprinting a new message into the many segments of its tiny mind. It could hold only one message and one destination at a time.

"Bring the prisoner to me immediately," he said.

Then he set the linguapede loose to return to Ackthor.

The creature skittered away across the rocks.

Then he waited, hoping they could reach him in time.

His flesh had nearly healed when he heard the goblins' approach. Jorath rolled to his feet to meet them. Four of them came mounted on their coyotes borrowed from the Penumbra, dragging a figure so tightly bound in dark ropes it looked like a cocoon.

The gnarled little creature in the most elaborate armor raised his hand in a stiff-armed salute. "Hail, my lord!"

"You have brought me a gift," Jorath said.

The captive's head lolled, barely conscious, as the goblins had dragged him by the feet across hundreds of paces of rocky ground and treacherous cliff. At the sight of the bright elf, at once so familiar and so hated, Jorath's fists clenched.

He drew his dagger and severed the ropes tying the captive to the goblins' saddles.

The captive's face was a beaten, bloody mess, one eye swollen shut, lips ravaged. His good eye focused on Jorath and bulged with surprise.

"Your arrival is fortuitous, cousin," Jorath said.

The bright elf spat. "Traitor! Vile, corrupt—"

Jorath silenced him by jamming a convenient stone into his mouth.

"Your orders, my lord?" the lead goblin said.

"Return to your people and await my signal," Jorath said. "We will attack again shortly, and this time, it will not be a feint. You will do your utmost to destroy the humans first."

The goblin bowed. "With pleasure, my lord."

With that the goblins wheeled their rangy, canine mounts and sped away.

Jorath knelt over the bright elf as the captive struggled feebly in his bonds, one eye wild with fear. "I would like to savor this, Cousin Arwyn, but alas there is no time."

He seized the bright elf's skull in both hands.

"No!" Arwyn choked.

Jorath gathered his will, focused his strength, and cracked the bright elf's spirit wide open. With a deep, sucking breath, he drew Arwyn's burst of life force into himself, centuries of life and experiences. The inrush of it, so steeped in fear and pain, hit him with a blast of ecstasy so profound he almost collapsed.

The lingering pain from his wounds evaporated, and fresh power rushed through him, pulsing through his flesh. Strength roiled through him in such magnitude he leaped up, seized the dead bright elf and flung the body out of sight into the night, laughing with glee. His teeth ached with it. His nails tingled. His toes curled.

"And that, cousin, is why I serve the Dark."

Still tingling, he strode to the precipice and surveyed the brightly lit camp far below.

But a tiny pinprick stabbed his mind. He clapped a hand over one eye, trying to squeeze away the pain.

His tendrils of corruption in the human's mind! Someone was trying to sever them.

There was no more time to waste.

Thirty

INSIDE THE HAUNTED HOUSE of his father's mind, Hunter and Bob searched for bugs. Creeping mist clung to corners and shadows. Shadows flitted across windows. The endless rooms and corridors, smelling of dust and decay, were full of ghosts.

The first time Hunter saw ghosts, he gasped and hid behind a dusty old wing-backed chair. In the spectral green light of a cold fireplace, a fat, burly man screamed and waved his fists at a boy about Hunter's age. Hunter couldn't make out words, only the tone and the rage. He could see right through them. The boy stood with his head hanging low, absorbing this haranguing.

So rather than running, Hunter gathered his courage and yelled at them, *You're not real!*

And they disappeared. Hunter moved on and continued his search.

The rooms were full of shouting or crying. Hunter saw the little boy over and over at various ages, sometimes running from monsters, sometimes fighting them, other times standing there while they sneered and belittled him. Hunter heard a baby crying once and ran through a door to see what was the matter. He found the little boy, maybe a year old, standing in a crib in soiled pajamas, surrounded by monstrous specters like tentacled, horned, screaming things, raging at each other, raging at the baby.

Then a beetle the size of a shoebox leaped out from under the crib and charged toward Hunter's feet. It tried to feint and dodge past him to escape out the door, but he caught it with his foot and kicked it onto its back. It lay on its back, spindly legs waving, until he stomped it.

The ghosts in the room disappeared.

The hunt continued.

At one point, a deep, subsonic rumble tore through the house, rattling the cobwebbed chandeliers and cracked windows. The floor heaved, and Hunter paused to steady himself. With the great rumble came a sudden rise in the ghost screams, as if they'd been given a fresh jolt of energy.

A different kind of noise snagged his attention, drawing him up a rickety staircase into a gallery of statues. Orange moonlight streamed through the panes of tall windows, casting crooked lattices on the floor. In the gallery, something big was moving in the darkness behind the statue of a man in a baseball uniform, ready to swing his bat.

Another ghost over there? Hunter seemed to find bugs wherever he found ghosts, so he readied himself for another squishing.

The ghostly cries and shrieks that had filled the house when he and Bob first arrived had diminished. Somehow, he could sense Bob zipping through the house leaving a trail of dramatic expostulations, his cane transformed into a sword, pinning bugs to walls, floors, and ceilings.

The noise here was like a deep, heavy scratching on wood.

He crept toward it, darting from statue to statue. The statues were all of men in heroic poses. Firefighters, athletes, astronauts, even characters from movies and books. The scratching grew louder and louder.

When he peeked around the last statue, however, he found not a ghost but a rhinoceros beetle the size of a horse. And not just a regular-looking one, but a demon one, covered in nasty spikes and blood-red whorls across its thick carapace. The scratching sound came from the beetle chewing on a pile of human bones.

The beetle saw him.

It rotated its ponderous bulk toward him, its ruby-red eyes glinting, its four-foot black horn glistening.

***

Jorath felt his hooks in the human's mind being destroyed one by one, but with his fresh infusion of power from the bright elf's life force, he would be stronger than before. Alas, he had no time to pause and reinforce the spell. The moment required more direct means. If he could kill Stewart's family before he awakened, the battle would be over.

He knew better this time than to give the bright elves a big, slow target to shoot at. They were dangerous with their flechette guns. Even now, he could sense their magical wards blooming below, spheres of defense that would weaken him if he got too close. The bright elves were well versed in magical defenses, but not with attack. He should know.

The goblins would make a suitable distraction and allow him to turn the tables in a way the enemy would not expect.

He sent a silent mental signal to Ackthor. *Commence your attack. Now.*

***

The enormous rhinoceros beetle tossed its horn threateningly, the sight of it freezing Hunter in place.

This beetle could crush him with its weight, impale him on that enormous horn, chew him to bits with its huge mandibles—which real rhinoceros beetles did *not* have.

He could run, but there was no one else who could save Dad from his own nightmares.

So Hunter stood his ground and pulled his hunting knife.

The monster beetle charged, horn aimed for Hunter's heart.

He leaped out of the way—as he'd been taught in taekwondo to avoid an attack—wishing he had a bigger weapon, a big, flaming sword maybe.

Rolling to his feet, he felt the knife grow heavier, the grip changing from hard ironwood to silk cords and ray skin.

The hilt of a sword, a katana.

He stared at it for a moment in surprise. Then the blade burst into flame.

The beetle skidded to a halt, spun, and charged again.

Hunter dodged and swung the sword with both hands. The fiery blade severed two of the monster's thick, powerful legs as it thundered past. The limbs fell and dissolved into smoke. The rest of the creature stumbled and struggled to right itself, the stumps of its legs glowing with embers. In that moment of hesitation, Hunter raised the sword above his head and brought it down onto the creature's horn. The horn fell away, and the beetle jerked away with a furious hiss. He struck again, this time squarely between the beetle's gleaming ruby eyes.

His flaming sword sliced through the beetle and into the floor.

The beetle's remaining legs collapsed under it, and the whole monster burst into a swirling cloud of acrid smoke.

Suddenly sunlight streamed through the windows of the house, dispelling the creeping mist lurking in all the corners.

Hunter thrust his sword high in triumph. *Yes!*

***

Stewart's eyes popped open and he gasped, flinging himself bolt upright. There was so much light, blinding him from a sky full of little suns, he shielded his eyes against it.

Two little yelps from behind him brought him around to see Hunter and Bob, both wearing expressions of joy and triumph.

"Dad?" Hunter said hopefully.

"Am I awake?" Stewart croaked.

Sounds of battle rose in the distance. Weapons clashing. Cries of warning, anger, and alarm.

"Dad, are you okay?" Hunter said.

Stewart said, "I think so. I—"

He was cut off by Hunter throwing his arms around his neck. "Mom's hurt, and Cassie's singing to her."

"What's going on? I went to sleep, and everything was fine. But then the dreams came and wouldn't let go. I tried everything to wake up, and now—"

A horn in the distance sounded like a hurried alarm. The roar of a bear echoed from the forest, a roar of rage. He surely wouldn't want to be on Pooh's bad side.

Stewart stood, lifting Hunter in his arms.

"Me and Bob, we woke you up," Hunter said. "There was a spell on you."

A faint memory flickered of Hunter wielding a flaming sword.

"Thanks—" But then he saw Liz, and all the blood, and heard Cassie singing, and a bolt of dread shot through him like the night Cassie had been born, a long-ago night of blood and fear still fresh in his memory.

He jumped to her side. Her eyes fluttered, unseeing.

He asked Claude, "Is she going to be all right? What happened?"

Cassie stopped singing—what a pretty voice she had—and said, "A monster came after us while you were asleep, Daddy. Mommy fought it off, but she got hurt really bad, and it got some poison in her, and we're trying to get it out so we can heal her."

The determination on her face, so grown up, so in control of her fear, nearly broke his heart. He hugged her close and kissed her head. "I'm back now."

"Good, but I have to keep singing. It's helping get the poison out."

Stewart let her go, and she crouched to take Liz's hand again. She opened her mouth and launched into a fresh rendition of "Let It Go," a song that always choked him up.

He traded glances with Claude and the bright elf who was tending to her.

Claude's expression was grim, tense. "There is something lodged within her now that's blocking our magic. It is of the Dark. Cassie's beautiful singing is keeping your wife stable."

"Will she be okay?" Stewart said.

"I cannot say," Claude said. The worry on his face was plain. "We can cling to her, for now, but she's lost a lot of blood."

"Can I help somehow?" Stewart asked.

"You can protect us from whatever attack comes," the bright elf said. "My brethren just sounded an alarm horn. The battle has turned for the worse."

Stewart retrieved his battle-axe from the wreckage of their hut, twirled it in his grip a couple of times. The diamond doublet under his shirt was still intact.

Hunter sidled up beside him. "There's goblins out there, Dad. And the dark elf is here somewhere."

Pooh's roars were coming closer.

How could they ever reach the Great Tortoise's mouth if they were pursued at every step?

"Bob!" Stewart called.

There came a small whooshing noise. "You called?" Bob said from the level of Stewart's knee.

Stewart said, "You told me that we've been walking on the Great Tortoise for days. If he's here, if we're on him, how do we get to him?"

"As I told you, he'll appear when he sees fit. The Cosmic Tortoise cares little for such things as humans and leprechauns and elves. We are but dust drifting over his eternal shell, fleeting and inconsequential."

"We could be waiting forever. How do we get him to appear?" Stewart asked.

Bob rubbed his chin. "It might be we could call him."

"How?"

"With a magical loudspeaker, we could tweak his ear perhaps."

"A loudspeaker how big?"

Bob scratched one of his mutton-chop sideburns. "Oh, perhaps the size of Mesa Roja."

"*What?*" Stewart said.

"We're talking about the Cosmic Tortoise, Stewart. He breathes eternities while he sleeps. To get his attention before he's ready to give it, you must use your magic."

Stewart's immediate reaction was to think, *I don't have any magic.* But he knew that to be a lie driven into his head by others who couldn't bear for him to believe it.

"I can show you how, Dad!" Hunter said. "Bob taught me."

Stewart's throat was thick with words that almost wouldn't come out. A thrill of fear shot through him. Was this moment what he'd always dreamed of? "Okay, then. Show me."

***

The bright elves fell back before Jorath's rage. He rampaged through the forest, smashing trees aside. Around him, the goblins cheered and cackled, charging after the retreating elves.

The elves' flechettes pinged and fell away from the stony carapace his fur had become. He had to credit his former brethren for their courage. Their unicorn mounts were nimble and fierce, but they could not stand against his huge claws. He had already crushed several of his enemies against trees or beneath his feet.

The elves tooted on their little horns, but Jorath simply laughed.

Somewhere deep within, the consciousness of the great bear

roared with frustration, tamped into a tiny hole, struggling desperately against the force of Jorath's will. The elves were the beast's friends, and its anguish at their deaths burned deep in its enormous heart.

He ran through the forest toward the bright lights glimmering through the trees, the campsite. That's where he would find his prey.

***

With Hunter and Bob instructing him, Stewart was able to find the sparks of the Source and draw them into himself, feeling raw, creative warmth tingling through him. It was a lot like when he was forging a blade and the process was going well, when he was in the Zone. The collected ball of sparks felt like he'd just dived into the Zone and was swimming in it.

More horns erupted from the blackness of the forest, quick, staccato notes. Warnings.

Stewart jumped to his feet.

The sounds of rending foliage came from the woods, elven shouts and goblin screeches.

Then it exploded out of the tree line.

Pooh.

Charging straight toward them like a freight train, eyes blazing with murder, its claws tearing up sod and stone.

"Oh, dear Source," the bright elf said with burgeoning terror on his face. "Pooh is possessed!"

Stewart's stomach knotted into an icy nest of snakes. He gripped his axe and positioned himself between Pooh and his family.

Hunter stepped up beside him, a flaming katana in his hands. His face was grim, resolved.

"Where did you get that?" Stewart asked.

"Inside your head," Hunter said with a little smile.

Down the slope, a line of bright elves formed an arc ahead of Pooh's charge, and raised their arms to the sky.

Saplings and bushes sprang from the ground, writhing and growing and thickening, forming a thick web of foliage. More elves came running. The crescent of the tree barrier spread and became a circle around the bear. Saplings became thick tree trunks, skinny branches became meaty boughs, closing around Pooh like a thicket of tentacles. The bear roared his frustration. The wet, woody sounds of splintering tree trunks echoed across the cliff face as the bear tore into them with his claws.

"That will not detain him for long," the bright elf said.

Goblins boiled out of the woods, firing their crossbows at the elves. The elves wheeled their red unicorn mounts and returned fire.

"Stewart!" Claude shouted. "You must go!"

"Go where? I can't leave you all like this!" Stewart shouted.

"If we fail and Pooh reaches us, *all* is lost, *everything!* Don't you understand?"

Stewart did understand. Unless he made it to the Dark Realm and brought back the Princess, not just he and his family would be lost, but the entire mortal world, and the Light Realm as well.

He had to get the Cosmic Tortoise to show himself.

Cassie's singing gave him an idea.

The enclosure shuddered and shook with the force of Pooh's rage. Whole trees were uprooted, but others grew to replace them.

The huge bear thrust his head through an opening and roared. The opening closed, forcing him to pull back inside.

"Cassie!" Stewart called, gesturing to her. She stopped singing, looked at Liz reluctantly, but came to him. "When I tell you," he said, "I want you to sing as loud and pretty as you can. I'm going to try making it louder. Can you do that?"

She nodded. "What song?"

"Your favorite."

"Hmm." She rubbed her chin. "How about 'Touch the Sky'?"

He had often heard her singing that one in her room while she played with dolls. Every single time, she would come out of the bedroom afterward and ask him for a bow and arrow like Merida's. He would always say *You're too young for a bow and arrow*, but after what he'd seen, he'd have to reconsider, maybe for Christmas or her next birthday.

If she had one.

If any of them did...

"That's perfect," he said, "but wait until I tell you." Could he pull this off?

She nodded once.

His chest still tingled with the ball of sparks. He felt like he could do anything, accomplish anything, wind, fire, all that kind of thing.

He was going to make the sky itself sing with Cassie's voice.

"Okay, honey, go for it!" he said.

She took a deep breath and began to sing.

Her voice rose into the night sky, echoing from the face of the cliff, down to the forest.

It was the echo he needed.

The magical globes still hung in the sky, shedding light almost as bright as day across the mountainside.

The bear ripped and tore at his prison, sending massive tree trunks and showers of leaves flying. The bright elves tried to dodge these even as they struggled to maintain the barrier and hold off the goblin attack.

The glowing globes held no substance, only light.

That is, until Stewart focused his will, extended his arms, and sent sparks shooting from his hands into the nearest globes. The globes took substance, becoming huge white beach balls. Cassie's powerful voice, cracking with the effort, caught among the globes and made them start to vibrate.

His next burst of will thickened the air around the globes, formed barely visible shapes like nets or cones, becoming an enormous, diaphanous structure floating in the sky, resonating with her voice. The melody spread across the mountainside, growing louder with each measure, churning and building among the globes until it sounded like a stadium rock concert at full volume, ringing through his flesh, his bones, the earth itself.

Cassie's face bloomed with surprise and glee. She took a deep breath and redoubled her effort.

The goblins screamed and held their ears.

The elves sang along, building the song to greater heights.

Touching her back, he could feel her little body straining.

Far above them on the mountainside, something broke loose. An avalanche of rocks thundered down, too far away to threaten them, but it came sliding and crashing in a cascade of earth and boulders. What lay revealed by the falling rocks was...beyond comprehension.

An eye.

But the eye stretched the equivalent of several city blocks. A hundred yards, at least, across the great, reptilian pupil.

But the tremendous volume of the song had distracted enough of the elves that the bear's prison regrowth slowed. The bear burst through the wall, roared with triumph and bloodlust, slew a shocked bright elf with a single swipe of his paw, and stormed up the slope toward Stewart.

The elves scrambled to catch him. Thick ropy vines sprang from the remnants of the enclosure, entangling the bear's legs, trying to drag him back into his prison. His claws tore up great furrows of stony earth.

The huge eye, high on the mountainside, blinked, and looked down at them.

The sight of it, so vast, so intelligent, so wise, dashed ice water through Stewart's legs. In that eye dwelled stars, planets, nebulae, the vastness of eternity, the birth and death of suns.

The entire cliff face, before which they had been camped, shuddered. Rocks and boulders dislodged and fell with a booming clatter.

The bear slashed at his bonds, scratching at the ground, breaking loose from more vines than could regrow to seize him.

Beyond the nearest mountain peaks, beyond the face of the Cosmic Tortoise, the sky was beginning to pale with the coming of dawn.

The ground heaved and shook, knocking Hunter off his feet. Liz gasped in pain.

Goblins swept up toward the elves, firing their crossbows with their gnarled little hands, eyes gleaming with desperation. The bolts glanced from the elves' armor, but distracted them from imprisoning Pooh. Royal Guards charged the goblin skirmish line on scarlet unicorns, obsidian horns out-thrust.

The cliff, all twenty-five hundred feet of its height, the whole mile of its length, rose into the air with a rumble like thunder.

Behind it lay not a cavern, but a mouth, filled with a great, coarse tongue and bony ridges.

Stewart knelt and hugged his daughter. "You did it!"

Her eyes were the size of big, blue golf balls, staring up at this wonder of the universe. "I *did?*" she breathed.

"You go back and sing to Mommy now, honey," he said.

"That was my first concert, Daddy!"

He hugged her again. "And it was amazing."

But just then, the bear ripped free of his bonds.

A line of unicorn cavalry set their lances and charged the bear.

Pushing Cassie gently away, he picked up his battle-axe and squared himself to the oncoming beast.

The mouth started to close.

"You must go!" Claude shouted from Liz's side. "Hurry, Stewart! We cannot follow you!"

"But—!" He couldn't leave Liz like this. He couldn't leave his children to face that *monster.*

The bright elf cavalry crashed into the bear, their lances splintering against its impenetrable hide. The concussion of their charge bowled Pooh onto his side, but his thrashing claws sent unicorns and elves flying.

It was a hundred-yard run to reach the cave. The cliff—or rather, the Tortoise's upper lip—was closing.

"Go, Dad," Hunter said, clutching his sword. "We got this."

He gave them each one last look, then said, "I love you all."

Then he took off running. He used to be able to run a forty-meter in football practice in five seconds, not professional speed but plenty fast. His throat was thick, his breath huffing as he ran up the slope toward the immense cavern.

He didn't dare look back.

The bear roared. The goblin drums rattled their tattoo. Elven trumpets rose in chorus, fewer than before.

He leaped between jagged boulders thirty feet high. They weren't boulders at all, but the Tortoise's stony lips. He fell at the foot of the mile-wide tongue as the mouth clamped shut behind him.

PART IV

Thirty-One

STEWART LAY IN TWO inches of squishy moistness, the floor of the Cosmic Tortoise's mouth, his eyes full of blackness, trying not to think about exactly what he was lying in. He had just seen so many incredible things all at once, had just used magic for the first time, had seen his children do incredible things, had seen Liz on the brink of death, and then *left her*.

It was a lot to process.

His breaths shuddered in and out as he wondered how he would be able to live with himself if he'd just left his wife and children to die.

Then again, maybe he wouldn't live long anyway, given where he was headed.

The vastness of the cavern around him staggered his sense of scale. He could sense its immensity as he lay there on his back, listening, breathing. As his eyes adjusted to the pitch blackness, he thought he could see motes of light above him, drifting, swirling. He reached for them—and they came.

The motes of light were the Source, and here in the blackness of the Tortoise's mouth, he could see them. Why he could see them so easily here and not outside was beyond his understanding. He still didn't know *how* the magic worked, only that it *did*. Bob and

Hunter had told him to trust his intuition, so he would try, maybe for the first time since he was small.

If the Cosmic Tortoise's body was in scale with its mouth, he might well have a twenty-mile hike through the Tortoise to reach the Dark Realm, and then, who knew how far to wherever the Princess was being held? Then again, maybe he shouldn't ascribe too many rules of Penumbral reality to the situation. The Light Realm had already proved such things as time and distance held less meaning here than in the mortal world, the Penumbra.

"Penumbra" made Earth sound alien, scary, and weird. Maybe it *was,* to creatures from other realms. It was pretty scary and weird to its natives, too.

He stood, coming out of the moisture with a slimy squelch, and collected himself. He still had his battle-axe and diamond mail doublet. He still had the shoulder pouch containing the oil and the baseball. What was he supposed to do with a baseball anyway? Claude had said he could use it to stop time, but how? He hoped his intuition would let him know. In his jeans pocket was the pocket watch Claude had given him.

As he gathered more and more of the Source into himself, he used it to infuse the head of his axe with light, not unlike how the bright elves had created the light globes. He held it high, as bright as a car's headlight.

Right beside him was the Tortoise's enormous tongue, like a massive, living hill. It looked like a grayish-pink boulder that moved with its own life, coarse surfaced, larger even than some of the rock formations and plateaus around Mesa Roja. But unlike most rock formations, this thing was contiguous.

Climbing up the side to the nominally horizontal upper surface took him several minutes, but when he reached it, he had
to pause and wonder at the vastness of the creature's mouth, so
deep and high and vast his light would not reach the interior's
limits.

It would be easy to get lost in such a huge, dark space, with no
landmarks to orientate him, but the great tongue had striations
that all pointed the same direction—down its gullet. So he walked,
guilt and urgency at war in his tread. Guilt for leaving his family in
danger. Urgency to reach the Dark Realm, save the Princess, and
thus, everyone else too.

Unfortunately, amid the frenzy of battle, he had not thought to
grab any food or water before lunging into the Tortoise's mouth.
He remembered well the warning against eating or drinking anything in the Dark Realm. How long he would be able to survive
there without any food or water, he had no idea. Physical reality
took liberties in the magical realms.

And then the lumpy hillock of tongue lurched and flung him
high. Yelling incoherently, limbs flailing, he arced so high his light
wouldn't reach what was below. He came down in a spongy mass
of phlegm at the back of the Tortoise's throat.

It was like swimming in Jell-O that smelled like a reptile house
at the zoo. When he finally reached more solid ground, he couldn't
help but laugh. It bubbled out of him in a guffaw at the absurdity
of it until tears streamed down his cheeks.

The Cosmic Tortoise had just swallowed him.

When the laughter subsided, he moved on into the immense
tunnel of the creature's esophagus. His light would not reach the

ceiling or walls, but a trickle of moisture ran down the concave center, marking his path.

Best not to waste time, so he set off at a jog. As time passed underfoot, he found the brightness of his axe was dimming, so he sought more sparks, of which there were plenty, and replenished it. Maybe he was getting the hang of this "magic" thing.

He jogged until he tired. Then he rested.

For a while he walked along the shore of a vast, dark ocean, its waters lapping at its edges. Occasionally he felt the breath of wind, neither warm nor cold, moist nor arid, but just an impression of air moving, but then he considered that it might be simply his *idea* of air, his *notion* of reality within this gargantuan creature, a construct of his mind, when it might be something else entirely. Things moved in the dark, fathomless waters. He could hear them leaping, splashing. He caught glimpses at the edge of his light of pale, scuttling things that fled before him, some of which were small and nonthreatening, some of which made him glad he had a weapon.

He thought several times that he heard the flap of great leathery wings, too high for his light to reach. The roof—the sky?— was utterly black, but distant cries tormented his ears, unable to grasp their nature or distance, cries so alien he couldn't imagine what sort of creature would make them. He dared not sleep, fearing what might come upon him, so he kept going. Without sun or stars, he had no sense of time. He knew only that he was weary and had to keep going.

From the ocean's edge, he reached a ropy bridge that stretched ahead into nothingness, just wide enough for him to cross, above a bottomless chasm. It lacked any sort of handhold, so the slightest lurch or a good gust of wind might send him spinning into the abyss. But his intuition told him this was his path. So he went forward. The bridge swayed and flexed with his weight, but its surface was rough enough for solid footing.

As he went, however, he imagined the soles of his shoes growing bony crampons and soon noticed that his tread felt surer. And there they were, inch-long spikes growing from the rubber soles of his hiking boots. "I could get used to this magic stuff," he chuckled into the abyss.

Below him, he heard wings, and perhaps sloshing, like great breakers against a shore.

And then stars appeared, not above him, but below. In a moment of vertigo, he dropped to his knees, clutching futilely at the featureless bridge. The gaseous streaks of a beautiful nebula, a cosmic gas cloud that engulfed many star systems, painted the darkness. His stomach leaped into his throat and hung there. In the vastness, things moved. Were they aware of him? Was he aware of the dust motes on his shoes? The germs on his hands?

He couldn't go back. What would happen if he simply jumped? Would he fall forever? Was there a bottom? Composing himself with a sweating effort of will, he kept on.

Awareness of a growing thirst crept up on him, but it was so difficult to tell because he had no idea how long he'd been inside the Tortoise. It could have been a day. It could have been a week, or a month.

The precariousness of the bridge stretched what felt like miles, stretching his nerves to full tension, even with his new crampons.

What did it represent? A tendon? A blood vessel? A nerve ganglion? When finally, he reached the far edge of the chasm, he collapsed with relief.

Beyond the chasm, a wind rose, bringing the stench of sulfur and ammonia. Crimson pinpricks appeared above him, like stars through a red veil, perhaps. They weren't sparks of the Source, however, because they would not come to him when he willed it.

But he had no notion of the direction to go from here, so he pulled out the gold pocket watch from his pocket and opened it. The outer dial still pointed toward the Sun, rather than the Moon, so he was still safe from turning to the Dark. The inner dial, the compass, pointed off into the black, so he set off in that direction.

Before long, the ground underfoot sloped downward. The light increased, but with a crimson cast, such that he could see features in the distance, like great cliffs perhaps a mile away on both sides. As he jogged, the cliffs angled inward and hove higher and higher. Clumps of what looked like thorny black brambles appeared on the landscape, thickening and clumping larger and larger. As he neared one, the light of his axe revealed them to have glossy, metallic exteriors, more like conglomerations of black razor-wire than anything living.

It was then he noticed that the light of his axe had taken on a reddish cast, as if filtered through blood. The air smelled of hot metal and sulfur and dust.

The cliffs became a canyon half a mile deep. The sky brightened like blood soaking dark cloth, until a sullen scarlet orb nosed above the horizon.

Atop one wall of the canyon, a cluster of lights emerged. Wariness made Stewart pause. The last thing he needed was to stumble into a town full of enemies. There were no friends here. His only hope was to remain unnoticed, undetected. Would news of the events at Chukwa's mouth have gotten back here? If so, given how much effort the Dark Lord had put into ensnaring Stewart, the entirety of the Dark Realm would probably be on the lookout for him, so he hugged the canyon wall, picking his way between boulders and clumps of metal thorns.

Growing closer, he saw the lights were part of a village. Smokestacks rose from the tumbledown assemblage of visible structures. Dark smoke poured from the smokestacks, and the acrid stench of ash and soot filled the air. Even though the place looked inhabited, it felt lifeless. The lights he'd seen looked to be flames burning atop long black staves. The rumble and chuff of churning machinery echoed over him. It was all too far away for him to see tiny details like inhabitants—or lookouts. Was this canyon seeded with magical detection methods? Were they already aware of him?

The ball of Source he'd gathered into himself had diminished but some remained. Could he conceal himself with magic? But if he used Light magic here, would it be like shouting *Here I am!* to every Dark Realm creature close by?

Then he heard movement echoing down the canyon, growing louder.

The orb in the sky rose grim and sullen, casting the landscape into lurid scarlet, so he no longer needed the light of his axe. He doused it and hid between two clumps of thorns. The thorns pricked at him, sharp and barbed.

But what if he tried to use Dark magic to power some sort of concealment? If he truly walked in both realms, he might be able to use Dark as well as Light.

The sounds of movement grew louder suddenly. Perhaps a hundred yards ahead of him, the canyon floor bent out of sight. Coming around the bend were mounted warriors. Their polished plate armor shone in the ruddy light, so smooth, so well joined that they resembled insects. Then he saw they were not riding horses, or any kind of sane creature, but elephant-sized beasts that looked like part centipede, part lobster, scuttling along on too many legs, with too many eyes, too many venomous-looking spines. The riders carried jagged-looking weapons Stewart couldn't identify. Having seen what the goblins and bright elves could do, he thought they were probably some sort of ranged weapon.

At least a dozen of the riders came straight down the canyon toward him.

There was nowhere to hide, except in the razor-wire bushes, but they would not conceal him from sight at close range.

He closed his eyes, took a deep breath, and opened himself to the Source. But the Source here tasted bitter, smelled like rotten cheese and metal flakes. Behind his eyelids he found spinning barbs of scarlet energy. Swallowing hard, he reached out to draw them toward him. Each one brought with it a sharp stab of pain as it entered him, like hospital needles and dental drills, fishhooks and broken glass.

But this Dark essence settled into him and congealed into a ball of throbbing power. It suffused him, sparking the impulse to charge out there with his axe and destroy all of the oncoming riders. With enough power, he knew he could do it. He could wipe them from the face of existence, squash them like the bugs they resembled, scatter their remnants for a hundred paces in every direction. He could set loose the gorilla-like beast of his dreams, clad it in impenetrable armor, and rip them all limb from limb and—

No.

The unwelcome grin of anticipation on his face brought him back to himself, and he felt vaguely ill.

He only had a few seconds before one of them spotted him among the steely bramble.

Camouflage. He needed camouflage.

From the Dark Source, he created a coating for himself that was striped and black and spiny like the bramble itself. Every visible bit of him took on this appearance, red like the rocks, black like the thorns, flesh and clothing alike, even his eyes.

As the riders drew nearer, their stench threatened to make him retch. They were like Death mixed with the sickly stench of worms and insects and corruption.

He froze where he stood among the brambles, scarcely daring to breathe.

The arthropoid steeds undulated across the uneven landscape, eyes glittering like dark jewels, carapaces gleaming. Vicious-looking mandibles and claws swept across the ground before them.

The riders wore featureless helmets with blank faceplates, slitted only for the eyes. If they had not exuded an aura of deadly menace, he might have thought them beautiful in the perfection of their plates and joints. He could appreciate meticulous metalwork. As they neared, he could make out the intricate scrollwork decorating their limbs and breastplates.

The way they carried themselves made him think they were searching for something. Did they have magical means to detect him?

The warriors dispersed among the tracks between the thorns and boulders covering the floor of the canyon.

He held his breath, heart pounding so loudly they *must* hear it, his teeth painfully clenched, as one of them passed within ten yards of him.

But it passed. And it kept going. He only breathed again when it was thirty yards past him.

He turned his head as slowly as he could to follow their movements down the canyon—away from him. His breath returned, ragged and painful in his chest.

For all those long years, he stood there, heart thudding against his breastbone, sweat trickling down his face, soaking the back of his hair. He did not move until the riders had moved out of sight.

Then he burst from the thorn bushes and darted to the next one.

And then the next one, pausing at each to listen for any approaching sounds, scan for any movement besides his.

It was eternities before the village on the precipice disappeared out of sight behind him.

He pulled out his compass to check it again, and discovered that the Sun on the dial had shifted significantly, rotating almost ninety degrees. The Moon was now ready to rise. When the Moon reached the midnight position, he would become a creature of the Dark. As he watched the device's inner workings slowly rotating, the Moon continued to creep upward. Even the little bit of Dark magic he had used was enough to make him almost irretrievable. He dared not use it again, and he didn't have much time. If he encountered another party of riders, what could he do?

At least the compass showed he was on the right heading.

"You are a lucky human, Stewart Riley," said a voice behind him.

Thirty-Two

STEWART SPUN, raising his axe in a two-handed grip.

A bright elf stepped out from behind a boulder, palms up. Its samurai-like armor was scored and dented in places, some of the laces sliced through so that a few of the lacquered plates were loose or missing. His helmet obscured his features such that Stewart couldn't recognize him, but then there were many elves whom he had not met among their party. Whorls of dark paint were smeared on his face, on his armor and helmet, like war-paint.

"You just about lost your head," Stewart said, lowering his axe.

"Apologies for startling you," the elf said with a weary smile, "I was just so delighted to have finally caught up with you. I am Tyr Ar-Chaheris."

"What are you doing here?" Stewart asked. "How did you get past that bunch of warriors?"

"Magic, of course," the elf said, "I've been following you. You got somewhat ahead of me in the belly of the Great Tortoise."

"How did you find me?" Stewart asked.

The elf smiled faintly. "Again, magic. I know you. I know what to look for."

Stewart sighed. "I have a lot to learn."

"Indeed," the elf said, with enough ill-concealed disdain in his voice to make Stewart's hackles rise, "but be that as it may, we must complete our mission, yes?"

"First of all," Stewart said, "what are you doing here?"

"The commander sent me to help you. You are quite fortunate not to have been spotted already. Do you know who those riders were?"

"How could I?" Stewart said sharply.

"I suppose not," the elf said with a shrug. "Those were El-Mithari Garkus Riders. Among the fiercest of the Dark Lord's minions. Vile creatures. Garkii can sense vibrations in the ground as faint as a human heartbeat. Had they caught you, you would have spent eternity being digested in the gullet of one of those beasts. How you avoided them, I cannot fathom."

"Magic," Stewart said with a wry smile, even as he shivered at the thought of being swallowed whole by one of those things.

"We should move quickly in case they return."

Stewart nodded and checked his compass, which still pointed down the canyon. "Let's go."

They took off running at a pace Stewart felt he could sustain.

As they left the immediate danger behind them, other thoughts and questions found space in Stewart's mind. "If we jumped into the Tortoise's mouth at the same time, how did we not see each other on the passage through?"

"Time and space hold little meaning inside that creature. It must be strange for a Penumbral human. It is strange even for me, and I was born and raised in the magical realm."

Stewart's breath puffed in and out. "You're a being of the Light Realm, so how are you able to stay here?"

The elf pointed at the whorls of dark war paint on his face, smeared all on his armor and hands. "I used the blood of the goblins to make this paint. It works as a kind of Trojan horse."

"How did you have time to do that before the Tortoise's mouth closed?"

A moment's hesitation before the elf answered, "I had some goblin blood on me. I used that once I was inside the Tortoise's mouth."

Stewart wasn't sure why his instincts were making him distrust this elf. After all, the bright elves had escorted him and his family all the way from the City. They were the Queen's Royal Guards. But he was grateful to have someone who knew the ins and outs of the magical realms. Ever since leaving the Penumbra—home—he'd felt lost and blinded by his own ignorance.

But there was one question foremost in his mind. "What about Liz and the kids? Are they all right?"

The elf looked away, his porcelain-smooth face cracking with sadness. "I am sorry. My brethren and I...we tried to hold back the bear. But it was too strong. It broke free and..."

Stewart's legs crumpled beneath him, and he sank to the ground like a burlap sack drained of its contents. His throat cinched shut. He couldn't breathe. Tears burst into his vision. His hands shook so badly he dropped his axe. Sobs wracked him like crashing surf.

"I am very sorry to give you this news," the elf said.

Images of his family blasted through his mind like shotgun pellets. His and Liz's first date. Their first kiss. Their first night together. Their wedding day. The day she'd told him she was pregnant. The day Hunter was born. All those nights they'd backed each other up feeding a colicky infant. Hunter's first steps. His first words. His unique expression of skepticism over a given course of action, as if to say *You want me to do* what *now?* The day he and Liz and baby Hunter had moved into the trailer. The day Cassie was born and he thought she was the most beautiful baby in the world. The day she'd fallen asleep on his chest for the very first time. The way she sat in her car seat singing gibberish and dancing along with "Uptown Funk" on the radio.

All of it gone, like smoke in the wind.

All these moments sleeted through his mind, each one razor sharp, cutting him deeper and deeper.

It was as if his soul itself were bleeding out around him.

The dark sun slid across the overturned bowl of the sky.

The elf stood back and let Stewart have his grief.

All those moments, lost. Beautiful lives, snuffed.

There was nothing for him anymore. He would never smile again, never feel Liz's arms again or hugs from his kids. Cassie and Hunter would never grow up. He and Liz would never grow old together.

It was over for him.

He got up and started walking. It didn't matter which direction. There were only two really, forward and back. He didn't know which direction he took, only that he could no longer bear to be wherever he was standing.

"Stewart—"

"Don't. Touch. Me," Stewart growled.

Bring on the monsters. Let them eat him. Let them digest him for eternity. He deserved it. It was his fault. He had left them. He should never have left them alone. Their deaths were on him.

Some part of him had always known it would end this way. He was not worthy of Liz, or of his kids. He was just a no-account orphan, a Bad Kid. He would never amount to anything else—that's what he'd heard his whole life. All those foster parents and school administrators had been right.

He should have done the things that were in his nature, all those dark impulses that would have made his life better. Liars and thieves ran the world. The news proved it every day. He should be one of those people.

Without having to see them, he could sense the scarlet fishhooks of Dark magic swirling around him like gnats to a flame.

"Stewart, what are you going to do?" said the elf.

He wiped the tears from his cheeks. His eyes felt so raw, so scratchy, he could barely keep them open.

"Sleep."

He seized all the scarlet motes and channeled them into his axe. The axe head gleamed with crimson fire. Then he approached the canyon wall. He raised it high, channeled his rage, almost feeling his arms swell with the power of it, and he brought the axe down onto the stone of the canyon wall with the clap of a thunder-stroke. Shattered stone blasted his face and body in a shower of gravel. As the dust settled, he saw the hollow his Dark magic-fueled blow had made.

A crater of about ten feet in depth and half as high, blown out as if with TNT.

And the noise of it had echoed for miles, up and down the canyon, no doubt drawing the attention of everything that had heard it.

He crawled inside. The elf hurried in beside him. For the first time, Stewart caught the elf's scent, like nothing he had ever smelled before, like the sharp tang of blood or metal.

Then he breathed deep, inhaling more crimson fishhooks until they seethed in his breast like liquid fire. Binding them to his will, he sent them out to gather all the rubble he'd just scattered across the canyon floor, bring it back and cover the opening he'd made. In a swirl of dust, the pebbles and stones gathered themselves in the cave opening, shutting him and the elf into darkness, except for a meager spear of lurid sunset shining through a tiny opening at the top.

In the darkness, he lay on his side on the jagged rock with a stone for a pillow and wept until sleep claimed him.

***

Stewart didn't know whether elves slept. All he knew was that Tyr settled into stillness so profound he might have been dead. But he didn't care. This elf meant nothing to him; he was a mere appendage.

His sleep was fraught with black abysses and leviathans writhing in the deep, shifting from an age-old slumber. Great eyes appeared and disappeared, cosmic beasts the size of worlds. But most of all was a sense of loneliness. In all the universes that existed, he was alone.

When he sat up, the sliver of lurid sunlight was gone.

He was still thirsty, and his hungry stomach had twisted itself into knots.

Barely discernible, Tyr's dim shape spoke: "What are you going to do, Stewart?"

His voice was a croak. "I'm going to do what I came here to do."

He didn't realize that was his intention until he spoke the words. Maybe it was habit. Maybe it was stubbornness.

As he was already a dead man, he was going to do everything in his power to do what he came here to do. And there would be no concern about going home again. Then, if he succeeded in saving the Princess, he would march into Baron Tyrus's castle, or whatever the hell he lived in, and cut his head off. Or else die in the attempt.

"I am delighted to hear that," the elf said. But was that hesitation in his voice? Maybe he could sense the Dark magic coalescing around Stewart.

Stewart gathered himself, peered out the small opening to check for anyone or anything outside. But there was nothing out there except empty canyon and cold stone. Not even the thorny brambles grew in this area. So he set about shoving away the rubble to enlarge the opening. As he worked, he told the elf, "You should probably turn around and go home. This is a suicide mission now."

"It always was. I am with you until the end."

Perhaps Stewart might have appreciated the sentiment once, but now it just annoyed him. Why did this immortal creature care what happened to him? Perhaps it was only self-interest, a desire to preserve the Light Realm. With one swipe of his axe, Stewart could cut this little man in two, save him the agony of what was coming. "Why are you here anyway?" He wanted no further company on this death-capade.

"It is my solemn duty to be here. Duty to...the Queen, duty to my house, duty to my honor."

When he had enlarged the opening sufficiently to crawl through, there was nothing to do but resume his way.

The sky outside was a forbidding expanse of blackness peppered with pallid pinpricks, empty of wonder or comfort.

One look at the dial of his compass showed that his Sun had long since set and the Moon was rising. He would soon become a creature of the Dark. Stewart's mouth was so dry, his throat parched, his voice became a rasping crow's. Or maybe it was just the grief that would dog him every moment from now until his end.

As they set out again, Tyr Ar-Chaheris walked with an upright stride, shoulders back. There was no doubt in him. But Stewart's feet felt embedded in lead. His muscles and soul screamed their weariness, willing him to lie down and just give up.

But he would not.

One more thing to do. Only then would he give up.

Thirty-Three

HUNTER GRIPPED HIS FLAMING katana with both hands, squeezing harder as his dad disappeared into the mouth of an entire mountain. As he watched the unbridled savagery of a bear that could shred entire trees, his legs trembled and his arms felt like noodles. He could hardly hear anything over the beating of his own heart. He ached with fear for his wounded mom.

And his dad was gone, maybe never to return.

He wiped a tear from his cheek with the back of one hand, then squared himself toward the bear again.

In the distance, the sounds of battle between elves and goblins continued, cries of anger and bleats of pain echoing against the Cosmic Tortoise's *face*.

He could hardly believe what he had seen his father do. Dad had made Cassie's voice come *out of the sky*.

If he could do that, anything was possible.

Behind him, Bob and the elf continued to work on Mom, with Cassie's cracked voice soothing and focusing them.

Then with a tremendous explosion of fury, the bear leveled an entire side of his living prison. The force of it threw elves in every direction.

Pooh was free.

And barreling straight toward Hunter. He could feel the pounding of the huge paws through the ground. Pooh's eyes blazed with bloodthirsty intelligence, straight into him.

He gripped his sword and raised it to strike. His flaming blade could cut through anything, even the bear's armadillo-like hide.

Tears of terror misted his vision, but he held his ground, breathing deeply as he'd been taught in martial arts, calming himself.

The bear's great maw gaped with slavering fangs.

Just then, a spear of dawn crested the nearby mountaintops, spreading across the valley, a line between bright and shadow sweeping toward him.

The bear was ten yards away, coming faster than a truck.

Hunter braced himself, holding his breath.

The moment the sunlight touched the bear's ears, its eyes rolled back and its legs collapsed under it. It fell onto its belly and tumbled toward Hunter. He dived out of the way, and the enormous beast came to rest within a few feet of Cassie and Mom.

Hunter scrambled to his feet and ran around the small hillock of Pooh's body to the head, raising his sword, ready for a desperate stab. "Is it dead?"

The elf's face was gray and sweaty, his eyes wide, but breathing heavily with relief. "The possessing spirit has departed, driven away by the touch of the sun."

Cassie said, "Will Pooh be okay?"

Claude answered, "I believe he will, my dear. That is, if Hunter doesn't finish him off. Easy, my boy."

Hunter lowered his weapon. "Just being careful."

The great bear's tongue, as wide as a trash can lid, had flopped out onto the ground. Its eyes were closed. Its stone-like armor became fur again. Deep breaths huffed in and out.

"What if he wakes up again?" Hunter said.

Claude said, "I daresay he'll be somewhat embarrassed."

"Is Mom going to be okay?" Hunter said.

"I think we can stabilize her," the bright elf said, "but it is beyond our power to heal her. That vicious beast last night left some sort of Dark sliver within her, and we cannot extract it. It is like a worm, eating at her spirit. Only the Queen can save her. We must take her to the City, but she might not survive the journey."

"Can't we call the Queen and bring her here?" Hunter asked. "All the things magic can do, can't we make a magic telephone?"

"The Queen is bound to the Source. We are too far from there," the elf said.

"There must be something we can do!" Hunter said angrily. Mom's face looked like gray paste. Her lips were the wrong color. Sweat sheened her face. Claude clutched one hand and Cassie the other. Cassie's lip was clenched between her teeth.

Then he became aware of the silence downslope. The sounds of battle had ceased. Bright elves were picking themselves up from the ground, lending aid to their wounded. Scarlet unicorns searched for their riders among the trees and the wounded. A few bright elf bodies remained still.

"Let's make a wagon for Mom," Hunter said, "with lots of cushions."

Bob approached, looking exhausted. His missing top hat let his hair fly into a black tumbleweed. "I reckon the boy's onto something. We daren't dally."

The bright elf nodded. "Then we shall fashion a carriage, power it with magic, and set out immediately. Cassie, my child, you must stay with your mother, keep her focused on you, make her as happy as you can."

Cassie nodded with conviction. "The Cassie Jukebox is open for business."

Liz chuckled, then groaned, "Oh, goodness, don't make me laugh."

"Yay! You're awake!" Cassie said.

"I'm not sure," Liz said faintly. "Everything feels like a dream..." Her voice trailed off.

"We can waste no time," Claude said.

The bright elf said, "I shall gather my brethren." Then he departed down the slope.

"What about Dad?" Hunter said.

Claude said, "The Tortoise's mouth is closed. If your father is to come back to us, he won't be returning this way."

Hunter sighed, skeptical. It didn't feel right to bug out. But then something sharp jabbed him under the arm, gently lifting him.

A red unicorn regarded him quizzically.

Hunter's eyes met the unicorn's dark orbs. Untold intelligence sparkled deep within them, like stars in black marbles. Its coat resembled red velvet cake. The obsidian horn looked razor sharp, as long as his arm, wet with something Hunter didn't want to think about. In that moment, he knew the unicorn's thoughts.

Its rider was dead.

Hunter gasped. "You mean—?"

The unicorn dipped its head and extended its nose to be

touched. Hunter was about the size of a bright elf, the perfect size to ride this creature. He reached out, hesitantly, and stroked its nose.

It needed a new rider.

He ran his fingers through its dark-red beard.

The red unicorns were drawn to bravery and stoutness of heart, Claude had said.

The unicorn stepped closer, and Hunter felt a moment of sadness at its empty saddle and scarred barding. He felt the unicorn's sadness, too.

Then it nuzzled him, and tingles of pride and gratitude dashed through him.

***

Stewart and the elf walked in the bottom of a dry, sandy riverbed. Tributaries branched from the riverbed, often populated by stagnant pools of black, tarry muck. Travelling in the Dark Realm felt just as abstract as in the Light.

Eventually the floor of the canyon rose to meet the land above, a bleak, undulating patchwork of black woods and jagged badlands. The only signs of intelligent habitation were conglomerations of machinery, smokestacks, and shantytowns clustered in haphazard heaps of metal and black brick. High, spindly torches belched black smoke into the sky. From a distance, movement was visible among the structures, but he got no sense of the nature of the inhabitants. They could have been semi-corporeal black smoke for all he knew. At random intervals around the landscape, bits of incomprehensible machinery poked from the ground.

The banks of the riverbed obscured their passage from any casual onlooker. Strangely, Stewart no longer feared being caught. He was a creature of the Dark now, traveling to meet the Master for the first time. Any creature he encountered would sense the darkness in him. If they didn't, he would kill them. He had the power now. His whole body throbbed with it, to be unleashed at his whim.

The elf was a taciturn companion, seeming to be focused on looking for threats. Stewart welcomed the quiet.

They stopped to rest, sitting upon the termite-ridden corpse of a fallen tree. Then Stewart saw the infestation was not of termites, but couldn't bear to look long enough to determine what they actually were.

The elf said, "Are you sure you wouldn't like some water, Stewart? I have a few drops left. A bit of bread perhaps? We've been traveling for days."

Stewart blinked and tried to clear his head. "We have?"

"Indeed, it's been six sunsets since we met, and I am weary and half-starved."

"So even elves have limits." Stewart's mind was a stagnant fog. Had it really been six days? He only remembered sleeping once, inside the cave he had made. He didn't remember marching nonstop through the night. It was as if he walked in a dream. Somewhere along the journey, he'd forgotten his thirst and hunger.

"We are nearing the Metropolis," the elf said. "Can't you feel it?"

For some time now, Stewart had felt something throbbing up through the earth into his feet, as if unspeakable things moved underneath, heading in one direction. "Yes, I think so."

"It is there." The elf pointed across the vast plain, up the river-bed, toward a single volcano rising out of the misty distance. But a volcano it was not. Its lines were too regular, its angles too unnatural, its sides too polished. It was an edifice of mind-bending proportions, reaching miles into the ruddy sky, even as it sprawled out of sight in the mist. From this distance, it was impossible to grasp the scale.

Tiny black things swirled like gnats around the Metropolis's jagged minarets and sky bridges.

"The Princess is somewhere in there?" Stewart asked.

The elf nodded. "The Dark Lord would keep her close, to gloat over her, feed upon her power."

How was he supposed to find one little girl in a city that size, a city crawling with enemies? Then again, were they enemies now at all? He was one of them. Would they even give him a second glance?

"Come," the elf said, "you shall need all your strength to face the Dark Lord's minions." He held out a chunk of dry, hard bread.

It looked darker than the elven bread Stewart remembered. But he took it. His stomach was a twisted fist. He gnawed on a corner of it. It didn't taste like the elven bread he'd eaten on the journey to the Tortoise's mouth. It tasted bitter, metallic. "It's spoiled," he said.

"Perhaps we have been in the Dark Realm for too long. The Dark essence has suffused the bread. Nevertheless, it will feed us."

The elf offered Stewart a nearly empty water pouch. Stewart lifted it to his lips and squeezed a little into his mouth. It tasted awful, like coppery medicine, but the more it swirled on his tongue, the more accustomed to it he became.

"The water, too," Stewart said, handing it back.

The elf took the pouch and upended it. Did the elf relish the taste?

Stewart's eyes went to the bread.

It was a corner of round, flat bread, but three or four finger-breadths thick. The bread he'd eaten on the journey to the Tortoise's mouth had been uniformly half that thickness, with a lighter, fluffier texture. This bread was wrong.

"No," Stewart said, immediately wondering why that was appropriate.

The elf looked at him.

"No!" he said, more forcefully, his anger gaining compression, like a corked bottle in a flame.

This was not a bright elf.

***

Jorath saw the snarl of rage twist Stewart's face in the moment of realization.

He barely had time to launch a spell of defensive aura before Stewart snatched up his axe and swung it toward Jorath's chest.

The spell turned the blow aside enough that the edge only grazed him, but the force of it threw him ten paces away. He rolled in midair and hit the ground in a somersault that bounced him back to his feet.

The veins and tendons of Stewart's neck bulged, his face reddening, teeth clenching. His fists twisted the wrappings of the axe haft with white-knuckled fury.

Jorath whipped out his sword. The illusion of bright elf armor dispersed like sand in water, leaving him clad in his own metal plate. Breathing a great inrush of Dark magic, he channeled the magic into his sword. A nimbus of sickly pale light exploded from the blade, where it glowed like magnesium fire, blinding bright.

"It's *you!*" Stewart snarled.

Rather than waste his breath, Jorath channeled still more magic into his blade and slashed in Stewart's direction. Shards of Dark essence flew from the edge toward Stewart, becoming tiny razor blades.

Stewart roared with pain, bleeding from a dozen wounds small and not-so-small. His chest deepened and his arms swelled. A blunt snout sprang from his face. His skin hardened into reptilian scales, sealing the bleeding wounds. His eyes blazed with primal fury, and Jorath's blood chilled. Stewart now resembled a cross between a silverback gorilla and a crocodile.

Until this moment, he had been certain he could protect himself from this ignorant human, but now...

Stewart charged with shocking speed, swinging his axe, its head leaving a streak of glittering Dark magic in its wake. Jorath's protective spell might not work a second time.

Jorath back-flipped to avoid another lethal swing and landed atop a head-high boulder. Stewart's next blow split the massive stone into halves, showering gobbets of molten rock in all directions.

How had a Penumbral human become so strong? And without real training? Stewart's dizzying speed, both reptilian and simian in its ferocious alacrity, kept Jorath on the defensive, unable to gather himself for a magical strike. With his sword, he deflected a blow that left his arm numb to the shoulder.

His purpose had been to draw Stewart close enough to the Metropolis that the Master would sense their presence and dispatch a "welcoming party," but Stewart had seen through his ruse too soon. The aim was still to recruit this powerful human, not destroy him, but he somehow retained his force of will against the wishes of the Master.

Jorath whipped his blade through an arc that released another shower of ethereal blades. This time, they bounced off Stewart's thick hide as he charged through the fusillade and seized Jorath by the arm.

***

This dark elf was a quick, wily little monster, but Stewart finally got hold of his arm.

This monster had killed Liz.

This monster had killed Hunter and Cassie.

He raised the dark elf above his head to dash him against the split boulder, but a searing pain across his forearm made him release his grip. The Dark elf skittered back like a monkey, gripping his short, curved blade. The elf's armor looked insectoid now, like a carapace or an exoskeleton.

"How squishy are you inside that armor?" Steward taunted. He intended to find out.

But he could not match the creature's quickness, faster than a human eye could follow. Worst of all, Stewart was tiring. His heart labored and his breath came in gasps. But he didn't dare hold back. If he let this dark elf get away, it would bring hell down upon his head, because even though he was now a creature of the Dark, only the elf knew his purpose was still to save the Princess.

Stewart could muster no magical attack, or the time required would give the dark elf an opening. This creature would cut his throat given the slightest opportunity, just as it had destroyed his family. It would not see another sunset.

He leaped forward again, swinging his axe with tiring arms.

The elf parried the rain of blows again and again and even managed a few counter-strikes at Stewart's arms and legs, leaving bleeding, searing furrows. Several obsidian shards, like slivers of darkness, were embedded in the coat of diamond mail.

Stewart drew back again and began to circle his enemy, axe poised.

If the fight went on too long, enemies would take note of the clamor. Maybe they already had and were incoming.

The look of fear on the dark elf's face bolstered Stewart's rage. To finish this, he needed to get his grip on the elf again.

The ground around them was a coarse mix of gravel, stones, and fragments of worked metal, as if mountains of great machines had exploded and scattered debris. Stewart snatched up a great handful of stones and dark metal fragments and flung them with all his strength, like a shotgun blast. Then another handful. Then another. The elf threw up an arm to protect his face, dodging left and right. But the speed and accuracy of Stewart's old baseball arm had not diminished. Finally, a fist-sized stone glanced off the side of the elf's skull, knocking him sprawling and dazed.

Stewart charged with a roar of triumph, the sound resonating in his mind with the bellow of the gorilla-beast he'd once become in a horrible dream. In an instant, Stewart's fists crashed down onto the elf's breastplate. Rather than a solid blow, however, it felt as if his fists had been turned aside, like the repulsion of two magnets. Nevertheless, the blow drove the elf an inch into the earth.

The sensation of it sent a pulse of Dark magic surging through Stewart, coming up through the ground as if drawn by a sudden vacuum. The influx burned like fire in his chest and turned his arms into pile-drivers. He slammed his fists into the elf again, this time solidly.

The elf's eyes bulged. Dark liquid flecked his lips.

"You!"

Smash.

"Killed!"

Smash.

"My!"

Smash.

"Family!"

Then he kicked the elf in the side, sending him crashing against a piece of machinery butting from the earth thirty yards away.

The elf lay still.

Stewart snatched up his axe. Why had he dropped it? One blow from it would have ended this fight long ago. Then he stalked toward the elf.

The elf flopped onto his side, limbs broken, but his eyes were open and aware. Dark blood poured from his nose and mouth. He spat broken teeth. He struggled to sit upright, crying out in agony with every movement.

Stewart's increasingly tuned magic sense detected a rush of Dark essence pouring into the elf.

He raised his axe for a finishing blow.

The elf's beaten, bloodshot eyes blazed with terror and hate.

Stewart swung the axe.

The dark elf dissolved into a figure of black smoke.

The axe swept through the smoke, meeting no resistance.

The smoke dissipated in the wind.

The dark elf was gone.

Stewart buried his gleaming axe head in the machinery as if it were an aluminum can, and roared with frustration.

Thirty-Four

JORATH LAY GASPING and broken in the pool of black water. His armor was deformed and smashed, compressing his flesh and bones. He couldn't breathe. He flailed with broken limbs at the buckles of his breastplate, finally freeing it so he might breathe again with shattered ribs. Every intake of breath ripped like fire through his chest. His breath burbled in his throat.

The vaulted ceiling of the Master's palace stretched into darkness above him. He sensed movement around him, curiosity at his sudden appearance in the Master's Hall of Triumphs, the place where the Baron Tyrus's greatest victories were enshrined in sculpture and paintings, where the heads of his greatest enemies were preserved and mounted on the installations throughout the hall.

So battered by desperation and the power of Stewart's fists, Jorath could only remember this place as a pool of Dark Source to be the target of his displacement spell.

He was broken inside, shattered by the power of Stewart's blows. Dark elves could heal far better than humans, but one more blow might have finished him. And now he lay in an open pool of Dark Source, drawing it into him like breath to mend his broken body.

As he lay there, feeling his splintered bones realigning, his pulped internal organs reconstituting, a shadow loomed over him.

The Master's voice echoed in the Hall of Triumphs. "So, Jorath El-Thrim, you have returned." The menace sizzling beneath the Master's words turned Jorath's flesh to ice.

He heaved himself upright out of the water. "The human is here, Master. But he is powerful." The shame of it cracked his voice. "He defeated me."

The admission gave the Master pause. A human defeating a dark elf in single combat was unthinkable. It had never happened before, ever, in any realm.

Jorath stood there, calf deep in Dark Source, trembling with the desire to flee, but there was nowhere in any realm the Master's minions could not find him. Better to die by his own hand than in the Machine. Better to die and spare the House of Thrim the shame of having one of its own suffer the stain of defeat by a *human*.

"Do you know where he is?" the Master said.

"Yes, Master," Jorath said. "I can take you straight to him." All around them, dark elves gathered. The pressure of his kinsmen's eyes upon him was like a physical force, crushing his already bruised body. There was no mercy in their gaze, no compassion, nor did he expect any. He had failed, and failure they would not stand. Centuries ago, the House of Thrim had welcomed him, a bitter, young bright elf fallen from the Light Realm, full of directionless rage and bloodlust. Anytime a Light Realm creature descended to the Dark was cause for a celebration, a victory.

The House of Chaheris had cast him out upon discovering his experiments. How else could they have known how much physical damage a goblin could withstand unless they tested its limits? He had experimented on only twenty human prisoners in the Penumbra in the days when Rome was at its pinnacle. After he had joined the Dark Realm, his proclivities had been right at home among the House of Thrim, except there, he'd been allowed to experiment on Penumbral animals and humans. His treatises on live human dissection were studied by younglings fresh from the crèche.

"Do that, and you shall be given your release. Your time in the Machine will be brief."

Jorath knelt in the black water at his master's feet.

***

Stewart had to find the Princess, and fast. That dark elf knew where he was and could be bringing the Dark Lord himself down on Stewart's head.

He pulled out his compass. It looked tarnished now, timeworn. Only a sliver of distance remained between the needle and the full Moon.

His closeness to the abyss of Darkness freed him to do whatever he needed to do without fear. And so he would. There was no going home.

He set off running for the distant Metropolis, knowing that any physical fatigue he might come to feel was only an illusion, something his human mind would tell him he should be feeling. He was no longer certain breath was truly necessary here. He could breathe in magical essence, and it would fuel him.

He could see now that his first impression of the city being a volcano was also correct. The Metropolis had been built upon a volcanic cone. A wisp of smoke rose from the crater at the pinnacle. Orange threads of lava trickled down through canals and lava-falls from the great heights.

But there was no visible cover between him and the distant city. In his approach, he would stand out like a hammered thumb.

Some instinct told him he had to change his appearance again or else find some sort of fast-moving conveyance. No doubt, the Dark Lord might have the magical wherewithal to detect him, wherever he might be hiding. No, he had to vacate this area as quickly as possible.

But how?

He tried listening to the quiet voices of his instincts, but the urgency of fear would not let his mind go still.

His eyes could not leave the Metropolis. He kept expecting a swarm of nasty somethings to burst forth and streak toward him.

But then he felt the earth shudder underfoot with the passage of some subterranean leviathan, as had often happened since coming out of the canyon.

Did that mean there were tunnels under there? In such a place, he might stay hidden long enough to reach the city.

But how to get down into the tunnels? He had no way of knowing how deep the tunnels ran, or even if he could reach one.

What about one of those conglomerations of derelict machinery scattered across the plain? Might they reach down into the earth with some sort of access hatch?

He gauged about two hundred yards distance to the nearest one, next to a copse of black thorny trees, much like the clumps of thorny brambles in the canyon. Running toward it, however, he could see thorns on the branches long and thick enough to impale a human, easily as long as his forearm and thick as his thumb.

When he arrived at the clump of dark, quiescent machinery about the size of a two-story house, he looked for a hatch or opening. Glancing up at the city for signs of pursuit, he noticed that the dark, winged flying things had stopped circulating and had fallen into a V-formation. Four of them. The V pointed straight toward him.

Redoubling his search, he scoured the tubes and enclosures for openings. He scratched the parched earth away, hoping to find a hatch or removable panel. But to no avail.

The V-formation of flying things had wings of enormous span, perhaps as broad as a passenger airliner.

The machinery's interior was a nest of tubes of various diameters and directions, elbows and spirals. But some of them reached down into the earth.

There were no openings, but he could certainly make one. He touched the cold, dead metal, and felt no vibration, no heat, but that didn't mean it wasn't filled with high-pressure acid or toxic gas or whatever else the Dark Realm felt necessary to pipe all through the barren landscape.

He had no time for testing. *Trust your intuition.*

He channeled magic energy into his axe until the head glowed crimson, then he chose a pipe that would be thick enough for him to traverse. Raising the axe, he cleaved a side of the pipe wide open, bracing himself to run to safety from what might come out. But there was nothing. Only black emptiness.

The creatures in the V-formation proved to be what he could only describe as dragons, except that they appeared to be made of metal. Their claws and the veins of membranous wings glinted in the ruddy light. Wisps of smoke trailed behind them like exhaust. And they were the size of an airliner.

After two more hearty axe chops, he'd opened the pipe sufficiently for him to crawl through. Inside was a vertical shaft about three feet in diameter. Bracing his feet on riveted lips of the pipe sections, he pulled his makeshift door closed as tight as the gap would allow. The jagged metal edges cut his fingers, but there was no time to worry about that.

The shaft below him was pitch black and bottomless.

With a deep breath, he hooked his axe into his belt and braced his hands and feet against the sides. With continual outward pressure, he was able to inch down the shaft until he reached the lip of the next pipe section.

From directly overhead, the thundering screech of the flying beasts echoed through the metal of the shaft walls.

Twice more, he was able to accomplish this, until fatigue weakened his hands and cost him his grip.

He fell.

Down and down and down, bouncing and scrabbling at the sides, ripping out fingernails on metal flanges.

And then, a bend in the pipe caught his plummeting fall and bounced him into unconsciousness.

Thirty-Five

STEWART AWOKE IN DARKNESS so complete, he couldn't tell if his eyes were open until he rubbed them. Half-nauseated, dizzy from the bumps to the head, he lay like a limp T-bone on the concave floor of a horizontal pipe. When he could manage control of them again, his questing fingers found the upward curve of the shaft down which he'd fallen. How far, he had no idea.

Composing himself, orientating himself with up and down, took time. When he tried to sit up, he slammed his pate into the roof of the pipe, sending multicolored bursts through his vision. He lay on his back and groaned.

Get up, babe. You got to keep going.

It was as if he heard Liz's voice in his ears, just as clear as if she were next to him.

Tears came into his eyes that weren't from physical pain.

But he slowly, painfully righted himself, doubled around and pointed himself in the only direction he could go. Before he went far, however, he gathered enough Dark essence to create a globe of dull reddish light that led the way before him.

Through endless tunnels he crawled, twisting, turning, branching, dropping. At times, the pipe would shake and shudder in the aftershocks of some massive creature rumbling through the earth.

This gave him hope, as a main tunnel had to be somewhere nearby. He only hoped he didn't encounter whatever was moving through those tunnels. The deeper he went, the warmer the air became, until it became uncomfortably hot. Sweat slicked his hands, lessening the surety of his grip.

Eventually a horizontal pipe ended in a cast-iron grate. Beyond the grate lay a vast open cavern. As best he could see, the floor was smooth and well worn, with a pair of fat, parallel rails set too far apart for any earthly train.

With his waning strength, he kicked the grate with both feet, over and over again, until it finally gave way and burst outward.

The clang of the grate echoed untold distances in both directions. The only other sounds were his own breathing and a subsonic rumble that rose and fell. The air smelled of brimstone, steam, and an acrid stench he could not identify.

Checking his compass, he headed in the direction of the needle, his fist-sized, floating globule of illumination pacing him as he ran. The tunnel was so wide that his light would not reach the far side until he moved into the center between the rails.

The rails stood perhaps a foot high and just as thick, with a distance between them of perhaps twelve feet.

The heat made breathing difficult as he ran, but he was growing used to the sensation of the Dark essence as it infused him, like being raked through fishhooks for a split second before it infused him with warmth and power.

But then the ground underfoot began to tremble.

The rails rang like tuning forks.

He charged for the side of the tunnel and threw himself as flat as he could against the wall.

What came thundering down the rails an instant later was not a train, but a thing of segmented, black-iron carapace, flexing like a millipede, with a hundred eyes gleaming like furnace windows, so fat and bulbous that it almost ground him to paste against the wall of the tunnel. It blasted past him going at least sixty miles per hour. The hot wind left in its wake scorched Stewart's exposed flesh and made his clothes feel fresh from an over-heated dryer. He smelled singed hair.

Whether it was some kind of transport machine or a living creature he could not fathom, but he ran after it toward the city with all the speed he could sustain.

After a while, the dull throb of noise ahead became the sound of machinery at work, gears grinding, pistons churning, the breath of steam and internal combustion. The stench of brimstone became so strong, he removed his shirt and used it for a mask. The diamond mail shirt gleamed like purity itself, catching the dimmest light like a cascade of tiny mirrors. At the next protrusion of machinery along the wall, he scraped handfuls of old grease from the unmoving joints and rubbed it into every square inch of the mail shirt, dulling its gleam.

The tunnel widened into a cavern of immense proportions. Lights gleaming in the distant depths, reflecting from haphazard planes and edges, suggested construction, but whether they were buildings or more machines, he couldn't tell.

The caustic air burned his throat. Without the filter of his shirt, he would hardly be able to breathe now.

He worked his way along one cavern wall, compass in hand leading him ever onward, keeping a lookout for any kind of smithy or foundry. He had been trusting his intuition that he might find such a place, or else how would he make the key he needed to free the Princess? He didn't know if he could forge such a thing with magic alone.

He was always on the lookout for entities that might raise an alarm against him, but the tunnels were strangely deserted.

That is, until after what must have been hours of following the compass and moving toward the Metropolis, he spotted an open doorway glowing orange from within. Creeping to the opening, he peeked inside.

His heart leaped for the good fortune of it.

Industrious little creatures filled the room with activity, banging on orange metal with hammers, quenching strange bits in dark water or oil baths, grinding with spinning wheels, sending showers of sparks in all directions. An immense, pot-bellied furnace dominated one wall, heat waves boiling from it. The room looked like a cavern hollowed from dark rock. The smell of hot iron made him feel right at home.

He was half-expecting goblins, but these creatures were not. They looked more like Bob's larger cousins, little men with smudged features, pale, sallow skin that had never seen the light of a sun, and hair singed to short curlicues. They stood about as high as his waist. They might have been cute had there been any humor or humanity in their eyes. Their faces were cruel, their eyes cold. He thought he'd read once that leprechauns were master cobblers. These fellows looked like master smiths, with thick arms, barrel chests, and gnarled, calloused fists.

This smithy was exactly what he needed.

He walked in, shut the thick steel door behind him, threw the latch, grabbed a piece of something resembling iron re-bar, and bent it around the bolt, freezing it in place. With the door locked, he turned to face the dozen or so dwarfish creatures who were all looking at him, first quizzically, then with growing alarm at the sight of his glowing axe.

Within himself, he unlocked a cage.

He threw their corpses unceremoniously into the huge furnace, trying to ignore the stench they made.

Now, he had his workspace to build the key. How long he would remain undetected, he could not guess, so there was no time to waste.

Searching the smithy, he found all sorts of raw ingots and assorted bits of abandoned, flawed pieces. As soon as he examined the metals closely, however, he felt the Dark essence inherent in each bar, each fragment. None of them would be suitable for the kind of key he needed.

The Queen had said his key must be infused with love. The Princess was bound to her cage, not just physically but magically, and only a key forged in love could destroy her prison. The Queen had burned the key's image into his memory. If somehow, he lived to be a thousand years old, he doubted he would ever be able to forget a single contour or barb of the jagged, spiny, wrought-iron thing. It had to not only fit the lock, but also destroy the cage itself.

He needed metal from the Light Realm.

He looked at the head of his axe.

His only weapon.

Had it yet been corrupted by the Dark? First wiping away the blood of the dwarfish smiths, he ran his fingers over the runes inscribed in the steel.

It remained pure.

With only a moment's regret, he used a hammer and chisel to remove the head from the haft. Then he found a crucible big enough for the axe head and threw it in. Around the smithy, he found dwarf-sized leather aprons, most of them ratty and discarded but better than nothing. He tied several of them around himself, fashioned two of them into makeshift mittens, then found a long-handled pair of tongs to lift the crucible into the furnace.

While he waited for the axe head to melt, he pulled out the lump of moist clay he'd brought from the Light Realm and began to sculpt the mold for the key. His mind knew its shape, and his concentration focused his fingers into recreating its exact size and shape. At first his fingers felt fat and clumsy, rubbed raw and blistered by stone and heat, but the more he focused, the more they obeyed his intuitions. He didn't know how long he worked the clay, but when he reached its final shape, it was correct in every detail as if summoned straight from his memory. The shape of it was more than a foot long, with a shank as thick as his thumb, a bow as broad as his palm, half an inch thick, and a bit as long as his middle finger, a thicket of barbs and spines. The finished product would be a hefty chunk of steel. This clay mold he placed into a kiln to harden. While he waited for his materials, he located a sand bed suitable for casting the key.

Then it was time to check his axe head, reduced now to a white-hot puddle in the bottom of his crucible.

So lost was he in his work, he almost failed to notice the sounds of scratching at the door. Something was outside.

The clay mold was not fully hardened, but it would have to do. He pulled it from the kiln and pressed it into the bed of sand, creating a negative impression of the key. Sweat poured down his face. He was feeling light-headed. Could it be heatstroke?

Then he removed the original and prepared to pour his molten metal into the mold. This was the trickiest, most dangerous part of the process. If he didn't get it just right, he would have to start over, and he doubted his increasingly insistent visitors were willing to give him the time.

Gripping the crucible in a pair of heavy tongs, he tipped the liquid metal into the mold. In his exhaustion, he almost fumbled the crucible and spilled molten steel down his legs and feet, splashing sparks and tiny gobbets in all directions.

Then he realized something was missing.

The axe head's steel was still pure from the Light Realm, but the Queen had told him it needed to be infused with pure love, and he doubted the touch of his hands and intention alone were enough. Sticky with the blood of the dwarven smiths, his hands were hardly pure anymore.

Around his left ring finger gleamed a golden band.

His breath caught.

He could never have afforded a wedding ring of solid gold, so this one was just gold-plated, but there was no purer symbol of love he could call his.

Tears misted his vision.

The pounding on the door intensified.

The love of his life was gone. He was never going to see Liz again.

And she would not have hesitated for this.

He twisted the ring free of his finger, leaving the pale groove of skin that hadn't seen the light of day since their wedding.

Then he dropped the ring into the molten shape of the key. The yellow-hot liquid metal darkened around the ring as it sank in, losing its rigidity.

The door shuddered under a rain of powerful blows. Pebbles and grit fell from the ceiling.

Then, abruptly, the ring liquefied and flowed into the molten steel. He wasn't sure those two metals would behave that way on Earth; perhaps it had been his magical intention guiding the metallurgical process. All he knew was that now he had the key he needed.

As a last step to the casting process, he pulled the vial of oil he'd gotten from Claude—so many decades ago, it seemed—oil that would guarantee the final purity of the key. He pulled the stopper and poured the oil over the liquescent surface of the casting. The oil sizzled and smoked and released a scent like summer mornings and dewy sage, pristine lakes and sun-dappled pines, cinnamon, cardamom and cloves. Sparkles stroked the surface of the semi-molten steel.

He didn't dare throw water on the key to hurry the process, or else it might turn brittle and shatter under the stresses of cooling.

Waiting for it to cool, to solidify, while something very large and very insistent was beating on the door, was the longest few minutes of Stewart's life. He braced all the bars and plates of steel and iron he could find against the door. Whatever was out there, it was big.

He pulled the baseball out of his satchel. Would it work at all? It was just a baseball. If it could stop time, how wide would the effect be? Whatever he hit with it? Ten feet? A mile? The entire Metropolis? He had no way of knowing.

Claude was right; this baseball had, in many ways, defined the first half of his life. It was *his,* in the way of an old, favorite shirt or a worn pair of sneakers or a treasured regret.

A metal spike jammed between the door and the jamb, and like a four-foot crowbar began to worry at the gap. Metal squeaked and groaned.

And he no longer had a weapon.

Or perhaps magic would be his weapon.

Hunter had conjured a flaming katana from a hunting knife, and there were plenty of chunks of metal around here that could serve as an improvised weapon.

By the time the key cooled to orange-hot, it had solidified. With a pair of tongs, he eased it out of its sandy bed and lowered it into a bucket of black water. The sizzle and hiss raised an acrid stench, but he didn't think it was from the key itself, rather the tainted water coming into contact with the oil.

Another spike stabbed through the crack in the lower half of the door, and both were now prying.

"Stout door," he mused with a parched throat, cracked lips, and swollen tongue.

The pounding at the door echoed inside his head, throbbing in his temples. He took the key to a grinding wheel, where he smoothed and polished its rough corners and flashing, breathing deeply to keep his hands from shaking. Sweat poured down his face.

Amid the polishing, the gold of his wedding ring emerged, amalgamated with the steel.

The door exploded inward, blasting an iron table out of its path.

A massive head filled the opening, too large to be fully visible.

The huge reptilian snout was either made from or sheathed in dull iron. Fangs as long as his hand chewed at the door jamb. Its scorching breath stank of brimstone and acid, hot enough to set paper afire.

An eye the size of a volleyball glowed like an orange coal, peering in at him.

Thirty-Six

STEWART STARED AT THE enormous beast trying to chew its way through the rock to get to him. His limbs turned to nerveless goo and his blood to ice water.

He clutched the key in his left hand, and the baseball in his right.

He wouldn't get another chance.

Winding up for the throw, he waited for the creature's eye to peer in at him again. Like a rat gnawing at a hole, it ripped away chunks of rock from the doorway. Soon it would be able to get its head through. The depths of its throat glowed furnace-orange. Could it breathe fire? Perhaps not, or it would have reduced him to charcoal by now. It was such a merging of flesh and machine, he wasn't sure if the creature was biological or mechanical.

Then it wormed its head through the hole, jaws agape and belching heat, reaching for him.

He threw the baseball with all his strength.

It struck the beast squarely in the eye.

All sound ceased, as if Stewart had suddenly gone deaf.

The dragon stopped like a paused video.

Sparks trailing from its nose held their place in midair.

"Holy crud, it worked!" Stewart croaked.

But for how long? A strange thought, considering he had just stopped time itself.

He hurried around the massive head, but took the chance to study the thing. It was indeed the merger of both a living thing and a machine, a kind of cyborg dragon. As he scooched around the armor-plated neck through the door, he noticed that he no longer felt the heat of the furnace or of this dragon, as if all transfer of heat had stopped. The key no longer felt warm in his hand.

He could hardly bear to touch the dragon's coarse, steel neck, but he had to wriggle out into the tunnel.

In the tunnel, he found a contingent of armored dark elves like the one he'd fought, as well as a dozen or so dwarven smiths, all waiting to rush in after him.

The urge welled up to steal one of their weapons and kill them all while they were helpless, or put out the dragon's eyes. But again, he didn't know how much time he'd stolen.

Without a backward glance, he ran, pulling out his compass as he went.

The air itself felt dead, unmoving, thicker somehow as if resisting his passage. And he could hear nothing, not even the sound of his own footsteps or his breath. The maze of subterranean tunnels engulfed him. When he encountered a fork or an intersection, the compass needle swiveled to lead him on. He hoped it wasn't leading him in circles.

Then the air grew warm again, and the sound of his footsteps returned. How far he had managed to travel away from the cyber-dragon, he could not guess in the warren of passageways. That beast couldn't follow him down these narrow passages in any case.

But the dark elves and dwarves could. Would they be able to find him? Could they sense his location? He wouldn't wait around to find out.

An orange glow drew him forward, along with a low, burbling, slurping sound. The source proved to be a river of lava crossing a cavern the size of a baseball field. Waves of heat rippled up from the orange flow. He paused at the tunnel mouth long enough to ascertain the cavern was empty of life, but the balconies and mezzanines along the walls and ceiling suggested this was a well-trafficked area.

He hurried to cross the stone bridge over the slow-moving river, checked his compass, and darted into the next passageway.

As he went, he gathered a sense that his path started to slope upward. The walls of the passageways grew uncomfortably warm to the touch and underfoot. Endless black pipes and conduits radiated heat, leaving him perpetually drenched in sweat. His head swam to the point of dizziness.

Then a thought punched through the haze of confusion. Perhaps with magic he could defend himself from this heat before he died of heatstroke.

He drew in a deep draught of crimson barbs and formed them into an invisible shield around him. At its edges, heat waves rippled and danced, but he no longer felt the heat. Sweat cooled on his skin.

The thunderous screech of a cyber-dragon echoed down endless tunnels from behind him.

The march of hundreds of armored feet rose and fell in the distance.

Then a fluttering rush sounded from up ahead, a cacophony of squeaks and wings.

He knew what a swarm of bats sounded like, and it was coming this way. There was nowhere for him to run. They would be upon him in seconds. What manner of bats might exist in such a place as this?

If there was anything plentiful here for him to use, it was Dark Source. So he drew in another scathing draught, hardened his protective shield, and expanded it like a balloon to fill the tunnel, creating an invisible barrier. Then he gathered all the heat from the area around him, collecting it, channeling it into his shield.

The air grew so chill he could suddenly see his breath.

An immense swarm of leathery wings and beady red eyes and tiny fangs exploded from around a bend in the passage, racing toward him. They were the biggest bats he had ever seen, larger than fruit bats and flying foxes. And like the dragon, they were augmented with razored steel claws and metal plating.

But there was no way for a single bat to alter its course in the narrow passageways. When they splatted against Stewart's barrier of focused heat, hundreds of them, they exploded into sprays of sparks, gobbets of molten metal, and smoking pellets of flash-cooked flesh, choking him with the stench of seared hair and meat. Every single one of them.

As the embers of the last one drifted over his face, he smiled grimly, shuffled through the blackened, calf-deep remains, and hurried onward, ignoring the increasing wooziness in his step. Turning the shield into a heat-weapon took too much power for him to sustain, so he let the shield return to its original state.

Perhaps those bats had been searching for him, spies or messengers for the Dark Lord. If so, the Dark Lord might now know exactly where he was.

He spurred himself into a run again, key in one hand, compass in the other.

The shield kept the increasing heat away from him, but he could still sense its presence, like knowing something bad is on the other side of a door, taxing him both mentally and magically. Every time he drew in another gust of Dark Source, the pain was worse and lasted longer.

And then, after what seemed endless hours of tunnels and searching, he entered another large chamber, this one much less finished in construction.

In the center of the chamber stood a half-spheroid block of obsidian, like an overturned bowl thirty feet high. The cavern walls were of shiny, half-melted stone, as if this were the inside of a bubble of once-molten rock. At the same time, the half-spheroid didn't look like obsidian, because the facets were moving, shifting, throbbing. His vision seemed to slide away from the facets, as if matter and solidity had no meaning for what they were.

The compass needle pointed straight toward it.

It was, however, surrounded by a moat of flowing lava.

The roar of a cyber-dragon echoed in pursuit.

The air in the chamber rippled with heat. Dark-streaked orange lava bubbled and slurped, catching the facets of the obsidian globe like slivers of flame.

This was it.

This was what he'd come all this way to do.

The rock around the banks of the lava river felt thin and looked brittle, ready to crack like an eggshell underfoot. If he leaped over a rivulet of lava, he half-expected his feet to break through the crust on the far side and plunge his legs into molten rock. His heat shield would not protect him from that.

So he summoned his will, and drew in a deep, scalding, raking breath of Dark Source. The pain staggered him and he sank to his knees, waiting for it to subside. Tears streamed down his cheeks. The pain was like having his lungs and organs shredded by shards of glass.

When he could bear to open his eyes and focus externally, the sounds of pursuit were closer. Dark elf voices. Dwarf voices. The subsonic dragon-rumble.

The Princess had to be in that sphere.

But first he had to get across the moat.

For him, magic seemed to work best when he could use it to manipulate something that already existed.

Like a physical form.

He closed his eyes and let his imagination play.

So infused was he with Dark essence that the transformation happened immediately.

Great, black, feathery wings sprang from his back to a span of at least thirty feet. He flexed and extended them a few times until they felt just as natural as if he'd had them all his life, as normal as his arms.

With two great flaps, he was aloft, lifting his feet and flying over the lethal lava flows.

The heat formed great updrafts that boosted him higher, and

from the air he could see a landing on one side of the sphere, as if there once had been a bridge. But there was no entrance.

The landing was about a ten-foot square of smooth dark stone. He landed there, folding his wings carefully to keep from dipping his feathers into the lava moat.

But he could find nothing resembling a keyhole. There was no opening at all, just irregular mirrors of shifting black glass, distorting his appearance.

Catching a glimpse of himself, he looked away. He couldn't bear his appearance now, haggard, emaciated, a ghost with red-rimmed eyes and a ferocious mouth. Would his family even recognize him now?

It didn't matter. They were gone. Better that they never saw him this way.

Strange lights glowed within the obsidian depths. Perhaps lava glowing within? Or something else?

Then one of the lights took shape and formed an image. Stewart as a teenager.

The image took life and movement, showing Stewart stuffing a sandwich in his pocket in a Mesa Roja supermarket. An old lady, who'd seen him do it, gave him a withering look. He fled the supermarket. When he ate the sandwich, it didn't fill the hollowness inside.

Other lights glowed from within nearby facets.

One showed him sitting up in bed, crying. It was the night he'd lost the baseball game. But he hadn't remembered crying about it for so long until just this moment. Nevertheless, the sadness and shame were like a fresh punch in the gut.

Another facet showed him throwing rocks through the windows of several houses late one night. No one had ever proven he'd done it, but one of his foster mothers had beaten him for it anyway.

There was the time at the quarry, when he'd wanted to push his foster brother into the deep water and watch him drown for being so awful.

There was the time he'd pushed the class Fat Kid off the hayrack ride at the county fair, just like the older kids had done to Stewart twice already that night. Everyone laughed with thoughtless glee, but the kid was too overweight to catch up. Stewart couldn't remember the boy's name, only that he sounded like he was gasping out his last breath a quarter-mile later, when the driver finally realized one of the kids was missing and stopped to wait for him to catch up. Stewart had felt awful and tried to apologize, but the Fat Kid never spoke to him again.

The time he'd tried to kiss Nancy Ellis at the eighth-grade dance, and she'd laughed at him like it was a joke and not an expression of his undying love.

The time he'd watched two high school boys beat up a Navajo kid who wanted to go to school off the reservation, and he had not stopped them. He still remembered the shame of not knowing what to do in that moment, so shocked by the sudden violence that it had frozen him in place on the sidewalk. He was twelve. They were seniors. He should have done something. He never saw the Navajo kid again.

The facets were filled with Stewart's failures. Everything that confirmed he had never been anything but a Bad Seed, a thief, a coward, a bully.

There was no way for him to get inside. He wasn't good enough.

But the noises of pursuit were drawing closer. He didn't have much longer.

He pulled out the key and tried pressing it against the obsidian surface. He tried hitting the surface with the key. He tried using magic to create a keyhole, but without effect.

He plopped down onto the ground, beaten.

The dragon sounded just outside the chamber, flanked by untold swarms of vicious dark elves and angry dwarves. Yeah, those dwarves might be pretty ticked off at him for killing a bunch of their buddies.

What was he thinking? Why would he have ever thought he could succeed? Him. The Bad Kid. Staring into the obsidian mirrors before him, he had seen only truth.

It was time to give it up, accept his nature, say "hi" to the Dark Lord. He was through running. He was done struggling to force the world to accept him, to believe in him. What was the point anyway? The only people who'd ever believed in him were dead. For once, it might be nice to be on the winning side. The good guys never won. All around him, all over the world, the absolute worst people were the ones in charge. Liars, cheaters, bullies, they were the ones running the show. Maybe there was a good reason for that.

His decision settled upon his shoulders like lead anvils, bowing his back.

A voice like the deepest thunder, deeper even than the roar of the dragon, because it carried with the voice of the cosmos, reverberated through nearby lava chambers. "Find him. He must be close. I can smell his blood."

He gazed into the obsidian mirrors and waited for the Dark Lord to find him.

A smear of light swam up out of the dark and coalesced into Liz's face, as if she were looking at him through a smudged window. "Hey, babe."

"Hey," he said.

"You've been through a lot."

The sight of her face, the most beautiful he'd ever seen, full of concern and kindness, brought a lump into his throat.

"You're in so much pain, I can see that," she said. "I wish I could be there to touch you. I want to help you."

"I can't do it," he said. "I'm done. It's over. I'm sorry. For everything."

He wished he could kiss her goodbye, stroke her face.

"It's okay," she said. "You've done enough. It's okay to rest for a while."

But at those words, he blinked and leaped out of his despairing stupor. His shoulders and fists clenched.

"No." It was a garbled croak of a syllable.

Liz would never have said such a thing to him. Not now, at a time like this. She'd have been yelling at him to get up, to *never* give up.

He rose to his feet, rage boiling up in him like a volcano.

"No more *lies!*" he roared.

An immense raking gust of Dark essence whooshed into him like a hurricane. His fist became a hammer of diamond, and he struck the face of the obsidian barrier.

A spider-web of cracks sprang the impact across the surface.

Movement behind him caught the corner of his eye. On the far side of the cavern, in the shadows of a broad entrance, a pair of orange-glowing orbs appeared, and then a metallic snout, and then the razor-tipped claw at the knuckle of a wing.

The cyber-dragon spotted him and growled.

But then beside the dragon appeared an austere figure, impossibly tall and thin, clad in robes of black and scarlet. Its face was parchment stretched over a skull, its eyes glowing coals of spite and greed. It raised a spindly talon and pointed at Stewart. The Dark Lord.

He was out of time.

He drew back his fist and slammed it into the barrier again with all his augmented might. The blow dislodged grit from the ceiling, and spread the cracks even further.

He gasped, breathless.

The dragon leaped fully into the chamber, stretching its leathery wings, heedless of its limbs that dipped into the rivulets of lava or broke through the crust into hidden pockets.

Stewart had strength enough for one more blow. He drew in another draught of Dark essence.

"*No!*" roared the Dark Lord.

Stewart's blow shattered fully a third of the immense obsidian sphere. Razor-sharp shards exploded in all directions, painlessly slicing across his body in a score of places.

Within the shattered globe lay a cage of dark, twisted metal. And within the cage, a small creature glowing with its own light, a light flickering like a faulty fluorescent bulb.

From inside the globe, Stewart couldn't see the dragon, but the noise of it lurching toward him rattled loose more shards of volcanic glass.

He pulled out the key, thrust it into the keyhole and twisted. The lock spun as if recently oiled, but instead of the cage opening, it dissolved into a cloud of black flakes.

Before him, on a stone pedestal, sat the most abused, disheveled, filthy child he could have imagined. Her limbs were rail thin, her face gaunt and haggard, her pale hair ratty and disheveled. Dressed in a grungy shift of coarse brown burlap, she looked as if she had shrunk within it. But even the grime could not hide the porcelain purity of her cheeks, or dim the brightness in her eyes, which flared anew with azure light. And her features brooked no doubt that she was the daughter of the Queen.

Freed of her bonds, she was already growing indistinct, her edges fuzzy.

But she took one look at her savior, and her expression of sympathy, empathy, and gratitude bespoke her heart breaking in that very moment. A tear like a shard of glittering diamond slid down her cheek.

The dragon's head reared above the globe on its serpentine neck, glaring down at him.

The Princess threw herself into Stewart's arms. Her eyes met his. And she smiled.

The dragon's jaws darted toward them, then slammed shut on empty air.

Thirty-Seven

THE EVENING BREEZE WAFTED the smell of flowers and greenery through the window as Hunter sat on a stool beside his mom's bed. Cassie lay in the bed with her, asleep, snuggled up along her side.

Jaclyn and Jazlyn sat against the side of the bed, motionless, as if they were only dolls.

Hunter had never been so tired. He'd caught himself nodding twice. The journey back to the City had been grueling, and his backside and thighs were chapped from riding on unicorn-back for so many hours.

His unicorn's name was Ainyr, and Ainyr resembled a horse, but did not move like a horse. The horse's gait Hunter had grown accustomed to on the journey to the Tortoise's mouth was not what Ainyr possessed. It was smoother, but with a different undulation.

On the return trip, they had ridden many more hours at a time to get Mom back to the City as soon as possible. It had been a journey as fevered as it was sad. The bright elves had lost half of their number in fighting the goblins and the possessed Pooh.

When Pooh finally awakened, having returned to his senses, he saw the destruction he had wrought, and how everyone was terrified of him, and the horror, guilt, and despair were so plain on his features he could have been human. He disappeared into the forest, and no one had seen him since.

Fortunately, they had arrived at the City in time, and the Queen had worked her magic to remove the poison the giant badger-wolverine had left in Mom's wound. She would heal normally now, they said, with a scar across her belly.

She had been asleep for hours, though, so Hunter couldn't help but be worried. Seeing her brought down like this frightened him, especially with Dad gone.

Hunter and Cassie could have become orphans. He didn't want to be an orphan. He wanted his parents alive and whole.

But would Dad ever come back? If something happened to him in the Dark Realm, how would they ever know?

Hunter walked to the window to admire the sunset painting the City with more vibrant colors than he imagined existed on Earth. The array of twinkling lights and sparkling lake and verdant forest was so beautiful. But still, he missed his own bed, his room, their house, the desert. He missed the raccoons, and the javelinas, and even the scorpions and tarantulas. He felt like he hadn't been home in years.

Their room in the Queen's mansion was three tiers up from the floor of the banquet hall where they had first dined. Their door opened onto a mezzanine with a stairway leading down to the floor. The place smelled like the inside of a living tree, fresh and green and alive.

Maybe he was just getting restless. Or maybe he was hungry. It had been a while since he'd eaten, so worried about Mom his stomach felt queasy most of the time.

He stepped onto the balcony overlooking the banquet hall. Golden-orange light poured brilliant shapes across the polished parquet floor. The hall was empty right now, the dining table and chairs pushed to one side.

Then he felt the entire room, maybe even the entire tree, shudder. A noise hit his eardrums, but he couldn't characterize it as a *pop* or a *whoosh* or a *wham*.

But something had appeared in the middle of the banquet-hall floor, a creature with two enormous, black-feathered wings, curled up into a ball as if in pain or terror. A single loose feather the length of Hunter's leg spun a lazy spiral toward the floor.

An alarm bell clanged furiously.

Voices rose throughout the mansion. Running feet pounded up and down corridors and stairways.

The winged creature unfurled its wings and rolled onto its back. It was a man with a little girl in his arms.

Hunter rubbed his eyes.

"Dad?" he whispered. He had tried to shout, but the sound choked off. His chest filled with emotion. "Dad!"

He bolted down the nearest staircase.

Royal Guards burst into the hall, weapons brandished, running with that super-human elven speed to circle the motionless, winged entity in the center of the room.

"Dad!" Hunter called.

He shoved between the guards and writhed free of their attempts to stop him. But now that he had a better look, he couldn't be sure this was his father. "Dad?"

The man's clothes were scorched, and he stank of old sweat,

burned feathers, soot, and something like rotten eggs. His skin was swollen, torn, bleeding, his face puffy, his lips cracked. And those wings... The tips twitched and flexed.

An emaciated little girl clung to the man's chest. She looked mostly starved, disheveled and filthy in a shapeless shift that looked like a gunny sack. But her eyes shone like stars and they were full of tears for the winged man.

Bob's voice called, "Hunter, get back, lad!"

Hunter took another step toward the man. "Dad? Is it you?"

Mom's voice called down from above, "Hunter! What are you doing?" She and Cassie were coming down the staircase, holding hands. She moved slowly and painfully, but he was happy to see her standing up and moving.

"I think it's Dad!" Hunter called back.

The Royal Guard edged closer, ready to act at the slightest warning.

The winged man's eyelids fluttered, and he stirred.

The Queen swept into the circle of Royal Guards, shining so brightly Hunter could barely stand to look at her. "Is it you, my daughter?" Her voice echoed as if from across the cosmos.

The little girl sobbed with joy and nodded, but kept hold of the winged man.

"Come away from him, child," the Queen said. "He reeks of Darkness."

"I cannot, Mummy!" the Princess said, in a voice higher-pitched than the Queen's, with the same ring of power. "If I let him go, he will fall back into the Dark Lord's clutches."

The Queen looked deep into the winged man. "Perhaps that is for the best."

"No!" Hunter and the Princess yelled at the same moment.

The Princess gave Hunter a look of such gratitude that it stopped up his throat. Then she said, "He saved me, Mummy."

"He saved all of us!" Bob said, standing at the edge of the circle, stamping his cane against the floor defiantly.

The circle parted to allow Mom and Cassie through. "Oh, sweet sagebrush, *Stewart!*" she cried as she stumbled to his side and sank to her knees. One of his wings twitched.

He opened his eyes.

"Dad!" Hunter breathed.

Emotions cascaded through his father's eyes, looking at Mom, looking at Hunter and Cassie. First joy, but then disbelief that flared into rage.

He struggled to get up, but his purpose wasn't to hug anybody. "No! Another lie!" he roared, more like a gorilla than a man.

Instantly, flashes of light engulfed him, and when they faded, his hands, arms, and legs were encircled by sparkling bands of starlight.

"Alas," the Queen said, "I fear he is more beast now than man. A beast with incredible magical powers."

"That's the Dark side!" Mom cried. "You have to save him! He did what you asked!"

"And this is the cost," the Queen said. "He paid it willingly."

Mom got to her feet and faced the Queen, eyes blazing, fists clenched. "*You. Fix. Him.*"

A hush fell over the hall. No one moved. The Queen raised an eyebrow, clearly unaccustomed to being ordered around. Hunter gulped. *Uh-oh.*

But Mom didn't back down. "You got your daughter back. You give me back my husband."

"Mummy," the Princess said, "if the two of us work together, we can draw the Darkness out of him."

"He stinks of it," the Queen said distastefully. "It will contaminate us all."

"You know there is a way," the Princess said grimly.

***

Stewart awoke to a sensation like a thousand fishhooks tugging at his flesh.

A deep, thunderous, feminine voice said, "The Dark essence is deeply embedded. It will take great power to extract it. And at great cost to him."

"Do it!" came another female voice, a human one.

"Please, Mummy, we must try!" said a child's voice, very close to him.

His eyes snapped open, and there was Liz. And Hunter. And Cassie. All looking wide-eyed straight at him. The Princess held one of his hands in hers.

Hadn't he dreamed them? He couldn't believe they were here. They were dead.

But if they weren't dead, if they were really here right now, that meant they could see him now, in his horrid state, a croaking, lurching thing, bound by chains of starlight that burned his skin like branding irons. He was a monster.

"No!" he cried, a choked, ragged sound.

"Oh, Stewart," Liz said, her eyes full of tears. She knelt beside him and squeezed his hand, clutching her belly with the other.

"You're dead!" he said.

She smiled and stroked his hand with her thumb. "Almost. But they brought me back here in time for the Queen to save me."

His breath came in desperate gasps. "He told me..."

"Whoever told you I was dead lied to you, baby." Her voice was soft and soothing as a rose petal. And he was nothing more than a chunk of scorched lava rock.

"You're all supposed to be dead!" he shouted.

Cassie gasped.

Hunter crossed his arms. "Dad! Snap out of it! You're scaring Cassie."

"It is the Darkness in him, child," the Queen said. "It has poisoned his mind. He cannot see the truth of his eyes."

"I wasn't supposed to come back!" Stewart croaked, his head sagging to the floor, his heart wanting to burst at the expressions of everyone staring at him. So much pain and fear, and all because of him. Especially Liz. Liz should never have seen him this way.

He struggled against his bonds. "Send me back."

"Elizabeth, children," the Queen said, "you must hold your father in the Light Realm. You must not let him frighten you. We can save him, but you must be strong. This is going to cause him a great deal of pain."

"Can't you put him to sleep?" Cassie said. "Like an operation?"

The Queen shook her head. "I am sorry, child, but no."

Small hands grabbed his shins, holding on tight.

His great wings flapped once, slamming against the floor, then they were bound, too.

"We're ready," Hunter said to the Queen.

The Queen reached toward Stewart with an open hand, and then made a fist as if seizing a handful of something. Then she pulled.

His bonds held him to the floor as a thousand fishhooks ripped a scream out of him. She pulled, the smooth muscles of her over-sized arms flexing, straining as if in a tug-of-war. He screamed and screamed. Then she relented.

"His Darkness is strong," she said, panting slightly. "It will not come willingly."

"I can help, Mummy," the Princess said.

The Queen gathered herself, then reached with both hands. The moment they made fists, Stewart gasped in pain. She pulled. Stewart screamed, tears streaming into his hair.

Hunter and Cassie were crying.

The Princess's glittering fingers began to work across one of his arms, gently touching, squeezing, kneading, plucking, and wher-ever she touched him, an invisible barb came loose with a sudden, vicious *pop,* immediately soothed by the Princess's gentle touch. One by one, they came loose, and each one left him gasping. She slowly, methodically moved her touch across his entire body while the Queen maintained the tension on her invisible ropes.

Eyes squeezed shut, he focused his attention on the touch of Liz's hand, that gentle but unyielding grip, the warmth of it, the softness of it.

Then with a great wrench, like ripping off a body-sized bandage made of barbed wire, the Queen tore something out of him.

Something...alive?

Not living, not exactly, but aware, sentient, scheming.

His wings were gone.

They belonged to the thing hovering above him trapped in chains of starlight. A vaguely human-shaped shadow with broad, black vulture's wings and a single eye that burned like lava. Its arms ended in hooks rather than hands. It struggled ferociously, its gaping black maw screaming its rage soundlessly.

The Royal Guard edged away from it.

The Queen held its bonds in one hand, and with a gesture in the other summoned a crystalline urn the size of Stewart's head. It fit in her palm like a soda can. She placed it upon the floor beneath the shadow of Dark essence. "You must help me now, Daughter."

The Princess stood and moved to take her mother's hand.

Stewart felt the power of their combined will wash through him in a great wave, the focused will of the universe itself, a pressure like the bottom of the sea, or under twenty feet of avalanche snow.

The shadow's bonds tightened, cinching, squeezing, compressing, forcing it down into the urn. It squirmed and writhed and thrashed, its awful eye blazing a vow of vengeance at those who dared to imprison it. But into the urn it went, squashed and jammed and tamped, until the Princess put the lid on.

The Queen knelt and laid her hand on the lid. There came a flash of heat and will, and the lid was sealed as tight as if it had never been separate.

Inside the urn, a shadowy fog swirled and churned, its baleful orange eye glaring out at them.

"It is done," the Queen said.

Stewart sagged back, spent, gasping and covered in sweat, staring into the vaulted ceiling. A suffusion of calm and tranquility spread through him the likes of which he had never experienced. He felt normal, if beaten up and exhausted. Maybe better than normal.

Liz threw herself on him and covered his face and lips with kisses.

Even though his arms felt like chunks of lead, he hugged her close. This time, the tears were of joy.

Cassie and Hunter were there, too, hugging him.

It took all the strength he had left to hug them all back.

After a time, Liz turned to the Queen. "Is he okay now?"

The Queen said, "The essence he accrued in the Dark Realm, we have removed. But he still bears most of what he brought with him. It is inextricably part of him. If he wishes to shed himself of that, it must be through his own efforts."

Liz pointed at the urn. "What about that thing?"

"We shall keep this prison safe in our vault. And may we all wish this entity never finds its freedom again. It was *powerful*. Given enough time and practice, his power may have grown to rival that of the Dark Lord himself."

"What happens if it does get loose?" Hunter asked.

"Then it will hunt your father across all realms, seeking to reclaim its fleshly seat. What would happen then..." She shook her head.

The Princess came and knelt beside Stewart's head, and laid a cool, soft hand on his forehead. "Thank you." Then she kissed him on the forehead.

Her limbs were fuller now, her cheeks less sunken, her eyes less hollow, as if being home was even now rejuvenating her.

Liz hugged the Princess. "And thank you for saving him. I can't imagine what he went through."

"He is a good person," said the Princess. "Sometimes, that is all it takes."

Epilogue

THE FAMILIAR SCENT of sagebrush and scrub pines came on a wave of hot, dry air as Stewart, Liz, and the kids stepped through the bridge back to Earth. Through a swirling, spinning tunnel of stars and gas clouds, they went from the Queen's mansion to their back yard.

It was a lovely Mesa Roja sunset, but couldn't hold a candle to the spectacular sunsets of the Light Realm. Nevertheless, Stewart breathed deep of the Arizona breeze. It smelled like fresh, clean air now, open and free, instead of relentless, scorching, dusty heat.

Cassie yelled, "Yay! We're home!"

Jaclyn and Jazlyn walked just behind her. She had grown so attached to them during their travels through the Borderlands and the Light Realm, none of them could bear to part with each other. The way they moved in mute silence still gave Stewart the willies, however.

"How long have we been gone?" Hunter asked. "It feels like forever."

"We'd better find out," Liz said. "We might have some explaining to do with the school."

"Or the landlord," Stewart said, wincing at the fact that he was still unemployed. They still had no money, and now, not even transportation. The truck had been destroyed, and he had no idea how to find out what had happened to it. The Park Service would not have left it to rust away in the middle of the campground road.

The Queen's voice echoed around them. "I think you'll find things are changing in your lives."

"How?" Stewart said to the empty air. "Did you do something? Change things?"

"No, *you* did," the Queen's voice said, fading like the whisper of a summer zephyr.

Liz hugged him. "I wasn't sure we'd ever make it back."

"Me, too," he said, hugging her back.

They'd spent two more weeks of subjective time in the City for Liz and Stewart to heal their wounds. Right now, Stewart felt better than any time he could remember, both physically and mentally. The Queen and the Princess had not extracted all the Darkness from him—it was too deeply woven into the threads of his life—but they had removed most of what he'd acquired in the Dark Realm.

In all this leisure time, Cassie and Hunter had spent many hours practicing their use of magic, or else in the City's library, lost in the endless tomes of ages past, learning the runes that helped manifest magic on Earth.

But now, they were home.

Hunter's eyes narrowed. "Did our house shrink or something?"

Liz chuckled, "No, it's the same as it ever was."

"Hmm, looks smaller."

Liz and Stewart exchanged glances and smiles. Stewart retrieved a spare key from under the back step. Their keys had been lost in the wreckage of the truck.

Walking into the house, Stewart took a deep breath. "Well, at least the mice haven't moved in yet. Any more of them anyway."

Liz flipped a light switch, and the living room lights came on. "Well, that's a good sign. We still have electricity."

"Okay," Stewart said, "time for a family meeting."

The children groaned.

"Yeah," Liz said, "now that we're back home, we have some things to discuss."

They all sat down at the customary family conference site, the kitchen table. How strange and diminutive their house felt now.

Stewart said, "We've all been through a lot of crazy, crazy stuff. Rule number one, the unbreakable rule. Are you ready?"

The kids nodded.

"We do not talk about *any* of this outside the family. Not to friends, not to teachers, not to anybody."

"Why, Daddy?" Cassie said.

"Remember what happened at school with Charlie and Joey?" Hunter asked. "They'll think we're crazy."

"Right," Stewart said. "From now until forever." He made a zipping motion across his lips. "Promise?"

Liz and both kids made lip-zipping motions.

"Can we see if the magic we learned works here?" Hunter asked. "We were studying runes while Mom was getting better."

"As long as nobody sees you and you don't use it to harm *anyone ever*, yes," Stewart said. "We've seen how the Dark magic works. It gets into you..." Here in the Penumbra, between the Light and Dark Realms, the magical essence they drew into themselves might come from either source, depending on their intention. He trailed off, the memory of it sharp as a forest of blades. He blinked and swallowed hard. "Promise?"

Hunter and Cassie said, "Promise."

"Okay, then," Stewart said, easing back in his chair.

"That's all?" Hunter asked.

"That's all."

Cassie said, "Mommy, can I go play with my toys?"

"Sure, honey. I think we all need to feel a little normal." Liz ruffled her hair and sent her on her way. Jaclyn and Jazlyn followed her.

"Dad, can I go get the mail?" Hunter said. For whatever reason, he had always loved to bring the mail from the mailbox, which stood on a post at the end of their driveway.

Stewart nodded a go-ahead.

Standing alone without the children now, Liz faced him. "How can we ever get back to normal? I mean, how normal can things really be with a couple of lethal dolls as playmates?"

"Why should we? Who would want to?"

"But what then? It's not like we can use magic to create food and lot rent."

He sighed and hugged her tight. "I wish I knew."

Hunter burst through the front door with a wad of letters and circulars in his arms. He handed it all to Stewart.

Stewart took them all with a sigh and started thumbing through. The date on one of the circulars caught Stewart's eye. It was dated the Monday after they had left for the camping trip. "We've only been gone a few days. No more than a week."

He sorted out a copy of the *Mesa Roja Messenger*, the local paper, which came out on Wednesdays. The headline read: "Search Continues for Missing School Principal."

Near the bottom of the front page was an announcement for the liquidation auction for Richards Locksmithing. That seemed awfully sudden. Could something have happened to Mr. Richards?

Liz shuffled through the letters. "Bill...bill...bill...overdue notice..." She sighed and deflated into the sofa. "Too bad we can't just conjure up a little gold bullion."

Among her fistful of letters, the next visible one was from a return address that he recognized, the company logo for Steel and Shield, Inc., one of the country's premier retailers of authentic, well-made swords and other medieval weapons, the kind of weapons that could be used, rather than costume pieces, the kind of weapons coveted by true collectors and medieval combat enthusiasts. The letter was hand-addressed to Stewart.

He tugged the letter free and looked at it for a moment, turning the envelope over and over, wondering what could be inside. More than likely, they were trying to sell him something. He moved to toss it in the garbage, but a tiny, quiet voice in his mind stopped him.

Instead, he opened the envelope.

The words in the letter wouldn't quite register.

He read them again.

"Huh," he said, flummoxed.

"What is it?" Liz asked.

"Huh."

"Stewart?"

"Huh."

"Oh, come *on*." She jumped up, yanked the paper out of his fingers, and read. Then she said, "Huh."

"I think it's for real."

"Well, yeah, it's addressed to you and everything."

She read aloud:

"*Dear Stewart.*

"*We are contacting you to verify that you are a smith skilled in the production of various styles of blades.*

"*We acquired one of your Damascus rapiers through an auction, and the previous owner indicated that you were the original smith. As you have no website or contact information readily available, we had some trouble tracking you down. Smiths with skills such as yours are in short supply.*"

He had made a couple of Damascus rapiers for collectors he'd met at a Renaissance Fair a couple of years ago.

"*If you're amenable,*" Liz went on, "*we would like to engage your services to produce blades for us on a bespoke basis. We have an extensive backorder list we would like to eventually clear, but we anticipate having enough customers to fill your schedule for years to come.*

"*Again, if this opportunity interests you, please contact us at your earliest convenience. Yours Respectfully...*"

Hunter, who had paused in the hallway listening, came back into the living room. "Dad! That's amazing!"

Liz jumped up and hugged him. "Maybe we're going to be okay!"

Stewart still felt a little shaky, but something was blooming in his heart. Excitement.

Hope.

He kissed Liz, trying not to think about his Dark essence imprisoned in a crystal urn far, far away, an entity bent on escape. Then he looked into her eyes and smiled. "Maybe we will."

THE END